◇ *GP* ◇

The Germania Press

Also by William Russell Sheridan

The Adamantine Heart
The Return of Wahkahchai
The Bavarian

The Spy from Livani

WILLIAM RUSSELL SHERIDAN

THE GERMANIA PRESS
Bavaria, Germany and California, USA

The Germania Press
Bavaria, Germany and California, USA

First Germania Press edition September 2020

Jacket design by Laura LaRoche: LLPix.com

Manufactured in the United States of America

Library of Congress Cataloging-in-Publication Data
Sheridan, William Russell.
The Spy from Livani: a novel/William Russell Sheridan

ISBN: 978-0-9909682-7-6

ACKNOWLEDGMENTS

My dearest critical readers deserve my continued gratitude for their unreserved feedback.

In the United States and in Germany: my parents Bill and Helga, whose stories I will always remember.

In California: Janet Immel, for whom I gladly write.

All my handball buddies who can read with minimal assistance. Jim Pfouts for our in-depth discussions of language philosophy. Paul Casale, new friend, for close reading and generous feedback.

Carl Grilli, master builder, storyteller, and dear friend. He tells me what to do and I do it. Nothing else need be said.

In the Midwest: Steve Doty and Marlene Ciorba, great teachers both; Steve and Judy Schultz for pushing me to be better and better.
In the Pacific Northwest: Daniel Lippincott for staying with me.

In Bavaria, Germany: *Erster Hauptkommissar* Roland Rüssel, one of the most important people in my life; mentor and protector. Martina Rüssel, whose English is far better than my German.

Continued appreciation for Marlies Reuther-Rüssel for taking care of Roland, Nancy, and me.

Gratitude to Ernst Baur for his gracious friendship. The best parts of four books were written at Villa Ernesto in the Italian Alps high above Cannobio, Italy, on the Lago Maggiore.

And, of course, whether at home in Bavaria or California, Nancy Clark, my favorite travel companion through life.

"We have to distrust each other. It's our only defense against betrayal."

— Tennessee Williams, *Camino Real*

CONTENTS

Ditch Bear 1

Rock Bottom 11

Offer Letter..19

Transition..29

Dean's Office 39

Squared Away..47

Handball 57

Butchery 67

Welcome 67

Making New Friends 87

First Day 95

Class Exercise 105

New Roommate 113

Thunderstorm 125

Deputy Sheriff.. 133

Lady's Choice... 141

The Hearing 147

The Defense Rests 161

Frame-up 173

Evaluation Day 183

Missing Persons 191

Lake Kabetogama 203

Confession.. 215

Spy from Livani 223

Enrollment in the CIA ... 233

Building Trust ... 241

Blood Brotherhood ... 249

Practicum ... 255

Assignments ... 263

Karin's Show ... 271

Breakthrough ... 281

Prisoner ... 295

Rumspringa ... 305

Interviews ... 317

Little Sister ... 325

High Heels ... 335

Grandmother ... 347

Decisions ... 359

Hostage Rescue ... 369

Longshot ... 379

CHAPTER ONE

Ditch Bear

Farley Nilsson downshifted the old Chevy pickup truck into second gear to get her up the slope of the hill. The engine stuttered and she lost a bit more rust from her flanks, but once over the gentle rise he popped the transmission into third and let her run a bit. In the ditch that ran alongside the blacktop he saw a bear. He clutched and braked bringing the pickup to a wobbly halt. He rolled down his window, took his Minnesota Twins baseball cap off and had a look back. No, he was wrong. Not a bear at all unless bears wore hats. "Now that's not something you see every day," Farley said aloud. He scratched a chin grizzled with three-day-old whiskers. "Not even out here in Minnesota's North Woods, where a man can see just about everything worth seeing and worth talking about."

He ground the gears as he pushed the stick into reverse, the old girl resisting as usual, and almost stalled her out as a result. "Goddammit," he groused. "I'll take a boat over a truck any day!" The tranny accepted his attempt to reverse the engine and as he gave her gas, the truck hopped back about thirty yards where he could take a closer look at the bear in the hat in the ditch.

Nope. Wrong again. Might not be a bear in a hat at all, he observed. Could be a man big as a bear lying in the ditch, but it was too soon to say with certainty and Farley was never one to jump to conclusions. The man-bear did have a hat on his head. Farley found the switch for the spotlight mounted atop his side mirror, swiveled it back and down into the direction of the ditch, and switched it on. The lemon colored light weakly illuminated the figure in the shallow ditch that paralleled the road. Farley said damn to no one in particular, got out, but left the engine sputtering and shaking the chassis so as not to draw down the battery too much with the spotlight.

He stood over the dark form in the ditch and poked the bear with the toe of his black and white canvas tennis shoe. The bear, wearing a University of Minnesota cap, grunted from the nudge in the ribs, in Farley's opinion a clear sign of life. "Sure sounds like a bear," Farley noted. His spotlight gained a false strength as dark ran in among the pines, firs, beeches, hazel nut trees, and willows that became a forest the longer and deeper you looked. He saw the lights of another vehicle cresting the hill. Farley could just make out the light bar on top of the National Park Service truck driven by Ranger Jim McManus, off duty and headed for home. The ranger pulled in behind Farley's truck, the color of a Lund walleye boat, still wobbling and puffing white smoke from the rattling tailpipe. A high-power flashlight struck Farley in the chest.

"That you, Farley?" NPS Ranger McManus asked.

"Who else would be driving that piece of junk at this time of day?" Farley replied, answering a question with a question. The ranger laughed.

"You hit a deer or a bear, maybe?" Bear season was not too far away and hunters were already in the woods setting out baits, preparing stands, and scouting, all the activity pushing the bears into movement.

"Didn't hit nothing, don't ya know?" Farley answered the ranger now standing at his side, "Not that you could tell by looking at my truck." While Ranger McManus tried to make sense of the figure prostrate in the ditch snuffling and snorting like a bear from time to time, Farley offered a piece of information. "Gonna try and sell her before the winter comes and get me something a bit more reliable."

"You mean a truck that wasn't made in the last century?" McManus teased. At that moment the truck coughed, farted through the tailpipe, shook and died. The spotlight temporarily brightened, dimmed to orange and failed.

"Goddammit," Farley exclaimed before he kicked the dented side of the truck in frustration. "Now you've gone and insulted the old girl."

"Hold on," the ranger cautioned. "Don't be getting your britches in a bunch. No insult intended. That old truck has been very good to you and she deserves a little respect. I'll bring you an extra flashlight from my vehicle and we'll see what we've got in front of us here this time." He remembered the corpse Farley had caught in Lake Kabetogama last year or so while he was out fishing for big northern pike.

Farley took the flashlight the ranger had brought for him and in the double circle of lemonade colored light, the two men examined Farley's new discovery in the ditch. "Damned if these LEDs don't throw a bright light," remarked Farley, impressed with the candlepower they were throwing into the ditch.

The ranger said, "Sure looks like a bear in a hat to me too." Farley nodded in agreement, glad to have someone else come to the same conclusion. But he shook his head despite the fact that his initial impression of the scene had been confirmed.

"I don't think it's a bear at all...but it could be if you were driving by on the road and you just happened to look down for a sec or two. It doesn't surprise me at all," Farley allowed, now more certain than ever of his new conclusion, "that you was so easily fooled." He missed the ranger's grin in the dark. Some folks said that Farley Nilsson was older than Lake Kabetogama itself and very few of the year-round residents could remember a time when Farley had not been fishing the Boundary Waters. One thing he knew for sure: Farley was there when the lake had become part of the national parks system in the seventies. He moved in for a closer look.

"Let's see if you found yourself another corpse."

The thought distressed Farley. One corpse discovery was sufficient for one man's lifetime and he assuredly did not relish the idea of another, nor the notoriety that went along with such a macabre finding. The notoriety of his previous discovery had cost him valuable fishing time, what with all the interviews for TV and all the locals forcing him to retell the same story over and over until he got so sick and tired of it that he had to take a day and drive into International Falls and have a hamburger. So he was glad the ranger had arrived to share this latest find. He was fully prepared to offer him full and first rights of discovery.

Both men, now duly convinced by the light that they had more man than bear in front of them, decided it would be in the creature's best interests to be removed from its present location. Farley took the lead, given the advantage of his experience in finding such ambiguous discoveries. "Come on over here and let's see if we can't get him turned over so we can check his breathing."

The ranger took the boots and Farley the shoulders and on three they managed to roll the man onto his back, unseating his cap in the process. Now there was no further doubt that they were working with a man and not a bear. Both men had seen a bear in a cap but never one wearing boots. Farley waved a hand in the air as if trying to swat away a pine fly. "Whooeee. He smells worse than any bear I ever shot and skinned."

"Must be drunk as a skunk," the ranger observed through rhyme. Both flashlights illuminated the stinking man's face.

"Well I'll be...," said Farley.

"Damn," said the ranger, finishing Farley's thought. "If it ain't the professor. What's he doin' sleepin' in this ditch and stinking up the place for miles around?"

Farley grunted. It didn't take a detective of the professor's stature or reputation to figure that one out. "I'd argue that he was trying to walk home from the Four Winds bar and he didn't quite make it," he said for the edification of the young ranger.

"Just like your truck, huh Farley?" the ranger teased, knowing his friend had a sense of humor.

"I'll give you that," Farley allowed.

The ranger slapped the bearded cheek of the unconscious inebriated man. "Wake up, Doc! You can't sleep here all night." All they got for their trouble was a bear-like snort and the gasoline-like smell of whisky mixed with sweat. "The two of us can't handle him. He's big as a grizzly. I know he has always been a big man walking, but damned if he hasn't put on a considerable amount of winter weight since the last time I saw him."

"Maybe that's why he's taken to hibernating in this ditch," Farley mused.

The ranger shined his light onto the bed of Farley's red truck, now black in the night. "That winch of yours still working?"

"Hell yah," Farley said, disgruntled that the ranger would think any of Farley's gear related to fishing would not work. "She works just fine," Farley explained. "It's the damned truck that don't work worth a diddly dippity damn." The ranger had no idea of the severity a diddly dippity damn might suggest, but it was nevertheless to his ear a handsome piece of alliteration in the dark of night.

Farley climbed into the cab of his tired old truck but no amount of coaxing or pumping the gas pedal could get her to turn over. He gave up and got out, cursing the truck's reliable failure, pushed up the hood, got his jumper cables from behind the seat and waited as the ranger swung the park vehicle into position for a jump. In a hail of sparks Farley simultaneously bumped the positive and negative poles with the metal end of one of the clamps. "That's a good sign," he observed. "She's still got some life in her old battery yet."

They got the clamps properly hooked up to both batteries, and the ranger gave his truck some gas to rev up the engine. Farley keyed the ignition and the Chevy's six cylinders rattled into a sluggish start. Farley goosed the gas pedal to get the rpms up and she settled into a trustworthy rumble. The ranger hopped out and disconnected the jumper cables from both vehicles, threw them into the cab of Farley's truck, then drove his vehicle around to the back of the truck and switched on his high beams to shed more light on the situation. Farley climbed into the back of his truck with much more agility than the ranger ever expected of a man Farley's age or one twenty years younger, and he prepared the electric winch for a pull. Farley used the winch to pull his johnboat up into the corrugated metal bed of his truck when he fished rivers or small lakes and ponds in the area.

"How we gonna do this without damaging the professor?" the ranger asked, deferring to Farley's greater store of backwoods knowledge.

"Looks to me like the damage has already been done," Farley philosophized. "He sure as hell ain't gonna feel anything in his condition. But we should be mindful of his boots. That's a fine pair of Danner hunting boots he's got on those big feet of his and he'll be angry if we scuff 'em up too bad when we skip-load him onto the truck bed."

The ranger agreed. Farley was right again as usual. His early years working as a lumberjack had given him a learned appreciation for a fine set of boots. It would not be neighborly to scuff or cause unseemly damage to a man's boots while you were winching him up into the truck bed, the steel worn shiny and smooth, scoured of all paint and rust by the johnboat sliding her blunt nose into the thrumming pull of the winch.

The two men ran the steel cable around the hulking figure's ankles, set the choke, careful not to set it so tight as to cause damage to his expensive footwear.

"I'll hold his head Farley, while you run the winch." It sounded like a good plan.

"Holler when you're ready, Jim," Farley hollered into the dark.

"Let 'er rip!" the ranger hollered back. The ranger straddled the professor's head and held it with two hands like a novice bowler trying to roll too heavy a ball down the middle of the bowling alley. He duck-walked along as the massive form slide closer to the rear end of the truck's open gate. "Stop! Stop!" the ranger yelled and gently lowered the professor's head to the tarmac. He rested, panted, and breathed in the heavy humidity the evening's clouds had brought down across the border from Canada. Recovered and with Farley's help, they angled the professor's legs, now bent at the knee, up onto the tailgate. As Farley put the winch back in gear, the ranger said, "Slow it down a bit. He's starting to corkscrew. You'll have to jump down here and help me lift his shoulders or we're likely to break the big man's back."

Farley saw the inescapable wisdom in that, and helped the ranger lift the professor's upper body, one man at each shoulder. Unfortunately, as careful and vigilant as they were trying to be with their friend in need, they inadvertently chunked his head on the rounded lip of the scarred tailgate.

"Ow! Goddammit!" the professor yelled. "What the hell was that?" he complained before passing out again.

"That, most likely, was the beginning of a concussion," Farley said to the unconscious man. The ranger could not keep himself from laughing.

"Goddammit, Farley," the ranger said, "please try to show the man some respect."

The ranger had a point and Farley walked back to the ditch, following the drag line they had gouged into the grass with the professor's body, his ass plowing a substantial furrow until it reached the road. The flashlight found the professor's hat and Farley put it back on the man's head where it rightfully belonged.

"You gonna leave his feet tied to the winch like that?"

"Yep," said Farley, self-evidently. "Don't want him to slide out the back on the way to his cabin. You lead the way," Farley directed.

They delivered the professor to his door, leaving him under the cover of the front porch like a UPS parcel. Farley covered the bulky man with an old canvas tarp that stunk of mold and fish. He stepped back to look at his handiwork. "Yep. Sure looks like a bear in a hat to me."

The ranger agreed. "He sure owes us one for tonight. Say, Farley. Don't you have a key to his front door?"

"I most certainly do."

Without giving that piece of information a second thought the ranger said, "Let's go home, Farley. Way past dinner for us both." They complimented each other on a job well done and wished each other a good night. They agreed to check on the professor in the morning.

Professor Doctor William Russell Sheridan, former professor of semiotic theory, special agent and consultant to the FBI, woke to the shock of the sun in his eyes. He tried to get his bearings and groaned, not so much from the pain of sleeping on his doorstep, but from the realization of what he had done. This fall down the stairs of excess was getting to be too much. He struggled to sit up and immediately threw off the canvas covering his lower body. It stank in the heat of the sun and the malodorous smell caused him to retch. He swallowed. He felt an instant of panic suffuse his stomach before he found the physical reassurance of his wallet in place where it should be. He took it out of the hip pocket of his blue jeans and checked his credit cards and cash. He found all the plastic and his driver's license but he had done some damage to his cash flow. Although the back of his head throbbed more than his stomach, he was reasonably certain he had not been rolled and robbed. He still had his boots.

A second twinge of panic abated when he patted his jeans again and found his keys and car fob. His cap had rolled off his head sometime during the night so he reseated it, grateful for the sun block the bill afforded him. He let himself in, removing his sweat stained coat, smelling not much better than the tarp he had slept under. As he pulled his boots off, the phone in the kitchen rang. Caller id notified him it was Farley Nilsson. He coughed and cleared his throat and assured his old friend he was indeed still alive.

He let Farley fill him in on the rescue. "I owe you one, Farley. I'll make it up to you," he promised.

"Oh hell, Will. You don't owe me or Jim nothin'. That's what we do up here. A man needs help, he gets it. I know you'd do the same for me, eh?"

Will thanked him all the same. "Do me one more favor, buddy, if you will. Call Jim McManus and tell him I'm alive and kicking but there's a lot of clean up to do. Tell him I'll call him tomorrow and thank him personally for helping haul my sorry ass home. I'm just not up to it today and I need a shower in the worst way.

Farley chuckled into the phone. "I can smell you from my house," he kidded. Will knew he was not far from the truth, if his own nose was a reliable judge. Farley continued. "It's been a long time since I've seen a man that stinkin' drunk. In fact, if my failing memory serves, it was you shortly after Sylvie returned to Germany." Will groaned his assent. He waited as Farley paused on the line, gathering his thoughts before he spoke.

"Time for you to do me one favor, big man...." Farley's tone had changed and Will knew he was loath to ask anyone for a favor unless it was absolutely necessary.

"You got it Farley. Just name it."

He heard his friend take a breath deep enough to pull the phone from his hand. "Time to stop, my friend. She's not coming back." He quickly added, "Though it's no damn business of mine and I sure don't want to be messin' in yours."

Will sighed into the receiver and sat on the stool fronting the island in the kitchen. "I know, Farley. She's not coming back and I'm not going to chase her. I got that figured out finally and for the last time last night. I was just trying to scuttle and sink that little ship of grief I was sailing on. And you are a true and dear friend. I'll tell you this much, dear Farley. I'm done like an Easter goose. Last night clinched it for me. I dreamt the bear was after me but I managed to fight him off. It's time for me to listen to the vision and act on it." He could imagine Farley nodding in agreement at the other end of the line.

"Let me know if there is anything I can do, or anything you need," Farley offered, good hearted soul that he was.

Will promised to call him if he needed anything, but right now more than anything else he needed time to put the locomotive of his train wreck life back on the tracks. They ended the conversation, two men doing what had to be done and saying what needed to be said on the shore of Lake Kabetogama in Voyageur's National Park on the boundary waters between Minnesota and Canada.

While he waited for the hot water to come in the shower, in his office Will sat in front of his computer, ignored the prompts to check his emails, found Bass Pro Shops/ Cabela's in his Favorites list, and ordered their top of the line walleye rod and reel. He wanted it sent by next-day mail to Farley's address. He ordered the same package for the ranger. For the first time in a very long time he felt good about something he had done. It was a moment that called for a celebratory drink; just one.

CHAPTER TWO

Rock Bottom

Three days later Farley Nilsson rattled his old Chevy pickup truck into the opening bay of Will's three-car garage and entered the house through the door into the main cabin. He walked through the washroom, the pantry, and into the massive room that held the open kitchen. Farley looked out over the kitchen island and into the living room with its cathedral ceilings of exposed and varnished oak beams. On either side of the stone fireplace, French windows opened out onto the lake. The afternoon wind agitated the waters into a light walleye chop. Farley stood for a minute and took a longing look out at the jade green lake, wind pushing a crown of white foam onto the waves. Like the bumper sticker on too many rusted chrome bumpers, Farley lamented he would rather be fishing, but his friend needed him now more than ever.

He spotted Will passed out in his oversized leather recliner facing the cold fireplace. He wore a pair of black underwear and a tattered blue terrycloth robe that showed its white stitches bright against the blue. His beard blackened his face and spittle had drooled from the corner of his mouth and dried, showing white like the threads in the seams of his robe. A bottle of Glenmorangie, his favorite single malt Scotch whisky, sat three quarters empty on a side table. There was no glass.

"Will!" Farley yelled and shook his friend by the massive bulge of muscle in his shoulder. "Wake up, Will!"

Will stretched his bare legs the length of the recliner, toes pointed, his white feet extending past the recliner's bolster. He managed to open one eye, then the next, and with a knuckle rubbed into each eye tried to clear the sleep fog occluding his vision. "Hey, Farley. It's good to see you." He blinked three or four times. The pleasure of seeing his friend was genuine. He tried to push the lever for the recliner so he could sit up. He gave up and Farley, shaking his head, did it for him. Farley had his own key and garage door opener to the expansive log cabin set at the edge of the lake. Farley had the full and free run of the house, whether Will was there or not. Will considered him more so a friend in residence than a caretaker and he knew the older man, deep into his seventies now, occasionally enjoyed company during the long cold winters in the Great White North.

Will managed to pull the open sections of his robe together in an attempt to cover the extended rise of his belly, which now sat higher than his chest, and once a great source of embarrassment. Farley noticed it did not seem to embarrass the man much anymore; a man he once knew to be as solid and tough as a Canadian maple. Farley slowly shook his head from side to side, while Will did the same, each man trying to get his bearings. Barely in control of his nervousness, Farley believed in letting people live their lives so long as they left him alone to live his. Now he found himself on the precipice of having to impose on the life of someone very dear to him. He justified what he was about to do on the grounds of their deep and abiding friendship. For Christ's sake, they were fishing and hunting buddies, and he could never forgive himself if he let such a dear friend come to harm through his own inaction. On the basis of this reasoning, Farley jumped in with both feet.

"We need to talk," Farley said, circumspect as always. Farley didn't waste words and he didn't waste fishing line.

"What's on your mind, old friend?" Now able to focus his bloodshot eyes, Will sat up in the chair, gripping the padded arms.

"You," Farley said.

"Me?"

"Yes, you. Have you looked in the mirror lately?"

Will scratched his beard with his thumb and forefinger. "Okay, so I haven't shaved in a couple of days. But you haven't either."

This perfectly logical observation flustered Farley a moment before he found a suitable rejoinder. "This is not about me; it's about you. You haven't shaved, your hair is longer than I've ever seen it, you haven't brushed your teeth for days and you stink of alcohol and sweat. And you need to burn that robe."

Will pulled away from Farley's verbal assault. "Dammit Farley, that hurts. This is my favorite robe. An old lover made it for me by hand from a sewing pattern. I love this robe."

Farley sputtered a bit. "Don't go and get me off the track of what I came here to say. I'm going to say it, Will Sheridan, and then I'll leave you to your miseries. You have grown fat as a sow bear getting ready to den up." Farley pulled no punches.

Will tried to cover the protrusion of his white belly, defending his physical condition. Begrudgingly he said, "I might have put on a couple of pounds."

Farley laughed derisively. "That's like saying a black bear puts on a few pounds before he hibernates for the winter. I know for sure that winter is coming, but you for sure ain't hibernating." Farley leaned back in his chair across from Will, having done what he came to do. He scooted forward and tapped Will on the one bony white knee still covered in terrycloth blue. "And when's the last time you wrote a word or solved a criminal case?" He said it more as an accusation than a question.

"I can't rightly say, Farley."

"You know full well how long it's been."

Will closed his eyes and put his hand to his forehead. "I know, Farley. Since she left and went back to Germany. I miss her and I miss my uncle."

"So why don't you go and see them both?" Farley asked, steadfast in his logic.

"I plan to see my uncle next summer."

"In the meantime?"

Will shrugged.

"You gotta stop drinking and you have to get back in shape, big man. I'm worried about you."

He yelled at his friend. "God dammit, Farley. You're not my mother, so stop acting like it!" When he saw the stricken look that swept across Farley's face like a hand slap across the cheek, he instantly regretted what he said. He struggled to lean forward over the impediment of his belly. "I didn't mean that, Farley. It's the god damn booze talking, nothing more." The look of misery on Will's face was almost too much for Farley to bear, a man not used to such naked and overpowering sentiment. He had to look away and clear his throat two or three times.

"Farley, do you want something to drink?" Will asked, trying to undo some of the damage that lingered in Farley's face, red with emotion or coughing.

"No, no. I do not want something to drink and I do not want to drink with you either. I want you to get over Sylvie and get on with your life. For the sake of us both, big man, it's time to get over her and move on. After a wildfire even a burnt-out forest starts to rebuild itself."

Will was about to comment on the quality of the old woodsman's metaphor but he thought better of it. He had at least that much self-control left in him. Will took a long hard look at his old friend and fishing partner. He knew what he had allowed himself to become as he slid deeper into the corrosive mud and wallow of self-pity since Sylvie and uncle Roland had returned to Germany, which he felt had been a cruel act of kindness.

Farley stood now that he had said what he had come to say and seen what he needed to see. "No more drinking

Will. Get your fat ass into shape so we can go fishing again."

"I promise, Farley," Will said to his back as Farley turned to go.

Farley raised a hand. "I've heard it all before. Just do it, big man; don't talk about it. Just get it done. And I left your mail on the German table. Looks like there's an important letter from some university down in Iowa. Don't forget to pay your bills. Now I'm going fishing and you ain't. And that's a sad state of affairs if anyone were to ask me."

"Don't go, Farley," Will shouted after him and tried to get up out of his chair. It took him two tries and a bout of hacking stopped in his tracks. By the time he blew his nose and cleared his eyes of tears, Farley was gone, the garage door closing itself. He stood there in bare feet on the cold concrete of the garage until the automatic light went out. He did not know what to do or what to do with himself. Never before in his life, not once, had he ever not known what to do. He needed a drink. Why was he so damn tired and why did he need to sleep all day? He stumbled back into the house, slumped back into his recliner, but he could not maneuver the mechanism to make the chair lay back. He was too weak. There had been a time when he could have lifted the entire chair and carried it upside down on his head. He gave up and stumbled into his bedroom and fell asleep atop the covers. It was three o'clock in the afternoon.

He woke up at ten minutes after eleven pm the same day and stood under the hot water of the walk-in shower until the steam cleared his head. He washed his hair, made a mental note to go into Ray and get a haircut the next day. He shaved in the shower, the new blade in the razor just able to pare down and remove the five-day growth from his face. He scrubbed himself with a washcloth, rinsed, and repeated. He walked out the shower, dried his long black hair with one towel, and dried his body with another. He looked in the mirror, combed his hair back, then shaved again. Finished, he reached for his blue bathrobe, thought better of it, and threw it in the laundry basket. He put on a pair of black underwear, a black T-shirt, and his blue cotton house shorts. He stripped his bed of sheets and pillow cases, gathered his dirty laundry and in the washroom past the kitchen, started a load.

His stomach could manage only toast and tea but it was enough. He returned to his en suite bathroom, cleaned the toilet, the sinks, and the shower. Then he mopped the tiled floors, warm below his bare feet from the embedded heating coils. Then he went into the kitchen, designated it a federal disaster area, and for the sake of his own environmental protection, cleaned it until every surface sparkled or gleamed in the light. He vacuumed the living room, recycled old magazines and newspapers, went through the pile of mail Farley had set next to three others trying to meld into each other like a pack of cards and did a quick triage.

Bills in one pile, in another correspondence or envelopes that interested him. Unopened, he threw the solicitations, ads, credit card offers, and subscriptions to new magazines into the large green recycle can already two thirds full with unread magazines and newspapers. Before he transferred the first two piles requiring further attention into his study—he refused to call it his office except for tax purposes, preferring the more seemly nomenclature of the academic world to the business world. His was a book lined study where he did his research, worked on his criminal cases, and wrote his best-selling books. Their international success was precisely one of the reasons why he had left his tenured position at the university.

He had seen and experienced too many fine universities ruined by administrators who had replaced a perfectly good and viable academic model of running an institution with a business model, which necessitated seeing students as consumers, faculty as replaceable workers without job security, and the university in general as a business organization headed by a CEO-like president who invariably hired a nearly infinite number of vice presidents, all making twice to three times the salary of a professor. No, he had seen and experienced too much of the corruption and malfeasance the business model engendered. The remembrance depressed him and robbed him of his motivation, already stretched dangerously thin. He left the rest of the mail for tomorrow's attention.

He finished cleaning the toilet next to the study, an apt metaphor in his opinion of the current pedagogical philosophy infecting university leadership and management. He sat on the leather couch, exhausted and sweating as the dark of the evening infiltrated the house. He turned on the lights, looked around and was pleased with what he had accomplished. He looked across the room to the liquor cabinet, standing in oak and glass against the far wall. He got up, switched off the lights to the living room and kitchen, changed his underwear and after a quick rinse in the shower went to bed at three am. He read a bit from Mark Twain's, "A Tramp Abroad," dropped the book on the night table and ten minutes later fell asleep, completely sober.

The next day, after a late afternoon fishing for northern pike behind Sugarbush island, he made himself a dinner of the fresh pike, floured and sautéed in butter and finished with a drizzle of lemon juice, served next to wild rice and a shrimp salad. He limited himself to one glass of sauvignon blanc. After he poured the wine, he replaced the cork and put the bottle back into the refrigerator without guilt or qualms. He read the newspaper at the massive oak table that sat in the formal dining room, and decided to make an early night of it. After almost one week since his epiphany and his trip into the ditch, he was able to sleep without first drinking himself into an insensate stupor. Falling asleep wasn't the problem; it was the dreaming. His decision to go to bed earlier than usual was a mistake. At dawn he woke up dreaming of her and sat at the edge of his bed, depressed, still in the nocturnal grip of her attraction. He could smell booze in his nose and for an instant wondered if he had fallen off the wagon and rolled back into the ditch of drinking. But no, it was an olfactory flashback. He had experienced one or two in the early days of his recovery. He debated whether he should just give in and reach for the Glenmorangie. He shook his head clear of that debilitating thought and put on a running shirt, jock, shorts, athletic socks, and running shoes under his Twins ball cap. Now that he had given his liver time to recover, it was time to whip himself back into condition.

CHAPTER THREE

Offer Letter

In the living room he stretched and was disgusted when his gut impinged on his attempts to limber up what was left of his muscle mass, much of it pickled and dissolved in alcohol. He noticed he had also lost a considerable amount of flexibility as his knees tented up when he tried to touch his toes. No worries. No rush. The athlete in him cautioned patience. He would start the run at a brisk walk.

Once out and through the ornate, carved oak double-doors to his cabin, he placed the spare key under a granite rock and shuffled into a fast walk down the gentle slope of the double-wide driveway. He decided two miles should be plenty for the first time out. After 200 meters of a brisk walk down the driveway and onto the county road, he settled into a plodding jog. Not so bad, he thought to himself. I'm still in pretty good aerobic shape. Wind is still good. After 200 meters of jogging, face red with exertion and gasping for air, he stepped off the side of the black topped road, crossed the ditch, grabbed hold of a small birch tree for support and let his stomach try to empty itself. The spasms over, he wiped the tears from his eyes, spat once or twice to clear his mouth, and swallowed the last of the bile as his stomach tried one last time to completely invert itself.

Good, he thought. No need to carry all that extra weight. Now I'm fast and light again. He managed another hundred meters or so before his labored breathing once again forced him to stop and wait for his heartbeat to drop under one thousand beats a minute. "I'm definitely in the training zone," he said aloud to the crows mocking him from their perch in the pine branches above him. He ignored their critiques of his fitness level and jog-walked the remainder of the way back to his mailbox. He stopped only because he needed to check the mail and it was a good thing he did because it was stuffed full. With no possibility of running with both hands full of mail, magazines, and advertising fliers, he walked back up the driveway to his front door. He allowed himself a cool down walk up to the front door. No sense in overdoing it on the first day, he agreed with himself. Don't want to get so sore that I can't move for the next three days. That would be defeating the purpose.

He found his house key, unlocked the front door, picked up the four bundles of mail equaling four weeks of no retrieval, each bundle wrapped in a rubber band, threw them on the kitchen table and went to take a shower. He did not want to leave the pulsating spray of the hot water. His muscles sang from the exertion of the run. As he washed his hair, grown too long for even a Northwoodsman, he laughed at his accomplishment. Not too long ago two hours of handball in International Falls, weights, and a sauna were routine workouts. Today he had barely managed half a mile. He shaved in the walk-in shower and as he toweled off, examined his gut in the mirror above the sink. From a side view he looked to be about six months pregnant. He patted his beer baby bump and said into the mirror, "Bye bye, baby. I love you dearly but I have to give you up."

After his shower he made breakfast: one egg instead of three; no bacon; one piece of toast instead of two; blueberry jam instead of butter on the toast because a man needed some sweetness in his life; a small glass of tomato juice and a large glass of decaffeinated, sugar-free black tea. For rehydration he drank a second glass as he read the paper at the kitchen island.

After breakfast he had restored enough motivation to attack the mail pile again, pleased with his success at the breakfast table. He sighed after surveying the work at hand. It was enough to drive a man to drink. Yesterday's labor had not made much of a dent in all the unwanted correspondence foisted on him through his mail box. Bills requiring immediate action were separated into a pile. Financial, music, fishing, and hunting magazines deserved their own pile; personal correspondence warranted another. All advertisements and junk mail went into the trash pile. Offers for mortgage refinancing—he had paid off his mortgage five years ago—joined the credit card offers in a shred pile. After his survey of the refrigerator's nearly empty shelves, he set aside the coupons for his favorite supermarket in International Falls. It was also time to restock the fridge with foods healthier than just yoghurt and celery.

Once the magazines had been sorted according to interest, he addressed the personal correspondence pile, the shortest stack, given his rapidly failing patience with the entire postal enterprise. An official envelope caught his eye. It was a university envelope from Iowa Polytechnic State University where he had last taught. Another dunning letter for contributions, he thought, and was about to throw it on the shred pile when he noticed the return address. It was from the dean's office of the Graduate College and he recognized the name of a former colleague, one of the very few he had liked and respected as a man and a scholar. It was addressed to Sheridan personally and the salutation properly included his titles. He gave the envelope to the letter opener.

After the address and the usual pleasantries, in the second paragraph the dean got down to business. Professor Doctor William R. Sheridan was being offered a position as a visiting adjunct professor with the rank of full professor. The temporary appointment as a member of the graduate faculty was to last one full academic year, including the Fall, Spring, and Summer semesters. The teaching requirement consisted of one interdisciplinary graduate seminar per semester with a focus on the application of semiotic theory to criminology, his area of expertise. There would be no restrictions on the design of the course. He was not required to teach during the Summer semester but toward the end of the appointment he was required to write an assessment paper to be submitted with his syllabus. The salary was one hundred twenty-five thousand dollars with fringe benefits equaling at least twenty-seven percent of the base salary. Benefits would include full medical and dental insurance, a small life insurance policy, and matching contributions to the university's TIAA pension plan. The total salary package was worth approximately one hundred fifty-eight thousand, seven hundred and fifty dollars. In addition, his moving expenses would be paid and he would receive a stipend to cover the rental of an apartment for one calendar year. The appointment was being financed by a grant from the National Science Foundation.

He dismissed the letter. Not interested. He had vowed never to have anything to do with the academic world ever again. During his tenure as a graduate faculty member responsible for educating Masters and Ph.D. students and his three years as Head of the Department of Interdisciplinary Studies, he had had his fill of political infighting, petty back-stabbing, whining, crying, and professional jealousy. When his first book on the application of semiotic theories to the interpretation and solving of crimes was published to world-wide renown, not one of his colleagues, except for the man who was currently the dean, had come to him and offered personal congratulations. When he resigned his position and left to work as a special consultant for the FBI, again only one man had made the effort to say goodbye and wish him good luck with his new endeavors: the current dean, Dr. Harry Carpenter. The money just was not worth the hassle of dealing with the people anymore.

He finished the personal correspondence pile, wrote a few checks to pay bills, two with apologies for lateness, read the reviews on the five latest hunting rifles, and as he fed the opened envelopes and offers for credit cards he neither wanted nor needed into the shredder, he picked up the letter again and was just about to feed it into the toothy machine when he paused. You know, he thought to himself, this might not be such a bad idea after all. In fact, it might be exactly what he needed: a chance to revisit some of his theories and methods derived therefrom; a chance to teach and work with some energetic and fresh young minds; perhaps a chance to once and finally break the pull of the woman in Bavaria, Germany, where he had been born and grew up.

He looked down at his pregnancy. Not so fast. He was in no shape physically or mentally to handle a graduate class of academically advanced students. Not that he was afraid of anything that they might throw at him. He had educated Ph.D. students who were now professors at major universities around the world. It's just that he wasn't ready. He would need time to develop a pedagogical philosophy of the course, a syllabus detailing reading requirements, exams, papers, and grading expectations. All this took more time and energy than most persons realized. He could not just stroll into an advanced graduate seminar and wing it, although he had seen many of his colleagues do exactly that out of laziness, to the detriment of the students and their education.

He gave the letter one more read, carefully this time instead of speeding through it. The appointment would remain open until filled, but the dean assured him he was the one and only viable candidate and the position had been written specifically with him in mind. Will knew the other verbiage was required to assuage the EEOC folks. The purpose of the position and ultimately the grant, was an effort for the first time to institutionalize Will's methods. Good point, he thought. If he could teach them to FBI field agents in Quantico and law enforcement officers of

Interpol, he saw no reason to think his theories, methods, and processes could not be taught to snot-nosed, fresh-faced, wet-behind-the-ears graduate students, brimming with energy and intellectual curiosity. Nevertheless, such a course would challenge his mental and physical stamina. His stomach betrayed a twinge of excitement, the same anticipation he felt after he analyzed a section of the lake and decided it had to hold good-sized northern pike. Then, the satisfaction of success as he burned a white three-quarter ounce spinnerbait with an oversized nickel Colorado blade through the water and felt the satisfaction of setting the hook and reeling in a forty-two inch alpha predator. When the big toothy fish slashed the bait and hooked herself, he felt an adrenaline rush like an epi pen loaded with naloxone stabbed into the heart of an overdosing cocaine addict.

He had one week to respond to the deadline given in the letter so the university could put things in motion to prepare for his arrival and list his course in the online catalogue available with his course description during Fall registration for classes. He set the letter aside. He checked the calendar on his computer. He was shocked to learn the summer was more than half gone. He looked at the date listed for the start of the course in the Fall semester. Last week of August, but he wanted to be there at least a week prior to meeting his class, if that is what he decided to do. He had about six weeks to get back in shape, develop a syllabus, plan lecture materials and assignments, and a bibliography of books and research articles students would be required to read in order to gain the credits the course offered. Okay. If after one week he felt the same way as he did now, certain that the twinge in his belly was not gas or the baby kicking; if that sense of anticipatory excitement still manifested itself, an excitement Sylvie Schumann often had engendered in him, then he would make the call and send the letter accepting the appointment.

One week later he wrote an email to Dean Carpenter and accepted the offer, setting in motion a return to a former life, a time before Sylvie, and a chance to forget her without the help, aid, or influence of binge drinking. Once his decision was formalized and made contractually inviolate by signing and returning the acceptance letter, he set about his recovery with characteristic discipline. He ate nothing white except a spoonful or two of handmade vanilla ice cream from the Bite'n Bait restaurant up the road to the main highway, his reward for giving up sugar and bread and rice, unless it was wild or brown. He kept Greek yoghurt for its probiotics but limited his milk consumption. He increased his protein consumption as his muscle mass grew, raiding the freezer for venison, pheasant, turkey, and quail. He added spinach to his salads and limited the dressing. Walleye, pike, or smallmouth bass, freshly caught, were on the menu three days a week. When he was too tired or too lazy to cook, he met Farley at the Bite'n Bait and had dinner with the owner, Heidi Popelka, on Walleye Wednesday, enjoying the fresh catch Farley routinely provided the combination restaurant and bait shop. After dinner he picked up a cannister of wriggling nightcrawlers for use the next day off Pine Island when the walleye bite slowed and Lindy-rigged bottom bouncers were not working.

He gave up drinking as medication, but rationalized a glass of wine from Paso Robles in California as food, one high in resveratrol. He limited his beer consumption to one Bavarian beer from Munich and then only after a two-mile run or handball at the Y in International Falls, which he used as a gauge for his return to fitness. In the second week of his reconditioning, he made it through one game of singles. In the third week he could play two games without taking a timeout. In the third week he beat the local champion. In week five of his recovery, he played a tournament in Kelowna, British Columbia and defeated the province champion in the finals, despite not having one member of the raucous and rowdy crowd rooting for him, the very same crowd of avid supporters for their vanquished champion who refused to let him touch his wallet during the celebration in a downtown tavern after the tournament.

By the end of his sixth week and one week away from his departure to Iowa he took stock. He could run two miles in six minutes each. He could bench press two hundred pounds at least fifteen times. He could now play three games of handball three days a week. He had lost a total of four inches off his waist, dropping from a 44 to a 40. Hell, while playing basketball in college he wore a 38. He could see the top four rows of his abdominal muscles again, needing one more week to bring the last row back into view. His manboobs, thankfully, were gone and he was pleased to see the cut of his pectoralis major chest muscles no longer larded with fat. He now measured fifty inches across the chest, which gave him a ten-inch drop to his waist, satisfying one of his goals. Lastly, he was less than five pounds from his target weight of 250, having lost thirty-five pounds over the course of his regimen. When he stood at the urinal in the locker room at the Y, he could now look down and actually see his Bavarian bratwurst.

As he stepped into his Levis, unworn for almost six months, they buttoned without him having to suck in his gut or worry about nearly killing someone when the brass button popped under the pressure of his gut like a rivet letting go from a steam boiler and embedding itself in the wainscoting of the Bite'n Bait one Wednesday deep into his tumble into alcoholic depression. And the loose-fit style he wore because of his muscular thighs once again had enough room to be comfortable, unlike the skinny jeans worn by so many of the emaciated, muscle deprived metrosexuals he saw in the Twin Cities. One last look in the mirror and the reflection of his image showed a man fit, sleek, and once again confident. He had his walk back, as Farley was kind enough to point out last week after fishing for smallmouth bass up in Hacksaw Bay.

Farley was on the way over for a dinner of porterhouse steaks to celebrate Will's accomplishments and give Farley the news about the appointment to IPSU. Over dinner, he broke the news. Farley was silent for a long time before he spoke, cutting, chewing, and swallowing a cut of the filet on the other side of the bone from the sirloin. "I don't have many friends, big man," he said putting down his knife and fork to swirl the glass of zinfandel, a wine he had never heard of until Will introduced him to it and taught him the finer nuances of appreciating the wine. "And I have even fewer guys that I like to fish with or invite in my boat. Losing you is gonna be tough on me. And who's gonna pull your ass out of the ditch when your next girlfriend leaves you?"

Will was stunned at Farley's reaction to the news. He had expected nothing but good wishes, encouragement, and shared happiness with the new opportunity. As Farley nuzzled the wine, it occurred to him. Farley thought he was leaving for good, picking up locks, stocks, and fish barrels. "I must have given you the wrong impression, good buddy. This is nothing more than a temporary teaching position down in northern Iowa. No way in hell am I leaving for good. I have to be there in early August, get an apartment set up somewhere, meet the dean and go through in-processing. I'll teach the Fall and Spring semester but will stay through the summer and write a paper summarizing my experiences with the course and the graduate students." He watched Farley's eyes brighten under a thin film of tear as he realized his dear friend was not leaving for good. "I will be down there for about a year but you know how many breaks college students get. And I'll be back for all the semester breaks, and all the major federal holidays, Thanksgiving and Christmas for sure. We'll get some ice fishing in during the winter holidays."

Farley patted the napkin to the corner of his eyes, then the corners of his mouth. "It was tears of happiness, brother." They laughed at the lie and clinked wine glasses, relief evident in the bronzed face of the older fisherman as it pushed out the last vestiges of the thought of loss.

"By the way, you old sentimental coot. You get the keys to the cabin while I'm gone. I would appreciate it if you would act as caretaker for the property. I'll help you move your stuff from your place and bring your boat over."

"That's a great offer, Doc. But I prefer the comfort of my own bed. If you don't mind too much, I'll stay on the weekends and look after things here during the week."

"Perfect," Will said, glad to see his friend restored to his natural good humor. "But no parties."

"Can't promise that," Farley said.

CHAPTER FOUR

Transition

A week later, having previously said goodbye to his other friends, he handed Farley a full set of spare keys to augment those already in his possession They went through a laundry list of vital information and things that needed to be done in his absence: the collection of unforwarded mail, the new code to the security system, and what plants to water indoors, and cell phone numbers with the promise to call soon as he had the address for his new digs in Iowa. He checked the Subaru Forester once again to make certain he had not forgotten his laptop or his handball gear or his two favorite pillows. He knew the Y at Waterloo, Iowa at one time had a contingent of pretty good ballplayers, but a lot could change in five years. He would find out soon enough if there were still any handball players around.

Satisfied he had not forgotten anything he could not buy down south, he took Farley's weathered hand into his own. Despite his age, the man had a grip of warm steel. Up here in the Great White North, lakers and lumberjacks did not hug in public, not even their wives and the women they loved, may they never meet, but Will said screw it and hugged Farley anyway. He could repair the social damage some other time. He got in the silver SUV and drove south a very long time.

Four and a half hours later he crossed the Mississippi at Minneapolis-St. Paul, and in homage put in a CD of Prince's greatest hits. Before reaching the Twin Cities, he had stopped for a bite to eat and picked up a few packs of artificial worms in case he wanted to do some drop shot fishing for largemouth bass on Iowa's many lakes. He intended to fish during his time off and had brought along his favorite baitcasting rod and reel. In the back he also had a six foot medium-fast St. Croix spinning rod with an Abu Garcia Revo SX spinning reel lined with 6 pound test for excursions to northern Iowa's more than thirty trout streams, most of them lightly fished since most Iowans preferred lake fishing for crappies, bluegills, catfish, and the big black bass found in almost every lake in Iowa. He had forgotten his tacklebox filled with Mepps trout spinners, Super Dupers, and Kastmasters, but he could buy those in the fishing section of any big box store in Iowa.

At Albert Lea, named after Albert Miller Lea, who had surveyed southern Minnesota and northern Iowa, he drove into a thunderstorm that nearly overpowered the electric motor pulsing the wiper blades that cleared the sluicing water from the Suby's broad windshield. The storm welcomed him across the border into Iowa, whose Meskwaki Indian name meant the beautiful land between two rivers, the Mississippi to the east and the Missouri to the west, both rivers carving out the state's borders. All respect to the tribe who had never been defeated by white soldiers and who had bought their own land to live on from the federal government, eschewing the forced and cashiered life lived on a reservation; but come on boys and girls, the rolling hills and forests of northeast Iowa certainly qualified for the beauty designation, but almost everything else had been plowed under and planted to corn or soybeans in service to the god of ethanol, on lands of rich black soil where corn had once been grown to feed people or livestock or provide seed for future growth and plantation.

Now the corn helped fuel the Ford, Chevy, and Dodge pickup trucks ubiquitous throughout the state. As a result of habitat destruction, much of the prairie grass was gone, carved under by gigantic industrial sized plows, and the pheasants were all but gone. The latest road count, according to one of his favorite hunting magazines, had recorded less than a hundred thousand birds where once he could remember counts of over a million birds. That thought and Prince's crying doves saddened him. At least the farmers had prospered, as did Monsanto, the conglomerate that provided the genetically engineered pest resistant, fast growing corn seeds and whose legal problems were now in the hands of the Germans at Bayer. And let's not forget John Deere, who sold the mammoth green combines and gargantuan tractors that pulled the plows, seeders, and fertilizers and allowed a man to farm four months a year on leased ground if he could not afford his own, work another job in town at the hardware store while his wife taught, and spend three months on the Texas coast or on the Florida panhandle during brutally harsh snow-blown Iowa winters.

No, he lamented to himself as he drove on through the purple rain lashing the Subaru, egged on by Prince's own funky soul lamentations, the second golden age of pheasant hunting in Iowa was dead as a racoon, roadkill on the side of I-35 south. Now pheasant hunters sought out Kansas and South Dakota or even parts of Montana, South Dakota alone earning millions of tourist dollars every pheasant season as hunters flocked in with their guns and dogs and trucks needing housing, ammunition, food, and licenses. Prince restored him to good humor with the hope of finding a girl like darling Nikki or one in a raspberry beret.

Dean Carpenter had put him in touch with a trustworthy landlord who rented a duplex to visiting faculty, preferring them to the destruction often wrought by university students who might pile in six or eight deep on each side of the duplex. He would rent to one or two students on the lease but they usually turned the lease around and sublet the apartment to others, two per bedroom and three or four more downstairs in the fully furnished and finished basement. After the neighbors complained of the numerous vehicles parked up and down the street of the family neighborhood, often blocking driveways; trash from empty beer bottles and dixie cups and full condoms after raging beer parties after football games, won or lost, littering front and back yards; coming and going at all hours of the day and night either to early morning classes or late night returns from the bars, he pulled the leases. The straw that finally severed the camel's back was the consistent call from local PD about noise complaints, the rock and rap music thumping from high powered speakers audible through walls four houses down in any direction. When he sat with the local police chief he was presented with a list of complaints, violations, and citations racked up by his renters. And so, after the chief said he was sick and tired of sending his officers out to take abuse and harassment from drunken rowdy revelers, most of them underage vomiting, urinating, and disrespectful examples of Iowa's best and brightest—and he was talking about just the females, who seemed quite content to goad the testosterone, beer, and energy drink fueled young men, with cowboys whoops and titty flashes—the landlord contacted the university and offered his rental to resident or visiting faculty only. He no longer advertised but enough local and transient adjunct and part-time faculty kept both sides of the duplex rented and he was now able to sleep through the night without getting calls from the cops or renters wanting him to come out at 2:00 a.m. in the morning to fix clogged toilets, broken refrigerators, or one idiot who called in a drunken stupor and wanted to know if he could get a deal on the rent since he had been going home on all semester breaks and holidays.

The landlord seemed like a nice enough guy on the phone and the photos he had sent of the apartment were attractive. Will took the time to commiserate with him about his stomach problems, now improving, and his headaches, which had gone away literally and figuratively now that he was no longer renting to students. When Will assured him the university would be covering twelve months of rent, including a damage deposit, his mood seemed to markedly improve. Will signed the lease over the computer.

The Subaru's on-board navigation directed him flawlessly past one of Iowa's few state parks where he had often fished the small lakes there and stretches of the Cedar River, or run on the excellent paved trails used by runners, walkers, bikers, in-line skaters, and cross country skiers in the winter, which meant about half the year; and on past Cedar City, home of Iowa Polytechnic State University. As he drove south along the river, he noticed the old ice house was gone, victim of a previous spring flood. It had once held a decent restaurant even by small town Midwestern standards, where the interview team had taken him to dinner when he interviewed for his tenure track position years earlier.

He drove out of town another mile or two and into a relatively new subdivision called Cherryglen just past the Pheasant Hill municipal golf course where he once had driven a par four hole of just over 400 yards. He could still see that drive in his mind's eye. He might even play a few rounds now and then if time, weather, and schedule permitted, but he would have to rent clubs. As much as he enjoyed the game—and as a younger man had played frequently with his father—golf was a time leech capable of bleeding off an entire afternoon and early evening. And since most clubs did not allow spikes anymore, court shoes would suffice and he had brought those along for handball. One way or another, after his work at the university was done, he intended to stay busy and out of earshot of Sylvie Schumann's siren call across the great green ocean, a call destined to crash him once again on the rocks of inebriation. He had floundered there long enough and now valued his sobriety and reconstituted health.

It was time to accept the fact that she had her life in Germany, and he had his here. She had spurned his offer to stay with him in the States and returned home to her fiancé, a lawyer, after he proposed marriage and she accepted. She worked as a plainclothes detective under the guidance of his uncle and her mentor, Roland Rieger, chief of detectives in the Bavarian State Criminal Police. It was time to accept the fact that she had not chosen him and as difficult as it had been to accept that fact of his life, it was now time to man up and grow a pair and keep the memory of her and all that had been good and beautiful about the woman and the relationship.

And that's what killed him: so much goodness and beauty in one woman. And with his uncle's help during a vacation visit, the three had solved one of his most difficult cases, now chronicled in *The Return of Wahkahchai*. This was actually the second case the three had worked on and solved. He had shared the first case with his readers in *The Adamantine Heart*. In the moment of remembering her, a cinder of despair flared into flame as the female voice of the GPS interrupted his reverie and pulled him back from a fall into the fire of remorse with the announcement that he had arrived at his destination. The Subaru was wise.

He pulled into the driveway off the blacktop, onto a wide drive half gravel off the road and concrete two car lengths long up to the side-by-side, two-door garage. His door was the one on the right but he did not yet have the opener. The incessant rain had followed him down from Albert Lea and into Cedar City. The skies reverberated with the crash of thunder after lightning stabbed its supercharged light across the sky and into the earth, bringing a temporary illumination to his situation. He turned and fumbled behind the passenger's seat for his green 10X Gore-Tex raincoat, one he never traveled without in the car, managed to get it over his shoulder with twists and turns of his body that would have made Houdini proud.

He opened the door, popped a collapsible umbrella open above the car door, and hustled up the two concrete steps below the run to the front door. He pulled open the outer glass weather door, tried the door knob to the wooden front door and found it locked, found the key under the welcome mat as promised, and unlocked the door under the flashlight of a particularly aggressive and energetic lightning strike. As the thunder cracked and rolled over the apartment, he felt the rumble in his chest, and by his calculations, less than a mile away. Dr. Will Sheridan pushed the door open with his booted foot, closed the dripping black nylon umbrella now heavy with water, which he tried to shake off before closing both doors, and entered the front room of the duplex, his home for the next year.

He fumbled for the light switch and once he found it, the rented furniture of the living room emerged. A blue three cushion couch ran the length of the window that looked out onto the street, a chaise longue of the same color faced the newer LCD TV above a cable box; good, he thought to himself, a high-speed Internet connection seemed possible for his laptop. He would need to buy a Wi-Fi router. Swirls in the tan carpet indicated the rug had been recently vacuumed and the furniture smelled of cleaning chemicals. He immediately opened a few windows a crack to let in fresh air. In the kitchen he found a round oaken table large enough to seat six by his count of chairs. A refrigerator, a stove, a dishwasher he was happy to see, a microwave in the corner, all GE and all were white and recently new. The kitchen was large enough for two to cook comfortably in without banging butts or elbows.

He walked back into the living room, turned right and flicked the switch to the bathroom. It contained a double sink and a long mirror lined with six rounded clear light bulbs illuminated the room, which he much preferred over the frosted when he shaved every third day or so. The toilet stood next to the shower, fronted by an unfrosted sliding glass door. The tub sparkled from a recent cleaning. He tested the plumbing; it had been a long drive indeed. At the end of the short hall a door opened onto a bedroom, the window looking out onto the short patio that served as a walkway to the front door of the apartment on the other side of the duplex. A double bed, chest of drawers and an armchair filled the room. He switched off the light and closed the door. Not for me, he thought and tried the last door on the right. This room held a queen-size bed, a full closet, a long chest of drawers of oak, a sitting table with chairs and a bathroom en suite. My room, he said, opening the windows that looked out onto the backyard. Perfect.

The rain had lessened enough for him to bring in his two suitcases, coats, boots, fishing gear, and lastly, his laptop computer. He found an Internet cable and hooked it up but he doubted that the connection was live. He tried it anyway. Nope. He would have to call and have utilities, cable, water and garbage placed under his name. He did get a dial tone on the phone, but he had his cell in his pocket, just in case. He made his bed from the garbage bag of bed linens he had brought in, threw his two favorite pillows on the bed, grabbed an oversize bath towel from another brown garbage bag, his toiletries kit, and took a long hot shower, read until midnight, and fell asleep.

He woke once to pee, disoriented in the dark until he turned on the lamp that lit his bed, and remembered where he was, thankful for once that the sense of not knowing where or when he was came from displacement in time and space and not the detachment of his emotions through the act of imbibing beer, wine, and whisky. He woke ten hours later refreshed and renewed, but he had dreamed of her again, all the same. Wish fulfillment dreams, he noted to himself, perfectly normal and to be expected. He had always deemed his unconscious self the smarter of the three parts of his Freudian personality. He needed to eat and satisfy the wishes of another basic drive altogether.

After breakfast of a single hamburger with lettuce, tomatoes, pickles, mustard, but no onions or cheese, at the nearest Hardees, he made a call to the graduate dean's office at Iowa Polytechnic State University or IPSU stenciled above the university's crest on the sweatshirts of the students on campus. When he last checked, about 14,000 undergraduate students were enrolled, with another 3000 or so at the graduate level, pursuing either a master's or doctoral degree. At one time the department in which he had labored—and he used the term decidedly—had been designated one of the three premier graduate departments in the university and he had the distinction of serving as a graduate professor nine of the ten years he had taught there. Dean Carpenter was pleased to receive him at Will's earliest convenience and Will assured him he could be there in in about fifteen minutes. Will offered to bring him a hamburger but the dean laughed and said he had just eaten.

The campus had not changed much over the years. A few newer buildings he did not recognize had risen. He wondered if the library had been expanded. A Research I institution like IPSU lived or died by the quality of its on-campus libraries. The football stadium, an enclosed dome supported by air seemed to have a new roof, and additional buildings formed a larger complex, no doubt other athletic facilities such as weight rooms and coaches' offices. One had the look of a new basketball arena. Always money for sports, he mused, and little for the academic side; these were indeed constants in the academic universe. Nevertheless, he enjoyed watching Division I collegiate sports and thought about buying season tickets for both.

He found parking in front of a large four-story building that housed the administrative offices for the university, unimaginatively named the Admin Building. He pulled the Subaru into one of the four spaces reserved for visitors, ignored the meter blinking at him, entered the glass doors of the administrative building and found the directory. He took the elevator to the fourth floor where the administrative offices of the graduate studies dean and the president of the university were housed. He walked through the open door and was greeted by a pretty work-study student at the front desk. "Please inform the dean that Dr. William Sheridan has arrived."

She stood and returned his smile and said, "Yes, sir. Please follow me. You are expected."

A good start.

CHAPTER FIVE

Dean's Office

The weather in Iowa is brutal, as it is in most parts of the north central United States, a brutality unsuitable for livestock and most human beings. The seasons are oppressive and weigh down on you and press into your bones hardening them at first, then making them brittle by sucking out all the calcium. Old people who have suffered through decades of weather begin to look like crows. Noses lengthen into beaks, eyes glass over, backs round and shoulders slump, legs and arms thin and walking gaits are reduced to stiffened waddles. If they have enough money, the lucky ones fly to Arizona, Texas, or California where the sun drills some lightness back into their bones.

The seasons shuttle in an oppressive heaviness not unlike gravity on a larger planet; they pull you down to the ground where you work the earth, plow it, till it, seed it, harvest it and repeat until eventually you can no longer escape the relentless weight of the earth and there you are laid to rest. Spring storms blow tornadic wind and rain strong enough to knock you down and moves the earth and fells trees. Rivers flood the farm and reposition houses further down the river. Your property becomes lakefront. The summer humidity lies heavy on your chest and infiltrates into your lungs like a pernicious virus, restricting your breathing. The summer heat boils the water out of your blood, thickening it like clay slurry at the bottom of a river, and deprives you of oxygen needed to think. The snow and cold retard your movement into a slow-motion film. Iowa is a land of Gore-Tex and air conditioning. And then comes the gentle respite of autumn before the approaching brutality of winter: the rains stop, humidity breaks, temperatures moderate, the winds die down, and the harvest is good and the sweetcorn fresh.

From behind a desk much too large for the room, the dean of the Graduate College came around to greet Will first by name and then by hand and clapped him on the shoulder. "My God, man," he gushed, "you haven't aged a day." He meant it. "You certainly seem fit enough," he remarked.

"Thanks, Harry," Will said. "The years have been kind to you, too," he lied.

The dean pointed to his nearly white hair. "I'm not so sure about that. I still had brown hair when you and I taught together here...," he paused for a moment, "some years ago." Will noted the careful formulation of the dean's statement. That's why he was the dean.

"How long have you served, Harry?"

As the dean waved Will to take a seat in one of the two upholstered chairs at either end of the glass coffee table, he paused a minute to count the years. "I took over the position of head of department from you after you left to go to work for the FBI. I did that for about three years until Dean Winston left, or to be more precise, was asked to leave. I served as acting dean until after a national search. I came out as the number one candidate and the university screwed up and hired me to take over the reins. I was then appointed by the president to run the Graduate College."

As Will settled himself across from one of the few faculty members he had truly respected as a scholar and as a man, he remembered. "Ah, yes. Wasn't she the one who in one year's time outspent all three head football coaches at all three of Iowa's Research I universities in travel expenses alone?"

The dean laughed. "She's the one. No one has yet figured out how the *Des Moines Register* got hold of those figures." He gave Will a sly wink. "Any ideas?"

Will smiled and ignored the question. "It is good to see you again, Harry. The fact that you are the dean of one of the largest colleges in the university speaks well of you."

Dean Harry Carpenter accepted the compliment with a smile and said, "Let's get down to brass tacks because I know that's what you're here for."

Will interrupted. "As a matter of curiosity and before we start, whatever happened to her?"

"Oh, you're not going to believe this," the dean said, leaning in closer and dropping his voice so the secretaries and work study students in the next room could not overhear what he did not want overheard. "If I recall, at the time, you were the president of the university Senate and thus charged with conducting her fifth-year evaluation."

Will nodded. "And once statistical services finished their analysis of faculty responses and sent them back to me, they were so shockingly bad that I took them directly to President Feinberg. He came to my office the next day and said that he would take care of the matter personally. What he did," Will added, "was promote her into the office of the president the next semester. But I heard that two years later she was gone. Any idea where?"

"Last I heard she was running a school for girls in Texas on the Mexico border down by Matamoros, I think," Carpenter said.

"Good riddance," Will said, "but the girls there have my sympathies."

"I'm with you there," the dean agreed. He laughed again. "I still can see you at the first all college faculty meeting when she introduced us to her plan to institute and support multiculturalism in our college, and you had the balls to ask her what exactly she meant by multiculturalism. I remember how shocked she looked that anyone could have the audacity to question her grand plan by first asking her to define her terms. She mumbled and fumbled for some nonsensical definition bereft of any logic or sense whatsoever."

Will nodded. "You know, Harry, it was a legitimate question and I absolutely had no desire to try to embarrass the woman. The intent behind my question was sincere as I am the product of two cultures myself, and as a Ph. D. with an interdisciplinary doctorate, and as a graduate studies professor teaching at a Research I university that recruits and educates, at least at the graduate level," he allowed, "students from all parts of the world, I simply wanted to know exactly what this grand design for multiculturalism was to be."

The dean reset a white plastic button on the cuff of his blue button-down long sleeve shirt, looked out the window and said, "I know there is always a subtext behind your questions, Will. I think you wanted to expose the fact that there was very little thinking behind her so-called grand design to institute multiculturalism at our university; that you wanted to show the rest of the faculty that this was simply another example of upper-level administration trying to institute vacuous, poorly thought through blather generated by education Ph. D.'s that have never been so much as a department head, to say nothing of leading a faculty or having a vision for the direction of the college based on the best needs of the students and the faculty." He looked at Will for confirmation.

"You already know what I think, Harry."

"And by the way, we don't call it multiculturalism anymore. We call it diversity." Harry gave Will a minute to chew that one over as just another example of how vacuous concepts morph into other terminology and gain traction in the slippery mud of pedagogical ideology. "Let's have a little fun at your expense," he said. "In order to better understand your motives in asking your question of the dean, please allow me to apply some of your vaunted semiotic analysis to the situation."

Will grinned and steepled his fingers. It was exactly this sort or intellectual interplay between two scholars that he found himself missing from time to time. "It seems you have been reading my books. I'm honored. This should be good." He opened his hands in welcome. "By all means, analyze away, but if you screw it up, I'm going to tell you."

The dean locked his fingers behind his head, arms bent at the elbow. The chain mail gauntlet of analysis and interpretation had been thrown down. "I find it a significant fact that you led the interdepartmental search committee for this particular dean."

Will demurred. "I was appointed to the committee and after we met the first time, they voted me chair and I accepted. That is the substantiated fact, but whose significance you have not yet demonstrated in your analysis. And you might add, in the hopes of bolstering your case, I served on numerous such committees over the years, some as chair, all of which resulted in the successful hire of quality, competent faculty or staff. On this basis, the president selected me for the hiring committee."

"In what you just said I hear the implication that our former dean was not a quality, competent candidate."

Will leaned forward in his chair. "Dammit Harry! It's not an implication at all. It's the result of a demonstrable proof. To wit: her fifth-year review was the worst I have ever seen for an administrator at this university. She had five years to show us what she could do and, in the end, it was consistently and dishearteningly bad. And as you know, the president immediately shut down the review process, asked me to forward any and all documentation to his office, by which he meant the stack of damning letters many faculty members took time from their busy schedule to write. And if I remember correctly, one of those letters, signed, was from you." Will pointed an accusatory finger at the dean. "So, let me ask you, Harry..."

Dean Carpenter opened his hands in welcome, at the same time condemning the poor leadership and direction of the previous dean.

"Had those results gotten out it would have caused embarrassment for everyone involved. That's how bad it was.

Have you ever heard of a college-level review process being summarily shut down because the results were consistently awful?"

"I am happy to inform you that I have not," he said remembering the results of his own fifth-year review. He paused for a minute and scratched his chin. "No doubt about that," Harry agreed. "We dodged a bullet there."

"No, Harry. We didn't dodge a bullet. I changed the direction of the shot before the pistol was aimed and fired. Now please continue with your analysis."

Dean Carpenter resumed. "It is a demonstrable fact that after all three candidates had been interviewed and received their trips to campus, your committee forwarded the name of an associate dean then at the University of Indiana, whom the committee decided was the most qualified and competent candidate."

"That is a fact, known to be true, and irrefutable," Will agreed. "He had served four years as an associate dean in their College of Social Sciences, a college three times the size of ours. His faculty had given him their unqualified support as an AD and during his tenure as the head of the Anthropology Department, I might add. Every single letter written in support of his candidacy lamented the fact that they might lose him, but thought he would make a wonderful dean for us. He had established a reputation as a published scholar before he moved into admin. Accordingly, I have no doubt that he was by far the best candidate and my committee agreed in full and with complete consensus. On that basis I advanced his name to the president. I have no doubt he would've led this college to even greater prominence."

Now the dean leaned in. "That, my friend, is an unsubstantiated hypothesis."

Will waved away the assertion. "Not entirely. I told you he turned us down, with regret, because the damn salary we were able to offer him at the time was an embarrassment. Why would he or anyone in their right mind take a pay cut of nearly $25,000 to come work here at IPSU?" Will asked, not expecting an answer. "And where is he now?" Will challenged the dean. "And this speaks to my claim that he would have substantially improved and advanced our college. He's currently a vice president at Stanford." Will sat back in his chair.

"I take your point," the dean allowed. "It is also a known fact," he said, returning to his analysis, "that the president of the university at the time asked for you to send a rank-ordered list of the top ten candidates, one that included at least one female candidate, and you had her ranked last."

Will corrected him. "She was the only female who applied! The committee ranked her last, but I agreed with their assessment. She had a doctorate in education, and took most of her courses online and, Harry, you know as well as I do, hers was not a research-based degree; it was an administrative degree and you also know fully well that she was not trained as a research scholar and that she did not understand the demands placed on a faculty of a Research I institution such as ours to publish or perish. In the social sciences, it is extraordinarily hard to get work accepted for publication. My book on semiotic theory took me three years to research and write.

"In addition, her recommendations were tepid, to say the least. And not one letter spoke of the woman in glowing terms either as a person or in terms of her accomplishments. My analysis of the letters indicated that the writers were writing in order to get rid of her. She was department head at some quasi-religious private college in Arkansas, for crying out loud." The intensity in Will's voice underscored the point. "I would in fact have been remiss in my duties as charged by the university had I not pointed out her shortcomings, as I did for all the candidates, I might add."

"And the university hired her anyway," the dean noted.

Will grimaced at the irrefutable truth of the statement. "She was an affirmative action hire, Harry. You know that as well as anyone. That's the ugly elephant stinking up the room that no one wants to talk about. And why did the president think we had to go outside the university to hire a dean? I argued we have more competent and qualified women right here in this college, Harry, many of whom I hired personally."

"I'm with you there, Will. But the analytical point is this: she was hired despite your recommendation against, and against the recommendation of the hiring committee, a fact that she no doubt got wind of. And when you stood to ask her to define and explain her notion of multiculturalism, she talked in circles for five minutes until she confused everyone in the room, including herself. Then she just stopped talking and stood there in a pile of excremental embarrassment until one of her future ass kissers lobbed her a softball question and pulled her out of her own drowning cesspool. My semiotic analysis of that event allows me to conclude you had intended the question as a warning for the rest of us and as a validation of your, and your committee's assessment," he asserted, here holding up a hand to thwart Will's interruption, "that she was intellectually unqualified, and not ready for the job."

Will crossed his legs and gripped both supporting arms of the chair. "There is no doubting your brilliance, Harry. "This is one of the reasons you always had my respect. And kudos on your analysis; you nailed it and you nailed me but let me say just one thing in my defense. I knew her; the woman was a fake and I was simply trying to warn others."

"And no one listened."

"And very few listened," Will said, correcting Carpenter. "And that is my failing and I take full responsibility for that. The woman set our college back ten years."

"That's a demonstrable fact," Harry agreed. "It has taken many years of hard work to repair the damage she caused and bring us back to the prominence students and faculty of the College of Human and Social Sciences deserve."

CHAPTER SIX

Squared Away

For the next few minutes both men sat in the comfortable silence of two men who had renewed a friendship, thinking through all that had been said and learned. Will was the first to break the mood of shared contemplation.

"To give you a bit more insight into those times, Harry, let me give you a significant interpretable example."

Harry crossed his long legs, pulled a cuff down over an exposed shin and awaited the example with genuine interest.

"This happened shortly after the president shut down Dean Winston's fifth-year evaluation and review. As you know, the Interdisciplinary Studies Department, which I headed back then, advanced to the dean the agreement that we needed to institute a new general education requirement, one that focused on the importance of language communication within the human and social sciences. After the curriculum committee for the college accepted the recommendation, we sent the recommendation under the signatures of all seven department heads and forwarded it to Dean Winston's office, as requested. And I have to tell you, in all honesty, she seemed genuinely enthusiastic about it. I thought great, it was a perfect example of our college and university taking a leadership role by offering a general education requirement course that would teach our students the importance of language communication whether the students be English, sociology, psychology, business, or physics majors, you name it.

"Then she said, 'tell me what you need and I'll give it to you.' I found that strange because our committee at the department level had already broken down the need for additional faculty and costs of salaries, hiring costs, staff and support expenditures, and so on. We argued that we were willing to take on the monumental and disruptive task of implementing a GER because it was a very good way for us to take our small department and grow it with the addition of more teaching faculty. As department head, I even volunteered to give up a graduate seminar and teach a section of the new course. After hearing her statement, it was evident to me she had not read the entire proposal or she would have never said that to me."

Harry nodded enthusiastically. "I remember you said at the departmental faculty meeting we were promised four new hires for the next year and two more each year thereafter until we got the ten we needed to cover all the sections of the course."

"Exactly," Will said. "We got funded in full the first year, hired four new faculty with enough expertise to teach the course, were sending out advertisements for the next year's positions when the money suddenly dried up, despite the fact that her signature appeared on the line below the budget for full implementation and rollout of the course as a general education requirement."

"I didn't know that," Carpenter admitted.

"You weren't in a position to know then. There's something else you don't know. After the program's successful implementation after the first year, it became one of our most popular courses, according to student evaluations. But there was an inherent systemic problem that I foresaw, after she had withdrawn the funding originally budgeted to successfully implement the GER as planned." He paused, waiting for the dean to ask the next logical question. When it came, he said, "By the end of the third year, as I predicted, because of her unwillingness to bring on the additional faculty and staff required to cover all the needed sections, we were swamped with seniors who could not graduate because they could not get seats in the course now required for their degree. We had 3000 students unable to matriculate because of a three-credit course they could not get into because there were not enough sections being offered. And every time I went to her office to beg for more money to hire new faculty, faculty which she had promised us and supposedly budgeted for, she was gone, attending a weeklong conference in Hawaii, Puerto Rico, the Caribbean, San Diego, or some or similar warm weather location while our problems grew worse in the department. Finally, one day after her return from a trip to Florida, where she was attending a conference on how to manage aggressive faculty unwilling to buy into her programs, I walked into her office and closed the door. I laid it out in black and white, in terms that even a person with a doctorate in education could understand. You know what she said?"

Dean Carpenter shook his head.

"'How are you going to solve this problem?' is what she said; as if this were somehow in some alternate universe a problem of my making. At that point I was irate and I told her in no uncertain terms that she was the cause of the problem because she was never here. She, not I, had signed off on the course and its budget and her inactivity and unwillingness to provide our department with the funds she had promised was now catching up to her, not me, to the detriment of 3000 seniors who would not be able to graduate on time.

"At that point in the conversation I thought she would shrivel up, dry up, and blow away like an oak leaf in December. To my dying day I will never forget what she said to me. 'You have to help me, Dr. Sheridan. We have to work together, you know, for the good of the students and for the good of our college,' she said, imploring me. Harry, I tell you I have never heard such desperation in an administrator's voice. What the hell was I going to do? I couldn't leave all those students in the lurch due to her professional malfeasance. It wasn't their fault that they were suffering due to inadequate and incompetent leadership from the dean's office.

"I pulled up my chair and said you have three possible solutions to this mess. Option Number One: withdraw the requirement for all students to take the course in order to graduate. Make it an elective. We have enough faculty on board now to cover the course as an elective. Know what she said? 'That's not going to happen; not on my watch. It would be an explicit admission that we failed.' No, I corrected her. It would be an admission that you failed. My department has done its job without failure. She ignored me and asked for Option Number Two. Okay. Temporarily waive the GER course for this year's graduating class due to a budget emergency. It's been done before. It surprised her to learn this. You temporarily waive the requirements for the 101 course only for the seniors who need it to graduate and this buys you time to hire new faculty according to the original schedule we gave you and you signed off on but have refused to honor. She looked away when I brought this little bit of an annoying fact to her attention. When she turned back to me, in a voice barely above a whisper she said, 'Professor Sheridan. The money isn't there.'

"What do you mean the money isn't there? I asked dumbfounded. I thought maybe I misunderstood her but no, she said again that the money wasn't there. 'I didn't ask for it at the last university budget meeting,' she explained. I could not have been more surprised if my dead grandmother from Germany had walked through the door wearing a dirndl and carrying six mugs of foaming Oktoberfest beer. I waited for her to continue with her explanation, letting the silence prompt her. She said, 'I didn't want to give the president and the other members of the budget committee the impression that our college couldn't buckle down, cut courses in other areas, be more efficient, and not always have to ask for more money when other colleges were having to do with less.'

"The illogic of her explanation made me furious. She could not have cared less about the course or the students hanging in graduation limbo, or the faculty working themselves to death taking on extra students, against contract rules I might add, in order to save her face in front of the committee. Later, I was told by the vice president who sat on the budget committee that he could not understand why she did not simply request the disbursement of monies for what they already considered a fully funded line item. In other words, Harry, they had the money set aside and the will to give it, but because of her lack of knowledge of the budgeting process, and since she didn't ask for it, they couldn't force her to take the money. They assumed she didn't need or want it. And since no one asked for the funds, they reallocated them."

Harry shook his head in disbelief. He had not known it was really that bad. He waited for Will to continue his account of the events. He wanted to hear the third option.

"'Next option,' she said, glaring at me. Okay. Option Number Three: Here's where we stood. The money to hire new faculty to teach the courses was gone. I did some fast thinking and some fast calculation. I said to her your next option and last option is this: both the Interdisciplinary Studies Department and our sister the Communication Studies Department in our college are two of the three designated premier graduate programs and, as such, are funded by a special recurring grant from the state that we can tap into. Here's what we can do: each graduate student, as you know, and I wasn't sure if she did know, can teach four 100-level introduction courses, two per semester as part of their teaching stipend. If we admit an additional ten graduate students into each program, that gives us twenty grad students in total. We pay them a standard graduate teaching stipend and that allows us to cover an additional eighty sections a year. With twenty students per class, that's an additional 1600 freshmen and with current faculty and graduate students already teaching the course, you will have demand covered for next year. And I might add, at a fraction of the cost it would require to hire the tenure-track faculty needed for the course. Problem solved. Both departments get new grad students, seniors graduate, and you come out of this looking like a genius.

"Harry. I am not exaggerating. She looked at me as if I were an idiot. She said, 'no,' emphatically. 'I want to maintain our student-to-professor ratios and if we put more graduate students in these new 101 sections, we lose our excellent ratio. I just can't do that. It affects the ratings our college gets when national magazines publish their yearly university rankings.'

"I was flabbergasted. So the reason she couldn't do it, as I understood it, was because she was deathly afraid that we would lose our ranking in the *U.S. News & World Report's* listing of the nation's top research universities. Screw the departments and screw the seniors. At that point I got up, left without saying goodbye, went to my office and typed my resignation letter. It was two words so she would not misinterpret it: I resign. And at the end of the semester I was gone and started my work as a special consultant for the FBI, and shortly thereafter published my first novel detailing some of my investigative work with them and Interpol."

"Amazing," Harry said, shaking his head. "I had no idea at the time. Thank goodness for the article in the *Des Moines Register* that came out the year after you left and detailed the hundreds of thousands of dollars she spent going to conferences all over the world. Nero fiddling while Rome burned. Despite her short and temporary relocation to the Office of the President, the scandal and the misuse of taxpayer dollars ultimately led to her dismissal."

Will grumped. "There was no mention in the paper of the 3000 seniors forced to graduate without having taken all the required courses. Or why this could possibly happen in the first place on Dean Winston's watch."

"No, that was never mentioned," Harry said, shaking his head as he remembered those times. "I sure as hell was sad to see you go. To this day the few of us from those times who still teach here wondered why you left so suddenly. We had no idea. Now I know."

Will avoided the opportunity to clarify his actions further. "One last question, Harry. How did they eventually solve the problem?"

Harry laughed. "You're never going to believe this. I found your solutions after you had typed them up, leaving them no doubt for whomever took your place, and as the appointed interim department head, I took your solutions directly to the president. He signed off immediately after he asked if you had shown all the options to Dean Winston and I said, of course, and she had dismissed all three as unworkable. The third option was initiated and implemented forthwith. It worked beautifully. In the year following we got the monies to admit twenty new graduate students. And two years later were able to put faculty back to teaching graduate courses. We were funded to hire an additional two graduate faculty members. And the icing on the cake: we ultimately received a grant to fund your current position as an adjunct visiting full professor, a direct consequence of the growth of our two premiere graduate programs within the college."

Now it was Will's turn to laugh. "We could conclude that I am both directly and indirectly responsible for my own hiring ten years after my resignation."

Harry chuckled, recognizing the delicious irony. "We could indeed, if we force that conclusion."

Will did not comment on the amendment to his conclusion, but instead asked, "Otherwise, how are things going in the Graduate College at good old Iowa Polytechnic State University?"

"Things are improving by degrees, pardon the pun, certainly now with the arrival of a research scholar possessed of an analytical mind even greater than my own." Will laughed again at his false hubris. "And I mean that sincerely. Your semiotic method of analysis enabled me to learn, interpret, and understand an event that very few of us here at the university could figure out or make sense of. Why in the world would a scholar and teacher of your reputation and rank suddenly leave the university? Now I know and I am greatly saddened by what I have learned. This makes me even more proud to have you here again."

"You know I'm the last person in the world who needs smoke blown up his ass, Harry. But I can tell you it is a pleasure to be sitting across from you again. I missed our conversations. But keep your hot lips to yourself or I might be tempted to file a sexual harassment suit with the Office of Affirmative Action." The dean threw up his hands in mock terror at that possibility and then after a short break for a snack together in the campus union, they got down to work getting Will squared away to take on his new teaching position.

Dean Carpenter walked with him down to the ground floor of the Admin building and led him to a convenient table in the Human Resources offices. To Will's surprise, Carpenter sat with him and personally walked him through the paperwork brought by office staff, indicating signatures where and as required. Normally, this was a job handled by staff, but when a dean said he wanted to do it, he got to do it. "When I wrote the grant initially, I put in the salary for a full professor on a nine-month standard contract, but on second thought, given that there might also be some administrative details left over that might take you through the summer—and here I'm thinking you might want to write up your experiences and possibly publish them—I changed the appointment from a nine-month academic year to a full twelve months, but you won't have to teach in the summer. Accordingly, what you have here is a new offer letter listing the starting salary and fringe benefits. Around here a full bull professor earns $125,000; add another $63,000 for the summer and in total you will be paid $188,000. You can decide to be paid biweekly or once a month." Will selected once a month. "In addition, you will receive full health and medical benefits, still no vision, I'm afraid, but we're working on that in the next contract, and you will have full dental benefits also, not that you look like you need them."

"I'm glad to have them," Will said. "You can never be too sure when a radical feminist might try to sucker punch a guy."

"Right," said the dean, hoping that none of the five women working in the office had overheard the remark. "Your pension will be fully funded through TIAA and you will have to select the balance between stocks and bonds."

Will thought for a minute about the market's prospects for the coming year. "Let's put 90% in stocks, half of that in the U.S. and the other half international, and put 10% in bonds." The dean looked at him under raised eyebrows. "You know something the rest of us don't?"

Will just grinned. "Semiotics, as the study of signs and symbols, can also be applied to the analysis and under-standing of economic indicators; in other words, signs that point us in the general direction the market might take. My analysis of current economic signs leads me to con-clude with about a 90% certainty that the market will improve over the coming years."

"How much?" The dean asked, writing a quick note to himself.

"That, I can't tell you," Will confessed. "Those predictions I leave to the talking heads on TV. But you know as well as I that on average, during the bull market, you can ex-pect a gain of about 7% or so in an index fund tied to the Dow Jones averages, and with the current yield from bonds under 25 basis points, it's a no-brainer for me."

"Okay. Almost done. For your information your fringe benefits calculated out to just under 27% of your salary thanks to our union statisticians, which would give you a total pay package of about...let's see," he patted his shirt for a calculator or his cell phone, but Will said, "half of one 188 is 94, half of that is 47, so add 47 to 188 and the pay package is worth about $235,000. Not bad, not bad at all and a helluva lot better than ten years ago."

The dean warned him, "Well, you haven't met your students yet. Then we'll see if this is sufficient compensation. I kept enrollment open and designated the course as enrollment at the discretion of the professor only. So you can pick and choose with whom you want to work." He looked up for confirmation that he had done the right thing and in Will's best interest.

"Very good," Will acknowledged. "How many do you want me to take on?"

"Entirely up to you but based on demand for graduate courses, I would suggest 5 to 7, but the course will fly even if you have only one student."

From his previous experience as a graduate studies professor, Will knew it was not unusual for highly demanding graduate seminars to be left with only two or three students. The work load of reading complex research articles and books, writing twenty-page papers that required in-depth analysis and critique, not to mention mid-terms and finals, often proved too much for some inadequately prepared masters or doctoral students. For that reason, most universities limited graduate course work to ten credits a semester if the grad student was also teaching two introductory courses. However, most undergraduate courses are self-supporting or they are dropped.

"I'll see to it that you get the class pre-enrollment list with student photos before you leave. You can make your selections from that pool. And now duty calls, my friend. I have to chair the university committee on committees," he said, without a trace of irony. I'll leave you in good hands to finish your in-processing. We'll talk again tomorrow. Just call the office and tell them when you're coming by."

"Thanks, Harry," Will said, as he stood and the men shook hands. "I'm looking forward to taking this on. It truly means a lot to me."

"My pleasure, Professor Doctor Sheridan. "Glad to have a scholar and researcher of your reputation on board."

CHAPTER SEVEN

Handball

Will had his picture taken for his official university identification card, one that also permitted him full access to the research libraries on campus. He received a set of keys, one to his office, the door to the building, and a master key that opened all locked classrooms given that the university was still on semester break. He signed another set of papers including his W-2 form and designated Farley Nilsson as his recipient for the modest life insurance policy in the event of his death. He checked the box for a one-year enrollment in the state faculty union.

He was given handouts covering salary, university codes of conduct for students and faculty, expectations for tenure, his rights as a professor, and a map of the campus. He kept a copy of the signed W-2 form, thanked everyone for the generous use of their time, and walked back to Hall Hall, known to the students as H2. The three-story building housed about half of the College of Human and Social Sciences faculty, but all the departmental offices and staff. It was named after the former dean of the college responsible for raising the monies that got the building built in the first place. At H2, he rode the elevator up to the third floor, ticked off room numbers until he found 345, easy enough to remember at the end of the hall that housed the offices of the Department of Interdisciplinary Studies, or ISD as students, the military, and other paramilitary organizations like the Marshals Service, CIA, or FBI abbreviated wherever and whenever they could. He had been assigned office space within the department, given the interdisciplinary nature of the course he was to teach, designated a 700-level course, reserved for doctoral level seminars but occasionally open to master's students as well.

At the personnel office he had been given a sign with his name etched on it in white letters against the black plastic: William R. Sheridan, Ph.D. and underneath, his rank of Professor. He slid it into the vacant slot next to his door, keyed the door and entered the office. A full bank of windows overlooked the grassy commons below framed by a series of other buildings whose names he would have to learn again later. Curtains, institutional brown and recently laundered, edged the long run of windows. The office was twice the size of the one he had formerly occupied as head of department. Signs indicated his office was previously used as a seminar room; it had been converted to an office for visiting adjunct faculty on temporary appointments.

On the left side of the room stood two rows of bookcases, metal, gray and empty. In the middle of the room, a desk gray, with a computer and keyboard, with a high back leather chair facing the door. To the right, a large tan couch, long enough to seat three comfortably fronted by a wood framed glass coffee table circled by three uncomfortable modern chairs whose blue color clashed with the couch in color and in form. He concluded each had been an afterthought and an attempt to fill the space of the large room more efficiently, but from university surplus. There were no pictures on the white walls. The phone sat next to the computer and the printer.

Good enough, he said to himself and took his watch from his pocket. Close to 4:00 p.m. Time to drive to the Y in the neighboring city of Waterloo to see if he could get a handball game and if not, hit the weights, the exercise bike, and take a Jacuzzi, despite the hot and humid weather.

After a workout of some sort and only then would he allow himself thoughts of dinner and at least one more night out, since he had not yet had time to set up a bed or provision his kitchen. He took the placard authorizing him to park anywhere on campus and threw it in the glove box. Was nobody's business who he worked for. He punched Waterloo YMCA into the navi; it had been ten years since his last visit, let it find and report the address, studied the route, and followed the directions to the gym. At the front desk he signed up for a year, including laundry service; he was given a locker number, a four-digit combination to the men's locker room door, a laundered white towel that smelled of industrial-strength dryers and cheap motels, and a white fishnet bag for his wet workout clothes and used towel.

He punched in the four numbers to pop the door to the men's dressing room, found his locker and dialed the combination of the painted locker door above the concrete bench that ran the length of the rows of tall blue lockers. He stripped, grabbed a towel, showered quickly and found the whirlpool. Screw the workout, he thought, as he lowered himself into the hot water, bubbles popping chlorinated spray into his face from the force of the jets pushing water under pressure into the cauldron where he sat. He slid in up to his chin, keeping his mouth closed and wrinkled his nose at the smell of heated chlorine. After exactly five minutes of soak time, he rinsed off quickly under a cold-water shower to close his sweating pores, toweled himself dry and dressed for handball. Still sweating lightly from the whirlpool, he walked out the locker room, red gym bag strapped over his shoulder, took a fresh towel from the stack at the laundry desk and walked down the hall to the five handball courts.

Through the glass back walls of the championship court, he saw three men playing a game of cutthroat. He watched them for a time to gauge their skill level and after they finished the point being played, all three players exited through the small rectangular door of the glass back wall and introduced themselves. They invited him in for a game of doubles, having noticed the eight pairs of handball gloves hanging from his gym bag. This was handball etiquette at its finest, and no matter where he traveled in the United States, it was always the same: a warm and genuine welcome back to the brotherhood of men and women who played one of the most physically demanding games in the world. Numerous physiological studies in sports medicine ranked handball among the top three sports for best conditioned athletes.

They gave him time to warm up alone in the court, went to get a drink while they rested a bit, and took a moment to judge his abilities as he progressed through his warm up routine. He started slowly, once the teams had been determined, playing the left side to complement his partner strong right hand. The game stayed close until the tenth point. He received a serve, which he let rebound off the back wall and rolled it out flat for a perfect kill shot called a blue mouse. This required striking the ball low enough so that it hit millimeters above the floor and the front wall simultaneously, the blue ball rebounding like a mouse rocketing from its home. "Great shot!" all three yelled.

When it was his turn to serve, he cracked out three serves just past the service line so that the ball rolled flat off the side wall, each for a service ace and an easy point for his team. He then hit two more power serves that crossed just millimeters above the short line, both unreturnable serves. During the next rally, with his left hand he hit a flat kill shot off the front wall, ending the rally and winning the game. All four players shook hands after the game, crab walked out through the door to get water, towel off the sweat, and change shirts. As they rested, one of the older players on the other doubles team sat next to him on the bleachers. He was the top player on the opposing team and as a left-hander, also played the left side. "Good game," he said, changing his gloves. "You said your last name was Sheridan?" Will nodded. "I remember a guy by that last name who played on the USHA Pro tour about 15 years back. I seem to recall he was a top five player."

Will smiled. "Top ten maybe, in my best year. That was me. I played mostly out of the Pacific Northwest back then and at the end of my tournament career I had a couple of years or so where I played pro qualifiers only here in the north central part of the country. I didn't tour any longer because of my academic career."

The man said, "Now I remember. You played the Tall Corn pro stop in Des Moines."

"Many times, and always one of my favorite tournaments. Great players, great hospitality, and great times." As the men rested a few more minutes before the next match, the gentlemen continued for the benefit of his buddies.

"I had the pleasure of watching you win one year. The tournament directors had flown in Bobby Owens from Ohio, who was the defending champion, and if I remember correctly, you beat Red Arlen in the semis to get into the finals against Owens."

Will shook his head in agreement. "That's right. Red and I often played against each other up in Seattle. At the time, Bobby was ranked number four on the tour and I had cut back tournament play as I needed to establish myself in my new teaching position at IPSU. Bobby was one of the fastest guys I ever played against. He could run down shots like a cheetah chasing a gazelle."

"Yeah, but you beat him with power and strategy."

Will laughed. "Bobby wasn't used to losing and I think I got inside his head a bit when I served seven straight aces to his strong hand."

The other man clapped him on the shoulder. "They wrote in "Handball" magazine that it was one of the greatest displays of power serving the writer had ever seen."

"And the one and only time I ever beat Bobby Owens. You guys ready for one more game?" Will asked, addressing the other three men, ready to change the subject from the past to the present. He knew that sharing handball stories with other handball players of tournament ability could run into hours. He was here to play, not to talk. After the second game, they thanked each other and shook the hands of each player personally. They all exchanged contact information with him and set up a match for next time. He joined the guys in the whirlpool, shared a few more stories but declined the offer of a beer together until next time. He explained that he had only been in town one day and needed to get his apartment set up. They offered to help in any way they could. From handball players, he expected nothing less.

He checked his phone for missed calls in the parking lot before he went to get a bite to eat. The dean had called. He punched redial and lowered the car windows steamed over with the heat from the handball play added to the humidity of the late afternoon. Looked like rain later in the evening. He welcomed the fresh air as the computer in his phone routed the call. The dean answered. "Hi, Will. Everything going okay?"

"So far, so good," Will reported. What can I do for you, Harry?" Will detested small talk on the phone.

"I forgot to share with you one thing during our meeting because I didn't think the situation warranted it and I wanted to talk privately with you about this."

Will said, "The NSA will know."

The dean chuckled. "I'll have to take my chances. Here it is, man-to-man. I would caution you not to screw any of the female students, even if they offer themselves to you, which is often a plausible scenario."

Will said, "Harry these are not eighteen-year-old freshmen still wearing white panties. They are graduate students in their late-20s and early-30s, most of them. They're all adults capable of making their own decisions."

"I know, I know," Harry said, "but things at the university have changed radically since you were last here. With the institutionalization of radical feminism, a string of Puritanism has reasserted itself within the collegiate system. And you know I'm not talking about the feminism you and

I respect and support, one that drives equal opportunities, equal pay for all, equal standing and respect for each other. No, Will, I'm talking about the radical element that has infused and infected our campuses here in the Midwest. They believe white males are the source of all evil in the world, and all female suffering is due to male oppression. To my mind, the most dangerous aspect of this sort of shallow thinking, which suffers from the fallacy of generalization as you might say, is the belief that all females are helpless creatures in the face of more powerful ravaging males."

Will nodded in agreement, caught himself and said, "Harry, this too shall eventually pass and women themselves will see the irony of these ill-conceived stereotypical conceptions of men and women. Rational thinking will prevail in time."

"The dean did not seem convinced. "You have to understand this, Will. These radicalized sisters have now risen to positions of power within the institution. Our current vice president, for example, is a card carrying member of the sisterhood, and she will smile in your face and welcome you publicly, but hate you privately because you are a man, and despite the fallacy of generalization, will hate you because she hates all men."

"I consider myself forewarned, Harry, and you know that I avoid all damaged souls whenever possible."

"It goes much deeper than that, dear Will. There are policies and regulations that prohibit fraternization between faculty and students, specifically between the student and professor who has power over the student because of grades."

"What does fraternization mean, Harry?"

"Well, it's kept undefined and ambiguous for purposes of control; you know, like requiring research and publication in order to achieve tenure but never defining how many articles actually qualify for tenure and promotion."

"Nothing ever seems to change," Will lamented.

Harry disagreed immediately. "That's why I'm calling, Will. Things have changed. Every sexual harassment complaint I receive reads almost the same, relying on the language of oppression. The sisterhood are determined to protect their helpless virgins from rapacious male professors and don't misunderstand me, their rhetoric is almost always in terms of an overpowering male taking advantage of the helpless, victimized female."

Will said, "I think I want to throw up."

"Listen, Will. We had a guy in the English Department two years into his tenure and one of his female students came to his office hours and said she wanted to do a professor as part of her sexual bucket list, no strings attached. Like an idiot, he agreed. When he gave her a B+ instead of an A- at the end of the semester, she filed a sexual harassment suit and claimed he had used grades to coerce her sexually. It took the union three years before they got around to defending him because of a backlog of cases. In the meantime, it ruined his family life because, of course, she detailed everything to her friends on Facebook and Twitter, essentially destroying his career. He was condemned in social media for forcing a female student, for coercing her to have sex for a grade, and even though the inquiry showed just the opposite, that kind of crap sticks like stink in a hog wallow. You know what he's doing now?" Will did not know. "He's driving for Uber in Des Moines and teaching part-time at the junior college. Do you want to be a taxi driver, Will? the dean asked.

Will laughed at the *reductio ad absurdum* conclusion but he was exasperated. "No one tells me who I can or cannot fuck, Harry. That is a privilege guaranteed to me in the Constitution of the United States of America, something called the pursuit of happiness."

"Granted, Will, but remember: the very unhappy persons at this university do not share your sense of democratic idealism."

"That's because they are fascists hiding behind politeness and civility and political correctness."

"That's right, Will, and what you saw coming as a tidal wave in your day is now a tsunami that has crested, broken, and swamped the towers of the university. We are no longer a liberal system, Will, despite what the press and media will have everyone believe; we have been transfigured into a rigid, radical, conservative institution."

Will thought for a moment, considering the dean's passion-driven polemic. "Have you been drinking, Harry?"

"Not enough. And by the way, I'm telling you things I don't ever tell Betty and this is for your ears only. And why am I telling you this?

Instead of taking the statement as a rhetorical question, Will replied, "Right now I'm the stranger sitting next to you in the airplane."

"Maybe," the dean said. "I really think it's more than that." Since they both knew what it was, Will remained silent. Dean Carpenter waited.

Then Will said, "You are indeed a good friend. I know there are islands of reason still afloat in this miasma of shoddy thinking. It's men and women like you who are willing to counter illogical and emotional arguments that rarely rise above the level of unsubstantiated opinions, persons who have the courage to refute such statements with logic, reason, and facts. Those kinds of thinkers, like you, have my continued respect. And now I want to thank you again for your guidance and let you get back to your wife, who loves you despite all your character flaws."

Harry said, "You're going to do whatever you want."

"I always have and I always will. One other thing you can be assured of. I've never in all my years as a professor ever taken advantage of or forced myself on a student for any reason whatsoever, and I don't intend to start now. This is my ethos as a professor and guides how I choose to conduct myself in my interactions with adults."

"Just be careful, Will. Sometimes your idealism cloaks you in a veil of naïveté and trust while evil stalks the halls of my beloved university."

"Got it, Harry. "Consider me warned and thanks again. We'll talk more tomorrow. Give my love to Bettina."

"She wants you to come over for dinner soon, once you get settled in."

"We'll do it soon. Bye for now."

"Bye."

Will shook his head as he rang off, put the cell phone on the seat next to him, and started the vehicle. What was he getting himself into? All he wanted to do was teach and refine his theories of crime investigation. He knew graduate students were often the most perspicacious critics, willing to ask the most difficult questions unaware of their difficulty, and eager to test proven and established ways of thinking. That is all he really wanted: to be tested, to have his methods and processes tested, to teach, and maybe, just maybe, escape the attraction of one of the most beautiful women he had ever known. No, this was about putting his head down, doing his job to the best of his abilities, and maybe having a little bit of fun along the way. At least the handball was good and that alleviated the bad mood Harry's call engendered in him, the cold fog of reality rolling over and dampening his sense of idealism. Harry's call had hit him like an unavoidable handball shot to the heart. It was time to take a more practical and pragmatic approach to his life.

CHAPTER EIGHT

Welcome

He went to his office in the Interdisciplinary Studies Department the next day and opened his computer, set up his passwords, opened an email account through the university, and edited his syllabus now that he had access to an official academic calendar for the coming school year. He was beginning to feel like a professor again. A professor is an expert in a particular field of study. A doctorate in interdisciplinary studies implies expertise in two or more fields of study. In the social sciences, or what the Germans more correctly call the human sciences in order to distinguish the field from the physical sciences such as physics or biology for example, a doctorate takes on average approximately eight years to complete. He thought back to his own training at the Edward R. Murrow School of Communication where he had received his interdisciplinary doctorate after five years of extensive and uninterrupted study.

After a master's degree that took three years of work because he taught during his graduate studies, he applied for and was accepted for Ph.D. work. Some Research I universities receive two hundred or more applications for doctoral work and select one or two students from the pool. The graduate student is then assigned to a graduate faculty member, a research scholar who over the years has established a record of publication and reputation within the field. Top graduate students at top schools might also receive both tuition waivers and a stipend for being a teaching assistant or a research assistant, and in rare instances, both. Ph.D.s trained as research scholars are like the Navy SEALs of the academic world. Very few are selected, and even fewer make it all the way through the rigorous and demanding academic training.

After three years of intensive classes called graduate seminars wherein the doctoral candidate studies with world-famous experts in their field, Will prepared himself for his written doctoral exams. This is a period of unrelenting study and preparation that took him more than six months. At the beginning of the exam week, he was placed in a small auxiliary office with a computer and printer. The head of his doctoral committee, having elicited questions from each of the faculty members on his committee and with whom he had studied, presented him with the first of the two questions he was required to answer, given four hours per question with a break for lunch after the first. He was given two new questions every morning, and his printed answers were collected in the afternoon. The written examination lasted five days.

When he turned in his last two answers printed off from the computer, he had written more than forty single spaced typed pages of responses. He felt his brain had been liquefied and was bleeding out from his nose and ears. He went home, got drunk, and slept for twelve hours. Now began the week-long agonizing period of waiting while his examiners read and evaluated the totality of his answers. Will knew that if any one of his examiners failed him on any one question, he would be given one more chance to pass the exam the next semester but every question would be new. Failing even one question on the retake would result in being washed out of the doctoral program.

Passing the exam permitted him to take the oral exam and thankfully this scholarly inquisition lasted only one day. His interlocutors, the same graduate faculty professors who had constructed the questions for his written exam, were permitted to ask him any questions relevant to any course taken during his three years of doctoral studies. At the end of fielding and responding to questions about theories, paradigms, philosophies, hypotheses, perspectives, history of the work in the field, what worked and what did not, he was excused and the committee voted. Any one professor voting for failure was sufficient to wash him out of the program. But Will passed by unanimous vote. Was he now a Ph. D., having passed his written and oral doctoral exams? Of course not. That would be too easy and everyone would want to do it.

Passing the written and oral exams conferred upon the graduate student an official status called "doctoral candidate." At this point in his training as a research scholar he was required to develop a proposal for a dissertation topic. A dissertation is a book-length formal manuscript that details the doctoral candidate's research program, its results and findings. The proposal, a formal document, is presented to the dissertation committee, professors who are experts within the fields the doctoral candidate is studying and wants to do research in, and is headed by a dissertation director responsible for guiding and mentoring the candidate through the process. The proposal is a formal written and oral argument that presents a persuasive case that claims the candidate's research will result in new and original contributions to the body of knowledge within the field. If a proposal for the dissertation is rejected by any one member of the dissertation committee, the candidate is washed out of the program. If the proposal is accepted, the doctoral candidate is given permission to begin the research.

It takes about a year to design the research study, develop hypotheses, test them, establish a theoretical perspective, review the state of knowledge related to the topic, collect data, analyze it, interpret it, draw conclusions and consider implications and directions for future research. The bound manuscript in the form of a book is presented to the dissertation committee and if any one member rejects it without calls for revision, in other words the dissertation has failed to produce new insights, understanding, or perspectives that advance the field, it is deemed a failure. The candidate is washed out of the program after having endured a month or two waiting for the outcome. It had been one of the most stressful periods of Will's life.

Will remembered quite a few doctoral colleagues who made it to the dissertation phase, but were then washed out, or were unwilling to dedicate another year of their lives to reworking and revising their dissertation. They simply dropped out ABD, an acronym that stood for All But Dissertation. This was not necessarily an academic kiss of death as many received teaching positions at state teaching universities, but it was the end of the academic road if one aspired to be a research scholar. Are we now a Ph. D., Will thought? Of course not. One still had to jump the hurdle of the oral defense of the dissertation. This was a public presentation and defense of the findings in the dissertation arranged by the university, which sent out a formal press release to the effect that so-and-so was prepared to defend a dissertation on such-and-such a topic.

This permitted other scholars in relevant fields to attend the doctoral candidate's presentation, after which the floor was open to critiques and questions from the scholars in the audience, including the dissertation committee. The questions were designed to test the candidate's grasp of the information and findings within the work and tested the quality of the candidate's poise during the defense of the work. In sum, it was the committee's last chance to determine if the doctoral candidate had indeed made a new and relevant contribution to the body of knowledge, and had in all ways and by all measures, conducted him or herself as a true doctor of philosophy. After the last question was asked and the audience left, the candidate was excused and asked to wait outside while his committee voted one last time, yes or no.

Will smiled as he remembered those last excruciating minutes. He stood outside the door of the lecture hall where he had presented and defended his work, shot the cuffs of his shirt, adjusted the tie he despised wearing, and rebuttoned the coat of his Armani suit. He took a deep breath and calmed himself. Yay or nay, and for whatever it was worth, he knew this: he had done one hell of a job and was pleased with his performance. He heard the door open and his dissertation director approached him, looking handsome in his suit, grey touching his hair at the temples. An avid poker player, his face was blank, devoid of any sign or indication of failure or success. He took a minute and looked Will up-and-down. Will noted a slight twitch of the micro muscles at the corner of his mouth. This might have been a nervous tic in response to the stress of the interpersonal interaction, having to tell a candidate that after eight years of rigorous and intensive study, research, writing, and analytical training, you have failed. Or it could have augured the beginning of a smile that signaled success. His director took one step forward, extended his hand and as Will took it in his own said, "Congratulations. Dr. Sheridan, you are now a Ph.D."

It was a day in his life he would never forget. He had matriculated into the top 1.5% of the world's educated elite. There were no higher academic degrees. Even M.D.s, if they were good enough to achieve a Ph.D. after med school, always signed their names M.D., Ph.D.

Iowa Polytechnic State University, home of the Tigers, was a Research I institution of higher learning. This differentiated it from a comprehensive university, where teaching and research were usually weighted equally in tenure decisions. Teaching universities were designed mostly to teach undergraduate students. At Research I schools, research and publication were the two overlords that ruled the academic kingdom, where teaching was considered or tolerated as a necessary evil by the court. Those who focused on teaching instead of publication did so at their own peril. Will remembered a colleague in the

Communication Studies Department who had received the Professor of the Year award for the entire university, given for outstanding teaching in the classroom, and the next year was denied tenure because he had not published enough research articles. He made the critical mistake of thinking that teaching and educating is more important to the institution than publishing. At many schools it was not, and it cost him his job. Research I schools put their focus and their money on research scholars whose mission is to advance knowledge, publish their work, write grants that enrich the university, and if they were competent in the classroom, so be it. So long as you didn't physically abuse anyone in the class, if you had merit as a scholar, you would receive tenure after six years, no matter how poor your teaching evaluations. Formerly a tenured professor, Sheridan prided himself on the quality of his teaching, the legacy of the many outstanding educators it had been his privilege to study with and learn from. He wondered if he still had the chops after so many years away from the lectern. Teaching highly motivated professional cops and special agents was one thing; teaching master's students and Ph. D. candidates was entirely another.

Iowa Polytechnic State University consists of six major colleges: the College of Agriculture, Physical Sciences, Human and Social Sciences, Education, Business, and the Graduate College. The Graduate College is a superordinate college that oversees all graduate programs at the university, but not all departments in all colleges have a graduate program. Dean Carpenter was responsible for graduate education in every college that offered graduate degrees and had faculty among the ranks of professors who had achieved graduate professor status. Such professors were tasked primarily to teach graduate seminars and an occasional upper division course for majors within the department to which they had been appointed. Most undergraduate classes were taught by untenured junior faculty or graduate teaching assistants known as TA's who had received teaching appointments as part of their graduate stipend. It was not a lot of money but coupled with a tuition waiver, most TAs and RAs, research assistants assigned to a graduate professor to help with research programs, graduate without any loans or student debt, unlike medical doctors, lawyers, or dentists, who are forced to pay their own way. In return for about $10,000 a semester, graduate students on a TA stipend teach two lower division courses per semester, usually general education requirement courses labeled 100, and Ph.D. students are occasionally allowed to teach 200 or 300 level courses for sophomores and juniors.

However, many universities do not provide teaching stipends for its graduate students and thus it is possible for a newly minted Ph.D. to arrive at a university and begin teaching undergraduates without ever having been in front of a student. This often results in a debacle for students and professors alike, but if publication is deemed sufficient and noteworthy, tenure can be won. This is just one of the many despicable ironies of working in the university system, Will had learned. Will recalled working with some professors in the physical sciences recruited from foreign universities who taught in faltering English coated with accents so thick students could not understand the classroom presentations, most delivered in monotone and Power Point. You can be a terrible teacher and still have a highly successful career at a university if you have the publications. If not, after your sixth-year evaluation you were gone, given an additional year to transition out of the school. Hence publish or perish, up or out. Winning tenure usually meant a promotion from assistant to associate professor and a small pay increase. It also meant you never had to research or publish another article during the life of your career or ever again revise your syllabus, as was frequently the case.

Here Will knew he was not being fair to the numerous professors who use tenure for its original intention: to give researchers the academic freedom and time to do research considered unconventional, radical, or unpopular. These scholars often did their best work in the years following tenure. It was during this time that most scholarly books were produced. Without tenure he could not have taken the chance to write outside his discipline, produce the book that was now being taught to detectives in the United States and internationally.

He pushed back from the computer and typing the schedule of events for his syllabus. The problem was this: the tenure system was rife with corruption because it was often abused. Some tenured professors simply showed up for work, stacking time like prisoners in the state penitentiary waiting for their release into the freedom of retirement. Conversely, some department heads and deans use tenure as a way of playing favorites. Will had heard horror stories where stated tenure requirements were as vague as "publication required within academic journals." When the candidate for tenure was subsequently denied, the reasons could be that the journals in which the professor had published did not have a high enough rejection rate, or only had two publications when the secret number was six. But the obverse could also hold. He remembered another example where a female Ph.D. received tenure after publishing one article, an editorial opinion no less, in the local city newspaper. And so it goes, he thought, glad he had publications in the top journal in his field and written a book—considered the holy grail of academic research and publishing— and glad he was out of that game for good.

CHAPTER TEN

Butchery

Business had been great at the Fort Charles, Iowa Future Ford dealership. Low interest rates were pulling cars out of the showrooms and into the garages of buyers. From his office on the second floor of the building that houses the sales offices and showroom on the floor below, Albert Young, owner, president, and CEO of the number one car dealership by sales in northern Iowa, swiveled his high-backed leather chair around to look over the expansive lot holding current year models of the F-150 pickup truck, SUVs, sedans, and the used car lot next door. White was the most prevalent color, as usual.

Despite last month's outstanding sales figures, Young was in a foul mood. In the middle of the month, walk-up traffic was slow, as expected, but even his bestseller, the pickup in its nearly limitless iterations: 150, 250, 350, super cab, eco, four-wheel-drive, and so on, wasn't selling as well as expected against the new Chevy Silverado and the Dodge Ram. Ford was offering rebates up to $10,000, killing much of his profit margin and some of his smarter shoppers were dealing right down to his holdback.

His younger, more aggressive sales guys could get by on the percentage of the holdback they earned coupled with their year-end bonus, but his older established salesmen with families, a mortgage, and a boat to pay off, were struggling. And the first snowfall was less than two months out.

Try to sell a car packed under two feet of snow and 20° below zero when more than half the state's farmers were sitting in Florida or Texas drinking mai tais and pina coladas. The light and tone on his office phone blinked and donged simultaneously. He swiveled back to face his desk, a dark highly polished oak. Iowans thought oak was a luxury step up from the pine cabinets most had in their farmhouses. He had nothing but maple in his own home on the outskirts of Fort Charles.

On the oak paneled walls that reached from floor to ceiling in his office at work, the ubiquitous framed photos and certificates one sees in every car dealership across the United States were hung. Here were photos of Albert Young presenting checks for scholarships, food drives, and an inordinate number of women's sports clubs and organizations. There were photos of the youth baseball teams and now soccer which he loathed and considered a prime example of the degeneracy in American sports. He preferred the summer corporate softball leagues Future Ford sponsored and played in, winning championships just often enough to keep him interested. The trophies, some more than four ostentatious feet high and built like skyscrapers from the fifties, lined the table along one wall. On his desk were three coffee mugs from the three state universities. Young himself had an associate of arts degree in finance from the branch of a local community college but was smart enough to know that most of the younger farmers who came in to buy from him were graduates of Iowa State. The coffee mug with the Cyclones emblem was slightly and subtly larger than the other two.

He answered the phone, pushing the blinking button. "Yeah?"

His receptionist answered. "Mr. Salerno is here to see you."

"Tell him I'm busy having my nails done."

"He insists."

"All right, for Christ's sake, send him in." The door to his office opened and his receptionist needlessly announced

Sam Salerno. In jeans and a windbreaker that smelled of gasoline, Salerno crossed the highly polished oak floors and approached the desk. Young did not get up but indicated to Salerno that he should help himself from the whisky bar. "Think I will, Al. You don't want one?"

Young said, "No. I'm giving a speech to the Rotary Club later today." He watched Salerno take down one finger of a two-finger pour of his best Scotch, then asked, "What can I do for you, Sammy?" although he pretty much knew what Salerno wanted, the second cause of his foul mood today. He expected it to worsen after Salerno sat down.

"We've talked about this before, Al. And I took the week to think it through like you suggested, but I haven't changed my mind. I can't eat, I can't sleep, I can't fuck my wife, even if I wanted to. I've lost twenty pounds, I'm depressed, and my hands shake. I need and I want to get out," he concluded, and finished his drink in one emphatic gulp. After tolerating the burn of the Scotch, he added, "For health reasons only."

Young did not say anything. Over the years he had learned the power of silence. Salerno got nervous, began to sweat, and pulled off his windbreaker, knocking a signed baseball off its presentation pedestal atop Young's desk. Young caught it before it rolled off the table. In Des Moines, some years ago he had paid Pete Rose a good amount of money for his signature scrawled on the milk white leather of the baseball.

"Sorry," Salerno quickly said, the misstep adding to his flustered nerves. "I really want you to know, Al, how much I've appreciated being with you and the other guys. I know you guys are responsible for much of the success I've had in town. Without your fuel contracts from the dealership, my stations would not have made it through the last economic crisis. As you know, Exxon would've been only too happy to shut me down and force me to close my pumps."

Young nodded. What Salerno was telling him was rancid butter spread over burnt toast. Then Young said something to Salerno that caught him by surprise. "I understand, Sammy. You've been an important member of our group and a good businessman for the town. Despite the fact that you took a blood oath, swearing to never leave the group, we can see how important it is to you and your health. Accordingly, we voted and we've decided to let you out."

It took Salerno a moment or two before he fully comprehended what Young had just said. He fully expected a further argument persuading him to stay in for the good of the group and for his personal and continued economic benefit. He stood as Young stood, came around the desk and hugged the taller man, much to Young's dismay. Salerno's breath reeked of soured whisky, his anxiety having fueled his drinking and fouling his breath. "Oh, man. I can't tell you how relieved I am."

"I know," said Young, pouring on the empathy. "Let's go ahead, you and me, and get this thing taken care of," and walked Sammy to the office door. "You leave first, and on the way out, tell my receptionist that next week you will bring by the new fuel contracts for the coming quarter. But don't dick around trying to schmooze her. Get in your truck and meet me in the parking lot of Patty's Pizza. We'll go from there.

"I brought all my stuff in the truck, just in case," Salerno said, trying to be reassuring.

"Good thinking. Okay, we'll drive out to the clubhouse, I get your contract from the safe, and you can turn in your stuff and I will watch you burn the contract. Give me fifteen minutes. I need to make a call or two and cancel some appointments for the afternoon. From Patty's follow me out of town. I'll be in the black Lincoln Navigator."

"Got it," Salerno said, washing the last of the nervousness from his wet hands. "I'll wait for you at the pizza joint." He went downstairs to speak with Young's receptionist about fuel deliveries the following week.

Young opened a smartphone and as he looked up a number thought to himself, asshole. He reminded his receptionist of his speech later that evening at the Rotary

Club and told her he was leaving to polish up his speech. He left through a door that took him down the stairs and out to the back of the dealership where he parked his massive SUV.

In his tank size black SUV now ahead of Salerno, Young drove the three or four miles outside of town on the blacktop, checking the rearview mirror to see if Salerno was still following in his white Ford F-150. An unmarked turn took them onto county gravel and one more turn onto a dirt road that required four-wheel-drive after two days of rain or snow, or until the road froze over for the winter. Today, conditions were still good. Now into the forested rolling hills, they approached the security gate that fenced in the property. Young entered the access number on the pad, and one half of the tall arched gate slowly opened. He waited until Salerno was through and the gate had closed behind him, then drove up to the renovated barn that served as the group's clubhouse.

They parked and as Young punched in the same combination on the keyboard next to the main entrance, Salerno waited with a backpack. The tumblers clicked on the door and Young heard the massive bolt locking the door slide back. From his pants pockets he pulled a set of keys carried only for meetings and opened a second lock on an inside door. Once inside, he quickly reset the alarm, and turned on the lights. There were no windows on that side of the building. He went to a gun safe tall as he was in cowboy boots and hat, dialed the combination, and pulled the handle. The opened door revealed a series of hunting rifles and shotguns. On a shelf lay pistols of various calibers and boxes of ammunition for all the firearms. A second lock box on a separate shelf required another key. He opened it, exposing a series of files. He leafed through them walking across the tops with his fingertips until he found what he needed, examined it, and pulled it out.

"Here it is," he assured Salerno, and handed him the document. As Salerno quickly read it and nodded, Young closed the file box, locked it, and with his back still to

Salerno, surreptitiously slipped a preloaded .22 caliber from the pistol shelf and stuck it in the waistband of his pants, covering it with his coat. He closed and locked the gun safe. As he turned, Salerno was still reading through the document. He led the man from the hunting room into the adjoining great room and flipped the switch for the gas fireplace. It whooshed and puttered into flame and Young added a few oak splits onto the fire. Together they watched it catch and take the oak logs from wood to flame.

"Your contract," said Young, pointing to the open fireplace after he had opened the glass gates. "You get to do the honors."

Salerno gingerly fed the two sheets into the fire, watching them smoke, curl to black, and disappear into the flames. "Man, I'm glad that's done," he said blowing ash from the tips of his fingers.

"Almost done," Young assured him. He picked out a small camera from a drawer under the fully stocked bar and turned to Salerno. "Get dressed, he said, indicating Salerno's backpack. "We need a picture of you in your robes to ensure that you don't talk."

Salerno thought for a moment and could only agree. As he pulled the red silk robe over his head he said, "I promise you once again I'll never tell a soul about the Brotherhood. But I think you're smart to have some insurance."

"Glad you understand," Young told him and walked with him through the back door that led onto a covered concrete patio. On the right side of the patio stood a barbecue built into a stone wall next to an outdoor utility sink; tables and patio furniture stood on the left. He had Salerno stand with his back to the woods on the grass that edged the patio. "Let's do one with your ceremonial mask on, hood up, and then one without." Mask and hood in place, Young snapped the photo with the digital camera. He checked the photo. "Good. Now one without the mask and the hood."

After dropping his hood and as Salerno had his attention focused on removing his black mask, Young slipped the small camera into the pocket of his corduroy coat and removed the .22 pistol. Salerno had just enough time to register surprise on his face and he no doubt heard the pop as the gun fired. Directly above his nose, a black hole suddenly appeared, its clean edges reddening just before he dropped onto his knees. His lolling head pulled him onto his back and his heart pumped twice more before it stopped, the trickle of blood at the edges of the hole marking its final effort. In the stillness, Young stood a minute or two, looked around, and watched the body. He walked over to the man, unzipped his pants and pissed in the man's face. Aloud he said to the corpse, "Read the fine print, bitch. No one gets to leave the Blood Brotherhood. No one!"

Murder is the easy part, Young thought. Now came the grisly work of disposing the body. He went inside and made two calls, one to Maynard Cheska, a local pig farmer, and the town's butcher. Then he called Buck Miller, the county sheriff and instructed Miller to meet him at the Cheska pig farm. About ten minutes later Maynard Cheska arrived with a white service van and backed it around the barn to the patio. Cheska walked up to the body and rolled the head over. "Good. No exit wound. Pretty good shot," he commented as Young extended the dead man's legs. They took the mask and together levered the robe off the body, putting both into the man's backpack.

"Why is the mask wet?" Miller wanted to know.

"I pissed on it after I shot him."

"Jesus," said the sheriff. "You are one kind of special psychopath."

Young grinned as they removed Salerno's car keys, wallet, change, pocket knife, his wedding ring from the third finger of his left hand, and a belt with an oversize oval buckle. Cheska was clad in green Oshkosh overalls that his stomach pushed away from his body. He had on work gloves, rubber boots, and a green John Deere cap, which he inverted to keep it from falling off his head as he reached down to grab Salerno's shoulders. Young stood between the dead man's legs and gripped them under the knees as if he were pushing a wheelbarrow. They lifted together and walked the dead man to the van where they placed him on a plastic sheet covering the back floor of the vehicle. Young returned for the backpack and as Cheska finished securing the load, threw the backpack in. Cheska closed the two rear doors of the van.

Young clapped him on shoulders thick as hams. "See you in about fifteen. I'll shut the clubhouse down and meet you at the slaughterhouse."

Sheriff Miller was waiting for them at the pig farm in his white Ford SUV, his personal vehicle, but he was still in uniform. Behind the slaughterhouse that stood separated from the pigsty, Young handed Miller the weapon. "No prints?" the burly sheriff asked, just to be certain.

"I wore my driving gloves the entire time," Young said.

The sheriff cleared his throat and spit. "I'll go put the gun in Deputy Sheriff Copeland's locker, the prick. I don't think he ever realized it was gone." He dropped the pistol into an evidence bag. "You guys get to have all the fun."

Young entered the slaughterhouse, took off his coat and put on a butcher's apron, clean for once he noted, and tied it off behind his back. He pulled a pair of latex gloves from the box on the table and put on a pair of clear protective industrial glasses. The plastic splash mask would come later.

Cheska, mask already in place, was hard at work. He had taken the head from the spine at the neck and put it aside on the slaughter table. The corpse had been gutted and bled, some of the offal and ichor running down into a drainage chute at the end of the table that discharged into a holding pond of fecal matter and black liquids outside the slaughterhouse. The larger pieces were separated out, run through the mincing machine, and the ground-up material was mixed with water and used as manure to be spread on the soybean fields surrounding Cheska's farm.

With a handheld control, the butcher repositioned the hook from which the headless and gutted body now hung. He took a long sharp butcher's knife, straightened the edge with a few expert strokes on the steel and set about dismembering the rest of the body.

It was a macabre pleasure to watch the man work, Young thought. He was really in his element. With three strokes of the razor-sharp knife he had the arm off. One slice under the armpit and up to the trapezius muscle on top of the shoulder; then another cut continuing over the deltoid and back down to the armpit to close the circle. His third and last cut laid open the joint and he had the arm off. He dropped the meat into a large aluminum pan sitting on a portable cart next to the butchers table, scarred and marred by a thousand cuts. Cheska said, "Your turn," as he made short work of taking off the other arm.

At the other table, Young took a somewhat smaller knife and opened the arm at the elbow, cutting through muscles, ligaments, and tendons to release the upper arm from the lower. He boned all the flesh from the humerus, ulna, and the radius. He had to be careful not to cut himself as he worked on the flesh between the two smaller bones of the forearm. They reminded him of the wing bones in a large turkey. Finished, he asked Cheska, "What do you want me to do with the hands?"

"Leave them. I'll take them off with the circular saw when I do the feet." He placed the other amputated arm on Young's table, took both legs off at the knee, and was working hard to dislocate the large ball joint of the hip. He had already taken the penis and testicles off during his first cuts to open the abdomen. He sawed through the heavy breastbone of the sternum and once through opened the ribs with a massive rib spreader. This gave him access to the heart, lungs, liver, and spleen when he was butchering deer, pigs, cows or steers for his customers and his retail shop. Even in the air-conditioned chill of the slaughterhouse, both men were sweating.

Cheska made frequent use of the steel to hone his blade. Finally, they had the hundred-and-fifty-pound man dismembered, filleted, and boned out like a ten-point buck. The totality of his material essence now lay in four aluminum pans in four separate and disjointed piles. They worked on the head last. All the bones lay in a separate pile; next came the hands and feet. At the base of the table, near the drain were placed the heart, lungs, kidneys, spleen, and liver; all the internal organs. Together they took the large muscles of the back off, the latissimus dorsi off both sides and the backstrap—erector spinae—the two lines of muscle that ran up both sides of the spine.

"Be careful not to cut yourself," Cheska warned as they worked with the flexible but thinner and longer filet knives. In good time, they were left with nothing but the spine, shoulder scapulae, and the attached ribs that curve out and down from the spine.

"This bastard was more trouble than he was worth," Young complained to no one in particular. After the bones dried, they would be ground into meal. The meat was chopped into cubes the size of a child's building blocks. They would later be fed to the hogs, along with the bone meal that helped constitute the daily slop he also fed to his hogs. Young detested the next and last chore: taking the head apart.

He held the head with one hand on the man's prominent nose, the other just under the back of the occipital ridge. Cheska ran a smaller handheld circular saw in a smooth cut across the forehead as Young, behind the plastic splash mask that extended above his eyebrows, turned away from the stinking smell of fresh-sawn skull bone. He wretched once as Maynard Cheska pried open the circular cut.

"You gotta puke?" he asked, kicking a large plastic-lined waste basket toward Young with his rubber boot.

"No. I got it. Just made the mistake of breathing once through my nose."

Cheska looked puzzled. "I always breathe through my nose," he said and uncapped the skull, exposing the brain. He cut through both optic nerves and the brain stem where it attached to the spinal cord, and pulled the brain out using both hands. He carried it like a large cantaloupe and placed it with the other internal organs. He popped the eyes out with his thumbs from within the skull, and cut out the tongue and took off the ears. "You want one for your collection?" Cheska joked. Young shook his head.

Cheska next peeled the skin from the skull, including most of the nose and lips, until they had a wet off-white half skull left, teeth included. Cheska took a large ball-peen hammer and loosened the teeth in the jaw enough so that the gums let them go with a sharp fast pull of the pliers. His grip slipped only twice. He broke loose the lower jaw from the rest of the face, fracturing the mandible. "Got them all," he said with satisfaction and threw the last of the molars into a large stone mortar.

Young took the pestle and began the labor of pulverizing the teeth. With magnetized needle-nose pliers he fished out the filings. There was a lot of metal in the man's mouth. As Young went about the task of dentistry, Cheska put the skull cap, which looked like an inverted sugar bowl carved out of wood, into a clear heavy-duty plastic bag, set it on the floor and then attacked it with a sledgehammer. Once broken into smaller pieces he fed them through the bone meal grinder. He finished the rest of the skull the same way. He then separated the ribs from the spine, dislocated the vertebrae through the discs, sawed the ribs into manageable pieces three inches long and threw them onto a pile of bone remnants from previously slaughtered pigs. It was hard to discern the difference except for the size. He fed the lot into the stainless-steel blades of the grinder with other bones from the pile. At this point he was ready for Young to add the pulverized teeth.

"You sure there ain't any more filings in that crap?"

"I put the whole lot through the sieve, just like you showed me."

"Good," said Cheska. "These blades cost a fucking fortune."

They sacked the bone meal and lifted the heavy bags to set outside. Later, after they were dried, he would mix them with other bags of bone meal from previous slaughters. Next, Cheska worked on the fingers with snips as Young disarticulated the toes, feeding them carefully, skin and all, into the grinder. This was not an ideal process, but it was a waste of time to try and skin and flesh out every toe and finger on a foot or hand. "Goddamn it. It takes a lot of work to butcher a man," Young commented, as he stood back and observed their handiwork."

"That's a fact, Jack," Maynard Cheska agreed. "A helluva lot more work than breaking down a young girl."

After helping Cheska clean up and wash down, Young divided the man's paper money equally. They each got $65 for their hard work, cheap bastard that he was. Credit cards, photos, and papers, they ran through the shredder in Cheska's office and added Salerno's wallet to the burn pile with the rest of his clothes. They kept his red robe. After the pile had cooled, Cheska would sift through the ashes and with a metal detector take out whatever metal snaps, zippers, or hardware remained in the furnace. This would be further melted down into ingots that he would hammer into metal spikes for his fences. He took pride in knowing that nothing about the man they had just butchered would go to waste; to his mind, the only redeeming thing about Sam Salerno.

After he showered and shaved at the meat locker, Albert Young drove Sam Salerno's white Ford F-150 pickup truck back to the dealership, stripped it of all VIN numbers, and had the boys wash, clean, and detail it. He then added falsified VIN numbers and prepared the vehicle for transport to a wholesale auction for used vehicles where it would be bought by an out of state broker who would turn around and sell it to some street corner dealership somewhere in the backwoods of Louisiana. Work done, Albert Young returned home, put on a clean blue suit, white shirt, and striped red power tie over polished black shoes and gave a speech that had the Rotarians at their tables laughing into the rubbery chicken atop their plates.

CHAPTER NINE

Making New Friends

A somewhat timid knock on his closed-door summoned his attention. "Wait one, please," he said, loud enough to be heard through the closed door. He saved his work and closed the file, then said, "Please come in." The door opened and a woman who looked to be about fifty or so entered. She wore a knee-length brown skirt, a coat that matched the skirt, and a multicolored scarf around her neck. The coat did not do a good job muting her portly figure. She had a pageboy haircut that an American figure skater named Dorothy Hamill had popularized years ago. It was died the color of a flushing red hen that most women of her age favored. He came around from his desk and offered a smile and an open hand. She took his hand, her fingers limp within his grasp. and he was forced to immediately moderate the power of his grip or risk crushing her fingers. Bob Hope used say put that fish back in the tank after experiencing similarly weak and timid handshakes. He introduced himself and offered her a seat next to the coffee table.

"I know who you are," she said, without introducing herself.

As yet he didn't know if this was a good thing or a bad thing, but from the dour look on her face and her impatient tone of voice, signs indicated the latter. He smiled and waited. When he did not ask for her name she said, "I'm

Dorothy Keller-Smith, head of the Interdisciplinary Studies Department," barely able to hide her exasperation.

"Thank you for coming to welcome me," he said, certain that this was not her intention.

"I didn't come here to welcome you, Dr. Sheridan," she snapped at him as if he were an undergraduate that had made a snide remark about her ugly scarf. "In fact, I consider it an insult when new faculty don't take the time to come and introduce themselves to me. Even if they are on temporary assignment." She recrossed her legs, the swift scissors of stretched nylon signaling her indignation. "And to say the least, I am not at all pleased that you are assigned here. In fact, your office was formally one of our seminar rooms, which we often use," she lied. He made no comment, further stoking her exasperation. He felt no comment was required. "Furthermore," she continued, "I've been asking around about you and it seems you left this university more than ten years ago under rather dubious circumstances." She made a deliberate point to vocally underline the last three words by lengthening their enunciation. He waited for a moment, gathering his thoughts, then looked her directly in the eye before he spoke.

"It may interest you to know," he began as he looked away from her, "that I have an appointment to the Graduate College under the aegis and at the behest of Dean Carpenter, one of your bosses," he added with emphasis by lengthening the last four words. "Not that it is any of your business, I'm here at the pleasure the dean and am funded by a grant from the National Science Foundation. I intend to have no interactions with the ISD, or with you for that matter, other than to make use of these facilities as directed by the dean." He looked back at her now and saw her face in full flush. "And it may further interest you to know for legal purposes that when I left this university the Iowa State Education Association formally closed all access to my files with explicit instructions that any inquiries concerning the circumstances of my leaving were to be directed first to the office of the provost, who is then required to immediately contact the ISEA. By legal writ and formal agreement, the office of the provost is permitted only to comment that I was a tenured professor here and left with the rank of full professor. As it appears that you have violated a standing legal agreement, after you exit from my office, I will call first the provost and then the ISEA and inform them of your violation, Dr. Keeler-Swift," he said, deliberately getting her name wrong.

"Keller-Smith," she tried to correct him.

"Whatever," he said, "and please be careful and don't let the door to my office smack you in the ass on your way out." He stood, turned, showing her his broad back as he returned to his desk and his computer work, not looking up as she slammed the door closed behind her in a fit of pique worthy of a seven-year-old. He shook his head grimly. And that's how you treat a bully. And this is what you wanted again?

After lunch, his office door open and once again at work behind the computer, Sonia Landsberg, Ph.D. stood in his doorway, legs crossed, arms crossed, shoulder resting on the door frame for support. She whistled softly. He looked up from writing on a yellow tablet into an authentic, teasing smile that came from artificially whitened teeth framed by lustrous red lipstick; her hair the color of wheat touched with rust at the end of harvest. She had taken the liberty of watching through the open door as he worked, his lips closed, his face relaxed, his eyes focused on the movement of the pen across the paper and on the thoughts he wrote so quickly and fluidly on the lined notepad.

"I hope I'm disturbing you," she said, and let her arms fall to her sides before clasping them behind her tan khakis.

"Why of course you are," he admitted, "but what a pleasant interruption indeed. I would invite you in for a chat, but as you can see, I'm really much too busy now to even talk to you. However, if you would leave me a signed photo and an email address, I'll be in touch with you in a day or so."

She laughed, her entire face alive with interest. She refused to be dissuaded, as yet a little unsure whether he was joking or not. "I know who you are," she said, her voice rising in a knowing lilt. "William Russell Sheridan, Ph.D. and Professor."

"Then you have me at a disadvantage, Mrs...."

She corrected him, "Miss Sonia Landsberg, Ph.D., Associate Professor, Interdisciplinary Studies Department."

"It is most likely a pleasure to meet you," he said, not getting up or inviting her deeper into his office. He pointed to the open door with his pen. "Nice job of reading my name off my name plate next to the door."

She affected a false pout, showing him her consternation as she pursed her lips into a rounded circle that made her seem more sexy than perturbed. "Only most likely?"

He shrugged, which she ignored.

"But I really do know some things about you," she said, shielding her face with her hand, speaking in a louder stage whisper. "Some really fascinating things. Would you like to know?" she asked, hoping this would pique his interest. She now had one hand on her left hip and raised her chin and chest to him all in one breath. She studied him for effect.

He put his pen down, placed his notes in the top drawer of his desk, put his computer to sleep, pushed back his chair and stood. He came around the desk careful not to bruise a hip on its metal edge and said, "If you insist, by all means come in and have a seat."

Finally. She turned her back to him, closed the door quietly but firmly and took a few quick steps as a dancer might before a jeté, and she plopped herself down on the end of his couch. She was pleased to see him scoot his chair around to face her. Not once had he stared at her chest. His eyes were a stunning blue-grey, his hair black and combed straight back in gentle waves. He looked like a movie star under the three-day stubble of his beard. His ears were slightly overlarge, but that just made her want to grab them with both hands, and his nose skewed slightly to his right. She wondered if it was the result of a sports injury or even more exciting, the result of a punch during a brawl.

"Both."

She was shocked and immediately blushed. How could he have known what she was thinking? Had she perhaps spoken what she was thinking out loud without having realized it? She put her hands atop of her thighs, contrite.

He urged her to tell what she knew.

"Okay," she said, with a soft flip of her hair. "Just because you asked." Her eyes widened, making her seem all the more attractive. Her pupils were already dilated with excitement. "You...," she began, pointing at him as if there could be any doubt, but he knew it was merely an expression of certainty. "You are a man of mystery and very much gossip up here on the third floor. You came waltzing in here with a walk like an old-time marshal in a Western, pardon the mixed gender metaphor. And Dean Carpenter is obviously enraptured by your presence."

"Somewhat overstated," he suggested, "and men can waltz."

She ignored him. "You don't talk to anyone except to acknowledge a greeting. You don't introduce yourself, and then...," here she stopped and looked around dramatically, "you tell our revered department head not to let the door hit her in the ass on the way out."

"Revered?" His tone expressed skepticism.

"Okay. Perhaps a more accurate word is despised." She clasped one hand over her cherry red lips in a futile attempt to hide her mock disbelief.

This time he blushed. "It was not my intention at all to publicly embarrass her or to have been overheard. I forget my voice carries at times."

"Every person who heard what you said to the old witch now has an undying respect for you. It's something we wish we could say at times."

"Tactically unacceptable, given departmental politics."

She nodded emphatically into her white blouse. He got it. "I do love the way you walk," she said, smoothly crossing a leg at the knee, but did not elaborate. Her thighs seemed impossibly long as she shifted her position a quarter in order to face him more directly. She took an unabashed minute to look him over.

He smiled at the eye rape. "Is there anything in particular you want to learn about me? Please feel free to ask, but understand that I am a very private person and don't let just anyone ask me questions."

"I'm flattered," she acknowledged and instantly took advantage of his offer. "Are you really from Germany?"

"Via northern Minnesota. How did you know that?"

"I've actually read two of your books."

"There are three available."

"Will you sign all three for me?"

"I have to clear it with my agent first."

She laughed as he checked his fingernails.

"How about you. Where are you from and where did you do your doctorate?"

"I'm from Dickinson, North Dakota and I got my doctorate at the University of Illinois. But I'm here to learn more about you. Rumor has it you used to teach here."

"That rumor is correct. I was formerly a tenured full professor here. I hold two doctorates, one an interdisciplinary Ph.D. in semiotic and communication theory. I took my first doctorate in clinical psychotherapy."

Her eyes widened. "I teach the com theory course here. One of your books is required reading."

He was impressed and told her so. "It's generally the hardest course to teach and the most difficult for graduate students. You have my respect. And thanks for choosing my work for your students."

She smiled at the compliment and recrossed her legs. She took a deep breath and decided to push her advantage. "Is it true you work for the FBI?" she dared to ask after she summoned up the courage.

"In the past, and on request," he said. "But please understand that for classified reasons I am not permitted to discuss my work until it has been officially declassified by the Department of Justice. Interests of national security, you know," he said affecting a British accent. "All very hush-hush."

Her eyes widened again and she looked stunned for an instant, as if the news had caught her by surprise. She leaned in close enough for him to smell her perfume and showed the curve of her breast as her shirt bloused open, revealing a glimpse of her pink low-cut bra. In his ear she whispered, "Do you carry a gun?"

"That is on a need to know basis, Dr. Landsberg." Besides it was obvious that in his IPSU tee shirt with its growling, leaping tiger emblem on the front, and in casual black slacks, he was unarmed.

Oh my God, she thought. She loved the way he smelled. "I need to know."

"No, you don't, and a pout won't help you."

She tried anyway. She thought for a minute. "Take me to dinner. I know a nice place in town. And if you're nice to me, I will let you be the man and pay."

How could he refuse an offer like that? As he rose, he said, "I have to tell you that I have made a decided and considered decision not to fraternize with any," he said, emphasizing the word any, "staff or faculty during my time here. I will be much too busy. But a man has to eat."

She batted her eyes at him, something she had not done since her boyfriend had asked into the rear seat of his Chevy after their high school junior prom.

"I promise I won't tell a soul," she had said then and now. He walked her to the door, and spent a full minute studying her. She turned in full bodily profile twice, chin up as though she were trying on new earrings.

"Meet me in the stadium parking lot by the front door in ten minutes. You can drive."

"Oh goody," she said, clapping her hands like a young girl waiting for an ice cream cone. "A man willing to compromise his principles for a woman."

"A man driven by the need to feed a ravenous appetite. Get out of here," he said, and whispered into her ear as she slipped by, brushing him with her hip. Acting the gentleman, he held the door and she did a sexy sashay on the way out, her hip gently brushing his thigh. "And don't let that gorgeous ass hit my door on your way out."

To let him know the compliment was appreciated, over her shoulder she threw him a smile that lit up her eyes and mouth with a radiance that caused him to inadvertently blink.

CHAPTER ELEVEN

First Day

Fall semester in the Heartland was one of his favorite times of the academic year. By late August most of the bad weather had spent itself in high humidity, thunderstorms, and tornadoes. A climatological respite had settled over the state and as the temperatures and heat moderated, Iowans enjoyed the beginnings of an Indian summer. In another two weeks temperatures would drop further, signaling deciduous trees to turn their leaves to autumn coloration before their branches released them, shaking in the wind, letting them fall to earth. If the good weather held, bicyclists, hikers, runners, and golfers would benefit until Halloween, or in rare cases, Thanksgiving, when the first snows were inevitable. But for now, the weather was good and the football team ran drills and practiced outside amid the whistles and coaches yelling encouragement or correctives. At noon the campus carillon in the bell tower chimed twelve times.

The campus was alive with activity. Students moved briskly now, moving in, enduring embarrassing goodbyes with parents until dad or mom or sometimes both slipped them a hundred in the last handshake. There were buildings to be identified and discovered, campus dorms to navigate, class schedules to study and revise, and books to be bought. And during the first week of orientation for the new students, friendships were forged and, in the evenings, those old enough or on fake ids filled the bars until closing, the alcohol and parties washing out the last of parental controls and strictures. And then it was time to get up, shower, put on clean clothes, eat breakfast in the dining halls, and go to class.

On the first day of class he walked into the classroom as the oversized hand of the analog clock on the wall ticked up to 7:00 p.m. He counted seven students in the black plastic wheeled chairs that flanked the seminar table. Two women who were talking together ended their conversation and one male folded the campus newspaper and put it under his notebook. Will took a moment to write his name on the whiteboard, getting a whiff of the alcohol in the black pen he used. He turned to greet his students.

"A warm welcome to all of you. This is the two-semester interdisciplinary—hence its 700 designation—graduate course on the application of semiotic theory to crime detection. In our first semester," he said, passing out the course syllabus, "we will cover semiotic theory and method and in the second, apply those theories and methods as we try to solve a real crime. My name, as you now know, is Dr. William R. Sheridan. You may call me Doctor or Professor. As we get to know each other better please feel free to call me Will."

He took a moment to remove the class roster from his black bookbag. "For the purposes of getting to know each other," he said from behind the oak half lectern sitting on his end of the seminar table, "I would appreciate the following from you when you hear your name called. Please share with us your graduate status and your emphasis, where you're from, and then one significant thing that you would like us to know about you. I'll begin. I hold two doctorates, the first in clinical psychology, the second an interdisciplinary Ph.D. in semiotic theory from Washington State University. I was born in Germany, but came to the United States to start college on a track and field scholarship. I want to share with you the highly significant fact that I am a special agent and consultant for the FBI. I am the author of the book, *The Application of Semiotic Theory to the Analysis and Interpretation of Crime,* which is on your reading list as a secondary work, and I have served as a special consultant to Interpol in Europe in addition to my consulting work here in the United States. My specialty is solving cold cases, that is, cases that have previously had no resolution. Now it's your turn."

He looked at the roster and called Jack L. Anders. No one responded as the students looked to each other, then back to him. He struck out the name. "Annalisa Allen, no middle initial."

A beautiful young woman raised her hand. "I am Annalisa Allen and I'm from the Dells, Wisconsin. Please call me Lisa. I'm a Ph.D. student in forensic psychology and criminology. The significant thing about me is that I enjoy making undergraduate boys ejaculate prematurely," she said, as if she had just described what she had eaten for breakfast that morning. She ignored the nervous laughter around her, and all eyes looked back on the professor, waiting to see how he would react to her blatant pronouncement.

He looked at her and calmly asked, "And how do you go about accomplishing that?" She smiled beatifically and raised a hand so white he thought it might have been dipped in marshmallow cream. She extended the index finger of her right hand and rotated it in gentle circles. "I understand," Will said.

Half the class looked puzzled, two burst out laughing, and the young black male with hair dyed orange shouted while wagging his own finger emphatically, "Honey, ain't nobody puttin' their finger up my ass. No sirree, and I'm gay," he said with a defiant smirk.

"And your name, sir?" Will asked, now that the young man had self-selected.

"Thank you, Master Professor Doctor Sir."

"Professor will be fine."

"Um hmm," he said, "Professor Sheridan is indeed fine," to the groans of two other males in the class. "Ya'll see before you the LaDamian Samson Baker, and y'all can call me LB. I'm a master's student in criminology with an emphasis in forensic analysis. I'm from Baton Rouge, Louisiana and I can cook me a mess o' gumbo so good you will shout whooee and run to lock da door so da neighbors cain't come in and get some." He patted his rouged lips with the pad of an index finger as he thought. "The most significant thing about me is that I love my *grand-mamam.* And in case you haven't noticed, I'm gay and here to be queer, so jus' deal widdit. I came out when I was five years old," he exaggerated and Will smiled. LB had an infectious charm about him, despite his affected flagrancy.

"You go, girl," one of the female students said to him in support and then went up top with a high five.

"Welcome to class, LB. Next, Michael Stephen Brisbane."

"Here, sir." A tanned and extremely fit older student signaled with a wave of his hand. "Please call me Mike. I'm working on a Master's degree in criminology and I'm from Apple Valley, Minnesota, just north of the Cities. I'm an ex-special forces Army Ranger and Green Beret. I served one tour of duty in Iraq during Desert Storm and one in Afghanistan. I'm a graduate of sniper school. I recently separated from the military as a sergeant first class but I'm now on active duty in the Reserves." The other students looked at him in awe. He continued. "The significant thing about me is that I love my country and I got my squad back from each mission without ever losing a man."

"Thank you for bringing yourself and your men back home safely," Will said.

"And thank you, sir, for not saying thanks for your service. I hate that."

Lisa turned to him and casually offered for everyone to hear, "If you want me to really thank you some time, just let me know." Mike blushed into his sunburned ears.

"I don't know about that, Miss. I'm married."

Lisa pulled at the nylon hem of her black tube skirt that had trouble reaching her mid-thigh as she crossed her legs. "Feel free to have her join us." At the blatant invitation Mike slumped into his chair and pulled his camo baseball cap down to his eyebrows.

Will smiled at the Green Beret's discomfort. "No cover indoors, soldier." Mike immediately removed his baseball cap and slumped a bit deeper in his chair with a sorry, sir; won't happen again.

Will smiled to let him know all was good. "You, sir," Will indicated to the young man sitting next to the Army Ranger.

"Larry Davidson. I'm from Boston and I'm a Ph.D. student in language philosophy."

Will smiled. "One of my areas of expertise. I'm a great admirer of Ludwig Wittgenstein's work."

Davidson looked away in disgust. "Nothing against you, sir, but I find his ideas incomprehensible."

Will nodded, careful not to take offense. "He can indeed be very difficult to read. Tell me something significant about yourself."

Davidson stole a surreptitious glance at Lisa Allen. LB steepled his fingers, widened his eyes and added, "Yes, Mr. Davidson. Y'all tell us something significant."

Davidson shot him a dirty look before focusing on Will. "There is nothing significant about me," he stated with finality. He stared. Will returned the stare until Davidson blinked and turned away, fumbling with his notebooks.

"I find that highly significant," offered LB, and everyone at the table laughed.

Will turned next to a young woman with shoulder length mouse brown hair highlighted with streaks of gold. Behind her large, oversized tortoise shell glasses, she was quite attractive. She said her name with a smile that turned up one corner of her mouth. "I'm Karin Gladstone, Dr. Sheridan. I'm just a poor farm girl from near Decorah, Iowa, working on my master's in criminology and anthropology. Significantly, I have worked every summer since I was thirteen on a corn detasseling crew and worked my way up to crew chief. This was my last summer after twelve years in a row," she said wistfully, then brightened. "Pardon the pun." As an afterthought she added, "I can drive a John Deere S700 combine."

Will understood now why she seemed so fit and trim. One or two months of hard work each summer walking through the cornfields, going down each and every row pulling the immature pollen producing tassels out of the tops of young corn plants grown shoulder high from sunup till the work was done, would indeed burn down a few calories in the heat and humidity of the sweltering Iowa summer. Corn plants have both male and female parts and in fields planted with two hybrids, all the tassels of one hybrid must be removed or the plants do not cross-pollinate correctly, causing thousands of dollars of lost revenue for the farmer.

High school coaches typically send their wrestlers, football players, basketball players, long-distance runners, and other athletes into the fields for off-season conditioning. It is a rite of passage for Iowa kids and a great way to earn spending money for the purchase of cars, gas, clothes, and music, and other life necessities for the 13 through 18 age group. The contractor places them under the direction of guides and crew chiefs, usually college students earning money for tuition. Many return to the same detasseling teams year after year.

A black-haired Asian woman went next. "My name is Yuriko Sumitomo and I am a Japanese doctoral student from the island of Osaka. I am a communication studies major." Her English, Will noted, although carefully measured and inflected, was nearly perfect. He stole a quick glance at his notes on the class list. She was a graduate of one of Japan's top universities.

"Tell us something significant about yourself, Yuriko."

She fluttered her eyelids and hid a smile behind a hand before starting. "I am the champion tennis player of my age group in Japan."

"You go, girl!" LB shouted and Yuriko bowed her head ever so slightly.

"Let's set up a game for tomorrow," Lisa said.

"With pleasure," Yuriko replied.

Will called one more name off the class list but received no answer so he crossed it out. "Let's take a moment to review," Will said. "Annalisa Allen, Ph.D. student in forensic psych and criminology. Safe and secure in her sexuality, she has no problem educating freshman as to the location of the prostate." The class laughed with the exception of Yuriko, who seemed puzzled.

LB was only too happy to elaborate for her. "Finger in da butt," he said, adding an explicit nonverbal illustration. Yuriko blushed, nodded her head, signaling her understanding, but Will doubted as much.

"Thank you, LB for the cross-cultural explanation."

"Everyone understands a finger in da butt," Dr. Sheridan."

"Practically universal," Will agreed. "So, we continue with LaDamian Baker, master's student in criminology and forensic analysis and uncompromisingly gay, especially in the kitchen." LB nodded violently.

"Mike Brisbane's next. Also a master's student in criminology; ex-special forces and a war fighter tried-and-true."

"Roger that, sir."

Will continued, "Larry Davidson, a Ph.D. student in language philosophy who hails from Boston. Karin Gladstone, another master's student in criminology and anthropology. And an Iowa farm girl through and through."

"Wouldn't mind seeing her in a pair of cutoff jeans and a redneck belly shirt," said Davidson. Before Will could say anything, the young Ranger sergeant first class stared him down. Davidson threw up his hands. "Hey, no offense intended."

"I take it as a compliment," Karin graciously allowed.

Will continued. "Yuriko Sumitomo, Ph.D. student in communication studies. An athlete and a scholar very much like myself," Will added. "Looks like we've got a pretty good and diverse crew. I think we're going to have a great semester working together and getting to know each other." All but one smiled back at him.

He took another ten minutes or so and walked them through the syllabus, Yuriko taking careful notes in the margins of her syllabus, writing in Japanese kanji characters. The other students dutifully took careful notes on assignments, readings, and exam dates, with the exception of Davidson, whose surreptitious attention now was centered in observations of Karin Gladstone. When she caught him staring, she did not return his smile. Finished with the bureaucratic work of taking roll and quickly shepherding the students through the syllabus, he gave them a fifteen-minute break. When he reconvened the class, he removed the half lectern from the seminar table, sat and began a lecture.

"As most of you may remember from other classes, semiotics is the formal study of signs and symbols. We can trace its origins all the way back to the ancient Greek rhetoricians. In fact, in Aristotle's great work on rhetorical theory he gives us an explanation of a *tekmērion,* defined as an unambiguous sign with an indisputable meaning. It can also be interpreted as an infallible proof. However, he also acknowledged that most signs are ambiguous. The great American philosopher of pragmatics, Charles Sanders Peirce, pronounced purse, and don't ask me why, defined signs as *aliquid stat pro aliquo.*" All but Yuriko seemed puzzled. "Ms. Sumitomo, do you have enough Latin to translate for us?"

"*Hai,*" she said inadvertently. "Yes. I will try. Something that stands for something else," she said.

"To somebody." Will helped her finish the translation. "Something that stands for something else to somebody. Let's look at the implications of the definition. The something is a sign. It represents something else. But the key to the definition is the last part. There must be an observer of the sign and what it refers to. This further implies a context and an understanding of the relationship between the sign and the thing that it stands for. Some signs are natural, such as smoke is a sign of fire; other signs are invented or created by humans, such as letters of the alphabet. This variety of signs is both arbitrary and conventional, which is our definition of a symbol." He paused to let them consider the implications of that statement.

Karin raised her hand. "What does it mean to say that a sign is arbitrary, sir?"

"Take the letter A. Why does it stand for and represent the sound Ahy?" She shook her head. "No one knows for certain. At some point in the development of our alphabet, some person decided that arbitrary figure should stand for that sound and once others acknowledged and accepted the relationship, the link was established and once so understood, became conventional."

"Lord Jesus" LB exclaimed, taking a logical leap. "It explains the establishment of our entire alphabet."

"It does, LB. And so we have the creation of the greatest symbol system ever created by the human mind. Remember, this kind of artificial sign, one whose meaning has become conventional is called a symbol. Thus, we have semiotics as the formal study of signs and their interpretation within some context of use. When we study the use and application of signs and symbols, we enter the realm of pragmatic theory and the ordinary language philosophy of Ludwig Wittgenstein, J.L. Austin, and his former student John Searle at UC Berkeley." Will noticed Davidson begrudgingly make a note or two.

Mike raised his hand. "Can the study of semiotics be applied to areas other than language as a symbol system?"

"Excellent question. It has a broad range of application as you will learn from your readings. My specific contribution to semiotic theory has been the application of semiotics to the analysis and interpretation of crimes. Each crime, usually murder, but not always, is a highly significant action. It has a context, always, and so is amenable to analysis and interpretation. Believe it or not, some of the work of Arthur Conan Doyle and his fictional detective, the great Sherlock Holmes, displays some aspects of semiotic analysis in the crimes perpetrated in the stories."

He thought of Yuriko. "Crimes that have been committed." He waited for her to correct her notes and continued.

"Doyle's contribution to analysis is his use of logical deduction. Doyle was actually trained as a physician and learned the skill of diagnosis, which he applies to the work of his great detective. However, Doyle sometimes confuses inductive logic with deductive logic, so you are advised to know the difference between both. Also, in your reading of Peirce's work, and good luck with that, focus on his treatment of inductive, deductive, and particularly his work on abductive hypotheses. Make certain you learn what an abductive hypothesis is, why it's based in observation, and how we use it. Understand that it is based in observation, or a series of observations that lead to the creation of an abductive argument that seeks the simplest and most likely explanation of the observations."

"This will become crucial to our work in the second semester when we take on and try to solve a real, existing cold case. One more thing of note. Semiotic analysis requires keen observation, as Sherlock Holmes will tell you. Moreover, certain criminals such as sexual predators are particularly keen observers, for example." Davidson was readying a snide comment but Will cut him off with the announcement that they were ready to take their second fifteen-minute break before they began the third and last hour of the seminar.

CHAPTER TWELVE

Class Exercise

When the students returned to the classroom, some carrying soda cans and open bags of chips or chocolate candy bars, he allowed them to settle before he gave them an assignment. "Please find yourselves in the following pairings. Lisa and Larry, pair off. Karin and Mike, then LB and Yuriko. After you introduce yourselves to each other and shake hands I want you to silently observe each other for five minutes. Then without speaking, write out your observations and conclusions, if any, and we will share these in class. Please find your partners now and begin. And remember: no talking or asking questions after introductions. You may, however, nonverbally direct the person so that you can get a better view of him or her Please begin."

The students pushed their chairs back and found their partners for the exercise, laughing and smiling nervously at the assignment. It took them a minute to shake hands and get used to each other's gaze after their introductions. Then the notetaking began with an occasional nonverbal request to stand or turn. LB seemed only too happy to pose; Yuriko blushed but pushed on anyway. Larry seemed bored, and with his interest focused primarily on Karin instead of Lisa, he wrote very little. Mike took meticulous notes, as did Karin.

When Will determined that the students were finished writing out their observation-based conclusions, he called the class back to order and announced, "Please begin by saying I observed, and then finish reporting your observations by stating, I conclude.... We'll start with LB and Yuriko."

LB was already waving his hand vigorously, wanting to be called on. "I'll go first," he graciously offered.

"Very well," said Will. "You go first."

LB looked once more at his notes. "Yuriko..." He stopped suddenly and restarted, remembering Will's directions to the class. "I observed...," he began the restart.

"Very good," Will interjected softly.

"I observed that Yuriko has shiny black hair and brown eyes. She is very pretty..."

"How is her hair styled, LB?"

"She has bangs across her forehead and the rest of her hair falls just above her mid-back. She wears very little makeup and just a touch of lipstick. Red," he added quickly. "She wears a collared shirt with blue edges on the cuffs and collar. I can just see the outlines of a white bra under the linen material of her shirt." He looked at Will and asked, "Is it okay to say that?"

"Of course."

"She wears an A-line skirt, cut fashionably short above midthigh and has on black pumps that are highly polished. She seems fit and smart."

"How can you tell she is smart?" Will asked.

LB said, "She speaks English, her second language, better than I do." The class laughed.

"What do you conclude from your observations?"

"I conclude that she is an excellent student, well-dressed and probably from a rich family, based on the quality of her expensive clothes." Yuriko hid an embarrassed smile behind her hand as if she were about to blow into her palm.

"Yuriko, you may now comment on LB's conclusions."

"He is correct, sir. My family is very rich and has lived for hundreds of years in Osaka. One of my forefathers was fortunate enough to serve the Emperor of Japan. I have the good fortune of being a graduate of Nippon's Osaka University...," she quickly corrected herself, "Japan's equivalent to Harvard or Yale."

"Thank you, Ms. Sumitomo. You may now share your observations of LB."

She read through her notes quickly, took a deep breath and began. "He is a very handsome black man."

"I love you, girl," LB stage whispered loud enough for everyone at the table to hear."

"He has dyed his hair orange. I see this sometimes among the young people in Japan who are very hip and cool. His ears are pierced and he wears a blue shirt with matching shorts like a young Japanese schoolboy. He wears black and white sneakers, I think you call them."

"Yes, ma'am," LB allowed, with a flip of the wrist. "That's to run away from the cops." Suddenly he turned as the realization of what he had just said hit him. "No disrespect intended, Professor."

"None taken, LB. We are being open and honest here. Yuriko, your conclusions please."

"I conclude that LB is a very modern and intelligent young man. He is very creative and he has the courage to express himself through fashion. I conclude that he is very gay also."

"Um hmm. You got that right, girl," LB said with a theatrical smirk. And Yuriko, behind the simile of a smile, seemed pleased with herself.

Will understood it had been her intention to try to make the class laugh and she had succeeded. "You both made a good start." After thanking the two previous students, he called on Larry and Lisa. "Your observations and conclusions, Larry," Will invited.

Without looking at his notes Davidson said, not looking at anyone in particular, "She wears a black tube dress cut so short I can almost see her pussy, since she obviously doesn't wear any underwear. Her tits are good and high enough that she does not need to wear a bra. Her hair is dyed black, cut pageboy short and she doesn't need to wear lipstick. Her eyes are sky-blue and her eyelashes are artificially lengthened. I conclude she is a slut." A nervous silence filled the room.

"Lisa?" Will prodded, watching carefully.

She began with a smile. "I take pride in my sluttiness." She looked Davidson in the eye. "My sexuality is my power as a woman and I'm not afraid to express it. I refuse to be cowed by people's expectation for how I should behave or comport myself as a female in this society. I am confident in who I am and I enjoy nothing more than exposing other people's hypocrisies and puritanical small-mindedness. Accordingly, I fuck whoever I want, whenever I want. And of one thing I am absolutely certain..." She paused for dramatic effect. "I am in fact a slut but if Davidson were the last man on earth, I would not let him fuck me. I would rather see the extinction of the human race." The class tittered.

"Lisa, your observations and conclusions of Mr. Davidson."

"Larry is tall and thin with dark brown hair and is trying to cover a bald spot. He thinks he is much smarter than people give him credit for and he fancies himself a rebel thinker. He is a narcissist, secretly hates women smarter than he is, which is all of them," she said with decided exaggeration. "And his insecurities are centered in his very small penis."

Will wondered how she had come to that conclusion. He reasoned that there was some virulent history between the two, now playing itself out in public. He decided he needed to keep an eye on these two.

With one more withering glance at him she said, "I both observe and conclude that you are an asshole."

Larry Davidson pushed back from the table, incensed. "I forgot to add she is also a bitch."

Before Will could say anything to take back control of the interchange between the two, Davidson stood and collected his things, shoving his materials into his backpack with obvious anger, his face gone red.

"I don't have to take this crap from anybody," he said and stormed out, pulling the class's attention along with him.

After a minute to let everyone reform their attention Will looked at Mike and Karin. "I assume that neither of you consider one or the other an asshole or a bitch?" The class laughed nervously and then relaxed again. "Okay. You two good to go?"

"Can do," Mike said immediately. "Ready to adapt and overcome." He looked at Karin. "And I promise not to call you any names."

"I can take it," she assured him with a smile.

"Okay, here goes. Karin has thick, light brown hair and eyes the color of honey. Her right eye is slightly off-center but no one but a trained sniper would see this. She wears glasses. She wears a tan, button-down oxford shirt over brown khakis. Her nails are the same color as her red lipstick. She does not wear an engagement or wedding ring. She wears her shirt unbuttoned to the third button down from the top and her bra is a light cherry red. Sorry," he added, for her sake. "I couldn't help but notice, and we were supposed to do careful and close observation." She smiled politely, nonplussed, and awaited his conclusions. "And by the way, she smells of lilacs and violets and freshly opened soap. I conclude that she is currently a single female, but interested. She appears more conservative than Lisa. Sorry," he apologized again.

Will directed him to stop saying sorry. "Yes, sir. I think she is extremely sharp and competent, but because she is a female from Iowa, dresses down more than Lisa or LB," he added with a touch of humor. The class laughed. They seem to have relaxed now that Davidson had left, Will observed. "I also conclude that as an Iowa farm girl pursuing a Master of Science degree, Karin is not only smart but tough. Any guy would be lucky to have her as a girlfriend," he added, with certainty.

Will indicated it was Karin's turn. "The first thing I noticed about Mike is the way he carries himself. He has the confidence and composure of someone who has seen and done it all. He keeps his dark blonde hair cut short military fashion. He's about six feet tall, but seems taller because of his cowboy boots. He wears blue jeans and a freshly ironed shirt so I conclude that his wife must love him a great deal." She paused to let the class laugh. "Personally, I find him to be handsome and he appears to be very strong as evidenced by the thickness through his chest and biceps. And he also has something tattooed on his bicep. I think it's a Latin phrase, *De oppresso liber*, but I'm not sure what that means." Mike blushed so she turned to Dr. Sheridan for help.

"Roughly translated it means to free from oppression. It's the motto for the United States Special Forces."

She waited while LB scooted over to ask for a flex from Mike, who acquiesced begrudgingly, and showed his guns, impressing everyone in the room.

LB said, "I want me one of those tats, too. I also need to be freed from oppression."

As LB scooted back to his place at the table Karin continued. "He is fit and tan, most likely because of his latest tour in Afghanistan. I conclude that he is a highly competent and smart individual or he would never have made it to or succeeded in the special forces and risen to the rank of sergeant first class. My conclusions are based on a very simple fact. He sits here among us." As she finished the rest of the class clapped quietly.

Will took the occasion to thank everyone for their participation in the exercise. "It will interest you to learn that your conclusions based on the observations you made, are examples of abductive hypotheses. What we would do next is seek information and facts that would verify those conclusions. Good work," he said and reminded them of the readings required for the next meeting of the class in one week's time. At that point he excused them into the night.

After he dismissed his graduate students and acknowledged their thank-yous and goodbyes on the way out, Will noticed Lisa hanging back, taking more time than needed to load notebooks and texts into her backpack. He stowed away his own materials, then erased the whiteboard. When he turned, she stood nearby. Behind an attractive smile she said, "I just want to thank you for not jumping in when Davidson and I went at it."

Will shrugged his shoulders. "You look like you can handle yourself."

"More than able," she said, placing the padded strap of her pack across one shoulder.

"If you don't mind my asking and just between the two of us, anything going on between you and Mr. Davidson that I should know about?"

"How in the hell do know that?"

He grinned. "That's what I get paid a lot of money to do."

"Nothing for you to worry about. I have it under control."

"I'm certain of that," he said. "One more quick question, before you leave."

"Shoot," she said.

"I noticed you have the traces of an accent. Mind telling me where you got it?"

She was momentarily shocked, but instantly regained her composure. Anyone else, she was certain, anyone less highly trained would never have noticed. She smiled and looked away. "My parents emigrated from Estonia to Wisconsin. We spoke a polyglot of languages at home: Estonian, Russian, German, and a lot of English at home and in school. I have a master's degree in foreign languages and literature."

The explanation seemed to satisfy him. "Walk you to the elevator?" She nodded.

On the bottom floor he held the elevator doors open as she stepped out ahead of him; he exited behind her and she said, "Thanks for the class tonight. I think I'm really going to enjoy learning about semiotics this semester."

Will laughed. "Thanks for the compliment and I do hope you have a great semester. And I hope you get things worked out with Mr. Davidson."

She looked at him with shocked surprise but made no comment. They wished each other good byes as the humid night and the parking lot separated them.

CHAPTER THIRTEEN

New Roommate

Over the next two weeks, he took them more deeply into semiotic theory and its applications. He led them into the minds and philosophies of Ferdinand de Saussure, Roland Barthes, Michel Foucault, Jacques Derrida, Julia Kristeva, and Umberto Eco. He showed them semiotic applications in textual hermeneutics and even biblical exegesis. Mike and Yuriko struggled with some of the material; the Army sergeant first class had not been adequately prepared in his previous studies, many of them online courses on various military bases around the world. For Yuriko it was simply a matter of learning enough vocabulary keep up with the readings. Both students, however, appeared to be highly motivated and did the extra work needed to keep abreast of the heavy reading requirements for the course.

Lisa and Karin seemed genuinely interested as evidenced by their thoughtful and insightful questions during his lectures. LB was a delight. Though he butchered most of the names from the readings and occasionally hid behind a flounce or a caricature, Will knew he had done his readings. He was high energy and had the courage to ask about what confused him in the readings. Will remembered from his own advanced graduate studies that there was ample opportunity for confusion in the work of the French, German, Italian, and American philosophers whose thinking was often transcribed into a writing and discourse intended mostly for other philosophers. Moreover, their works often suffered from less than sterling translation into English. Will would have been surprised if there had not been some confusion and misunderstanding among his students. Larry Davidson missed the week following his tantrum, showed up in the third week, but offered no excuses or explanations or apologies for missing the class. He said nothing and asked no questions and took few notes, in contrast to Yuriko, whose pen, taken from a white plastic container of five, flew over pages and pages of yellow notepaper.

In the fourth week he gave them a ten-question short answer essay exam that took the entire three hours. Davidson bullshitted his way through three of the questions and left the other seven unanswered. For some reason, his face was bruised and swollen as if he had been in a bar fight the night before. The other graduate students were stunned when he pushed back from the seminar table after only an hour of writing, picked up his backpack, ubiquitous on the shoulders of graduate students, handed in his exam and answers and the next day dropped the course, to Will's relief. He had prepared himself to meet with the young man in an effort to discern just what the problem was and, perhaps in his best interests, have him drop the course. He later learned that Davidson had withdrawn from all his coursework that semester and thus would not qualify to sit for his doctoral exams, effectively bringing an end to his Ph.D. studies.

Nothing to be ashamed of, Will thought, when he heard the news from Dean Carpenter. Very few students are accepted into Ph.D. programs and less than fifty percent of those make it all the way through their programs. That explains why less than 1.5% of the world's educated elite hold a doctorate. The road is too damn hard and too damn long. The average doctoral student needs eight years to finish the Ph.D. if also teaching or working as a research assistant. He wondered if he would ever do it again, knowing now what he did not know then. But he had other things on his mind.

During the exam, while he had the luxury of observing his students while they wrote, he noticed for the first time Lisa uncharacteristically wore jeans and a halter top, despite the chill in the air-conditioned room. She appeared sleep deprived and for once she had applied her makeup like a first-year undergraduate away from home for the first time, and too far from the small mirror in a dim light. Moreover, to his chagrin, it seemed her heavy makeup was hiding a bruise or two on her face. As she handed in her answers ahead of Yuriko, the last student writing and whom he had permitted the use of a Japanese-English dictionary, he asked Lisa to come back after Yuriko finished. When Yuriko left ten minutes later with apologies for taking so long, Lisa returned to the seminar room.

"Sit, please," he directed her. "I need a minute to do a close observation of you; with your permission, of course."

She took a deep breath, nodded her affirmation, her breasts peaking under the sheer material of the black halter top. She crossed her long legs to get more comfortable, the muscles of her thighs pushing against the tight fabric of her skinny jeans. She resigned yourself with a wry smile. He confirmed the bruises. He gently took both her hands from atop her thighs and held them in his own, examining her knuckles. Both hands were swollen and when he gently touched the knuckle of the first finger on her right hand, she winced. "Please close both hands." She did so. "Good," he said, "probably not broken. Ready to hear my analysis?"

She nodded, genuinely curious. "Based on my observations I conclude that you have been in a fight, most likely with a friend, boyfriend, or sexual partner, as it may be. Whoever it was—and I think it was your roommate—I believe you had an argument two days ago based on the development of your bruises. Despite his promises to you he has been unable to handle your sexual freedom, and you are unable and unwilling to deal with his jealousy, which you disdain. He grabbed you roughly by the shoulder, leaving a bruise." Here Will touched the purple blemish near her neck, now infused with yellow. "At this point your martial arts training took over and you hit him with an elbow strike, probably on the nose," he said and touched the bruise there, the elbow still slightly swollen.

"I reason from my inductive observation that you have studied some form of martial arts that permit you the use of an elbow strike. You laid him out with a left jab and a right cross, which grazed him," Will said, touching the fourth knuckle of her right-hand, "most likely because at that point he was falling back onto the bed." The surprise registering in her face signaled that he was correct in his detailed analysis. "You don't put up with assholes," he emphasized, "so you pack your clothes and books, throw everything into your SUV where you have been sleeping and living, until you can make arrangements for another place to live. This leads me to a conclusion in the form of an abductive hypothesis, as yet unproven, that the fight took place with your roommate in your shared apartment.

She uncrossed her legs and as he sat back, she leaned forward. "How could you possibly have known all that without having been there?" She shook her head in disbelief. "But your conclusion has my stomp of approval."

He chuckled at the malapropism, unsure whether it was an intentional well-designed play on words or if it was an unintentional misuse of the idiom. "This is what I do," he said simply. She ran her fingers through her hair and sighed. "I know," he said in sympathy. "You had hopes that this one would be different and could accept you on your own terms. Like too many men, he got jealous and then violent."

She forced a laugh. "And you know what, Dr. Sheridan? Some of the women I've slept with have been even worse."

He nodded his agreement. "But we have more immediate problems to solve at the moment. "If you want to press charges, I will have him arrested by the campus police."

She shook her head no. "He had to go to the medical center for his busted nose. Let's leave it at that."

Will could tell she still had some emotional attachment to her now ex-roomie. His loss, Will thought, as he gathered exams and placed them in his book bag. "I'll walk you down to the parking lot. As they rode the elevator down to the ground floor, he said to her, "Not easy putting makeup on in the car is it?"

"Not when you have to shower in the gym and try to hide a blooming shiner before going to class. How did you know?" she asked, then stopped him with a laugh as the elevator door opened and she answered her own question. "I know, it's what you do." He was too humble to reply.

He handed her into an SUV, a Honda Pilot stuffed to the windows with clothes, books, computer, bed sheets, sleeping bag, and pillow cases that doubled as curtains, purses and other bags. "How's your courage?"

"Coming up fast," she allowed.

"Follow me then."

"Where to?" she asked, keying the ignition of the older vehicle and checking the gas gauge.

"You'll see." Under the mercury vapor lamps in the parking lot fronting the Hall Center for Communication Studies, he drove ahead and onto University Avenue. He drove past the Crenshaw all sports dome and out into the dark of the night, past the municipal golf course, a farm on the left, and eventually to the start of the stand-alone housing subdivision named Hawthorn Acres. He turned onto Cherryglen Street, checked the mirror to make sure he had not lost her and turned into the driveway of the duplex. He pulled into the garage and she parked three car lengths behind him but he motioned for her to pull up onto the concrete apron. He invited her in, holding the door. Sleeping in the car or not, she smelled wickedly good.

"Thank you," she said, pushing past him face-to-face, a hand on his shoulder as he held the door for her.

He flipped the light switch and closed the doors. "Living room," he indicated. "The kitchen," he said, dropping his book bag on the circular oak tabletop. From the living room he opened the door to a bedroom that stood empty across from the bathroom. Past the bathroom he opened the door to a larger bedroom that contained a closet with two sliding closet doors, a queen mattress on the floor, and a chest of drawers. "You can crash here for the time being. This room is quieter than the other bedroom. The three graduate students living next door come and go at all hours, and walk past this bedroom's window to get to their front door. Otherwise, they are relatively quiet."

"This is so very kind of you, but I couldn't put you out. Just let me park in your driveway tonight, surf the couch in your living room, and I'll be on my way tomorrow."

"You're not putting me out," he assured her.

She stood up very straight, arms at her sides, and squared her shoulders. "Very well, then," she said, accepting the inevitable, relief evident in her voice, a bed far preferable to another night trying to sleep on the reclining seat of the Pilot.

"What time do you usually go to bed? I need time to move my things out. Shouldn't take me too long."

"I'm flexible," she added magnanimously, with a touch of tease thrown in

"I'm sure you are," he said, appreciating her long limbs and athletic figure. "You can go to bed whenever you want," he told her.

"In any bed I want?"

He laughed at the innuendo. "I will be sleeping downstairs while you are here."

She blushed into her cheeks pancaked with too much makeup, which had the effect of making her into an even more attractive clown, as if that were possible. "I see," she said to Will, genuinely disappointed and a little shocked at her false presumption.

"Come on," he invited her. "I'll show you the rest of my digs, then get you unloaded and squared away." He opened the door to the stairs reaching down to the finished basement from the kitchen. A carpeted room with a couch, two end tables, a TV and a stereo emerged from the darkness as he flipped on the lights. "Utility room," he indicated off to the right. He let her look in and as she leaned in her breasts brushed his forearm. She was not wearing a bra, he confirmed. "Washer, dryer, utility sink."

"I can't wait to wash out a few things. I've been living in these blue jeans."

"You don't need to tell me," he said, and on impulse she playfully punched him in the shoulder. Immediately she apologized. "Don't know if I should have done that."

"The thought of doing laundry makes me violent, too," he said, and she laughed while he opened an adjacent door. "My office." Some books and a desktop computer wired to the Internet caught her eye.

"You have Wi-Fi?" she asked. "I have a laptop."

"No. But tomorrow I'll go and buy a router and hook it up for you. That way you can work upstairs at the kitchen table or in the living room if you want."

"I'll gladly pay for it."

"No need. I was going to put one in anyway," he lied. "I'll see to it that the university gets billed for it."

"Oh goody," she giggled like a young girl getting her first bottle of perfume on Christmas.

He opened the next door over. "My bedroom." She peeked in because he allowed it. It was a mirror image of the room upstairs with a two-door standing closet, a night table with a reading lamp next to a queen bed on the floor, a pine chest of drawers and a coffee table along one wall past the end of the bed. He turned out the lights and walked back into the enormous living room. "Through that door on the left is my little bathroom and that one on the right leads to an authentic root cellar. To orient yourself it's under the front of the house and the porch of the front door."

"Got it," she said.

He took her upstairs and offered her a seat on the couch. Before she spoke, she took both his hands into her own. Her blue eyes went liquid. "This is so unbelievably sweet of you."

"Just hang on a minute. There will be a couple of house rules."

"Of course," she said, immediately sitting upright, but curled a leg underneath her, both sneakers now on the carpet.

"No music that I can hear when I'm downstairs, ever, please."

"Of course not," she nodded affirmatively.

"I don't care how you keep your room, but our common living areas including the kitchen, living room, and your bathroom will be kept clean."

"Promise," she said.

"As far as the bathroom is concerned, although I have my own, I don't want to run all the way downstairs every time I'm up here just to take a leak," he explained.

"I fully understand," she agreed.

"When I'm in the house there will be times when I need my privacy and I will disappear downstairs not to be disturbed. Of course, I promise to be conscious of your privacy needs too." She nodded. "Anything else before we go and get you unloaded?" He did not wait for her answer, remembering something else. "Oh, and one more thing. I prefer that you keep this on the down low." She agreed vigorously.

"It's nobody's business but our own."

"Exactly. So, any questions for me?" he asked, anticipating her inquiry.

"How do you feel about me bringing people to the house? You know I like to fuck boys and girls."

He laughed at her audacity. "The Germans have a saying. *Das ist nicht mein Bier.* That's not my beer but I ask only that you be discreet and if you introduce me it should always be as your roommate and nothing more. Understood?" Lisa made the nonverbal sign for zipping her lip. What a beautiful and refreshingly open woman, he thought. "Let's go and unload your car."

Half an hour later the Pilot stood empty except for the smell of a pretty woman who wanted to smell good. He marveled at how much the SUV could hold. After the last bag had been transferred inside, he took her to the phone on the kitchen wall. "I know you have your own cell phone but this is our land-line and this is the phone number. The phone has a neat little intercom feature. After you are settled, ring me downstairs. I'll be grading exams and when you're ready we can go get a pizza if you want. I don't feel like cooking after moving three tons of your junk."

She laughed at the hyperbole. "Pizza will be fine. And I'm buying. Oh, and lest we forget, what's my half of the rent for this dump?"

"Easy girl. Disparage my dump and I'll throw you out to sleep in your truck. The rent is paid as part of my grant from the university. In exchange for your portion, you will cook as needed, clean as required, and as necessary you will help me with the laundry."

"Sheesh," she said. "Now I have to learn how to cook."

After a pizza and a pitcher of beer at the local pizza joint in the city they returned home. Will welcomed her once again and excused himself for the evening, leaving her to finish unpacking and setting up her room. Around 2:00 a.m. he put the last grade on the last exam, gathered the papers and placed them in his book bag. He would officially record them at another time. He visited the bathroom, brushed his teeth and took his flashlight into the bedroom. When all the lights were out downstairs it was as black as the inside of a bowling ball. He needed the flashlight to find his way. He left the bedroom door open for circulation, turned on the table lamp, and started a new novel by James Lee Burke. At the top of the stairs he heard the door to the kitchen open gently. After a sufficient amount of time to let her blue eyes adapt to the pitch black of the basement living room, he heard the soft tread of bare feet on the carpet covered stairs. She paused at the bottom, seeing the reading light leaking from his bedroom.

"Dr. Sheridan," she called quietly in case he was asleep.

"Yes," he answered." He heard her run to his bedroom door, which she closed behind her after she entered his room. She wore a white, men's ribbed strap T-shirt. As he looked up at her, she pulled it off over her head and shoulders, and dropped it on the floor. Before he could think to protest, she lifted the covers and buried herself in next to him, positioning herself face-to-face.

"You're very sweet to offer, but this is not required. We are roommates and I have no further expectations of you." In order to lessen the sting of the rejection, he kissed her cheek, already hot and flushed.

"Sorry," she said, "nothing personal and please don't take offense. This isn't an offer, nor does it have anything to do with expectations. I have had a very stressful last few days and when I get stressed, I need to fuck," she explained as a matter of fact. As he readied a response in the face of that alarming information, she took his penis in her hand and slide her sweet breath onto his lips.

"This is what I do," she said, emphasizing the personal pronoun. He reached over to turn out the light and she reached over to turn it back on. "I want to observe you. I want to watch you fucking me." Once trapped within the gentle bite of her kiss, once within the insistent pulse of her hips, she pressing him from above, elbows locked, both hands on the muscles of his chest, fingers splayed, pushing and pushing, her eyes never leaving his, he gave in and gave as good as he got.

Lost in the rise of heat and in the swell of her intensity, he wondered how could nature at once be so kind and so cruel to give so much to one human being and so little to so many others. It was a problem best left for another time. As she repositioned herself atop him and leaned back so he could take both her breasts in his hands, she worked her hips with increasing urgency. He knew they had a long night of pleasurable discovery and experimentation ahead, with the luxury of no classes or office hours to prepare for the next day.

At 4:37 a.m. he kissed her cheek one more time. "Go find your own bed. I need to sleep."

Now on her side, she curled herself into his arms, and pressed her bottom up against him. "Don't want to go."

He said firmly to her, "I sleep alone, no offense and nothing personal. And if you sleep here with me with that outstanding ass of your pressed up against me, I will get no rest and no sleep whatsoever."

"Just once more," she entreated," and I promise I go." The smooth tight press of her ass against his penis had the desired effect and she repeated, pleading a bit, "just one more time."

He gave in, accepting the inevitable. "Okay, but you get to do all the work."

"Oh goody," she said and went to work.

At noon the next day he went upstairs to get a glass of orange juice and found her SUV gone. He read through the exams again to double check his evaluations before he recorded the grades into his laptop. Finished with his work, he went to get a hamburger at the Hardees in Waterloo, sat there and wrote for two hours, after which he headed for the YMCA to find a handball game. After three games of doubles and a good long soak the in the whirlpool, he drove home, wondering what he might have for dinner.

Her SUV was in the driveway so he drove around it and parked in the garage. None of the neighbors were home yet. She was in the kitchen, cooking spaghetti. Good girl, he thought, he needed the carbohydrates. He went to the refrigerator after correcting the sauce at her invitation; a little sugar did the trick. She put the lid on the spaghetti sauce to let it bubble in the pot and joined him for a cold beer. They clicked bottles but before she took a drink, she kissed him full on the lips.

"What was that for? he asked, surprised.

She practically overwhelmed him with a smile. "I'm stress free. And I have you to thank for that. I feel great today and I want to thank you so much for last night, and for letting me stay here." She got it all out but was too breathless to take a drink. He shrugged his shoulders.

"But can't fuck you tonight," she explained, stating the matter as a fact. "My pussy is too damn sore. I'll be happy to blow you, however," she offered magnanimously.

He nearly snorted his beer through his nose. "Thanks for that wonderful offer, but my penis is rubbed raw and it's not from playing handball. Let's finish our beer. I will open a bottle of a red wine I bought for us, a nice cabernet sauvignon from Paso Robles on California's Central Coast, and we'll drink it with dinner. And so I don't forget, here," he said, presenting them to her, "I had keys to the front and back door made for you. And remember, no obligations. You do whatever you please. But I'm not interested in having a girlfriend."

"Oh goodness," she said, accepting the gift of the housekeys. "I think I love you already," she said facetiously and dragged him into the kitchen. "Too soon?" she asked, making sure he got the joke.

CHAPTER FOURTEEN

Thunderstorm

Lisa came and went as she pleased. She attended her other graduate seminars and never missed a class. He often found her studying in the living room or at the kitchen table when she needed to use her laptop. She kept the kitchen clean and the living room vacuumed when he was gone, the upstairs bathroom spotlessly clean but cluttered with hair dryers, razors, shampoos, lotions, mascara pencils, deodorant, perfume, tissues, makeup removing wipes, and panties on the floor, but not often. Once he found one of his T-shirts from the FBI Academy at Quantico. As he held it up and appreciated its new smells, she walked by the open bathroom door, stopped and said, "Hope you don't mind. I found it when I was doing our laundry. I'm wearing it to sleep in."

He threw her the shirt. "If anything, I'm jealous." She laughed, her eyes sparkled, she threw the T-shirt on her bed, closed the door and with an I will see you for dinner tonight promise, she was gone into the fog of the morning.

The next day, working in his office downstairs on a new manuscript for a book, he heard the doorbell ring. He remembered Lisa was home but on her way to the library to do research for a paper in another one of her seminars. Lisa opened the front door and greeted Dr. Landsberg.

"Oh, hi Lisa. Is Dr. Sheridan home?"

"Come in. Come in. I think he's downstairs working on his book. Can I get you anything to drink before I give him a call to let him know you are here?"

Landsberg entered, unzipping her raincoat, not sure yet what to make of the situation. "A beer, if you have it."

Lisa took her coat, hung it in the coat closet and said, "Coming right up."

Dr. Sonia Landsberg sat and considered the circumstances. When Lisa brought her a beer and a glass, she said casually, "I didn't know you were living here. I thought you were sharing an apartment with Larry Davidson." She poured the glass half-full as Lisa sat and crossed freshly shaved legs now showing too good and shiny effect under a short white skirt and blue cotton sweater. Dr. Landsberg marveled for a minute at the young woman's audacious beauty. For just a second or two she caught herself staring as the young woman spoke.

"That's right. I was. But he was too high maintenance," she said, running her long fingers through her black hair. "The bastard had the gall to slap me one night when he smelled another girl' s perfume on me, so I had to kick his ass when he grabbed me. Then I moved out." Dr. Landsberg covered a little gasp. "I had been sleeping in my car for a few days when Dr. Sheridan deduced, or induced, I should say," she said laughing at the correction, "that I was homeless. He offered me a room here until I can make other arrangements. But, as you know, the university over-enrolled this year and graduate student housing is full with extensive waiting lists. And, of course, there is nothing left to rent in town at this time of year."

"I know exactly what you mean. It took me almost three years to find a decent place to live in Cedar City." Before Lisa stood to call Will, she placed her hand quickly on Sonia's thigh, at once a familiar and sympathetic gesture between two females who had shared similar circumstances and understood each other; on the other hand, a gesture that excited Sonia Landsberg and caused her quickly to flush red.

"I'll go and ring Dr. Sheridan," Lisa said, inwardly smiling at the unintended effect, "and let him know you are here." She excused herself.

When he received the call Will said, "Tell her I'll be up in five minutes or so. I'm still in my bathrobe. Offer her a beer or something to drink while she waits."

"Already done," Lisa informed him.

"Okay. Give me ten."

The two women were deep into a conversation about the enervating toll needy men put on a relationship when Will came through the kitchen into the living room and greeted Dr. Landsberg. Lisa stood. "I was just out the door and on my way to the library when Dr. Landsberg arrived," she explained. She went to her room and got her backpack and keys to the SUV, closing the bedroom door behind her as they waited.

Sonia cautioned her to take along a raincoat. "It's starting to look dangerous out there." With a thumb Lisa indicated she had one in her backpack.

"Lisa, can you do me a quick favor?"

"Yes sir," she said. "What do you need?"

"In the latest journal of *Semiotica*, there is an article by Finkelstein on critiquing the work of Kristeva. I need a copy of that article, please."

"Done," she said.

"Here. Let me give you money for the copying charge."

She waved him off. "You can pay me when I get back tonight. You two have fun." They waved her goodbye out the door and told her not to study too hard.

As Will and Dr. Landsberg sat on the couch, she said, "I had almost forgotten what a stunning young woman she is."

"I never noticed," Will said glibly. "Have you had her as a student before?"

Sonia nodded. "She took the communication theories graduate course with me two semesters ago, I think." Dr. Landsberg shook her head in disbelief. "And I can't believe what that bastard Davidson did to her. He was in the course with her and I think that's where they met. I'm glad he's gone."

Will nodded. "I can't believe what she did to him. Granted, she's athletic and tall, but Davidson weighs easily a hundred and seventy pounds, and yet she broke his nose and knocked his ass out."

"Oh my God, I didn't know that. She seems so sweet."

"Don't let the exterior fool you; she is one tough kid inside. Now, not to change the subject, but to what do I owe the pleasure of this visit?" he asked, gallantly.

"I just want to add quickly that I think it was very nice of you to come to her rescue and give her a place to stay."

"I didn't rescue her in that sense. I only gave her a place to stay so that it doesn't interfere with her studies while she gets back on her feet. Sleeping in a car at night and having to shower in the women's gym in the morning is not a good way to get through doctoral studies. Besides, I'm sure you would have done the same for her had you known her circumstances."

She nodded. "I came by to invite you out for lunch," she said, a touch of shyness and anticipation in her breathing.

Will shook his head no. "You know that I don't fraternize with colleagues," he said. The sudden slump of her shoulders signaled her disappointment. He said immediately, "Unless they are extremely intelligent and attractive and I know I can fully trust them." She blushed at the compliment and smiled, relief evident in her face.

He excused himself for a moment to go downstairs and when he returned with his jacket, he caught her in a reverie. "Still thinking about Miss Allen?" he asked, smiling.

She nodded self-consciously. "How could you possibly know that?"

"It's what I do. Lisa certainly has a way of affecting a person's thinking, I have discovered," Will said with a laugh, holding the door for her.

"I would do her." Sonia clapped a hand over her mouth as if to stifle herself. "I can't believe I just said that to you."

"Why Dr. Landsberg, there is a side of you that demands further exploration."

"In your dreams, big boy. We'll take my car."

"As you wish, madame."

After a lunch that lasted two hours, she dropped him off at his place with a date set for a home football game against Iowa on Saturday in the dome.

The following Friday she came by for dinner with Lisa and Will. Outside, the evening wind howled like wolves signaling each other after a moose kill in the great Northwoods where he lived in Minnesota. Then came the lightning storm that cracked the sky, rain that lacerated the trees, and hail that pounded the grass flat. They stood at the living room window watching through the porch light and marveled at the ferocity of an Iowa fall storm. When Lisa begged off after dinner to read and study in preparation for her Monday seminar, Will invited Sonia downstairs. Even in the depths of the basement, they could not escape the sounds of the full fury of the thunder that boomed and thumped through the sky like heavy artillery cannons firing in sequence.

After sharing a bottle of white wine, she made ready to leave. "It's getting late and I should go. I've had a wonderful time tonight and you and Lisa did a great job on the steaks." She kissed him quickly on the cheek.

He pulled her back down onto the couch. "I don't think it's safe for you to drive through a storm of this magnitude. For all we know roads and bridges might be washed out. For your safety I think you should stay the night. I have the guest bedroom across from Lisa's bedroom available and you are welcome to use it. I certainly don't think Lisa would mind, if you don't snore," he teased.

"I do not snore," she informed him in no uncertain terms. "And given the ferocity of this freaking storm, I accept your gracious offer. However, I feel it is in your best interest for me to at least put you to bed so that you do not cry every time lightning flashes and thunder shakes the house."

Will tilted his head from side to side a millimeter as he considered her proposition. "I do so admire a protective and caring woman. I'll go and get you a T-shirt to sleep in. Don't worry, it's freshly laundered."

"No need to bother. I sleep nude," she explained when no explanation was necessary.

He showed her to the bathroom, showed her the flashlight, and while she went about her preparations, awaited her in bed. He was just about to pick up a crime novel from one of his favorite authors when she came in behind the flashlight. She had worn the T-shirt for the trip into the bedroom. She closed the door behind her, flipped off the flashlight, put it down on the night table where Will's book lay unopened, and made a fine show of taking off the borrowed cotton shirt. She stood still while he took the time to admire her splendid figure.

Now in her late thirties and single, he noticed gravity had worked little or no effect on her breasts. Her arms were firm and tight, and he could count the muscles in her stomach. In the summer she rollerbladed the many paved miles of track along the Cedar River that the municipalities of Waterloo and Cedar City had been smart enough to pave for bicycle riders and skaters, bringing in thousands of tourists and millions of their dollars to the area and its state park. In the winter, also an ardent cross-country skier, she used the same snow-covered trails to pole and ski for miles through the forests that lined the groomed trails. Once out of her chair and away from long academic and scholarly hours seated behind her desk reading, writing, doing research, and grading papers and exams, her strenuous exercise regimen had kept her sexy, fit, and confident with her body's shape.

Under the covers of the heavy comforter, usually reserved for winter cold, they warmed each other, kissed, snuggled, and talked. "I've read two of your books now," she confessed. "I'm thinking of assigning them both as interdisciplinary readings in one of my seminars."

"Poor students," he said, deflecting the compliment with a little nip at the nape of her neck where she had touched it with perfume.

She raised her chin to give him more exposure. "If you don't mind my asking, whatever happened between you and that amazing detective from Germany, Sylvia Schumann, I believe?"

"Sylvie," he corrected her. She looked at him, expecting further elaboration but he was busy teasing a nipple into prominence between his lips. After a short gasp, she pulled his head up with both hands. "Sylvie?"

"I never discuss past relationships." He flicked the other nipple with his tongue. She lifted his chin with a finger. With gentle exasperation in his voice he said, "You read the damn book. She returned home to Germany after we closed the case we were working on with my uncle during their vacation with me in Minnesota. Last I heard, she got married and had three unfortunately ugly and retarded children with the guy she married. She also got fat and gained fifty pounds."

Sonia laughed. "I don't believe you."

"Believe this," he said, and transferred his attention from her nipples to her clitoris. No more questions ensued.

A timid tap on the bedroom door open a crack for ventilation amidst the tumult of the storm caught them both by surprise. "Come in," Will said to the furtive figure standing and waiting in the dark. Lisa slipped through the door and stood before them. Sheepishly she said, "Thunderstorms scare the living crap out of me."

If anything, the storm had worsened in intensity as the night had lengthened. He decided to let Lisa stay, but not before Will looked over at Sonia. "Oh, what the hell," she said and threw open the covers.

"Oh, goody," Lisa said, inverting the FBI T-shirt, and climbed in between them. As she made a production out of climbing over him, she let her body press against him and there was no mistaking her excitement as she slid her vagina across his genitals.

As she lay between them smiling like a coquette, Will asked, "What should we do now that baby is in bed with us?"

"Baby needs love and comforting," Sonia said.

Naked between them, Lisa said in her best little girl voice, "Baby says both of you should kiss me," and they did so as thunder shocked and concussed the house above them.

CHAPTER FIFTEEN

Deputy Sheriff

By his count Deputy Sheriff Delbert Copeland had been a working cop on the force almost twenty years in total now, and things had not always gone smoothly. He had resigned his position as a sergeant in the Des Moines Police Department after serving there for fifteen years. With a young daughter almost sixteen at the time, and after his wife had run off to Wichita Falls with a John Deere salesman, he decided the time was right to move to a smaller venue with less crime, less methamphetamine on the street, and a better chance to survive the routine of police work.

Despite the fact that he had recently been promoted to detective, when a deputy sheriff position opened in Fort Charles in the north-central part of Iowa close to the Minnesota border, he jumped at the chance and applied. Given his exemplary qualifications: five years in the Marine Corps, and fifteen years on the job as a Metro cop in Des Moines, he was hired just before his fortieth birthday. He had enough money saved up to buy a small house with acreage just south of town. It was his dream to work the forty-acre farm after retirement, settle down and become a gentleman farmer in the best Jeffersonian tradition.

The job, as expected, gave him ample time to put down roots in his new community in more ways than one. He leased thirty of his forty acres of arable land to a local established farmer, who planted half the acreage in seed corn used to create ethanol, thanks to the generous subsidies Iowa farmers collected from the federal government by their Republican senators, political action groups, and farm lobbyists. Their Republican senators and representatives showed no qualms in railing against big government's interference in the lives of farmers and beat the war drum against socialism even as they accepted millions of federal dollars in subsidy payments. The other half of the acreage was given over to soybeans, most of which he sold to Archer Daniels-Midland. With the subsidies and tax breaks, the farm produced just enough to make a small profit and although his salary as a deputy sheriff did not stretch very far even in small town rural Iowa, he had a retirement plan and a medical and insurance package, just right for his teenage daughter, happy to grow up on a farm and very quickly become the smartest student in the Fort Charles high school. Any year the farm managed to turn a small profit became a contribution for investment in her college fund.

Deputy Sheriff Copeland cruised the backroads on evening patrol outside Fort Charles. Even a deputy sheriff with detective qualifications was required to patrol and work night shifts from time to time given the five men and one-woman staff. This included the sheriff elected by the good citizens of Fort Charles and the surrounding county. Shortly after the only bar in Fort Charles kicked out the last of its desperate drinkers, Copeland caught a black Lincoln Navigator bouncing against the yellow line demarcating the side of the road and traveling 15 over the posted speed limit. He hit the lights on the cruiser and called it into dispatch as a 10-55, a possible drunken driver. After traveling two miles with no response from the big SUV, he went to the siren, and only then did the mammoth vehicle deign to pull over. He unstrapped and checked his Heckler and Koch 9-millimeter, tucked on his baseball cap emblazoned with the Sheriff's Department logo, and hit the spotlight illuminating what appeared to be a dealer's plate on the Navigator. He called numbers and letters in. He removed his flashlight-baton and as he approached the vehicle, shined the powerful LED beam into the back of the vehicle. It seemed clear. No passenger. Good. He walked up to just behind the driver's door, tapped the window with the butt of the foot-long metal flashlight. The driver was slumped forward and passed out over the steering wheel, high beams still on, engine running. Deputy Sheriff Copeland opened the door and the stink of alcohol turned him sideways. On the passenger seat he noticed an open container: a three-quarters empty bottle of Jim Beam sitting upright in the well of the upholstered leather seat. He checked the man's pulse, then pulled back an eyelid with the finger of his black leather glove. With a pen light taken from the pocket of his uniform shirt he shined the light into first one and then the other of the man's eyes, checking for pupillary response. At least he saw some dilation, but both eyes displayed micro tremors called nystagmus, a clear medical indication that the man's blood-alcohol level exceeded the legal limit set by the state of Iowa.

Convinced the man in the vehicle was merely drunk and not seriously ill, he pushed the snoring man off the steering wheel and back into his seat, reached across and switched off the engine and killed the lights. Leaving the door open to air out the stink in the cab, he returned to his cruiser and said to Sally, the rotund nearsighted blonde working dispatch that night, "1.6."

"Noted," she said, taking Copeland's best guess on the man's blood-alcohol level before using the field sobriety test. If he was within .1% of the official reading, she bought the beer. Otherwise it was on him. He got the test kit and returned to the vehicle. He took a fresh test tube out of its plastic container, put the plastic wrapper in his pant pocket and inserted the tube into the field breathalyzer. He flicked the man's ear once, twice, and with the third flick the unconscious man snorted and opened his eyes. He looked around as he tried to find his bearings, raising a hand against the blinding light of the flashlight shining into the cab.

"Everything all right, ossifer?" The man slurred.

"Step out of the car, please," Copeland directed. The man tried to get out but his seatbelt restricted him from traveling very far. Holding his breath Copeland reached in and released the belt. The man stood, staggered and fell into Copeland's arms. "Usually I athk a guy to buy me a drink firtht," he slurred, pleased at his attempt at humor. Copeland decided to dispense with the standard physical field sobriety tests, given the man's obvious level of drunkenness.

"Take just a minute, sir, if you please, and we'll soon get this over with." He directed the man to blow into the tube the required time. It took him four attempts. He finally got a good reading of 1.56. He advised the drunken man of his Miranda rights, asked him to turn and cuffed him.

"Ith that really nethethary?" the man asked, burping and giggling like a young girl. "Thorry," he said, suddenly contrite. Copeland waited to see if the man would puke himself, but no such luck. He would rather have him spew here on the side of the road than later in the back of his cruiser, which he would then have to hose out himself.

"Afraid so, sir. At this point I have determined that you are a danger to yourself and to others due to your current level of inebriation. I'm afraid that if I let you drive in your condition you might cause serious harm to yourself." He decided to re-cuff the compliant man's hands in front for better balance as he shuffled the drunkard to the back of his cruiser, opened the door and handed him in, hand on head so he wouldn't bump the back of his head as he sat down. He helped the man load his boots in, pointed toes capped with silver filigree, and secured him with a seatbelt. Once he saw that the drunk's knees were clear, he closed the door and went back to the Lincoln and did a visual check for drugs or paraphernalia. He called in Albert Young's driver's license for a 10-27, a vehicle registration request and dispatch reported Young had a record of numerous moving violations, including one prior operating while intoxicated, an OWI or DWI. Copeland shook his head. This one would cost the man thousands in insurance and court costs. He would be surprised if he avoided jail time.

Such was Del Copeland's first interaction with Albert Young, owner of Future Ford in Fort Charles, Iowa. It was not the beginning of a long and lasting friendship. On the contrary, Copeland, already considered an outsider, a big city cowboy trying to make a name for himself in a small town, was not deemed worthy of trust from the locals. In spite of the cold shoulders shown him at work, he went about the Job professionally, using discretion when warranted, but come on, when a man blew a 1.6 for Christ's sake, he was going to take him to jail. That was the law. After the blood draw came back confirming the breathalyzer reading of the amount of alcohol in the man's system, Copeland gave the case over to the DA's office and collected his free beer from dispatch.

Two things happened next with his righteous DWI stop. That morning, his shift over, as he was going off duty, he was called into Sheriff Miller's office and dressed down.

"Any idea who you arrested and threw in the drunk tank?" he asked, pointing to the incident reports.

"A guy named Albert Young. He had one prior DWI and blew at least twice over the legal limit."

"I don't give a shit if he blew a kangaroo. He's the mayor of Fort Charles, goddammit!"

Copeland looked at the man's face swelling with belligerency. He decided to back down a bit. After all, the man was his boss. "Sheriff, I just did what you and all the citizens of Fort Charles expect me to do: my job."

"Don't give me that self-serving, self-righteous attitude. What you did is put the Citizen of the Year in jail to the embarrassment of his family, the city, and this department. Just so you know. Now get out of my office. I do not want to see your ugly face anymore today."

Copeland was glad to leave.

The second thing that happened is Albert Young walked. At his trial hearing, his lawyer, a Creighton law school graduate with silvered hair and Italian calfskin shoes, argued that the chain of evidence had been compromised at the lab that had tested and analyzed Young's blood. He offered into evidence the fact that the original blood sample and the backup sample had been given different numbers, casting doubt on whose blood had actually been tested. "Reasonable doubt, your honor, due to chain of custody having been broken," was his closing statement.

The judge hearing the case was none too pleased. "Albert Young," he said, "please stand." Young, in a blue suit and new brown Tony Lima cowboy boots tipped with silver at the toes, stood. "I have no doubt in my highly trained legal mind that you were once again driving drunk. But because the idiots in the lab can't properly label their blood samples, despite Deputy Sheriff Copeland's testimony and the fact that he did everything by the book, I am forced by law to release you on a technicality. Albert," he admonished the defendant, pointing his gavel at the mayor, "you got a lucky break this time. If you are brought before me again for a DWI, I will see to it that you are prosecuted to the fullest extent the law allows me. Do we understand each other, sir?"

Young shook his head. "Absolutely, your honor. You will not see me here again."

Judge Robert Franklin seemed skeptical but his point made, he cracked the gavel on its wood base. "Case dismissed."

The young assistant DA trying the case closed his leather-bound notebook, a graduation present from his mother, and sighed. "Sorry Deputy Copeland. I really hated to lose this one. Wasn't your fault."

Del Copeland shrugged into his shoulders and took off his testimony tie and suit coat. He was no stranger to fuck ups in the criminal justice system. He had been naïve to think things might be better here in the backwoods. "If you don't mind me asking," he said to the kid, no more than a year or two out of law school, "what kind of car does Judge Franklin drive?"

The question puzzled the young lawyer. "Last time I checked, a white Ford F–150 pickup truck. Why do you ask?"

"Just curious."

Towards the middle of the semester, Sonia came into his office and quietly closed the door behind her. "What's up, Dr. Landsberg?" Will asked, looking up from behind his computer screen, happy for the interruption.

"Just came by to give you a quick heads-up." He noted the concern in her eyes. He put the computer to sleep and since he had the blinds to his window drawn closed behind him, she came around the desk and sat on his lap. She kissed him with authority and intent. She searched his eyes and smiled. "You are such a handsome man. I love your shiny coal black hair and those blue-gray eyes."

"You aren't so bad looking yourself," he said, unbuttoning the first two buttons of her blue silk blouse. She gently slapped his hand away but left her blouse unbuttoned, giving him a view of the swell of her breasts. The push-up bra had been worth the investment. Credit to Victoria's Secret, she thought. She put her hand around the back of his neck.

"Will, I have it on good authority that someone is planning something against you. I know it's nothing more than a rumor, but please be careful," she implored.

He took the time to study her face. She was not being dramatic. "I take you seriously. I'm no stranger to academic politics... academic jealousies, I should say. I'll keep my eyes open and my ears on." He kissed her affectionately. "It sweet of you to be so concerned about me." That said, he slipped his right hand into the bra cup of her left breast and held it in the cool of his palm. As he waited for the nipple to grow between his fingers, she kissed him on the neck.

"I don't know what it is about you that makes me so wanton and wet." She breathed a sigh of resignation onto his neck.

"Might be a good idea for you to come over later tonight," he suggested.

"I don't know," she deferred, feigning disinterest. "Will Lisa be home?"

"As a matter of fact, she did mention to me this morning that after her classes she needed some computer time at home tonight," Will said. "Maybe you'll get lucky."

"If I get lucky, big boy, you get lucky too."

"Then let's hope our luck holds for us both," Will said and kissed her forehead. "I'm playing handball at the Y until about seven. I will bring a pizza for three," he said. "7:30 then?" he asked.

"That's fine and maybe you should think about not playing so hard and save some strength. I think you're going to need it."

She was not exaggerating.

CHAPTER SIXTEEN

Lady's Choice

The next week during his office hours before his seminar, he looked up to a knock on the open door. A young woman of about twenty-five or so stood waiting expectantly.

"Please come in," he invited and came around the desk to greet her.

She introduced herself. "I'm Amber Kleinfeld, a Ph.D. student in social psychology and communications."

"Please come in and sit down," he said, offering her a chair at the side of his desk. He observed her for a second or two. She was wearing what his students called a fuck-me dress. The red fabric was stretched skintight over her ample frame and just covered the curve of her ass. Her breasts were pushed up into a shelf of flesh by her low-cut padded bra, which at the moment seemed superfluous. Her legs shined from the razor in the shower that morning and glistened with body lotion. She wore too much perfume, her eyelashes seemed unnaturally long, and she had not blended her lip liner well with the brick red lipstick she had finished with a gloss. Her badly dyed blonde hair fell to her shoulders and she flipped it to one side over a bare shoulder that showed her red bra strap. Then not without difficulty she crossed her legs. As she bent forward to the side of the chair to take a notepad out of her large red purse, he saw the full extent of the woman's overly ample breasts, a view obviously staged for his benefit.

"You were highly recommended to me by a friend who knows you and said that I should contact you if I have any questions about communication theories or semiosis." She stated the word as if she had spent a great deal of time practicing its pronunciation. "I'm getting ready to put together my proposal for my dissertation, and I would love to ask you a few questions."

"With pleasure," Will said, "if you would be so kind as to give me just a minute to finish off an email to a student, I can then give you my full and undivided attention." He quickly typed her name into the computer after he opened a file accessible only to faculty checking student records. Her picture came up. She was a student in the Women's Studies program. He knew that department had no Ph.D. program. He made a show of putting the computer to sleep, and with a flourish put a large ballpoint pen into his left shirt pocket next to two others. "And how can I best help you today, Miss Kleinfelder?"

"Kleinfeld," she corrected him, a hint of irritation in her voice. She paused for a minute and recrossed her legs, letting the material of her short dress slide further up over her ample thighs. "I would be so grateful if you could help me get started. I'm really getting desperate," she said, emphasizing really, her eyes widening and locking onto his. "I would do just about anything, because you know yourself as a Ph.D. how important the proposals for a dissertation can be."

He nodded emphatically to show her she was right about that, despite her garbled syntax. "I certainly appreciate a grateful student," he told her. "You know, Aristotle said that for learning to take place the student must meet the teacher at least halfway."

She flipped her hair to the other shoulder. "Oh, I'm more than willing to meet you halfway," she said, leaning forward and touching his forearm.

"Well then, let's get started," he said. "What theoretical basis do you want to use as the foundation for your dissertation research?" The question puzzled her. He elaborated. "That is to say, what is the object and intent of your study? If we know that, we can develop a theoretical rationale and a method for designing the research program." This seemed to make her happy and she scribbled something onto her notepad.

"Can you give me just a minute?" she asked and stood, looking at her watch. "I'm getting cold." She went and closed the door to his office. Hope you don't mind," she said, agitation replacing the treacly sweetness in her voice.

"Not if you don't mind," he allowed. "I certainly wouldn't want you to get cold."

She came back and sat and it took her a minute or two to get re-orientated. She took a deep breath. "I'm really interested in sexual relationships between men and women," she said, knowingly, despite an uncontrollable flush that painted red up into her cheeks.

That really narrows it down, Will thought to himself. "Can you be a bit more specific, please?"

"Oh, you know," she said, pulling at the hem of her dress that had slipped too high up her chubby thighs even for her sense of à la mode fashion. "I'd like to know what really gets guys off during sex. Is it like a power thing? I mean guys see us as a sexual object to be used for their personal gratification, right? I mean I love sex and everything," she explained, "but I also want to be respected for my mind."

"I couldn't agree with you more," Will said, confusing her. She didn't know if he was referring to her love of sex or her need to have her mind respected. She was getting more flustered and looked at her watch again.

"Here's what I recommend, he suggested. "Take a look at the work of Ludwig von Bertalanffy and his original contributions to systems theory. In other words, a relationship is a system and can be studied as such. Ask what could we learn about the link between power and sex, for example, in relationships between men and women."

She wrote with enthusiasm. "Oh, this is great," she said. "Power and sex. I love both." She looked up at him, smiling. "I think powerful men are very sexy," she said, dropping her voice into a sultry register.

"As are powerful women," he added, smiling.

She flipped her hair once more, then sat forward again, fumbling through her massive red purse before she replaced her notebook. It seemed to take her an inordinate amount of time. Finally finished with her rummaging, she looked at him, stood and said. "How can I show you my gratitude? I'm really willing to do just about anything to thank you for your important help."

"This is what I do," he said, opening his arms in humility as he stood. In that instant she kissed him, deliberately smearing her lipstick across his mouth. Will broke the kiss and held her at arm's length. "That is not necessary at all, Ms. Kleinfelder.

"Well, we will just see about that," she said, emphatically. "And it's Kleinfeld," she said, anger flushing her face. Just before she turned away from him, she lowered her dress over her bra, which she pushed down. Her breast unfolded like a soufflé rising in the heat. She turned and ran to the door, threw it open and screamed for help. "I've been raped," she screamed and started to cry. As luck would have it, Dr. Dorothy Keller-Smith just happened to be standing by his door, speaking with another female professor from the women's studies program. She took the young woman now sobbing hysterically into her arms.

"You will be held accountable for this," she said, pointing an accusing finger at him. "We have witnesses." She indicated to the black female professor who stood at his door.

Will said calmly, "I'm certainly glad of that," and closed the door in Keller-Smith's face, took a deep breath to compose himself, and sat down at the computer. He thought for a minute before he made a call to Dean Harry Carpenter and immediately apprised him of the situation.

The dean asked, "You okay?"

Will laughed into the phone. "The cheap perfume of that woman almost overpowered me. Other than that, I'm fine." He explained in more detail what had just happened.

"Okay," Dean Carpenter said, "you can expect that they will file a formal complaint and there will probably be a disciplinary inquiry by the end of the week. By the way, as the Dean of the Graduate College I will be presiding over the hearing, but it will be run by the head of the Affirmative Action office."

"Oh no," Will exclaimed in false shock, "perhaps I should just resign now."

"That would sure as hell save me a ton of problems," Dean Carpenter said. "And Will, make sure you write all of this up and then send me a copy as quickly as you can."

"Already on it. And Harry, there will be a surprise or two at the hearing."

"I'm certain of that," Carpenter allowed and hung up after a good luck wish.

Will immediately called Sonia at her office. Will told her the story. "That bitch," was all Sonia could sputter. Will wasn't sure if she meant the graduate student or the head of the Interdisciplinary Studies Department. It didn't matter.

"But boy do I have something to share with you, but not over the phone," Landsberg said, dropping her voice into a whisper. They agreed to meet later and discuss the situation in detail.

Will wrote out a narrative of the events in clear, exact, and cold clinical detail, met with Sonia, who decided to take a rain check on dinner, given what had just occurred. He agreed with her decision and they promised each other they would meet again when things cooled down. After the meeting and a goodbye kiss for Sonia, he went to play handball at the Y.

After he returned home from his workout, he cooked Lisa a dinner of *Wienerschnitzel* and an authentic hot Bavarian potato salad. After dinner with her, he excused himself and went downstairs to work. Before he turned his light out to go to sleep for the evening, she was at the bedroom door, completely naked.

"I know you have a lot of stress that needs relieving," she said, and that in her best little girl voice.

"Lots of stress today," Will could only agree. "But how did you know that?"

"The right people know" she said cryptically. "I know it must suck to be you right now, but too bad for you, big man. Tonight is lady's choice and tonight Lisa wants it here," she said, patting the tight swell and sleek curve of her gorgeous behind.

"All night long," Will promised.

CHAPTER SEVENTEEN

The Hearing

Two days later he received an official letter from the Affirmative Action office informing him that a formal complaint had been filed accusing him of sexual harassment and sexual assault. The letter called him to a formal hearing that would determine the validity of the complaint and given the seriousness of the charges, decide whether to remand the incident over to the campus police for formal charges and arrest. Will typed an email reply that said unfortunately on the date and time set by the AA office he was occupied with previous commitments with the FBI in Minneapolis, where he would be seeking counsel as to whether or not his civil rights were being violated. He wrote that he would be back the next day in the afternoon and would be more than happy to meet at that time.

The AA office wrote back immediately via email chastising him and informing him in no uncertain terms that they set the time and dates for hearing official complaints. Will wrote back in that case they should feel free to conduct the hearing without him. Two hours later came a short and succinct email stating that the meeting was rescheduled.

Will was pleased. The email was followed by one from Dean Carpenter. "Congratulations, Will. You have succeeded in pissing off the director of Affirmative Action." Will noted the smiley icon. Nevertheless, he had achieved what he intended. By taking control of the meeting time and date he had exerted a modicum of dominance. This was a significant act, one of many Will knew he had ahead of him in the coming days. He also knew from previous experience that to extricate himself from the quagmire he was bogged down in he would need to fall back on his years of training, discipline, and preparation.

Will sat on the couch watching one of his favorite survival shows. Lisa snaked her lithe body over the back of the couch until her head rested in his lap. "I'm naked and you should be very afraid." She turned over on her back and slithered closer to flick her long tongue against his neck. He looked over at her perfect taut breasts, her hard, flat stomach, and sleek, well-muscled thighs. With her black hair and feral green eyes locked onto his, he felt himself stirring. It was like looking into the eyes of a panther. He reached over and pulled a nipple into his lips, then let it pop out after it had stiffened into its full length. After he had achieved the result he intended at the tips of both her breasts, he gently pushed her to the side.

"I want to see if the hippie dork who thinks he is a survivalist taps out in the next few days, as I think he will. And if I am any judge of character, I also think his partner is better off without him and has a better chance of surviving if they carry his ass out on a stretcher."

Lisa was nonplussed. "Why don't I just blow you while you watch?"

"Why don't you just sit in my arms and I'll caress your hair until the show is over?"

She pulled his blue house shorts down over an erection that belied his disinterest. "My favorite lollypenis," Lisa said, with admiration in her voice. "Why don't you watch your show while you are inside Lisa? She'll keep you hard while she does her Kegel exercises and promises not to say a word."

One thing he had learned about Annalisa Allen. She was nothing if not persistent when she needed sexual stimulation, and this insistence was highly significant. He picked up the remote and turned off the LCD TV. "What's the matter, honey?"

She impaled herself on him with a suddenness that was almost painful. Now face to face she grabbed first his right arm, then his left, and wrapped them around her. She placed her head on his shoulder, looking away from him.

"Annalisa?" he said.

When she lifted her face to be kissed, tears pooled in her eyes. She searched his face. Instead of using her little girl voice she used her grown-up fully mature, I am a powerful and competent female voice, and said, "Please don't think less of me, but I am afraid for my warrior champion. I know the fear is irrational and I trust you will be able to extricate yourself from this morass of bullshit, but tonight for consolation I need just a little bit of love with my sex. One cube of sugar in the tea."

He kissed her again, and kissed the tears from her cheeks. "Your concern for me is heartwarming. But please put your fears to rest. I know these people and I understand their psychology. I have dealt with their like before and know how to deal with them. Much as I appreciate your concern, I promise you that with the help of some very good people, I will get out of this. I know I don't have to say this to you but nothing inappropriate happened in my office," he assured her. "Despite that, they know an accusation is enough in these times to irretrievably damage a reputation even if I assert nothing wrong happened. Their mindset, and that of too many others in academia now, is that an accusation is enough to warrant a finding of guilt, regardless of proof or fact. Ironically, it never works the other way around. It has gotten that bad and my accusers will do everything in their power to take advantage of this. So, dry your tears and trust me. And because you care and have shown me you care, tonight Lisa gets all the love she needs. The sex can wait," he said.

She shook her head emphatically. "The sex can't wait. I need it even more when you love me like this."

Will noticed with mild surprise she had not forgotten her Kegel exercises. "Whenever you need it, you just let me know."

She nibbled at the lobe of his ear. "I don't need it often," she admitted, sharing one iota of the truth of herself. "But tonight, I am still deeply affected by what happened to you."

He marveled at the woman's ability to multitask. As he tried to move inside her, she clamped down.

"Don't come," she implored, "until I'm ready."

"Don't worry, darling," he assured her. "I won't until you want me to."

"Despite what you told me, I'm still afraid," she said, and little Lisi is very much afraid. "We're afraid that very bad people will take you from us. We don't want to lose you now." She shuddered against his neck on a downstroke.

"This message is for Annalisa and little Lisi, both of whom I love. Not to worry. I've been in worse situations in my life and I have always come through; not always un-scathed, but I've always prevailed when the truth is on my side."

"I know the truth is on your side," she said. "Logically, I have reasoned this through and I know I should not be worried, but I am. I know most people can't be trusted. I need to tell you that."

"I'm glad you did. You and I will not withhold anything we need to tell each other. This is Lisa and Will's agree-ment. And anything you tell me in confidence remains a secret between us."

Lisa leaned back, put both arms around his neck and asked sincerely, "Anything, William?"

"Anything, Annalisa."

She allowed one more tear from each eye to slide over her rounded cheeks to the point of her chin before she took a deep breath and said, "Lisa needs to tell Will she loves him."

"Annalisa or Lisi?" he asked gently.

"It doesn't matter." Then she added, "Both. But just for tonight," was all she said in explanation.

"Say it when you're ready, then."

"I love you," she said.

"I love you, too," he said, looking deeply into her eyes.

She gasped and shuddered, thighs trembling as she once and finally lost control of herself. After she had regained her composure, she looked into his eyes and saw his love and concern for her. She sighed heavily into his chest. She kissed each of his eyes closed and said, "You may come now."

On the day of the hearing, Will arrived early. He had requested a venue change as well; one that permitted him the use of multimedia technology. This also had been begrudgingly granted. He had LB with him for his expertise in all things requiring cell phones, computers, social media, and any other technological devices. LB was attired in a look that could only be called gaucho, right down to his cowboy boots and yellow scarf. Will made certain LB set up a laptop computer at the front of the seminar tables that had been arranged in a small rectangle. He knew the director of AA would normally want to sit at the head of the table in order to control the hearing. Today he would be displaced. LB informed Will that all the connections were made, the computer powered up, the correct files accessible, the multimedia projector ready. Will gave him a thumbs up.

Dean Harry Carpenter was the next to arrive. As they shook hands he said to Will, "Be on your very best behavior today. These people, like all ideological fanatics, don't screw around. They live in a world that is black or white with nothing permissible in between."

"The truth will set me free," Will said, grinning. At that moment he turned to greet Glenda Martin, chief counsel for and representing the Iowa State Education Association. She kissed Will on the cheek in greeting and shook hands with Dean Carpenter. "So very glad to see you again, Dr. Sheridan."

Martin had been assigned to Sheridan during their investigation of the former dean's misappropriation of funds for her travel ventures. She placed her attaché case and matching bag on the table next to where Will would be sitting. Five minutes before the meeting was to start the director of Affirmative Action, Joshua Singleton, a slightly built man with a thin mustache and glasses entered the room followed by administrative assistant, Mary Brandt, who would record the meeting. He was followed by three other faculty members who would sit as independent judges hearing the case.

Will greeted each in turn as Harry made the introductions after everyone sat, no one shaking hands. Harry then called the meeting to order after Dr. Keller-Smith, head of the Interdisciplinary Studies Department arrived, representing and speaking for the complainant, who had been traumatized by the actions of Dr. Sheridan, and as a victim of sexual assault and harassment, was not required to attend the hearing. Keller-Smith was accompanied by Dr. Leticia Cook, head of the Women's Studies Department, a witness for the complainant. The two women wore scarves large as serapes around their necks. Glenda Martin wore an expensive, beautifully tailored Donna Karan pantsuit.

Dean Carpenter opened the proceedings after a nod to the recorder who leaned into a dictation cone. "We are here today to consider the complaint filed by a graduate student in the Women's Studies program alleging that Dr. William Sheridan sexually accosted her and created an atmosphere she found oppressive and sexually intimidating, to quote from her complaint. At her request, the complainant will be represented by both Dr. Keller-Smith and Mr. Joshua Singleton, director of the Affirmative Action office. Mary Brandt, also from AA will act as official recorder. Hearing officers include Dean Shirly Broadmoor, College of Education, Dean Claude Crenshaw, College of Physical Sciences, and Dean Donna Dorsett, College of Business

For the record I am Dean Harry Carpenter of the Graduate School. As the presiding officer, I have recused myself from voting as I am the one responsible for hiring Dr. Sheridan. Let the record show that Dr. William Sheridan, whom the complainant alleges perpetrated the actions as set forth in the formal complaint, is also present. Dr. Sheridan's attorney is Ms. Glenda Martin, chief counsel and representative of the Iowa State Education Association and she will speak for Dr. Sheridan. Mr. Singleton, you may proceed."

Singleton, a thin man almost to the point of emaciation, addressed Dean Carpenter. He was obviously upset. "Dean Carpenter, I must strenuously object to the presence of Miss Martin at this hearing. We received no warning that Dr. Sheridan would be represented by counsel nor that it would be chief counsel from the Iowa State Education Association. With respect, we ask that she be removed from these proceedings."

Miss Martin stood and addressed Dean Carpenter. "The union contract, of which the Iowa Polytechnic State University is signatory, and thus within my purview, specifically states that in such hearings at this, it is the right of the defendant to have a representative to speak on his or her behalf, and that such representative may in fact be a lawyer. Dr. Sheridan has chosen to exercise those rights as expressly detailed within the document." She sat.

Dean Carpenter said, "Counselor Martin is indeed correct. Dr. Sheridan is fully within his rights as stated within the binding contract. As does the complainant, Dr. Sheridan too has the right to representation. Miss Martin stays."

Singleton forced a smile and nodded his acknowledgment of the ruling. He began again. "Dr. Sheridan, would you be so kind as to characterize for us in your own words exactly what you believe happened on the date of the sexual assault and sexual harassment."

Glenda Martin rose from her seat look to at Dean Carpenter. "We would ask that the recorder please strike Mr. Singleton's comments. No sexual assault or sexual harassment has been established. Mr. Singleton no doubt meant to use and include the word alleged."

"Of course, Dean Carpenter, my apologies," Singleton said. Indicating quotes with the first two fingers of his hands he amended his statement to the alleged assault and sexual harassment.

Miss Martin again spoke for Dr. Sheridan. "It is my understanding that Dr. Sheridan has submitted a formal response in writing to the complaint and that you have copies of that response before you. My client has nothing further to add."

Will noticed Dean Dorsett let the semblance of a smile leak into her face. In addition to having earned a Ph.D. from Stanford, she was also once the CEO of a Fortune 500 company before leaving to lead the College of Business at IPSU.

"Granted," Joshua Singleton said, "we all have before us and have read his narrative of the events, but we would like to hear what you have to say in your own words, for the purposes of the record, you understand."

This time Sheridan spoke, placing his hand on the arm of Martin before she could stand. "My response to the complaint was written in my own words. It is not based on my belief as to what happened. It is a recounting of the facts as I observed them. I have nothing further to add. Feel free to read it into the record at your leisure." At this Dean Claude Crenshaw coughed away a grin. Dean Shirley Broadmoor sat stoically, swamped in a yellow and purple swash of nylon wrapped around her throat and draped over one shoulder like a sash worn by a pilot in the Lafayette Escadrille. Will wondered if she had arrived by biplane.

"Dean Carpenter, I suggest that Sheridan is being uncooperative," Singleton said, "and not taking this hearing or the complaints against him seriously."

"Not at all. He has every right to stand by his narrative. Moreover, there is nothing in his request to do so that suggests such action is anything but serious."

Singleton was perturbed to the point of stammering. It had been his intent to try and catch Will in a series of contradictions, thus undermining the force of his narrative statement. "Very well," he allowed, "your narrative will be considered as it stands and as it reads, noting for the record that no proof whatsoever has been offered in support of Dr. Sheridan's version of the events." He looked accusingly at Will and then tried to judge the reaction of the three independent hearing officers. Broadmoor nodded in sage agreement and Crenshaw took a drink of water from his glass.

Donna Dorsett looked puzzled and at that point Glenda Martin stood and said, "I want to state for the record that Dr. Sheridan in any court of law in the land is not required to provide proof. Were we sitting here today before a formal judge and jury as a defendant in the case, it is in fact you, Mr. Singleton, who carries the burden of proof. Once we are presented with your proof of the alleged actions, we will provide a defense. Until that time, we have nothing but the complaint from the student and Dr. Sheridan's response to the complaint." Now Dean Dorsett nodded and smiled, and sat back in her chair between Crenshaw and Broadmoor.

Dean Harry Carpenter said to Singleton, "I assume you have evidence to corroborate the complainant's version of the events, using your terminology."

"We most certainly do, your honor," he said, and before he could correct himself, Harry said, "Dean Carpenter will do just fine."

Singleton tried to play off his gaffe and ignore Carpenter's comment but everyone else smiled. "We would like to call Professor Keller-Smith and Professor Cook to recount what they heard, saw, and were told by the victim."

Before the two women could stand and begin their testimony, Martin interrupted. "Again, Mr. Singleton has yet to demonstrate that there is indeed a victim. Moreover, their account of what they were told by the complainant constitutes hearsay evidence and would not be allowed in a court of law."

Dean Carpenter said, "I agree. For the purposes of this hearing let's use the word complainant instead of victim. However, since this is indeed a hearing whose purpose is fact-finding, I will hear Professors Keller-Smith and Cook's version of the events. Keller-Smith, you may begin.

"I witnessed the horrible events exactly as the complainant describes in her narrative. I happened to be standing in the hall of the Interdisciplinary Studies Department near Dr. Sheridan's closed office door while I was having a conversation with Dr. Cook. She also witnessed the events as described."

"Dr. Carpenter, please," Martin said, the frustration showing in her voice.

Carpenter agreed. "Keller-Smith, please limit your testimony to what you saw and heard. I'm certain that Dr. Cook is fully capable of expressing herself and she will be given an opportunity to do so."

Keller-Smith, in a steady voice continued unperturbed. "The student came to the door screaming that she had been raped. Her lipstick was smeared and her dress had been pulled down over her left breast," she said with clinical detail. "She was in complete disarray and sobbing hysterically. I took her in my arms and tried to comfort her best I could, but she was obviously traumatized by the sexual assault she had experienced."

Martin quickly responded. "How does Keller-Smith know that the complainant's hysteria was the result of a sexual assault?"

"I saw her, too," Dr. Cook said imperiously. What else could it have been?" asked the large black woman with a sniff through flared nostrils.

"My point exactly, ladies. What else could it have been?"

"Well. we both know what we saw," Keller-Smith said and Cook affirmed.

Martin asked, "Did you not say you were standing next to Dr. Sheridan's closed door?"

They both nodded in the affirmative. Dr. Carpenter instructed them both to indicate orally either yes or no for the record. They both said yes.

"Did either of you see what might have transpired behind a closed door?" Martin asked.

They both nodded no, forcing Carpenter to admonish them again to respond orally.

"So for all you know, the student could have assaulted Dr. Sheridan."

Both women looked exasperated. Everyone knew that it was men who were the rapists and women the victims. "What you're saying is absurd and suggests to me Dr. Sheridan's guilt," Keller-Smith said with self-satisfaction.

At this point Sheridan posed a question to both Singleton and Dean Carpenter. "If I am in fact found to be guilty of the charges by this committee at this hearing, does this constitute grounds for my dismissal from the university?"

Singleton immediately said yes but Carpenter said it would depend on the circumstances.

"Very well. If I am indeed found guilty," Will said, now looking directly at Keller-Smith, "I will resign immediately." He withdrew a sealed envelope from his briefcase. "In fact, as a man of honor I have already written my letter of resignation to Dean Harry Carpenter, to be opened in the event that the charges against me are substantiated. That is and has always been my ethos."

"I would expect nothing less," huffed Keller-Smith, showing her self-righteousness to all in the cast of her head.

Will looked again at Keller-Smith. "Before I hand this to Dean Carpenter, let me ask you this. You believe I am guilty of the charges as set forth in the complaint?"

"One hundred percent without doubt," she said emphatically.

"One hundred percent," Will repeated.

"Absolutely. There is no doubt in my mind that you are guilty." She was encouraged now by the direction the proceedings were taking and Joshua Singleton's smile to her confirmed her thinking.

"Very well," Will said. "If you are one hundred percent absolutely certain of my guilt, then surely you would be willing to put your job on the line too. You see, I am one hundred percent absolutely certain I'm not guilty of the charges to the degree that I am willing to risk my job and my reputation and have stated so for the record. And as a quick aside, I do find it incongruous that no one at this hearing has yet seen fit to ask me directly if I am indeed guilty of the charges. I will state for the record that I am not, and that my guilt has merely been assumed and taken for granted."

At this point Dean Dorsett spoke. "Your point is taken, Dr. Sheridan, but you may be assured that I, speaking for my two colleagues, have not yet formed a conclusion as to your guilt or innocence. She looked to Crenshaw who nodded and Broadmoor, who nodded after a significant pause.

"Thank you, Dean Dorsett. I am reassured. In fact, I am so confident of my innocence that I propose this to Keller-Smith. Let's see if she will put her money where her big mouth is."

Carpenter admonished Will. "No need to get insulting. Let's keep it civil, please."

Will took a minute to regain his composure. He could only take so much of the woman's outright lying and self-righteous smugness in her effort to hide her prevarication. "I did not intend it as an insult, sir; it was merely an observation."

Dorsett and Crenshaw smiled. Broadmoor did not get it.

"I challenge Keller-Smith. Is she willing to put her job on the line? If I am indeed found innocent of the complaint, I expect that she will resign her position for conspiring to create and having supported a false accusation against me. A professor of honor and high ethics would do nothing less."

Carpenter spoke. "Dr. Sheridan poses an interesting scenario. He addressed Keller-Smith. "Are you in fact willing to put your job on the line, and I might add, the same applies to Dr. Cook?"

In the face of the question and the decision she was required to make, Keller-Smith had gone red with rage and there was only one answer for her to give without completely suffering a loss of face. "Absolutely," she managed through a choke and a forced swallow.

"Very well," said Carpenter, passing over a sheet of paper to both women. "Please write I resign forthwith if Dr. Sheridan is found innocent of the charges listed in the complaint."

Keller-Smith made a show of writing fearlessly; she signed, and pushed the paper over to Singleton who had the recorder read it into the record. "Let the record show Professor Keller-Smith has offered her resignation in the event Dr. Sheridan is found innocent of the charges as listed in the complaint. Dr. Cook?"

She stood up, her cheeks trembling. "I sure as hell didn't sign up for this. I will not allow myself to be bullied by this rapist," she said, picked up her briefcase and left.

"It seems Dr. Cook's conviction is rapidly crumbling," Dean Carpenter noted. "Let the record show that she has refused to sign and left the hearing without being excused. For that reason, none of her testimony will be considered. We will deal with her actions later," Carpenter noted wryly.

"Let's see where we are in the proceedings. I will recap. I have before me a signed and sworn complaint presented to Joshua Singleton, director of the Affirmative Action office alleging that Dr. Sheridan sexually assaulted a graduate student while in his office and created an unwelcome environment of sexual harassment. Singleton, as required by our code of conduct at the university brought the matter immediately to my attention, for which he has my thanks."

"Just doing my job, sir."

Carpenter ignored him and continued his overview despite the self-serving interruption from the little ass kisser. "Singleton interviewed the complainant and subsequently interviewed Doctors Keller-Smith and Cook and on the basis of their eyewitness testimony determined there was merit to the student's complaint." He looked to Sheridan and Martin. "Is this a fair and accurate recounting of what we have heard so far?" Both nodded yes.

"Please let the record indicate that all agree. Moreover, as an act of good faith, Dr. Sheridan has kindly offered his resignation if he should be adjudged guilty of the complaint by this committee. Dr. Keller-Smith has likewise tendered her resignation if it is determined that there is no merit to the charges, and she was in any way complicit in fabricating the complaint on the student's behalf, we note for the record," he said.

"In his defense Dr. Sheridan has presented for the record a narrative of his version of events stating that he made no advances and that in fact the complainant kissed him and then pulled her dress down over her breast exposing herself, and only then ran to the door, which she had herself closed, whereas in the complaint she says he closed the door. After opening the door, she then ran into the waiting arms of Keller-Smith and Cook, screaming that she had been not just sexually assaulted, but raped."

CHAPTER EIGHTEEN

The Defense Rests

At this point Keller-Smith interrupted vehemently "It's still a form of rape," Dr. Keller-Smith said. "He raped her sense of trust. She can never trust a male again nor can she ever be the same woman again."

"Please strike Dr. Keller-Smith's editorializing from the record," Counselor Martin requested of the recorder. "Her personal ideological opinions have no bearing on the issue at hand."

Carpenter indicated she should do so. Broadmoor looked shocked at the Dean's instructions.

"It seems we have arrived at a stalemate. It is obvious to any reasonable person that despite what Keller-Smith and the now absent Cook have said, their claim is merely conjecture as to what happened behind closed doors. It comes down to he said, she said, unless there is some other evidence to the contrary in this case."

Dean Claude Crenshaw spoke, "However, Harry, be that as it may, the mere fact that Dr. Sheridan has been charged brings both his character and reputation into question. Even if we are unable to make the determination of whether or not he is guilty of the charges, there will remain lingering doubts in the minds of some others and his reputation as a scholar and professor will suffer as a result."

There was general consensus around the table that Dean Crenshaw was correct.

'Therefore, and because I agree with much of what my colleague Dean Crenshaw is saying, it would certainly be in his best interests if Professor Sheridan could offer some or any proof for that matter, that supports his version of the events," added Dean Dorsett. "Proof I would gladly look forward to hearing."

"I don't know," Dean Broadmoor said, knowing for certain that saying something was expected of her. Everyone in the room now looked at Will.

"Glad I have your attention. I would ask that Mr. LaDamian Baker be permitted to assist me with an audiovisual presentation that will confirm the facts of the events as I have described them in my narrative. It will establish my innocence. Moreover, it will show conclusively that the entire episode in my office was in fact contrived and planned by three co-conspirators, Keller-Smith, Cook, and the enlisted cooperation of the graduate student, with malice of aforethought and with the intent to smear my name and reputation in an effort to get rid of me."

"Really? Now who would go to such lengths to do that?" Broadmoor asked sarcastically. Will could not thank her enough for the question.

"Using semiotic techniques of analysis, I will demonstrate that this entire tawdry affair was a plan conceived of and executed by Keller-Smith and Cook, enlisting the aid of a graduate student from the Women's Studies Department."

"These are very serious charges, indeed," Joshua Singleton said with great gravitas, "and I suggest to Dean Carpenter and the other members on the hearing committee that this is merely Sheridan's attempt to divert attention from his complaint by accusing the three innocent women."

Will glared at him, fury rising into his eyes. Glenda Martin spoke before he could.

"Are his claims any more or less serious than the charges against him?" And did you not previously state that he should provide evidence proving his innocence? Please give him a chance to do so. LB had taken the time to set up the laptop so that the video contained on a memory key would project onto a larger screen that dropped down from the ceiling with the push of a button. As LB saw to it that the lights were adjusted, Will started with an introduction. "The video you will see was taken from a micro video camera embedded in the pen I have here. It is standard issue for FBI agents in the field." He removed it from his shirt pocket and offered it for observation.

"I strenuously object," Keller-Smith shouted, standing in front of her chair. "This recording was done without the prior consent of the victim and further speaks to the perversity and guilt of the perpetrator. You cannot allow this to be shown!"

"Calm down, please," Dean Carpenter said to her, an undercurrent of warning behind the politeness. "I permitted your testimony to be heard, now I will permit Dr. Sheridan the same latitude."

Will continued, "As soon as Amber Kleinfeld entered my office and introduced herself as a doctoral student in social psychology and communication studies, my semiotic alarms were triggered and I became suspicious." He had LB show a still photo taken from the video of Kleinfeld in full seduction regalia. Dean Dorsett covered a discrete laugh with her hand and Crenshaw inadvertently said my goodness, like a grandfather seeing for the first time his granddaughter dressed up for a night out at the local bar with her girlfriends. Even Broadmoor could not hide her surprise.

"I had pretty much the same reaction when I saw her. In terms of a semiotic analysis, her clothing and makeup choices were anything but subtle." As he spoke, Will had LB bring up more stills focusing on the woman's outlandish eyelashes, her overly made-up lips, and a shot of her breasts barely contained within her dress. "Granted," Will said, "at this point it is still within the realm of reason to assume that she has not dressed specifically for the meeting with me; rather, for a night out after the meeting. However," Will said, "immediately after she introduced herself as a doctoral student, I took the liberty of quickly looking up her name and bona fides on the computer. You see here a snapshot of the screen with her real information. She is a master's student in the Women's Studies program and her advisor is Leticia Cook. At this point I knew she had lied to me.

"In semiotics we call this a significant action. There is intent behind the lie. I next had to determine why she had intentionally lied to me about her graduate status and her major affiliation. I concluded that she was trying to hide something." Here he paused for a second or two before he continued. "Or she was trying to protect someone. I then picked up my surveillance video pen and put it in my pocket so." He demonstrated the action. "At this point, I had enough information to conclude that something was clearly not right and I should take measures to protect myself. Note that Kleinfeld has gotten up and closed the door."

He looked directly at Keller-Smith before he continued. "That was my only intent in videotaping the meeting." She furled the flag of her voluminous scarf more tightly around her throat. Will thought he could smell goose roasting. He immediately controlled himself. There was still work to do. LB ran another minute or so of Kleinfeld speaking.

"Her speech pattern here is semiotically significant. She stumbles, she loops, she wanders, and notice how intently she fixates on me. Notice too, the twitch of the micro muscles around her eyes and lips, indicating her deception. These are all indicators of lying behavior used by FBI and police interrogators when interviewing suspects and persons of interest. I can cite the relevant research articles, if required." Carpenter looked at the three deans sitting in judgment. All shook their heads no.

"All have indicated no," Dean Carpenter said for the recorder. He had decided it was a waste of time to try and remind everyone to speak instead of nod. "Please continue. I find this highly informative." With the push of a button, LB let the video continue.

"Notice now that she has looked at her watch on three separate occasions. One could deduce that she is thinking ahead to her next appointment, or it is also possible that she is checking her timing. Remember that she has purposely closed the door to my office behind the pretext of being cold, certainly a possibility in our building. LB please run the time hack."

At the bottom of the video a digital timestream counted off. "The numbers you see are elapsed time indicators. She runs to close the door and checks her watch. About ten minutes later, she checks it again. Shortly thereafter she once more checks her watch and immediately thereafter initiates the charade of sexual assault. She initiates the kiss, as you can clearly see from the video, although the video does not capture the actual kiss as her proximity to me has covered up the video recorder in the pen. However, it does show clearly that she came toward me and that I did not approach her. And it also shows me holding her at arm's length and saying that isn't necessary at all Ms. Kleinfeld, whereupon, as the video decisively shows, she lowers her dress over her bra, lowers her bra exposing her breast, and runs for the door."

"She screams she has been raped and conveniently finds Professors Keller-Smith and Cook conversing outside my door. Kill the video LaDamian, if you please, and thanks for the assistance." LB shut down the projector, packed up the laptop, but left the memory key containing the video with Dr. Sheridan. All eyes were now on Keller-Smith.

Sheridan summarized for the hearing committee. "You have now witnessed a video recording of the events that I described in my narrative. You now know my description of the events to be a true and factual rendition of the meeting as it actually transpired. It is a factual rendition of the truth that materially contradicts the version of events recounted by Kleinfeld and sworn to by Keller-Smith and

Cook. You can conclude therefrom that no sexual assault took place and there was no sexual harassment."

"I respectfully disagree, Dr. Sheridan," Dean Dorsett said. "If anything, the video recording shows incontrovertibly that you are the one who was sexually harassed and assaulted."

"I appreciate that, Dean Dorsett. But there is yet another conclusion that is warranted by the evidence, if you will allow."

Harry nodded, caught himself and said, "By all means."

"Based on the facts and evidence before us, we can conclude that Keller-Smith, Cook, and graduate student Kleinfeld have colluded in an effort to have me fired." Will retook his seat.

Counselor Martin took over. "At this point, in an effort to corroborate Dr. Sheridan's claims of collusion and entrapment we should like to call as witness Dr. Sonia Landsberg of the Interdisciplinary Studies Department, whose office happens to be three doors down from Dr. Sheridan's."

Joshua Singleton got up, went to the door of the hearing room, opened it and said to Sonia, "We are ready for you." She came in, took her seat across from Dean Carpenter and faced the other members of the hearing committee.

"Please state your name for the record," Dean Carpenter directed her. "You may begin when you are ready."

She thanked the committee and the dean for permitting her to speak. She glanced quickly at the notes she had taken from her briefcase. "On the day of the alleged sexual assault, I was working in my office and had the door slightly ajar. I heard voices talking sotto voce in the hall, but loud enough for me to hear as they were unaware of my slightly opened door. Curious to see who it was, I got up to take a look. I saw Professors Keller-Smith and Cook but they were no longer talking as they had moved closer to Dr. Sheridan's door. They could not see me watching them through the opening in my door."

"What were they doing if they were no longer talking?" Dean Crenshaw asked. Dr. Landsberg did not answer immediately.

"They were both listening intently at Dr. Sheridan's door, and I can only surmise, waiting for something."

"What makes you think they were waiting for something, Dr. Landsberg?" Dean Dorsett asked.

"They both checked their watches repeatedly, as if they were waiting for something to happen at a specific time. At this point I checked the time on my smart phone."

"What happened next?" Dean Carpenter asked.

"They moved slightly away from the door, as if they expected it to open and checked their watches once again. Shortly thereafter the door flew open, I heard the graduate student screaming rape and saw her run into the arms of Keller-Smith, sobbing hysterically."

"What did you do next?" Dean Carpenter asked.

"I quietly closed my door and wrote notes about what I had just witnessed."

With her first question of the hearing, Dean Broadmoor asked, puzzlement evident in her voice, "Why didn't you assist Keller-Smith and Cook and come to the assistance of the graduate student?"

"Because the entire drama looked to me as if it had been carefully staged. And even if my conclusions were incorrect, Keller-Smith and Cook, both superior to me in rank as full professors, were already there. That concludes my testimony."

"Thank you Dr. Landsberg. One more question for the record," Glenda Martin said. "You consider yourself to be a friend of Dr. Sheridan?"

"I do."

Will spoke next. "In order to further corroborate my claim of collusion and entrapment, I would ask Counselor Martin to present to the hearing committee the cell phone and office telephone communication logs given to me by my friends at the Minneapolis, Minnesota FBI office. Please note the preponderance of telephone calls between Keller-

Smith, Cook, and Kleinfeld on the days preceding and immediately prior to the incident."

Glenda Martin distributed the call record and removed a voluminous document from her attaché case. "Because the FBI considered this a clear case of entrapment, a subpoena was issued that provided us with access to the phone call logs and to NSA recordings of the conversations. If required we will also submit these to the hearing committee for their perusal."

Dean Carpenter spoke. "With the consent of the members of the committee I believe we can forgo reading the transcripts of the telephone calls." All three members of the committee, including the director of affirmative action, agreed to Dean Carpenter's stipulation.

Glenda Martin looked at Will, who shrugged his consent. "Very well, we will hold the transcripts but reserve the right to use them if needed.

After writing a note to himself, Dean Carpenter put his pen down. "I think we have all heard enough today for us to render a decision. Mr. Singleton, would you please take all concerned into the anteroom with the exception of the recorder, Ms. Brandt? We will need about fifteen minutes to confer, whereupon we will reconvene and I will present my ruling. We will adjourn until 3:15 p.m.," Dean Carpenter said, looking up at the large clock on the wall of the hearing room.

Precisely on time Joshua Singleton brought them all back into the conference room and Dean Carpenter gave them time to retake their seats before he spoke. "After conferring with the hearing committee, we have arrived at the following decision. Having heard both sides of the complaint we find it entirely without merit. Dr. Sheridan is absolved of any and all wrongdoing. Although this was not a court of law, we find him to be innocent of the charges leveled in the complaint against him. In fact, we find that he is the aggrieved party in the matter and we would therefore encourage him to file a complaint to that effect with the Affirmative Action office."

He held up an envelope and motioned to Dr. Sheridan with it. "Your resignation is hereby rejected." With a dramatic flourish for all to see, he tore the envelope in half. He picked up the other envelope holding Dr. Keller-Smith's resignation letter. "I don't want to editorialize, but this entire tawdry affair has left a very bad taste in my mouth. In other words, I'm disgusted with you Keller-Smith. Your resignation is accepted immediately. Please see to it that your office is vacated within the week. At that time facility services will rekey the locks to your door. You will leave your keys with your executive secretary. A representative of Mr. Singleton's office will be there as you remove your personal belongings and nothing more."

She stood ashen faced. "You can rest assured that I will sue you bastards for every dime I can get. You have not heard or seen the last of me."

"Good luck with that, and given your threat of a lawsuit against this university, I instruct counselor Martin to provide this committee with a full record of the telephone transcripts. Mr. Singleton, please see Dr. Keller-Smith out. And please let me know if you need a copy of the videotape Dr. Sheridan has provided in his defense," he said, as she brusquely walked out, defiantly flipping her scarf over her left shoulder.

Sonia watched Will breathe a deep and slow sigh of relief and she smiled inwardly. Justice had been done today. She found herself relaxed now as well. When Singleton returned, Carpenter addressed him.

"You will see to it that Dr. Cook steps down from her position as chair of the Women's Studies Department. She will no longer serve as a graduate faculty member and will limit her teaching to undergraduate courses. She will receive a formal reprimand to be placed in her permanent records file. The graduate student will lose her graduate stipend. If she recants her complaint and writes a formal letter of apology to Dr. Sheridan, she will be permitted to continue her graduate studies after serving a one semester suspension beginning next semester. Otherwise, she will be dismissed at the end of the semester. And finally, after consultation with the hearing committee, whose time and patience have both been sorely tested today, we have decided that all records of this hearing will be placed in my office as a private personnel matter. The Affirmative Action office will purge its file of any records of this matter, is that understood Mr. Singleton?"

"Understood Dean Carpenter. I will see that it is done."

"You will do it yourself and then report to me," Carpenter directed. "With a formal apology to Dr. Sheridan, this hearing is closed and this meeting is adjourned!" he said with finality.

In the anteroom after Will accepted a quick and discrete hug from Dr. Landsberg, who looked on the verge of tears, Singleton and his recorder came out. She smiled at Will. Singleton passed, ignoring them both. Dean Crenshaw shook his hand and said, "Well done, son."

Dean Dorsett shook his hand, took him by the shoulder and said, "Impressive. I think I would enjoy working with you."

Dean Broadmoor shook his hand because the others had done so and muttered a goodbye.

"What a day," Harry Carpenter said. "Let's go get a beer, you two."

"Amen to that," Sonia and Will said in unison.

Three days later, after the dismissal of Professor Dorothy Keller-Smith, Sonia came over for a visit. Will was downstairs writing and Lisa was watching a favorite soap opera in the living room. Sonia jumped into Will's oversize blue lounger and sent her two friends to sit next to each other on the couch, two significant actions, noted Will to himself, pleasantly surprised to see her and curious as to what information she had brought.

"I have some news I want to share with you two. This just came down the wire. Dr. Leticia Cook admitted her duplicity in the sordid affair, giving Dean Carpenter further support for his decision to fire Keller-Smith. A formal reprimand was placed in her permanent personnel file and she was asked to step down as head of the Women's Studies Department and is no longer permitted to teach at the graduate level. Kleinfeld has recanted and withdrawn her complaint and has written a letter of apology to Will. Shortly after she submitted her letter to the Affirmative Action office, she withdrew from all her courses and left the university. The next part is strange. Just between the two of us, when I saw her walking from the Affirmative Action office, she looked like she had barely survived a train wreck."

"What do you mean?" Will asked.

"It looks like somebody beat the crap out of her. She was battered and bruised," Landsberg explained. "And there's one more small bit of good news I want to share. At the direction of the provost, the faculty of the Interdisciplinary Studies Department met and selected a new interim head of department." She stood and did a perfect pirouette, her white linen skirt twirling above her thighs.

Lisa jumped up from the couch and kissed her full on the lips. "Girl power," she said, and Sonia blushed into her cheeks. Lisa stepped back and gave Will a chance to congratulate Sonia.

"Tonight, we celebrate," he said, "and the university is buying."

"I know just how we can best work up an appetite before dinner," Lisa said, and added, "let's make it Sonia's choice." All agreed. "And I volunteer to go first," Lisa said, raising her hand.

"You know, you really are shameless," Will said.

"That's why you two love me so much," she said, already out of her sweatshirt and shorts.

In Lisa's arms that night Sonia asked Will lying next to them, "Do you know if by any chance your graduate student Mike Brisbane has any qualms about beating up women? Just asking."

Will said, "No, I don't," wondering where this was taking them. "But I can tell you that as a highly trained and highly professional Green Beret, I would consider it highly unlikely that he could do such a thing unless his family was under a direct threat."

Lisa rolled out of Sonia's arms and into Will's. She whispered into his ear. "If you were to ask me the same question, here's what I would tell you. I don't," was all she said and stretched out on top of him. She felt light as a feather against him. Sonia kissed them both.

CHAPTER NINETEEN

Missing Persons

The phone downstairs rang. It was Lisa on the intercom. "You busy?" she asked.

"Who wants to know?"

She giggled. "Annalisa."

"Can you give me five minutes to finish a paragraph?"

"Ten. Then I'm coming down there to kick your ass," she said and hung up the phone.

"Right," he said to no one in particular. A 5'10" woman of 135 pounds is going to kick my ass. One thing about his Annalisa—and he was thinking of her now in those terms, his Annalisa, which he would never say aloud to her—she was full of surprises. He found himself wanting to spend more and more time with her. About fifteen minutes later, he came out of the bathroom to see her walking down the stairs. For once she was not naked, except for her bare feet. She was clothed, for once, in a well-worn karate gi. She had an oval patch of the Isshinryu school on one shoulder of her white uniform jacket and her gi was held closed with a black belt, the two ends frayed and drooping from the perfectly tied and executed knot.

Lisa put both hands palm down on top of her thighs, and bowed deeply. Once more upright she lunged forward on her left leg, executing a downward block with her left hand, simultaneously pulling her right fist into a punching position above her right hip, the palm of her fist facing up. The thumb was in the correct position on the second knuckles of her tightly clenched hand. "Lisa wants to fight."

In a T-shirt and cotton house shorts, Will took off his sandals and socks. "It is inappropriate for a person of go dan rank and who wears a fifth-degree black belt to attack an untrained and helpless person like myself."

"Defend yourself," she commanded. "There is no honor in kicking your ass if you don't fight back."

"Okay Missy, but I am required by law to inform you that I am a highly trained martial artist who has earned black belts in Taekwondo, Aikido, has studied Krav Maga in Israel, and once trained with mixed martial artists and Navy SEALs. And don't forget my hand-to-hand combat training in the Army Special Forces."

"When Lisa kicks your ass, you will be humiliated."

"No full contact," he said. "I weigh 255 pounds, you 150."

"135, you bastard. You know what I weigh. Okay, no full contact on Lisa; trembling shock only. Full contact on Will." Trembling shock was a term used in officially sanctioned Taekwondo tournaments.

"All right, let's make this interesting, girl warrior. If you win, lady's choice for the next three times."

"And if you win?"

"If I win, Lisa brings me a prize from the bar and gets to watch."

"Done," she said, and executed an inside ax kick to the head with such speed that he barely had time to get a hand up to absorb some of the power of the kick as he stepped back. His hand smarted from the blow.

"Damn girl. You are fast."

She tried a front snap kick to the solar plexus. Had she been aiming for his balls, he would now be down on both knees trying to find his nuts. As it was, he had just enough time to turn one quarter and the kick grazed his hip. Now she came out of her classic karate stance and began to dance around him, both hands loose at the wrists, like a female Bruce Lee. Will knew jeet kune do when he saw it, admiring the hybrid form Lee had developed to maximize his natural speed and Will knew what was coming next.

She crossed her legs once, gaining forward momentum for a vicious side thrust kick. As he sidestepped the kick, simultaneously he hit the top of the side of her extended leg just above the knee with a downward hammer strike, the ball of his fist rebounding off the taut muscles of her thigh. She immediately whirled from left to right, trying to tag him with a spinning back fist. Had the strike hit him on the temple where it was aimed, the blow would have knocked him out in a second. Using an aikido maneuver, he leaned back out of the circular path of the fist and as it whistled past his nose, he added to her forward momentum by pushing the inside of her forearm, the extra unexpected momentum upsetting her center of balance and exposing her back to him. He grabbed the back of her gi jacket with the other hand and pulled her down onto her back. The force of the fall onto the carpeted floor stunned her, and in the instant she needed to regain her senses, he stole a kiss as he straddled her waist. She kneed him in the back, causing him to pitch forward and she used the momentum to roll him on his back as she inverted their positions. "Now Lisa ground and pound," she said, as she straddled him.

Before she could execute a downward elbow strike to his nose, he caught both her arms at the elbow joint and drove both his massive thumbs deep into the ulnar nerve of her arms. To his immediate regret, she screamed in pain and jumped off him to break the hold. "My beautiful darling," he said. "I didn't mean to hurt you like that."

She backed up, dancing and taking a moment to shake the pain and numbness from both arms, trying to get feeling back into her fingers. As he stepped forward to comfort her, she snapped a left-footed kick against the inside of his left thigh, a perfectly executed Muay Thai kick. "See how you like that, Yankee dog."

"No need to get insulting, little girl. Now it's on," he said, feeling blood rush into the left side of his thigh as a bruise formed, swelled, and grew hot. Goddammit, he thought. This girl can do some real damage. Time to end this. He stood, knees slightly flexed, on balance, hands held just above his thighs as she continued to dance and taunt him.

"Want some more of this, round eyes? Come get some." With a speed that shocked her more than the force of the blow, he slapped her hard across the right side of her face with his open left hand. In a real street fight he would have hit the ear, hand cupped, the force of the blow exploding his opponent' s eardrum. Even as she withdrew to recover from the shock of the blow, he hit her again, this time on her left cheek with his right hand. Both times he took just enough off the blow to make her appreciate the contact but not break the cheekbone.

For an instant, he saw a scintilla of fear in her eyes, but she instantly replaced it with a controlled fighting rage, which was exactly what he hoped she would do, a testament to her training and teachers. As she tried a vicious roundhouse kick, he stepped into the perimeter of the kick thereby blunting its force and direction, grabbed her extended leg, stepped in closer and kissed her startled face for good measure before he swept her leg and tripped her. As he executed the trip, he released his hold on her extended leg and she fell once again onto her back. The force of the fall knocked the breath from her lungs and as she fought for air, he dropped to her side, and put her into an arm bar that could dislocate the joint at the elbow. He gradually but forcefully increased the downward pressure on her hyper-extended arm, and she was forced to tap out, breathing heavily.

Out of respect, he lay down next to her. She toweled the sweat off her forehead with the sleeve arm of her gi jacket. Her face was flushed from the exertion and she blew air out through slightly pursed lips naturally reddened by her exertions, controlling her breathing. She turned to him on the ground. "I have never in all my twelve years of fighting ever experienced someone with hands as fast as yours. I never even saw the blows coming."

"That's just what George Foreman said about Muhammed Ali after the Thriller in Manila."

"No human being can be that fast, cowboy."

"Don't feel bad, vanquished noble warrior. I once patted a rattlesnake on the top of the head as part of my training with the Army Ranger snake eaters," he told her. "All right, Lisa. What was this all about?"

She ignored him. She rolled over on top of him, straddling him at the waist, her knees at his sides. She grabbed him by the ears. "I need to know that you can protect me. I can't respect a man if I can whip his ass." She untied the knot of her black belt, removed it, folded it, and put it aside. She opened up her karate jacket, found the inside tie, pulled the overhand knot loose and shouldered out of her jacket. She glistened with sweat, her breasts rising above the sleek muscles of her abdomen. "Now Lisi will have her way with Willie boy. Resistance is futile." She leaned forward to kiss him on the mouth. "Tomorrow night, Lisi brings Will home a present." She pondered for a moment, finger to her lips. "A blonde, I think."

"A blonde will do rather nicely."

With his daughter Karin away at the university, Del considered the possibility of getting himself into a relationship. As much as he dreaded the hassle and time suck of dating again, not to mention the expense—the price of a movie ticket and a tub of popcorn today was outrageous—he missed female companionship. He knew he wasn't getting any younger and, to his chagrin, the hair under his ball cap was moving further back off his forehead. No, it was now or never, he thought to himself, looking in the bathroom mirror as he combed his hair back. He trimmed his mustache and checked his teeth. The whitening solution the dentist gave him seem to be working. Satisfied with the result, he decided he still had a lot to offer the right woman. His decision made, he asked himself, now what? He took stock. He had a nice place with acreage just outside of town and kept the house reasonably clean, particularly the bathrooms. Karin's bedroom was neat and tidy for her visits during semester breaks or when she came home to work in the cornfields during the summer. The basement was a mess, but that's where he kept his guns, his loaders, presses, and tubs of wads, gunpowder, shell casings, brass crimping machine, and everything else necessary for loading his own pistol and rifle bullets, and shotgun shells for the pheasant season. He enjoyed the hard work of loading his own ammunition and it afforded him respite from the drudge of police work in the county.

The occasional bust of a meth head, a petty theft, a talk at Fort Charles high school trying to persuade the kids to stay off drugs, investigating the disappearance of a tank of anhydrous ammonia off a nearby farm, which the tweakers needed to cook their meth, these things occupied his time at work. He finished trimming his mustache, wiped out the sink, brushed the hair on the side of his head, and lamented the male pattern baldness that seemed to run in his family. His work in the bathroom done, he went into the kitchen and put together a cup of coffee and made certain he had enough for his thermos to take to work.

One specific case among the papers waiting for him on his desk in his office had caught his eye and interested him. Down in the Amana Colonies, according to a bulletin sent out across the net, a young girl had been reported missing some time ago. He remembered the bulletin only because a similar missing person report had come across his desk, this one closer to home just north of Fort Charles. He was struck by the similarities. Both young women under 18 years of age, both members of Iowa religious sects, both disappeared seemingly without a trace.

His routine inquiries to date had not turned up much to work with. Getting church members to talk about anything to the English, as people outside the cult were called, was difficult enough. Most just wrote it off as another youngster taking off after licking the juicy peach of freedom and heading for the big city of Des Moines, or north to the Twin

Cities. A few came back to the routine security of the farm, the family, and the religion. Some were never heard from again, all too happy to escape the regimented indoctrination that would otherwise be with them their entire life. He couldn't blame them. He had tasted enough of that life in the Army as a military policeman and that was enough for him.

He wondered if he were seeing a pattern emerge like a pre-digital photograph immersed in a processing solution. His instincts told him he was on to something and the pattern would bear close watching. He closed the folder he had been reading and pushed it away from him, taking the time and the luxury to finish his coffee before he mounted up and went on patrol. He made a mental note to give the case more thought later. He secured his service weapon, put on his ball cap, repositioned his bulletproof vest, grabbed his briefcase and settled into his mobile office. He checked his electronics, radioed dispatch and informed them that he was on patrol and available for duty.

Albert Young seethed and drummed his fingers on top of his highly polished oak desk. He couldn't believe the gall of that bastard, Copeland. Another DWI would have cost him his driver's license. His called Sheriff Miller, a rant more than a call, which only added to his frustration when the sheriff assured him with apologies that Copeland could not be fired without cause. On top of that, according to Miller, the little prick was asking too many questions around the county about young women who were turning up on missing person reports. It was a dangerous threat to the Blood Brotherhood that needed to be eliminated.

On his smart phone, he checked his calendar for the rest of the afternoon. He usually sat in on the sales meetings, but the sales manager would handle it unless Young was there to introduce incentives for staff to move some metal off the lot. Every day a car sat on the lot cost him money. Last week, for example, the sales person who sold the most vehicles in one day during the week got a paid trip down to Branson, Missouri to see the shows.

After he thought about what had to be done with Copeland, he called Sheriff Miller back and arranged to meet him at the Brotherhood's compound outside Fort Charles. There, in the privacy of the clubhouse, the two men put together a plan.

The next day, the president and CEO of Fort Charles Future Ford, the number one Ford dealership by volume in north-central Iowa, and the mayor of the town, called Penny Prescott into his office. He indicated to the open bar. "Get yourself a drink."

Her legs were good and showed well under her black short skirt. She wore a white blouse stretched tight by her black bra, three buttons open down the middle. Her hair was pulled back into an easy pony tail and she smelled good. No wonder she was one of his top sellers. He waited while she poured two jiggers of Jack Daniels into a cut crystal shot glass and added one ice cube, lightening the dark molasses color of the whiskey in the glass, and swirled it.

"Want me to make you one?" she asked him, over a sip of the amber Tennessee whiskey.

"No thanks," he said, patting his stomach in explanation. "Too much Mexican last night."

She grinned as she sat, holding a napkin under the crystal glass. You did not need to tell her about Mexican food; her ex was from Juarez.

"I need you to take one for the team."

Without pause she said, "Whatever it takes, boss."

He considered her comment. She had come to him about three years ago, desperate for a job, pleading for a chance. No one in town was willing to hire her. She had no references, no background to speak of, not even a GED to show him, but she was willing to do whatever it took. That first day when he put her under the oak table, she blew him like a professional, her eyes on his just before he unloaded into her mouth.

Even now she was still good for stress relief once or twice a week and for the first year or so smart enough to keep her mouth shut and her lipstick on. He showed his appreciation with a small bonus at the end of the month from time to time if sales were good. Unfortunately, over time she began to act as if a blow job now and then in the office or on the road had somehow elevated her status with him. She had even gone so far as to suggest to the other sales staff that she might have some pull with him. Much as he enjoyed the oral pleasuring, she had become bothersome.

"You need some tension release today, boss?"

"When we are finished here," he said. "You know the new deputy sheriff that came into town about the same time you did?"

"Copeland?" she asked.

"That's the guy. Got a kid at IPSU," he added. "A girl, I think. Nice kid everyone says, real smart."

"I've seen him around," Penny Prescott said. "Not a bad looking guy, a bit short, and he strikes me as something of a loner and a bit of a square. I've seen him occasionally at the lunch counter but I really don't know the guy. Never met his daughter."

"Would you do him?"

She thought about that one for a minute. The list of either eligible and/or attractive single males in the area in and around Fort Charles was disconcertingly short. "Hell yeah," she said. "I'd do him in a heartbeat. Any particular reason why?"

He ignored the question and she was smart enough not to ask it again. "Let's keep this on the down low. I'll consider it a personal favor." He pushed across an envelope of ten new $100 bills. "Dating expense account."

She opened the unsealed envelope and riffled the bills Her eyes widened at the sight and smell of the money. She closed the envelope and put it in her purse. "Hell, boss. For you I would do him for nothing."

"That's exactly the kind of attitude I expect from my people around here. Now come around here and show me exactly what you do so very well, then I'll fill you in after."

She finished her drink with a flourish, unbuttoned her blouse and opened her bra at the front for him, her nipples seeking his attention. He was already poking out through his pants and fully stiff when she covered him with the icy coldness of her mouth.

CHAPTER TWENTY

Frame-up

Penelope Prescott could not believe her good luck since coming up to Fort Charles from Cedar Rapids. She had kicked her cocaine habit, though she still smoked a joint for relaxation when a sale fell through. She had kicked her old man out, Harley and all, and decided that since he had left her nothing but bruised and alone, it was time to move north and find a way out of her hard life. She wanted to give a new direction a fair shot before succumbing to the seduction of drugs and gang life. Now in her late thirties, she had put together some semblance of a life that did not require hooking when her old man's benefit check ran out and the last of the food stamps was gone.

Granted, there is a certain thrill and allure to life viewed from the back of a thundering Harley Davidson motorcycle, and the yearly runs to Sparks, South Dakota were always good for laughs when the gangs gathered. She missed the pilgrimage to Burning Man in the Black Rock desert of northern Nevada, where she could give her breasts to the sun and have sex with a guy who was not a john. Here in Fort Charles the money selling cars afforded her the softer life she had been looking for and she was even thinking about having some of her tattoos lasered off, at least the one with her ex's name on her left ass cheek or the eight inch cock running up the side of her spine.

She had the boss figured out from the get-go, and if a weekly blow job or two was what it took to keep him happy and on his good side, more power to her. Her father had taught her those lessons early on and she was proficient already before her breasts swelled. By age sixteen she was through with school, out of the house and on the back of the shave tail, wind in her hair, breasts pressed tight up against the leather jacket of her old man.

They gave her a choice when it came to joining the gang: she could either be jumped in, or sexed in. Who the hell wanted the crap beat out of them to join a gang? Tough dikes and girls who hadn't found their own pussies yet, that's who. Hello? You didn't have to be a genius to figure out sex was the way to go. Truth be told, it hadn't been so bad in the gangbang, her choice to get it over with sooner, except for the jerk-off who wanted to take her rectally. Her good luck held that day when the tweaker showed up to the clubhouse stoned out of his mind. He couldn't get it up and damned if she was going to help him but he had to try anyway, substituting his finger for his limp dick. She could still get off when she fantasized about the rest of that experience when she was alone doing herself with her favorite sex toy.

So now, having to fuck a reasonably good-looking deputy sheriff and get paid for it to boot was a no-brainer. Like she told her boss Al Young, she would've done him for free. Another dab of perfume between her breasts, a tendril of brown hair dyed blonde replaced behind her ears to show off her new earrings, a quick look in her purse and she was at the door when the bell rang, in high heels and a black leather skirt tight enough to show her ass off to good effect for a woman getting closer to forty than she wanted or expected.

Before he pushed the buzzer to her apartment door, Del checked his zipper, tried to calm his heart rate down under 200 beats per minute, looked at the wine label one more time and hoped she liked plum wine from the Amana

Colonies, but then who didn't? With his index finger extended, he pushed the buzzer next to the door.

She answered with a smile that made him smile. "Well hi, Del. My, don't you look handsome tonight." He pushed the wine bottle at her. She accepted it with a kiss on his freshly shaved cheek for being so thoughtful, ran inside and put it in the refrigerator. "We'll drink it together later," she promised, and his heart rate hit 200 again.

He took her to the only restaurant in Fort Charles, with the exception of the Hardees or the local diner that served only a breakfast and lunch and where he occasionally stopped in for a cup of coffee and a piece of pie in the early afternoon during his break and before they closed. They each started with beers before the salads and he loosened up a bit. She had a disarming way of touching the back of his hand to emphasize a talking point. They both ordered the New York strip steak, his medium rare, hers medium. As they waited for their salads, they shared the freshly baked bread from the plastic wicker basket, talked about life in Fort Charles, sharing the fact that neither were natives and both fairly recent immigrants. They shared a chocolate mousse for dessert. She offered to pay her half of the dinner but he would not hear of it. He held the door of the Chevy, his personal vehicle, one that Karin mostly drove when she was home from school. Penny Prescott gave him a good look at her legs as she lifted them into the SUV. He was such a gentleman, unlike many of the sexists she endured every day at the dealership.

Back at her apartment she invited him in without a second thought. The sweet fruity wine made them giggly and led to bad puns and slaps and tickles on the couch. She took off her glasses and pulled him in for a kiss, opening her mouth and touching his tongue with hers. This gave him the courage to slide a hand up her skirt. With apologies, he told her he had not thought to bring a condom, not expecting the remotest possibility of her wanting to have sex with him. She slapped him on the back of the hand and told him not to worry about that for a minute.

She quickly excused herself, ran into the bathroom and got a condom, opened it and put it in her mouth. She came back, smiling to see if he was still hard, got on her knees between his legs, and then rolled the condom onto his penis and gave him a blow job, a little trick she had learned from a Thai hooker she had once engaged for a threesome on her old man's birthday.

Delbert Copeland, still in his white T-shirt and black socks, could not believe his good fortune since coming to Fort Charles. Eyes closed, he let Penny do what Penny seemed to do best and less than two minutes later tested the bulbous end of the condom with an impressive discharge, but not without apologies.

"Just don't you worry about a thing, honey," she said as she carefully removed the prophylactic, pinched the opening so as not to spill a drop and said she would be right back with a warm wash rag. In the bathroom, she dumped the condom and its slimy contents into a small plastic bag Albert Young had given her. She sealed it, pressing the seams together once, twice, three times until she was satisfied with the seal. As instructed, she inserted everything into a separate bag one size larger than the first. She placed both in her makeup bag and put that in her purse. She ran quickly into her bedroom and got another condom, just in case. When she returned to the living room Del had revived enough from his post orgasmic plum wine and blow job induced stupor, to offer her another drink from the sweet wine as she sat next to him.

"Your turn," he offered magnanimously, slid down to the floor and on his knees, opened her legs. He peeled her red panties down over her legs and over the rounds of her heels. She widened her legs for him and he searched for her clitoris with his tongue after he remembered to open his eyes. She slid down the back of the couch to give him better access and gasped at the first, wet touches. Her old man had never done that to her. Real men don't eat pussy, he used to say. She sighed after a climax that almost broke Copeland's nose but he was too much of a gentleman to complain. As she floated in the afterglow of her climax, he wiped his face with the other side of the cold wash rag and they cuddled on the couch, thinking how good things were now that they lived in Fort Charles, Iowa.

After a good long cuddle and more silly small talk, she led him into the bedroom and to her surprise, he was hard again without any help from her. To his surprise, she guided him into her without a condom this time and he could not believe how wet and hot she felt long the entire length of his penis. And despite his clumsy attempts that required her assistance to achieve successful docking, he was determined not to come so quickly this time like a teenager on his girlfriend' s couch while the parents were at the Saturday matinee in the only theater in Fort Charles. He held out just long enough to feel her belly rise into his own and hear the quickening of her breath in his ear. When she grabbed his buttocks with both hands and pulled him in tight, he exploded into her heat and darkness, mixing his wetness with hers. She held his ass tight as he came, legs crossed at the heels behind his butt and he could feel her pulse as her pussy fluttered and pulled at his cock. After the socially appropriate amount of time for holding each other, with nibbling and kissing thrown in for good measure, he offered to stay the night, but she shushed him. Both had to get up early for work. She waited for him to get his clothes and redress in the living room. There they exchanged cell phone numbers, hugs, and more lingering kisses at the door, and he promised to call the next evening.

"I'll be mad if you don't," she gently warned him, and he happily took the imprecation with him.

He drove home through a lingering emotional fog, in the haze of well-being and it was almost ten o'clock when he got home. All the talk and sex had tired him out, so he got ready for bed. In an act of selfish indulgence, he decided not to shower for the very simple reason that he wanted the smell of her with him at least until the morning. He would shower then before work.

Not five minutes after Deputy Sheriff Copeland left in a haze of perfume and endorphins, Penny called Al Young as agreed. He instructed her to get dressed, but no panties; otherwise, wear exactly the same clothes she wore on her date with Copeland. "You know where the blacktop crosses the Wapsipinicon west of town?" She knew it. "Meet me at the bridge by the dirt road the fishermen drive down to access the river." She seemed unsure. "Don't worry, I'll direct you when you get there. Don't forget the package." She promised and said she would meet him at the Wapsi bridge in about fifteen minutes.

He flashed the lights of the big black Navigator as she cautiously approached from the east. Directing her with a flashlight, he had her park below the bridge and out of sight of the blacktop. In the cool of the evening she could see his breath and black driving gloves. She exited the Ford Taurus, once parked, and handed him the package. He put it in a large black leather satchel.

"Make the call," he told her.

After calling Del Copeland on her cellphone, she returned to Young. As she waited expectantly, hoping to be complimented for doing a good job, he smashed her in the face and on the point of her chin with the butt end of the massive steel flashlight, immediately knocking her out. He caught her before she fell, dropped the flashlight and then choked her with both hands until she was quivering and dead. Before he dropped her into the dirt, he ripped open her blouse and lifted her bra over her ample breasts. Too bad, he thought. She still had good tits for a woman her age. On the ground he splayed her legs and pushed up the black leather skirt. Good. No panties. He returned to the SUV and retrieved the satchel. Like a doctor making a house call, he carried it with him to Penny Prescott. He opened the clasp and from the black leather bag he removed the condom. He kneeled between her legs, inverted the prophylactic and smeared the contents across her thighs and lower belly. Impulsively, he inserted a finger into her vagina. He didn't know why he had done that, but after he withdrew his middle finger, he wiped the surprising amount of moisture off on the inside of her thighs. He found some brush on the side of the road and used it to erase his footprints all the way up to the blacktop. Young threw the satchel in back of his SUV parked on the side of the highway and took off without a look back. He was already thinking about who to call to fill in for her tomorrow.

Del got the call in bed, reading light still on, enjoying a detective thriller by Martin Cruz Smith. He liked that guy Arkady Renko, but Copeland was sure as hell glad he didn't have to work in Moscow. Prescott seemed in a panic. Her car had broken down at the bridge that crossed the Wapsipinicon River. Was there any way he could come and help? She didn't have AAA.

"Of course," he assured her. "I'll get there soon as I can." He took the police cruiser but decided not to call it in because this was a personal and not a police matter. Copeland liked the thought of that very much. He was there in just under fifteen minutes. He saw her car lights down by the dirt road where the fishermen backed their trailers and unloaded their boats on the ridged concrete pad that sloped into the river. He drove down the dirt road, got out with his flashlight. He was shocked by what he saw. He quickly checked her vitals. To his horror, she was dead. He saw the bruises on her neck. It appeared to him she had also been raped. He gulped to swallow and tried to control his breathing. His impulse was to hold and comfort her, but thankfully his training took over. This was now a crime scene. Before he could reach the patrol SUV and call it in, the sheriff's SUV rolled up, lights and siren on. Copeland was glad to have the backup, but wondered why it hadn't been another deputy sheriff. He also wondered how Sheriff Miller could have gotten there so quickly as he had just called it into dispatch. He must have been out on patrol or on personal business.

Miller parked and walked up with a quick nod, flashlight on. Copeland gave him a verbal report of what he had found at the scene. After a quick look at Penny Prescott, the sheriff withdrew his revolver and pointed it at Copeland. "Turn around and put both hands behind your back." Without a word, Copeland complied, shocked at the brutality of the command. He felt the cold steel of handcuffs encase his wrists and heard the ratcheting click as the gears locked. "I'm arresting you for the rape and murder of Penny Prescott." He even mirandized Copeland.

"What's this all about?" was all Copeland could manage.

"You shut up and get in the truck. You know the procedure."

He was taken to the county jail and in-processed, to the overwhelming surprise and shock of the staff at the jail. He sat on the hard cement bench of his holding cell and wondered what the hell had just happened. Maybe things were not so good in Fort Charles, Iowa after all. Poor Penny, he thought, and then the full consequences of the evening struck him and he slumped down like a guilty man.

CHAPTER TWENTY-ONE

Evaluation Day

During closed week, the week before final exams, Will accepted research papers from his students. They had been given a rubric to follow as they researched and constructed their paper. Using their semiotic training, they were required to describe a criminal case they considered a miscarriage of justice. The paper required a persuasive argument derived from their semiotic analysis of the case and a supported claim that qualified it for re-examination. Sheridan provided the graduate students with access to LEXIS-NEXIS, Google Docs, news services, and other relevant criminal justice databases as they ferreted out the details of the crimes being researched.

During finals week, the last week of the semester, he had scheduled interviews with each of his students two days after their final exam for the course. In the last formal meeting with his graduate students before the month-long winter break, Will would share his evaluation of their work in the seminar, and make the decision whether or not to invite them to take the second half of the course, a ten-credit practicum by invitation of the professor. In the practicum, they would be offered an opportunity to put their semiotic training to work. This was a chance to move from theory to praxis, the practical application of what they had learned in books, scholarly articles, and lectures, to solving a real crime Will had selected from among the research papers.

Mike Brisbane was precisely ten minutes early for his appointment. Since Will was ready to receive him, he invited the former Green Beret into his office and they started the evaluation. "Please be seated."

"Thank you, sir. And before we begin, I would like to say what a pleasure it has been having you as my professor. I have thoroughly enjoyed our time together even though you worked my ass off."

Will looked the former Army sergeant first class over. He was clad in freshly pressed khakis and a brown denim shirt. He had removed his Army ballcap before entering Will's office and set it on his desk. In his early thirties, his fine, light brown hair, still cut in the military style, was already in full retreat from his forehead, hence the cap, which made him look ten years younger. Before he shared his evaluation with the young war fighter, Will needed to ask a few questions to verify what he knew about Brisbane.

"If you don't mind, I need to ask you a question or two about your background and training in the military."

"Not at all, sir, but you understand there are some topics I have taken an oath to keep secret."

Will smiled. "As have I. We will avoid any mention of deployments or downrange missions. Tell me a bit about your Army training."

"Yes, sir. I was selected by a Special Forces recruitment team after I completed Jump School qualification. They sent me to Camp McCall, North Carolina for the Special Forces Assessment and Selection course, twenty-four days of the most hellish training I ever experienced. Even though I nearly failed the land navigation segment of the course, I passed and I was assigned to take the Special Forces Qualification Course, or 'Q' Course as some call it. After passing the Robin Sage final examination, which ties all of our training together in Phase III of the SFQC, I was inducted into the 1st Special Forces Regiment and awarded my Green Beret and the badge for my Special Forces

Group." Brisbane looked away and took two or three deep breaths, controlling the emotions engendered by the memory. "I then joined with an operational detachment alpha—my ODA—with eleven other men."

"What language did you qualify in? Sheridan asked.

"They sent me to CENTCOM where I learned Arabic. From there I got sent to the Survival, Evasion, Resistance, and Escape school at Fort Bragg where, by the way, I got to eat my first and last snake. Before I was deployed, I had a chance to attend advanced parachute training in Yuma, Arizona. I was then assigned to the 5th Special Forces Group out of Fort Campbell, Kentucky and from there to Afghanistan and Iraq. The rest, as they say, is history."

Will nodded. Everything Brisbane had said squared with his own knowledge of Special Operations Command. "One last question and I will know what I need to know. What was your MOS?"

"My military occupational specialty, sir," he said with a grin, is 18B Sergeant/Weapons with qualification in both Army sniper courses. I was one of two snipers in my ODA." Brisbane grinned again. "And if you don't mind me asking sir, what was yours?"

Sheridan looked into the NCO's calm brown eyes. The young SFC had evidently completed a semiotic analysis of Will's questions. "18A."

Brisbane smacked the closed fist of his right hand into the open palm of his left hand. "I knew it. You commanded an ODA."

"That was a long time ago, soldier, and we shall not speak of it again."

"Understood, sir." Brisbane barely controlled an urge to salute.

"And thanks for taking me through your progressions. As you well know, most civilians have no idea whatsoever of the intellectual and physical training Special Forces soldiers must endure."

"Roger that, sir."

"Now that we're finished blowing smoke up each other skirts, let's get down to it. I'm going to be brutally honest with you, Mike."

"I expect nothing less from you, sir."

Will nodded. "Your preparation at the undergraduate level was in many respects deficient; this, however, was not your fault. It is the fault of those who taught you and a limitation of taking an on-line degree through military contractors. After I pointed out your research and writing deficiencies, you have been diligent in trying to correct them. Your hard work, without complaint, I might add, has impressed me." The young sergeant first class smiled. "Your first two papers, unfortunately, did not quite achieve the standard I expect from graduate students even at the Master's level. Your third and final paper, I am pleased to say, hit the mark. Your exam scores were both excellent." Will thought for a minute. "You have achieved a B for the course." The young man's shoulders slumped a bit. "Chin up soldier; there is better news to come. On the basis of your hard work, your consistent improvement, and your unflaggingly positive attitude, including your excellent contributions during class discussions, I would like to invite you to join us for the practicum."

Mike returned to his smile. "I would like nothing better, sir, than to be part of your team."

Will stood and they shook hands. He clapped him on the man's massive deltoid. "And don't take the B so hard. It's an honest and fair evaluation of your work to date. The important thing is you are improving by leaps and bounds. And if you survive the practicum, you most likely will walk away from that segment of the course with ten-credit A."

"The grade is not important to me, Dr. Sheridan. What I care most about is the opportunity to keep learning from you and to keep improving. As you know, not everyone makes it through each rotation in Special Forces training on the first try. That was easy compared to a seminar on semiotic theory." They both laughed. Mike had a point. He continued, "I certainly look forward to serving..." he corrected himself, "working with you next semester."

Will walked him to the door. "Have a great break and pay some attention to that sweetheart of yours, okay? She's feeling a bit left out, what with all the time you have been dedicating to your studies."

"How did you know, sir?" he asked, genuinely surprised.

"You double shaved today for this meeting, the first time in a while. In my experience, a three- or four-day stubble means fewer kisses. Yet I know you are very much in love with Regina. She has been very patient in giving you the time to pull the all-nighters you needed to get yourself up to full speed academically. I can tell when a man is sleep deprived. Hence, fewer or no kisses. Conclusion, she has sacrificed her time with you because she knows how important it is for you to succeed. Otherwise, you would never have made it through all the evolutions of your Ranger training and become a Green Beret Special Forces Operator. So take good care of that girl, if you know what I mean. She deserves it."

"Booyah!" Mike said as he walked out the door and into the hallway.

After a hug and a thumbs-up from Mike, Karin Copeland came in next wearing a short denim skirt and pink sweater over her white blouse. Her hair was pulled back into a loose ponytail and tied with a big black Chanel ribbon.

"Welcome Karin," Will said, inviting her to sit. He spent a moment or two observing her. His students had come to expect it from him. "Here's what I know," he said. "Your exam scores were near 100%. Your first two papers showed deep analytical insight and demonstrated an admirable grasp of semiotic theories. The poor work on your last paper, then, is an aberration. In sum, because I give A's only to students whose work has been consistently excellent throughout the semester course, on the basis of your last paper, I'm forced to give you a B+, despite the fact that the rest of your work was at an A level. I've also factored in your two missed seminars. That's six hours of class time, dear Karin. That's too much to miss in a graduate seminar."

She did not cry; she did not pout; it was evident from watching her that she had received exactly what she expected. "Before we continue, Karin, I have to ask you, what's going on? My analysis of your last paper, which was incomplete, by the way, and did not meet all the requirements as set forth on the protocol sheet, was poorly researched, hastily written, and seemed a last-minute effort. Please correct me if I'm wrong...."

"No, no," she admitted, "you got it exactly right."

He waited for her to continue and offer an explanation. When she did not, he continued. "My analysis shows further that something serious happened to one of your family members, most likely your father."

She was shocked. "How did you know that?"

"In every class before the two you missed, you have worn your hair tied back in your favorite red bow, a gift from your father, I think." She nodded almost imperceptibly, giving him the reinforcement he needed to continue his train of reasoning. "Something very bad has happened to your father, hence the black bow. You are obviously dealing with a stressful and traumatic situation which has caused you to miss two classes that I know you greatly enjoy based on your participation and enthusiasm. It has also pulled you from fully attending to your course work. This is because you are in psychological mourning of sorts." This time tears pooled in the well of her eyes but still she refused to cry. "I respect your need for privacy, Karin, so I will not probe further. However, if there is any way that I can help you with this problem, please let me know. I am here for you. You are my graduate student."

"Thank you so much, Dr. Sheridan, but right now I just need time," she said, a touch of pleading in her voice. "I have to wait and see how things work out with my father back home. Then I promise to tell you everything." She reached for her backpack sitting by the side of her chair, pulled out a Kleenex and dabbed at the corners of her eyes.

"I will be patient and wait," he said. "In the meantime, taking into account the personal situation you find yourself ineluctably immersed in...," he paused and she used the opening to say, with a little laugh, "I don't know what ineluctably means," and finally let loose a crooked smile that started in the middle of her mouth and moved up to take residence in the upper right-hand corner.

"And this is why I want to invite you to join us for the practicum next semester, if your situation permits. And by the way, ineluctable means, in this sense, unavoidable or inescapable."

She covered her surprise with the front of her hand. "OMG," she said. "I thought I had completely blown any chance of being accepted for the practicum. You are great, Dr. Sheridan. And I want you to know I will completely redo that paper and have the revision ready for you next week."

"This is exactly why I have invited you, Karin. And my invitation is indeed conditional. It becomes official only after I receive your rewritten paper. You will send it to me in two weeks, no later than. And even though it's a bureaucratic pain in the ass for me, I will submit an Incomplete for your grade, to be changed once I receive and evaluate your revised paper. And I wish you the best of luck with your dad's situation."

They shook hands in agreement and as he walked her to the door, before he could open it, she turned and kissed him quickly on the cheek. "I can't tell you how much this means to me."

The kiss was a highly significant action. It was a sign of trust. He was humbled. "Please stay in touch over the holidays, Karin. You have my email."

Now up on her toes again, a habit of hers when she was excited, as she exited, on the way out she gave LB a high-five that smacked like a pistol shot. He watched her walk down the hall. "You go, girl," he shouted after her.

"Come in, let LaDamian. I'm ready for you. But not ready for that outfit." Today LB was clad in what could only be called policeman, right down to the shiny polyester black pants, the dark blue field shirt, the polished brogan's, and to tie the look together, he even sported an authentic Sam Brown belt, replete with not one, but two sets of handcuffs, a Taser, mace, and a field flashlight. Will invited the patrolman to sit. He observed him for a moment, the young man grinning. "You have really outdone yourself this time, LB. But two sets of handcuffs, really?"

LB unclipped a set, normally holstered on the belt. "One for you, sir."

"Why thank you, LB, I will add them to my collection. Now a word, man-to-man, before we start. You are, of course, resplendent right down to your blue hair, which you have dyed to indicate the blue lights on a patrol cruiser."

"Knew you would get that, sir."

"And you're dressed today specifically for me, even though I am a special consultant to the FBI, and not a cop. But a cop is a cop, right LB?"

"You got that right, man, I mean Professor Sheridan," he quickly added.

"One thing. You have to lose the badge. Don't know where you got the uniform, but you can't wear the badge."

"Friend of mine stole it for me from the dry cleaners in New Orleans after the big hurricane," he admitted in all candor, again a sign of LB's respect for his professor.

"But son, that's a live badge. Belongs to an officer of the New Orleans Police Department and by law you are not permitted to wear it. You can be arrested for impersonating an officer."

"I had no idea, he said, chastened, and unbuttoned the right-side breast pocket of his shirt and slipped the badge into it.

"No harm done. But it would be a nice gesture on your part to use those phenomenal research and technical skills of yours, trace the number on the badge, get a name and address, and send the man his badge with a note of explanation that you found it on the street or some such thing.

Those badges are handmade and individually numbered and specifically designed for each department. The men and women who have earned them are proud to wear them."

"Done deal."

"Now for your evaluation. You are an enthusiastic and highly motivated graduate student. Everyone in class likes and respects you, as do I, but I don't need to tell you that. Your papers were all three excellent, your exam scores just a bit below. You will receive an A- for the course and an invitation to join the practicum next semester."

LB was up and out of his chair in a flash and in his best Michael Jackson imitation did a spin, a moonwalk, another spin and a moonwalk back to shake his professor's hand. "Let me get some love from my favorite professor," he said, hugging Will unabashedly.

"Now don't go getting your blue panties all in a bunch," Will kidded LB and walked him to the door.

"Police officer blue," LB said, "to match the hair and color coordinate with the uniform."

"Nice touch," Will admitted, and wished him a *Joyeux Noel* when back in New Orleans.

Yuriko was waiting next and accepted a high-five up and one down from LB in passing. Will turned and entered into his office, walking ahead of his student according to Japanese custom and culture. They exchanged bows, hers much deeper than his, and he indicated she should sit. He took a moment to observe her. "I see LB's influence is having of an effect on your fashion choices."

"*Hai. Domo arigato gozaimasu,*" she said, using the formal expression of thanks to a superior, nodding her head once. She was dressed in what could only be called a schoolgirl's outfit, or to be more precise, the uniform of a junior high catholic school girl from the '50s. Her glistening black hair was pulled back into twin ponytails tied by matching red bows, her lips startlingly red, and an expensive black and white checked wool skirt fell to her mid-thighs as she sat. She had finished the look with Snow

White bobby socks and shiny black patent leather shoes. She wore a pink cashmere sweater, unbuttoned, over her shoulders as if she were dressed for tennis.

"Very chic, I might say."

"*Hai.*"

"To begin. You are an excellent student. You are highly motivated and extremely disciplined. Your papers are carefully researched and your analytical skills are excellent. Your test scores hurt you just a bit, but this is a language and translation problem, given the highly difficult and complex terminology you have had to learn."

"*Hai,*" she nodded again.

"You will receive an A- for the course."

This time she bowed deeply in the chair. "*Okini sensei,*" she said, honoring her teacher and thanking Sheridan in the Kansai dialect spoken in Osaka.

"I invite you to join our practicum next semester." This time a hand flew up to hide an uncontrollable smile of happiness.

As they stood, she bowed again, more deeply this time. "You honor your humble student, Dr. Sheridan–san."

As he walked her to the door he said, "Yuriko, I've greatly enjoyed our tennis matches together. And I thank you for letting me win now and again."

"How did you know, Sheridan-san?"

"I know," was all he said. "But next time, full speed Miss Sumitomo."

"*Hai,*" she said grinning again.

He had finished a bit early with Yuriko so he had enough time to go down the hall and get a Diet Coke from the machine. He was pleased with the way the evaluations were going but to be honest he was just a bit nervous as he waited for Annalisa.

At precisely the hour of her appointment she knocked on his door. "Come," he said, "it's unlocked." He stood to greet her as she closed the door behind them. She had her hair professionally styled, her nails immaculately finished and hand-painted with diamonds to match her diamond earrings. She wore a bespoke blue pinstripe men's suit by Hugo Boss with nothing worn under the suit coat. The effect was both elegant, sophisticated, and sexually daring in the way supermodels carry themselves when dressed in haute couture.

"Dr. Sheridan," she said in formal greeting as she accepted his offer to be seated. She crossed one long leg over the other in suit pants whose crease was pressed in so sharp he thought she was in danger of cutting herself. Around both ankles, above Italian open-toed high heels, she exposed a diamond ankle chain.

He took more than his normal minute or two to behold the power and the glory of the young woman. He could hardly bring himself to speak, he was so overcome by the full force of her personality.

"Lisa got your tongue?" she teased gently.

He studiously ignored her. "You are, as ever, significantly beautiful, and if you use your mirror at home you do not need me to tell you that. But I do need to tell you is this. Your work has been exemplary in every regard, and I do not say that lightly. You are an outstanding doctoral student, one of the finest it has been my pleasure to work with, and I've worked with many. Your papers show exemplary analytical and critical skills. Your scores on the exams were with the highest in the class." She had not yet broken eye contact with him. "Your last paper on applying Wittgenstein's theory of natural language philosophy to the micro sociology of Harold Garfinkel, with some changes and edits, is potentially publishable." She blinked twice and blushed. "In particular, a more in-depth treatment of Garfinkel's influence on the micro analysis of interviews, that is, the talk between suspects and law enforcement interrogators needs more theoretical support."

"Would you be willing to help me with that?" It was both a serious question and an invitation.

"Normally, I do not collaborate with anyone, but I might make an exception in your case, given the quality of the paper. However, and you need to think about this for a moment, scholarly ethics would require you to offer me second authorship on the paper."

She took a deep breath, the rise of her breasts accentuating the slim European cut of the Hugo Boss suit coat. "I would be honored to co-author the paper with you."

"I look forward to a possible collaboration, then, if I have time. On to other matters," Will said. "You deserve and have earned an A for your work. Congratulations. I rarely give A's. You are invited to join next semester's practicum."

She ignored the formality of his extended hand so he could further admire her. "I bought the suit just for the occasion."

"I know you did. The effect is profound, a heady admixture of powerful femininity wrapped in the guise of masculinity."

"That was the balance of Yin and Yang I was shooting for. I call it my elegantly sexy but professionally competent look."

"It suits you," he said deadpan.

"That little pun will cost you. But before it does, I do want to say how much I enjoyed having you as my professor in the class. This was the most demanding graduate course I've ever taken, and I can't wait to start work with you, on the paper, and then the practicum."

"Hang on," he said, walking her to the door. "I haven't said yes to the paper yet."

She looked back over the sculpted shoulder of the worsted wool suit. "You will after tonight."

That's my Annalisa, he thought to himself, pleased with the way all the evaluations had gone. Now all he needed was a worthwhile case to test his new team when they returned next semester.

CHAPTER TWENTY-TWO

Lake Kabetogama

At the dinner table over a pork tenderloin cut into medallions and grilled outside on the portable gas-fed hibachi, with gnocchi on the side under a hunter sauce with sautéed mushrooms, he saved his shrimp salad for last. Lisa watched him eat.

"Do I have something on my chin?" he asked, dabbing with the cloth napkin just in case.

She shook her head. "Here in the United States, we eat our salads before the main course and not for dessert," she gently chastised him.

"I'm a recent immigrant," he explained. "And if you don't mind my asking, where are you from?"

Ahead of a smile she said without further elaboration, "You know I'm from Wisconsin."

He noticed a flush tinge her face a light berry crimson. He looked at her as he swirled his zinfandel. "You don't like talking about your background."

"Quit reading me or I'll finish my dinner in my room," she said half in jest, half in earnest.

"Because I value your company at the dinner table, and because we have other matters to discuss, I will revisit the theme of your origins narrative at another time."

She cut a tender bite of the pork tenderloin medallion and took it from the fork with the front of her teeth. "Is here the only place you value my company, big man?"

He ignored the question. It was time to confront the elephant in the room. "Do you have plans for the Christmas vacation?"

He noticed a subtle relaxation through her shoulders after he posed the question. "As you know, my dissertation proposal has been accepted, and with the ten credits from the practicum next semester, I have enough coursework to qualify for graduation."

"This implies you already passed your written and oral doctoral exams before I arrived."

"Correct."

He raised his glass to Annalisa. He knew what she had accomplished and what she had been through. Respect to her. That's why research scholar Ph.D.s were considered the academic elite. "Don't you think taking on the fieldwork of the practicum and beginning your research for the dissertation will be too much?"

"Not at all," she said sipping her wine. "I designed the dissertation around fieldwork, and the practicum with you will serve as a research base for my work, a wonderful synergy of events." They clicked classes again, celebrating her serendipity.

He said, "Of course you may stay here and have full use of the duplex while I return to Minnesota and reconsider the cases the students have presented to me."

She nodded slowly and sighed. "That's very kind of you as I have a ton of preparatory work to do, you know, reading and researching and thinking."

He sipped his own wine. Was her lack of enthusiasm a result of her upcoming workload or was it the result of his offer to give her the duplex over the vacation, the implication being that she should accept it and stay there to work. "I do have another option for you if you might be interested. I want to take you with me to my home on Lake Kabetogama in Minnesota. I have all the research tools you might need: fast computer linked to the fastest broadband Internet available, Wi-Fi throughout the home, access to my own professional library and, of course, your own room with bathroom en suite. But before you answer, I fully understand if you say no. I know what you still have ahead of you. At this time in your life you must be very selfish with your time, energy, and emotion or you won't make it."

She thought it was indeed a time required for personal selfishness. She looked him directly in the eye and said one word, "Yes." Her eyes were swimming with tears of happiness. She came around the table, sat in his lap, her hands wrapped around his neck, and kissed him until his legs fell asleep.

The next day they packed the Subaru with his one suitcase and laptop. It took five trips to load Annalisa's junk and he grumbled while she smiled and flirted in the cold of the morning, on the grasses a hard frost almost white as snow. Now December, the first snows had come late in November but had since melted away. The daytime temperatures warmed into the 40s but at night on cloudless evenings temperatures low as 28° froze the moisture on house windows and on car windshields sitting outside. She wore a pale blue cashmere sweater above a black leather miniskirt that caused him to shake his head as he stood watching her load the last of her things inside the open hatch of the Forrester.

"What?" she demanded.

"Are your legs cold in that skirt?"

"Of course," she said, "I love the feel of the cold on top of my thighs and in the wells behind my knees. It's invigorating. And thanks for noticing."

"Is there any other reason you're in a skirt today?" he asked, handing her into the front seat, admiring the length of her legs.

"You know what the reason is," she said cryptically.

He had a hunch. "Stove off, sink cabinets open and house temperature set so the pipes don't freeze?" He quizzed her as they drove out of the driveway and onto the street.

"All done," she confirmed with a smile and turned up the heater. Ten miles up the road he turned it down and she giggled. "Road trip," she said.

"Yes," he agreed, warming to her enthusiasm. "An essential part of American culture. But I'm sure you learned that wherever you went to school."

She turned and glared at him, punching him just below the last rib. "Don't you start with me. This is my vacation too, and I want peace and harmony and Christmas cheers in the car."

There it was again. The usage of an idiom but slightly incorrect or a creative manipulation and modification of the phrase. He logged it into deep memory with the other slight errors he had detected in her speech and then nodded. She was right. Neither the time nor the place. He let her pee in Albert Lea, Minnesota after indulging in the pleasure of asking, "Do you have to pee in Albert Lea?"

After she returned from the convenience store facilities, he asked, "Geez, what took you so long?"

"Why are you so grumpy today? she asked.

"Flashbacks," he said.

She scrunched up her face. "School or war related?"

"War in a sense," he allowed. "If you see relationships as war."

"Tell me about it," she encouraged him, pushing her back against the passenger door, angling her legs at the knees toward him so she could watch him in profile as he drove.

What the hell, he decided. The talk would eat up a few more miles. As snowflakes settled on the windshield, he switched on the wipers just before crossing the I-35 bridge over the Mississippi in the Twin Cities. "Not too long ago I drove this same stretch of road to pick up my uncle at the airport."

She interrupted. "*Erster Hauptkommissar* Roland Rieger of the Bavarian state criminal police," she said with exactitude.

He was not surprised she knew his uncle and his rank of chief of detectives. She had read his novels depicting the two men's work and adventures together. "The same. I expected to pick him up from the airport. I had finally convinced him to take some time off, come visit me for a holiday and some fishing, and help me with the notes for my next book. Instead, who do I see walking through the doors at the baggage terminal?"

She knew. "Sylvie Schumann, *Hauptkommissar,* and your uncle's colleague. You previously worked a case with the two in Bavaria as described by you in *The Adamantine Heart.*

He nodded. "You can imagine my surprise. I'm expecting Roland and here comes Sylvie in all her tall blonde, blue-eyed Germanic glory. What a shock. Evidently, uncle Roland was at the tail-end of an important case he was working on for Interpol and could not get away, so he sent Sylvie in his place, until he was finished."

"I know why he sent her," Annalisa said, knowingly.

"Do tell," he prompted.

"Because she loves you."

He dismissed her statement with an offhand whatever. "But there she was and I had to deal with her after I thought I most likely would never see her again. It was like a summer romance when you meet a girl, fall in love, and then both have to go back to school at different universities. You write letters, you call, you Skype or FaceTime but the time and distance always drags the relationship apart. And then slowly and subtly, you get on with your lives. And there she stood, beautiful as ever. No." He stopped himself. "Even more beautiful as she had matured into her competency as a detective under my uncle's tutelage and mentorship. Now her beauty was substantiated and supported by a newly found confidence. I fell instantly back into the river of love, swept downstream by all the memories of our time together in Bavaria. Her presence there washed over me like a tsunami. It was as if we had never been apart. She almost fainted in my arms she was so happy to see me again."

"Now you're just exaggerating."

He grinned, caught in the act. "Not much," he said.

"You sure it wasn't just jet lag?"

"Maybe on a flight east to Germany, but not so much on a flight west to the United States." They were north of the Cities now and heading for Hibbing. "We caught a case the three of us worked together shortly after Roland arrived. And the relationship blossomed. We solved the case, which you have read in *The Return of Wahkahchai*, Roland and Sylvie had to return to Bavaria and sometime later she told me she was going to marry her longtime boyfriend. I think she was waiting for me to ask her to stay."

"How did that make you feel?" Annalisa asked.

He glowered at her. "I hate those kinds of questions."

She rephrased the question. "How would that have made you feel, had you been a man with normal feelings in exactly the same situation?"

He signaled her to lean over and gave her a quick kiss on the cheek. "After she left, I kicked myself for not having the courage to ask her to stay. I decided to play the role of a devastated man, one who could not eat, sleep, or think. One who stumbled from day to night in a fog of alcohol in the routine of living just to live. My old friend Farley Nilsson, whom you will meet, pulled me out of the deadly spiral into oblivion. Once you get to know him ask him to tell you the story of the man-bear he discovered sleeping in the ditch not too long ago."

At Hibbing, they stopped for a bite to eat at the local Hardees. With two hands around a hamburger that an NFL linebacker would have had trouble eating, she asked, "You still love her?"

He pursed his lips, the agony showing in his face. Or was it just his disbelief at the way Lisa demolished her hamburger. "It's okay," she said, after a long chew and swallow. He wiped the mustard delicately from her chin. "You don't have to answer. I know you do."

He took a French fry and covered it in shiny blood red catsup. "You need to know this about my personality. When I fall in love, I fall in love deeply and completely. Love is not a temporary phenomenon that comes and goes with me. I've always been that way in my relationships and sometimes when they end, I suffer. I will love her until the day I die. She has a beauty of place, spirit, of mind and body that will stay with me until I take my last breath. Just so you know." Almost as an afterthought he added, "One other thing you should know about me. I am fully capable of loving more than one person at a time." He took a bite of a grilled chicken sandwich that was surprisingly good. "There, now you know. I hope you're happy."

Annalisa engulfed the last two inches of the monster burger and thought as she chewed. "Lisa is very happy and Lisi is very full, but would like a cookie for dessert."

He went and bought them each a chocolate chip cookie and refilled their Diet Cokes to take along. She looked around the restaurant, now nearly empty after the lunch rush off the freeway. "From your description, Will, I would do her."

"I don't know about that," he said, shaking his head. "I'm not sure she would let you. She's very shy and very choosy. But you would most certainly fall in love with her." Lisi leaned forward so that the blue sweater fell away from her chest, exposing her breasts above the low-cut bra. He picked out the chocolate chip that had fallen on her right breast and placed it on her tongue.

"Just one more question," she said, savoring the rescued morsel. "Is Sylvie more beautiful than I?"

He shook his head. "Honestly, no. But I don't quantify beauty that way. Beauty is about aesthetics and is thus relative to the observer. Her beauty was earthly, of the time and of the place. Your beauty is otherworldly, ethereal, surreal and as rare and strange as a newly discovered sub-atomic particle. Your beauty is paradoxical, elemental, both finite and infinite, a quantum beauty that as I begin to comprehend it, I lose more understanding of it. You are my otherworldly alien girl who was fallen to earth from outer space. I can only say that I am happy I was there to catch you as you fell to the ground."

In the car, Lisa cried a little bit but she said it was only the Minnesota cold stinging her eyes. On the way to Cloquet, Lisa showed him her legs, took his hand and showed him why she had worn a skirt and no panties. Stopping in Virginia to take a break, she never left his side.

Another hour or so brought them to the drive leading to Will's enormous log cabin on Lake Kabetogama. Farley Nilsson, good man that he was, had kept the driveway plowed. The snow banks on either side of the blacktop driveway indicated there had not been much snow yet in the Great White North. Lake Kabetogama was part of Voyageurs National Park, which constituted the boundary waters between Minnesota and Canada. Here on waterways that stretched all the way to the eastern seaboard, the French trappers and hunters of the 18th and 19th century had made their way west in birchbark canoes, trapping for beaver and other furs, and after iceout, paddled their heavily laden canoes back to the East Coast to trade. These trappers were known as *voyageurs*. To the west lay International Falls, and across the border into Canada, Fort Frances. Lake Kabetogama joined Lake Namakan and eventually the massive Rainy Lake, where Will often fished the walleye opener with Farley once the ice came out in Spring.

The south side of the lake was populated with fish camps for tourists, walleye fisherman, and in September, bear hunters. Some private building was still allowed but carefully regulated along the shore. To the north, nothing was permitted and even pre-existing cabins that had been built before the land and water became a national park were eventually bought by the government and torn down. Even Farley had given up one of his hunting cabins up the creek from Slatinsky's Bay. By that time, Farley had grown tired of continuously bear proofing the cabin. Early one morning he was awakened from a sound sleep by the racket of a big sow that had pulled off the shutters from a window at the back of the cabin, torn through the screen with her powerful claws, and retreated back into the woods behind the cabin only after suffering a swat or two on her glistening black nose from Farley's broom.

Farley Nilsson was there to meet them as they pulled into the three-car garage, parking next to Farley's rusting pickup truck. "I thought you were going to sell that beast," Will said, hugging his old friend after shaking his hand.

"I am," Farley said, delighted to see him. "You must be Annalisa Allen. I'm very pleased to make your acquaintance," he said, gallantly taking off his hat before offering his hand.

"The pleasure is mine," said Annalisa.

Farley took a step back and appraised her. "I don't know how he does it miss, but each woman is more beautiful than the other," he commented. Lisa beamed and prodded Will in the ribs.

"Do you have a girlfriend, Farley?" she asked.

"Not at the moment, Miss, sorry to say."

"You do now," she said in no uncertain terms and let Farley take her by the elbow and hand her into the house. "Will can see to the bags."

Farley had the house warm and a fire burning in the living room fireplace for them. He had prepared a walleye dinner, caught that morning after an ice fishing trip out onto the lake. He promised to take her but most likely she would need to get into a warm pair of pants or at least some leggings. She promised she had brought suitable clothes and looked forward to a new experience out on the vast, frozen lake.

After dinner and catch-up conversation, Farley got his truck started after appropriate cursing and pumping the gas, let it warm up and then rattled down the driveway to his little house across the street from the Pine Aire resort where he kept his boat docked during open water. Before the first freeze he took the boat out at the Kab ranger station and parked the trailer in his one truck, one boat garage. He promised to come and take them ice fishing in a couple of days once the storm blowing down out of Canada headed south and east. Will knew the wise old man was also giving them time to settle in and get used to each other under a new roof for Lisa.

With a touch of pride, Will showed her to the house. She got her choice of the five bedrooms, selecting one with a bathroom en suite and a stunning view of the ice and snow-covered lake, which he promised she would be able to see first-hand in the morning light. His room was on the other side of the cabin, near his study. Already familiar with the kitchen that opened into the enormous dining room with fireplace, where she stood with her rear to the warmth of the flames jumping behind the glass. He pointed out the bar at the end of the kitchen and asked if she wanted a glass of ruby port to top off the evening.

Glasses in hand, he showed her his office and study, lined with his research books on one wall and on the other an extensive collection of literature from many countries, English, American, French, German, Japanese, Chinese, Spanish, and Russian, some in translation, some in their original language. Interspersed on the walls, he had hung his framed degrees, certificates of award for excellence in teaching, and commendations from the government of the United States, Germany, and Austria. It was almost too much to take in all at once. He took her to the leather sectional in the living room and they enjoyed their port, unable to stop smiling at one another.

They spent their days reading, writing, and studying in the warmth of the massive oak log cabin on the massive slab of granite overlooking the wide expanse of the frozen, snow-covered 25,000-acre lake. For recreation they cross-country skied on the lake or snowshoed across and onto the many islands in the lake. One clear bright days so cold ice crystals danced in the air, they took the snow machines and went ice fishing with Farley. He taught her how to hook the live minnow so that it could still swim. And using micro-light fishing gear and not the standard tip up gear that most ice fishermen used, put her on walleye deep below the hole augured into the ten inches of ice that served as the cold floor of the fish hut.

Being outside in the cold was a real struggle, she learned, for something as simple as having to pee. A normal, natural bodily function became a complicated and intricate dance. Gloves off but glove liners on, pants down, tights down, panties down, toilet paper in one hand, the cautious and careful bend at the knees so as not to spray her new Sorel hunting boots rated warm and good down to 40° below zero, as if it could ever get that low, until one day in late December, it did. A quick wipe before the urine froze where it should never freeze, then panties up, thermal tights up, pants up, anorak down, and paper wipe placed into a plastic bag. Gloves back on and hood up, with one last quick look back and a quick kick to cover the snow tinged orange like a snow cone, a hurried tromp through the crunch of snow and a return back into the relative warmth of the hut.

Her eyes widened when she felt the line being taken and let it drop from her index finger as she had been taught, waiting one second, two, three, until no more line went off the small spinning reel and she closed the bail and set the hook. Through the hole in the ice she pulled up a 16-inch walleye and screamed with unabashed delight as the men jumped to release the fish from the hook. She had the pleasure of taking it outside and placing it in their external deep-freeze with the other fish Farley and Will had caught earlier. She was proud to have made the transition from a walleye fisher to a walleye catcher. That night they ate lightly floured walleye fillets sautéed in butter with Minnesota wild rice Will paired with a sauvignon blanc with a nice blend of acidity, minerality, and ripeness from Santa Barbara on the Central Coast of California.

In the evenings they retired to their separate stations in front of the computer screen, Will in his book-lined study, Lisa at the table in the formal dining room under a gigantic chandelier of elk antlers. They had each made good progress on the academic work they had brought north with them. Will had completed three chapters on a new book and Lisa her outline for her dissertation. She had also written the intro and assembled the beginnings of her bibliography and literature review, thanks to Will's library and the Internet that enabled her to access any university library on the system in the United States. Both were pleased with what the other had accomplished, sharing documents and helping with edits and feedback.

CHAPTER TWENTY-THREE

Confession

On a day bright, clear, and cold as the heart of a diamond, the sun useless for anything but light, Will got the snowmobiles ready. In the heated comfort of the snowmobile shed next to the garage, two powerful pulls on the black cord on his machine and the engine turned over. He let it warm as Lisa came out through the massive oak doors of the log cabin with a cooler in which they had packed a picnic lunch and added drinks. He stowed the cooler and strapped it down securely on the back of his idling machine. He showed her to a snowmobile borrowed from Farley, and somewhat smaller than Will's sled. "Have you ever ridden a motorcycle?"

She nodded. "I used to ride a Honda Ninja."

Of course, he thought, why do I even ask. "Good. Principle is much the same. Power switch on. Headlight switch on. Throttle here. No brake for the front skis, of course. The brake lever operates hydraulic discs that stop the rear tracks. Don't go over fifty, to be safe. Pull start cable here."

"Why not an electric start?"

"Reliability," he said. "Electronic ignition is nice but in the extreme cold up here they often fail."

She braced herself and gave the handle a pull. The engine chugged but did not start. She tried again, but no luck. She looked at Will, but he did not move to help her.

"Use both hands," he suggested.

Gripping the handle with both gloved hands, she pulled like a sawyer pulling a two-handed saw through a green Douglas fir. The engine stumbled and caught as Will boosted the throttle. Into the ear of her parka he yelled, "Go slow to start until you figure out the steering and the throttle. It's a heavy machine. Whatever you do, keep me in sight." She hugged and kissed him, wiping moisture from the tip of his nose with her waterproof overgloves. "Ready?" he asked and she nodded.

"Let's ride these bitches!"

He laughed at her enthusiasm and watched her straddle her machine. Even bundled in her black and red snowsuit under her parka, she looked sexy in the adamantine heart of the winter's cold.

They rode north and east to the front side of Sugarbush and he took her through the cut, avoiding the danger of the rocks that fronted the island like a series of submerged mines. On a neighboring island, he pointed up to an eagle's nest the size of a Fiat 500. As they left Sugarbush behind, he opened the throttle and she kept pace. To his surprise, as he was looking left at Cutover Island, she ran past him, carving large graceful S-turns in the snow above the ice that had knitted the water of the lake together. He let her go until it was time to angle toward Ellsworth Gardens, their destination for the day.

As they neared the north shore of the lake, he saw the boat dock and pulled ahead of her. She dropped back and they beached both snowmobiles alongside the dock. Will stood on his seat, put the Igloo cooler on the dock above them, grabbed one of the poles alongside the dock and jumped up. She watched and did the same, taking his hand to pull her up into his arms, and in thanks for the assist she gave him a kiss from icy lips. Knowing the trail, he had let her ride without her helmet, the windshield giving them enough protection from the windchill. The high for the day in the heart of the cold was forecast to be 10° above zero. She would be wearing her helmet on the ride home.

He carried the superfluous cooler—more useful now to keep their lunch from freezing—to the first of the green metal and plastic picnic tables designed to survive the elements of a Great White North winter. With his long arm he brushed the tabletop clear, though most of the snow had already fallen through the openings in the mesh of the picnic table, giving it the appearance of a great white waffle. He cleared them a seat. He handed her a thermos of hot cocoa, a ham sandwich, a plastic bag of small pretzels, and another bag filled with candy bars. Flocked with snow, the trees behind them blocked the wind, enabling them to drop the hoods of their parkas back onto their snowsuits and sit facing the sculpture of the stone gardens. Topped with a hood of snow, the myriad stone figures Jack Ellsworth had patiently and painstakingly built by hand during his time on the island in the forties took on a magical quality in the winter. In the summer, lilies and other flowers bloomed among the granite stone sculptures of bears, squirrels, deer and human figurines, all maintained by the National Park Service staff.

After a quick lunch he led her to the outhouse building, unzipped her parka, took it off, then unzipped her snowsuit, pulling it down over her shoulders and below her knees after he unbuckled her belt. With cold fingers that made her jump, he opened and removed her bra; then he pulled her panties down, worn for warmth only. With two cold fingers he stroked her naked clitoris and she gasped, but opened her legs wider to give him better access. Naked from the knees up, she quickly helped him undress. Before she could finish, he picked her up in the cradle of his arms and took her outside, putting her down on her feet gently so she had a view of the gardens. He bent her over with a push and entered her from behind. She came first but he was not long to follow, her ardor pulling him into his own climax. They stood pressed against each other, exposed skin still hot, steam rising from their bodies into the cauldron of the cold.

"That was certainly a wonderful and unexpected winter surprise," she said, warming his mouth with kisses.

He knew she wanted to go again but he said, "Don't expect anything for Christmas. We better go in now, clean up and zip up, or we will both be frozen joined at the belly, two new statues part of the winter landscape. They'll put up plaques commemorating our union." She felt the bite of frost on her erect nipples, the tip of her nose, her ears, and across the tops of her thighs and decided discretion is the better part of freezing.

Back on the snowmobiles, he took her on a loop behind Cutover Island past the Grassy Islands and then along the south bank and back home, throttles open. In the north sky behind them, out of the Canadian wild a black mass descended toward them. They parked in the snowmobile garage and covered the machines and she watched lightning arc through the snow clouds. The wind pushed snow off the branches of the firs as if preparing them for the new storm blowing up around them. They stamped their boots clean of snow and ice, listening to the wind that howled like wolves gathering around a kill in the forest. The entire sky darkened and the snows came through the thunder. After they stepped into the foyer of the mudroom, shedding their outerwear, she did not stop with gloves, boots, parkas, or snow suits. Lisa stood before him, naked and glorious in only her red and gray wool socks. She led him in front of the fire in the living room overlooking the lake and in the middle of the blizzard raging outside and quickly flocking the windows closed, dropped to her knees and covered him with the warmth of her mouth.

Annalisa was flushed with happiness. The research for her bibliographies for her doctoral dissertation was going well, and despite everything she had been taught and trained to do, or not to do, she was inexorably and unalterably in love. She loved exploring the vastness of the cabin, more rightly a small mansion, to her mind and in her experience at least, with its vaulted ceilings and exposed beams and girders. Sometimes at night while he slept she patted on bare feet from room to room opening every door, even those that gave entry to the four bathrooms, turned on the lights, lay on the beds, sat on all the couches, ran her fingertips over the cold slick marble of the countertops and hugged herself with happiness, a private exultation of pure and undilute joy like the late afternoon shimmer of light gunmetal gray on the fast-moving river of love that a woman has for a man.

During one of her nocturnal forays into the deep chambers of her happiness, exploring the rooms of affection and unbridled passion, anguish tossed Will from side to side, disturbing his sleep, buffeted by the high winds of doubt and uncertainty. He woke in a cold sweat, searching for his covers. He could bear it no longer. For the sake of them both he would confront her tomorrow morning with the truths derived from his semiotic analysis, his reading and interpretation of the signs that led him to his conclusions and fomented his nocturnal turmoil. Until he did so he could not trust her further. His doubts were becoming corrosive, an acid etching at the surface fringes of their love for each other. Until the issue was resolved he would not proceed one step further with her as best friend, as mentor, or as lover. Anything less would be unfair to them both. He went into the en suite bathroom, toweled off the sweat, and when he returned to his bed found the covers had been kicked to the floor in the unconscious despair and anguish of his doubts. His decision made, he fell asleep, planning his approach to her, trying to balance his needs and wants against the facsimile of truth and veracity persons in love want each other to believe and are willing to believe.

After quick morning kisses the next day and breakfast, he led her by the hand into the great room that looked out onto the lake made still and quiet by last night's snowstorm, the morning cold pushing fog off the frozen water and back up into the morning sky. In his oversized, stuffed leather recliner, she sat quietly, unsure, uncertain, hoping against hope, dreading what was to come. She had convinced herself that she did not deserve her happiness and most certainly she did not deserve this man. There was nothing for her to do but listen and wait for the heavy black hammer of certainty to strike and spark the anvil of her doubts.

After a heavy sigh that settled her shoulders, against the coolness in the massive open room and despite the fireplace pulsing flame and heat, she pulled up a light cotton blanket over the top of the black cashmere sweater she wore without a bra. She pulled her legs up in a curl next to her pink panties, forced a smile and waited. She was now enough of a trained semiotician to know her man was deeply troubled.

He began with a preamble. "Without a doubt you are one of the most brilliant graduate students it has been my pleasure to work with. You are highly intelligent, incisive, analytical and creative in your problem-solving and in your solutions. It is an honor to have you as my student and to teach you." She took a single tear from the edge of her right eye on the knuckle of her forefinger.

He took a deep breath. "When Sylvie left here with Uncle Roland to return to Bavaria, I thought I would never love again; in fact, I was certain I never wanted to love again. I was done with it. Then you came along and without realizing it insinuated yourself beneath my skin, compromised my thinking, and altered my philosophy and perspective on relationships and love. Understanding this and accepting this understanding, I cannot for the life of me comprehend why you have consistently and blatantly lied to me." He took a drink from his morning iced tea, carefully gazing her reaction to his words. He refused to let her run and hide.

"You are not originally from the Dells, Wisconsin as you have claimed, though I am certain you lived there for a time. I deduce this because I notice that your speech patterns are not derived from any Midwestern linguistic speech community. And although your English is excellent, as I would expect of a graduate student of your rank, it is tainted by the Queen's English as opposed to American English. This tells me you learned English not here in the United States but somewhere else. Every so often you make a little mistake of phrasing or use a word whose meaning is just a bit off. I also discern the relics of an accent in your speech, which you think is undetectable. If anything, my semiotic analysis of your linguistic and speech patterns indicates to me that you are from one of the Baltic states, most likely Latvia or Estonia." She gasped slightly in shock and disbelief at how close to the truth he had come.

"Moreover, your confidence as a woman in the company of men, your ability to fight and take care of yourself, your fitness and martial expertise, leads me to conclude that your training is professional. When I muster the courage to take a step back and attempt a stab at self-observation, when I am able to overcome my inherent biases and perspectives clouded by my training and experiences as a man, I allow myself just for a minute to disallow the idea that I have any meaningful effect on the opposite sex, by dint of charm, personality, or attractiveness. It then occurs to me in this sobering light of humility and self-effacement, that maybe it's not me at all; rather, it's you who has been the pursuer, not me. It's you who has taken advantage of my vanity, my loss, and as much as I hate to admit or say it, my vulnerability, even though I swore to high heaven that I would never again put myself in such a position of compromise." And as she quietly wept, his voice rose and he yelled at her, emphasizing each word. "Tell me I am wrong!"

She started and stiffened in the chair as if struck by the nearly physical oral manifestation of his anger, a psychic punch into the solar plexus below her breasts of such force that it drove the wind from her. Now she cried more freely even as she wrapped her arms around herself, trying to make herself small and insignificant within the confines of the great leather chair. As she sobbed, her tears pulled out the raw truth from the wellspring of her emotional core, from deep within the essence of her sense of self and being. She raised her chin with the last semblance of strength left in her, looked him directly in the eyes and said defiantly, "You're right. And the only reason I can tell you this is because I love you more than any human being I have ever loved. Please, please don't leave me," she pleaded.

CHAPTER TWENTY-FOUR

Spy from Livani

He watched her carefully and waited and knew at last the truth had emerged like a mirage from the desert of her lies. "Then tell me the true story of who you are, and maybe, just maybe, we can start to rebuild the trust between us."

With a speed that surprised him, she was out of the leather chair and on his lap. She took both his arms and put them around her shoulders before she drowned his face with kisses. "Without you in my life, there is no me," was all she said. He kissed the herbal spice still in her hair, her shiny wet lips swollen and naturally red with emotion. Then he gently pushed her to the farthest reaches of the couch. She took a throw pillow onto her lap, hugged it, took a deep breath and began.

"I was born in a little village in Latvia..."

He held up a hand and stopped her in midsentence. "To give you just one small example of the power of semiotic linguistic analysis, an American would almost never say 'a little village.' A local would say, I was born in a small town."

She thought about it, sniffed and began again, uncertain why he was lecturing her now. No matter. Only the truth was important now. "I was born in a little village south and west of Riga, the capital of Latvia, formerly part of the Soviet Union." He laughed at her audacity, secretly pleased with her resilience and defiance. "My mother was a professor of Music at Riga University. My father, who was trained as an engineer, became a party apparatchik before the dissolution of the USSR. He was then recruited to work in the intelligence service, technical branch, and rose to the rank of major. He was killed by a suicide bomber in Chechnya. I was a very young girl at the time of his death and I remember its horrifying effect on my mother. My father also worked part-time as an auto mechanic who kept the cars of the local politicians and police running. We were poor but did not know it because we had more than most, and the luxury of owning a car, an old Skoda that my father kept in good repair. I seemed to have a natural talent for music and languages and was a very good student at school. My scores were good enough to gain me entrance into Riga University." She paused to blow her nose and Will went into the kitchen and got them both a fresh glass of iced tea.

She took the tea with gratitude and nursed a sip from the oversized glass. "As I was saying, I attended university in Riga where my mother still taught and was there recruited into the Russian FSB, formerly the Soviet Union's KGB. Because both my mother and father spoke English in the home and were occasionally given permission to travel to the United States and Canada for work, I grew up speaking English as my second language, Russian as my third."

"Now I understand the presence of a tinge of accent on certain vowels after you drink too much."

She wrinkled her nose, her pride wounded, not at all convinced she had any accent whatsoever. She had tried for too long and too hard to rid herself of any accent that might give her true origins away. "In my second year of language studies one of my English professors and I started up a...relationship." It took her a bit of searching to find the word she wanted to describe their affair. "I was swept up in the romance of the moment, and he was a very good-looking older man," she assured Will as if this detail of the affair somehow attenuated her role or responsibility in the relational drama. He nodded, wanting her to move the narrative along. "He wasn't my first, you understand. I don't want you to think I was just some young naïve backwoods girl swept off her feet by the first good-looking roué she meets at university."

"Most young women at university don't sleep with their professors, unless they are trying to improve their grades," he commented. "And most American girls don't say at university, they say at college, just to give you another example."

She glared at him for being so mean, sniffed and took a sip of her tea. "It wasn't like that at all. I was in love with the romance of being away at school, of meeting so many bright and eager new friends, of learning, learning, learning everything I could and wanting to learn more. This was my way out of the doldrums of a small-town life lived among the pines," she said, emphasizing the words small-town life. "I was not just in love with my professor, I was in love with life." She paused to check her memory and the truth of her memory, and showed him a face flushed with consternation. "I didn't learn until later that he was also a Russian agent of the Federal Security Service (FSB). And by the way, she said snottily, the full and official name is Federal Security Service of the Russian Federation."

"In Russian, *Federal'naya sluzhba bezopasnosti Rossiyskoy Federasti.*" It is the immediate successor of the Federal Counterintelligence Service, the FSK, which replaced the USSR's KGB in 1991. The FSK became the FSB in 1995."

"I hate you."

He ignored her. "And your boyfriend's job, in addition to being your English professor, was to recruit his best and brightest students for service in the FSB."

"Please understand, dearest Will, I was not some wide-eyed, addled-pated young Bolshevik in thrall to the Soviet Union or to mother Russia. I went along because I was in love with him and with the possibilities of having an exciting cosmopolitan career that afforded me travel and freedom in my life." She leaned forward and looked him directly in the eye. "I didn't want to end up like my poor dear mother, made old and haggard before her time by vodka and teaching the music of the proletariat to the proletariat, music highly censored and vetted by the apparatchiks sworn to protect the people from the divisive and corruptive genius of Beethoven, Liszt, and Grieg, to mention just a few." She laughed now as she thought of the idiocy of it all. "To this day, when I hear Shostakovich I want to throw up."

"And that's why you have such an affinity and love for funk, hip hop, and rap."

Her face lit up. "I love Prince and all the gangsta rappers."

He shook his head and chuckled. "Give me Elīna Garanča or Kristīne Opolais any day, but I have to admit there are times when you do bring to mind darling Nikki."

She shot him a coy look below a raised eyebrow. "I am a sex fiend, not a mezzo soprano."

"I know you are. It's the only reason I put up with you and your lying," he teased. She pouted a little but he coaxed her back into her story.

"Okay. I was slotted for training within the Russian FSB after my graduation from Riga University. Because of my abilities with language and, to be frank, my exotic looks as I was later informed, I was slotted for further training in the Yasenovo district of Moscow with the SVR, the Russian Federation's Foreign Intelligence Service and the successor to the KGB's First Chief Directorate. "Given that I had matured into a reasonably attractive young woman..."

He interrupted. "That's the understatement of the century."

"The purpose of my training was ultimately to establish friendships and relationships in the United States in order to gather knowledge about financial, corporate, and economic issues, and now given my academic aptitude, I was tasked to gain admission to a reputable American university, first as a master's student, and then as a doctoral student. My studies would gain me access and the research skills necessary for gathering human intelligence. I was given a five-year contract, long enough to finish my Ph.D. after I graduated from the University of Wisconsin with my Master's degree."

Will nodded. "The SVR and the KGB before them have always prized HUMINT over SIGINT or signals intelligence."

She sipped again from her tea, and stretched her legs out gently probing and touching his hip with her bare feet. "And before you ask, no I was not sent to sex school in order to recruit men and women in the west in an effort to gather intelligence for our side. But in all truth, I was briefed on all aspects of seduction and how to use my womanly skills to entice and to persuade. Otherwise, when it comes to sex, I am entirely self-taught," she said with pride. "After graduation from spy school, to put it in a nutshell, I arrived in New York City, was assigned to my handler and station chief in the Lenox Hill neighborhood and began work under nonofficial cover. In other words, I became a sleeper spy. After I got accepted into the doctoral program at Iowa Polytechnic State University, I was tasked to report back to the *rezidentura* at our secure Russian UN office on East 67th Street."

"Why there?" he asked.

She now crossed her long sleek dancer's legs at the knee. "It's considered the equivalent to your Sensitive Compartmented Information Facility, and is supposed to be free of any electronic listening or surveillance devices, at least that's what my *rezident* tells me."

"Keep believing that. Bugs in phones or lampshades or behind paintings on the wall is old-school James Bond technology. Now the NSA can intercept cell phone conversations, download them directly from spy satellites stationed in geosynchronous orbit above the earth, or use lasers to lip read conversations behind closed doors in rooms through windows without any wiretaps."

Her eyes widened. "How do they do that?"

"Lasers," he explained.

"Lasers?"

"During a conversation the human voice produces sound waves. The sound waves contact the glass of windows in a room and cause a minute vibration. A laser focused on the windows from the outside is sensitive enough to record the vibrations from the glass, just like the cone of stereo speaker pushing out sound waves, and software programs in high-speed computers reproduce the voices, and translators decipher the conversation." She shook her head in disbelief. "As good as you guys are in human intelligence gathering, our technology is still a step or two ahead of yours. Now back to the story, please."

She huffed, thinking she was finished and that everything between them was good again. "There's really not much more to say. I arrived at IPSU, got a boyfriend for additional cover, started my scholarly studies and began gathering political intelligence and accessing financial and corporate data that the Russians don't have access to, but a Ph.D. student does."

"Yes," Will commented wryly. "One of the drawbacks of a so-called free society."

"Yes," she marveled. "It's amazing the amount of information a doctoral student has access to through the Freedom of Information Act. And then on a whim and a lark and because I needed 10 more seminar credits of coursework to fulfill my graduation requirements, I found an interesting and I hoped challenging course called Semiotic Theory taught by the internationally renowned scholar Professor Doctor William R. Sheridan, who also just happened to work as a special consultant to the FBI. What a gold mine of information that would be, I thought at the time." She lowered her eyes. "Unfortunately, I made one rather critical and crucial mistake."

She paused so he could ask, "And what might that be?"

"I fell in love, you big lug, as if you have to ask."

He laughed at her distress. "I agree. Love can indeed be a critical and crucial mistake."

"No, silly. That's not what I meant. It was a professional mistake, one that could compromise my ability to continue my work for the SVR as a NOCON. My cover is irretrievably blown, no thanks to you. And I no longer know what is to become of me. All I know deep down in my core is that I want only to continue loving you and, if any way possible, maybe continue my studies."

He gently shook his head. "Most likely you will be asked to disclose the ID of your controller in exchange for being allowed to return to Russia. Otherwise, you will almost certainly be prosecuted for high crimes against the state, tried and sentenced, and then incarcerated in a federal penitentiary."

He watched all the color drain from her cheeks and after the reality of the situation slapped her full in the face, she began to cry again, exactly the reaction he was hoping and looking for. In the depths of her despair, she came to the realization that her life as she now lived it was inevitably over. And in the darkness of her shame and regret at her loss, he offered her a soupçon of hope, the first ray of sunlight touching the face of the sea after the storm has passed. "There might be another possibility," was all he said.

She did not ask him to clarify further. She put her complete trust and faith in the man sitting at the opposite end of the couch. She came back into his arms and sat in his lap again eager to take him, he eager to respond as she tended to their clothes, and in spite of their urgent, unfettered and uninhibited lovemaking on the couch, after the storm of pleasure washed over them, he was troubled once more.

As a federal officer in the employ of the Department of Justice, it was his sworn duty to report her to the authorities. Anything less would compromise his integrity and put him in legal jeopardy. But he had a plan that might save them both if this was what he truly wanted. He needed to decide soon.

Later, still naked in each other's arms on the couch, the blanket pulled up tight below her chin, she cried out a little bit of her misery into the cup of his neck where it rounded down into his shoulder. He stroked her hair. "I've never had to depend on a man like this." She sniffled. "It makes me feel so helpless and small and I am anything but. I'm a big girl and I'm strong," she said defiantly.

He kissed the top of her head. "Needing a friend doesn't make you weak; it just makes you human."

She didn't seem convinced but with her sleek length stretched out on top of him, he was willing to attest to the undeniable certainty of her humanity. She lay there coordinating her breathing with his, exhaling as he inhaled. Half off, half on him, her one cool leg between his permitted her to gently pulse the slick wetness of her vagina against the rounded length of his quadriceps. In almost everything the woman does, he thought, she imposes some element of her sexuality.

She took a deep breath that pressed her breasts into his chest and spoke into the side of an ear. She pressed harder against him and he responded by tightening the bulge of his thigh muscles. She moaned a bit into his ear. "Don't stop that," she encouraged him.

She gripped his penis and squeezed. "I have no accent at all, do I?" She stroked him into an erection that touched his belly.

"*Nyet*," he said in Russian. "None at all. Now that we have that settled, tell me what you want to do."

She moved further atop him, reached down and slid his penis up into the welcoming moisture of her vagina. For a moment neither was able to speak. What she said next substantiated his decision.

"Now that we're together I can't think of doing anything but being with you." He pulled her up for a deep and long kiss that pushed her into a wrenching, gasping climax, never breaking the kiss. When she recovered her breathing, she was able to whisper into his ear. "I've never been so scared," she admitted, "since the night we got the news that my father was killed by the explosion from the bomb triggered by the Chechnyan terrorists." Her internal muscles fluttered and pulsed around his erection. "Don't you want to come?" said Lisi, in her little girl voice, just the slightest inflection tinging her vowels.

"In a minute," he said. "What do you want me to do now that I know?" he asked.

"I want to go to ground and get out. I don't want to be a spy for Russia against the United States." She moved her legs up and down just enough to keep him hard.

"I think I might have a way out for you, but it means you will have to double for a while."

She lifted herself to look into his eyes. "You mean me with Sylvie and you?"

"No, silly," he said, grabbing her taut ass with both hands. "As attractive a picture as that brings to mind, it means I have a friend in the CIA, for whom you would become a prized asset. In return I will bargain for your citizenship and placement at a university of your choice after you finish your doctoral work." She searched his face for the truth. He nodded.

"Now do you want to come?" she asked.

He touched the two most beautiful lips he had ever kissed and said, "Between these two gorgeous lips."

"See you later, alligator," she said, throwing up the blanket and two minutes later he almost passed out with pleasure.

He did not wait long to make the necessary calls. It was the only way to save her, and in a very real sense, save himself and their relationship together. He was bound by federal law to inform the authorities of his contact with a foreign agent, inadvertent though it might be, he explained to her. This was not about exposing her or ratting her out, it was about doing his duty to his country and obeying the sworn oath he had taken. She understood and accepted the inevitability of what was about to happen. Once she had decided that she must tell him everything, she was fully prepared to accept the consequences of her actions. She had fully resigned herself to accept whatever punishment was coming. She felt vulnerable, uncertain, and entirely dependent on his love for her. Now that the mask of deceit had dropped and she had confessed the truth, there was no going back. As the great German poet Rainer Maria Rilke wrote after looking upon the sublime form of the statue, the Archaic Torso of Apollo, she must forever change her life.

CHAPTER TWENTY-FIVE

Enrollment in the CIA

The early winter afternoon light faded into the snow-capped trees. The stillness outside was punctuated by an occasional crack of ice that fissured the frozen lake, or by a massive pine forced to drop its snow load and swish back into position. Evening stealthily darkened the windows of the cabin and an early rising moon was hung up in the branches of a large oak. Lisa sat at her computer in the dining room and Will played a CD of his favorite opera arias. He played the music loud enough to be heard in the living room but not loud enough to bother Lisa working at the dining room table. Nevertheless, the intrusion of an aria drew her attention away from her research and she sat upright and listened. The music haunted her, the beauty of the soprano's voice caused chills to tickle her spine and the melody mesmerized her. To her surprise when she heard the soprano sing the lyrics "*Mesiku na nebi hlubokem, svetlo tve daleko vidi,*" Annalisa recognized the language as Czech. Moon, high and deep in the sky, your light sees far, the artist sang.

She quickly closed the lid to her laptop, and stood in the middle of the living room. With her thumb she signaled to Will that he should turn it up. Music enveloped her in an hypnotic cocoon of sound, music, and emotion. She went to sit on Will's lap, arms around his neck, enthralled by the music. When the soprano finished the last perfectly held note in an exquisite crescendo, Will paused the recording. Lisa kissed him on the cheek through a three-day stubble, moonlight pushing tears from her eyes.

"That was the most beautiful song I've ever heard. Surely it is a song about love and longing."

Will kissed the top of her white blond hair, her natural color. "It's from an opera by Antonín Dvořák called *Rusalka*. The title of the song in English is "The song to the moon." There are many outstanding versions but this one by Renée Fleming is my favorite."

She looked up into his eyes, pleading. "Please let this be our song. And promise me you will never play it for another woman. Only for yourself or for us."

"Why Lisi, I didn't know you were such a romantic sentimentalist."

She nicked an ear with her teeth. "Promise!"

"I promise," he said and with a finger checked his ear for blood.

She settled her head on his great chest and sighed, placated.

"Please play our song again. For us."

"As you command, my princess," he said, and the music played again, the first haunting notes plucked from the harp strings calling to the violins. Rusalka, a water nymph, has fallen in love and wants to become human. She sings a song to the moon and asks it to reveal her love to her prince.

Will kissed Annalisa but did not tell her that in the opera the Prince learns that kissing the beautiful water nymph will result in his death. Nevertheless, at the edge of the lake he calls to her and when Rusalka finally kisses her prince and experiences human love, the kiss is fatal and the prince dies.

The next day, Will and Lisa drove to the FBI offices in Minneapolis to meet the CIA station chief who had flown in from Langley, Virginia. He was a former colleague of Will's during their doctoral work together at Washington State

University. James Dawson had risen through the ranks of the spy agency, working the counterespionage desk in Berlin after duty in Bonn, Germany, Seoul, South Korea, and Helsinki, Finland. After entering the building, where they were wanded, and had their appointment checked and verified, they were led to a secure room where an agent sat awaiting their arrival. Will introduced her to James Dawson, COS, or Chief of Station, equivalent to a Russian FSB *rezident*, and they all shook hands. After taking a few minutes to catch up on each other's lives, in a modern room with no windows, thin tables and thin chairs, Will explained the circumstances for their visit, giving Dawson time to observe Annalisa. He was stunned by the woman's beauty and the way she carried herself. If she was any indication of the quality of persons being recruited into the SVR and FSB, we're in trouble, Dawson thought as he listened to Will.

After he finished taking notes on Sheridan's recitation of his relationship with Annalisa Allen, Dawson began the interview by allowing Lisa to recount the circumstances of her recruitment by her professor at the University of Riga in Latvia and her subsequent training once in the SVR, the Russian foreign intelligence service. She made a deliberate point of stating that she had received her spy training in the clandestine services because of her intelligence and her facility with languages and that she was not forced to attend spy school for agents trained in the arts of sexual seduction. "I come by my talents naturally, honestly and as the result of practice, much study, and more practice," she said without artifice. She acknowledged that she knew and expected there would be times when she would be required to put those natural talents to use. Dawson asked how was it that she had been assigned to Dr. Sheridan.

"He first came across the desk of the SVR as a person of interest after his work in helping break the case of two Russian citizens assassinated by the Bulgarian State Intelligence Agency, the SIA, their foreign intelligence service. We learned Sheridan's analytical work showed that the two Russians, then living in the United Kingdom, were double agents working for MI5. After they were mysteriously killed, the report Sheridan wrote for the Brits surfaced arguing that the directive to remove the two agents could only have come from the desk of Vladimir Putin. The SVR could not explain how Dr. Sheridan had figured out what was considered a top-secret, black operation."

Will raised an eyebrow and Dawson smiled, knowing his old buddy. He had read a brief of the report.

Lisa continued with her narrative. "Accordingly, after my first year in the United States while I was still at the University of Wisconsin working on my Master's degree, I was tasked to find Dr. Sheridan and ultimately develop a relationship with him, however long that took. The problem at the time was this. He was living and working at his cabin on the Boundary Waters in Minnesota. I had been accepted into the doctoral program in forensic psychology at the University of Minnesota in an effort to get closer to him. At the last moment I accepted a position at the Iowa Polytechnic State University when I learned he had been a graduate studies professor there before he resigned his position and went to work as a special consultant for the FBI. It was my belief that once I became a graduate and alumna of the university, I would have a much better opportunity to forge a relationship with him. At the time it was my intent and my plan to begin a series of interviews with him concerning his understanding of the criminal mind and criminal behavior during the course of his work in the United States and internationally. I had at that time already read his published works detailing his declassified cases. This would have been the subterfuge on which I would base the development of a friendship with him."

It was increasingly obvious to both men that the telling of her story was causing Lisa intense emotional trauma. Her face had grown sallow and a note of desperation had crept into her voice and set into the corners of her eyes. Noting the beautiful young woman's increasing distress,

Dawson suggested they should all take a fifteen-minute break. She looked over at Will.

"It's up to you, Lisa. You're doing fine." For support he reached over and took her hand in his. She did not let it go.

She said, "Thank you for your kind offer, Mr. Dawson, but I prefer to continue and get this over with as quickly as I can." She thought for a moment trying to recall where she had left off. "Ahh, yes, my plan for getting in contact with professor Sheridan up in Minnesota. In the meantime, I was to send any information that might be of value to my resident, using my research access as a graduate student, first as a Master's student and then as a doctoral candidate. And then in one of those strange serendipitous coincidences life throws at us Dr. Sheridan showed up to teach a graduate seminar in semiotic theory at IPSU and I immediately sent him my credentials and my desire to be enrolled in his course."

Dawson made a quick note and said, "Please characterize for me the kind of information you were sending back before Will appeared on the scene."

"Anything related to oil was highly prized. For example, anything about the oilfields in North Dakota, in Texas, or in Pennsylvania. How many barrels per day were being produced by fracking in the Permian basin, the Marcellus Shale and Eagle Ford. Anything, especially technical papers or reports that discussed oil drilling technologies such as rig counts, or number of derricks and new wells, received high marks from my handlers. Any new oilfields being opened, anything about oil transportation such as pipelines, the number of tanker trucks and rail cars hauling oil were considered the highest priority. And the political positions regarding new construction in the opening of new oilfields and pipelines was also highly prized."

"Ironically, despite the fact that I was in the process of developing a relationship with Dr. Sheridan, the more information I discovered about oil economics and oil politics, the more it seemed the SVR's interest in my relationship with Will was put on a back burner. I believe this was the result of the United States placing sanctions and embargoes on Russia after the invasion of the Ukraine and the annexation of the Crimean Peninsula, which as you know was once the location of a secret Soviet submarine base."

She paused to take a sip from the can of Diet Coke Dawson had thoughtfully provided for her. "However, midway through the Fall semester, I was asked for a full and formal report of my progress with Dr. Sheridan. It seems another highly confidential action was being planned on foreign soil by the FSB and they wanted to be certain that Dr. Sheridan was not aware of it and would not involve himself once the action was successfully prosecuted." She stopped to take a deep breath and look over at Will, his hand still firmly trapped in hers. He smiled at her in support.

"What did you do next?" agent Dawson asked.

"I fell blindly and stupidly in love, thereby compromising my status as a deep cover agent. This week I decided to tell Will everything and hope for the best. I had no idea that he was harboring suspicions about me and had already figured out that something was not quite right with me. Because I was in love, and for that reason only, I confessed everything."

"Despite what you have said it is in our best interest to remain somewhat skeptical," Dawson said. But your subsequent behaviors will tell the tale and I want you to understand something. When Dr. Sheridan came to work for the FBI as a special consultant and agent, he was and is required by federal law to report any contact he has had with any agents foreign and domestic. Most likely his doing so has saved you. Although your official status as an SVR agent of the Russian Federal Security Service (FSB) confers on you diplomatic immunity, we can expose you, to the embarrassment of the FSB, and have you sent back to Russia. There is also the possibility that you can be arrested, tried, sentenced to prison, and then be used as leverage for a subsequent spy exchange with Russia." She nodded and slumped a bit in her chair. "After discussing your situation with Dr. Sheridan, whom I know and trust implicitly, I have decided there is another option available to us." Her interest piqued, she sat up straight again in her chair, waiting expectantly. "You can come to work for us."

She looked immediately at Will, now holding his hand in both of hers on her lap. "I will do anything to be able to stay here in the United States and continue my relationship with Will. I hope eventually to finish my dissertation, complete my doctoral work, and become an American citizen."

"Very good," Head of Station James Dawson said. "That's exactly what we hoped you would say. We will begin the process of enrolling you as a double agent working for the CIA in service to the United States of America. We will supply you with information that you will submit to your resident, and within the FSB to the Russian Foreign Intelligence Service, the SVR's ER Directorate, their branch for dealing with economic issues such as oil production and the like. Ready to go to work for a new master?" he asked with a wry grin.

She shared a smile of relief with both men and nodded eagerly. "Just tell me what I need to do."

"We will be in touch after we finish vetting and processing you," Dawson promised. "You will also have to take and pass a lie detector test." He pointed a finger of accusation at Will. "And you, big man, are not to teach her how to defeat a polygraph."

Will held up his hands in a mute protest of innocence. "I have no doubt she already knows how to do so."

Lisa nodded to both men in a show of honesty. Dawson turned back to Lisa who had crossed her legs at the knee under her black leather skirt.

"In the meantime, if I hear of my old friend Sheridan coming to any grief because of you, I will hunt you down personally, and see to it that you are prosecuted to the fullest extent of the law. That is my promise to you both."

"Thanks Jim, but I don't think it will come to that," Will said, turning and looking at Lisa. "I think I know my girl well enough now to say that to you with confidence." Lisa unconsciously squeezed his hand. "There are interesting days ahead of us. The ball is now in her court."

CHAPTER TWENTY-SIX

Building Trust

All too soon it was time to return to Iowa, the days faltering until they were almost gone, shortening by the minute, the nights under the aurora borealis were gone, and it was time for the trip back to the university. Farley Nilsson presented Annalisa with a going away gift: a pair of handmade and handsewn deer hide gloves he had tanned himself from the 10-point buck he had taken earlier in the season. Lined with the mink Farley had trapped, she could not believe how soft and warm the gloves were.

She kissed him goodbye on both cheeks, to Farley's embarrassment, and said, "I'll never take them off." She promised and thanked him again and Farley chuckled as he handed her into the car. He shook hands and clapped Will on the back as he waved them so long and closed the garage door against the blowing cold of a northern Minnesota snowy winter day and lost them in a flurry of white.

Despite temperatures in the low teens the snow stopped as they passed through Virginia, the clouds cleared, the weather held and the roads were soon clear of ice and snow, pushed to the side by the diligent and persistent workers driving massive snowplows whose blades curled the snow into dirty banks on either side of the freeway. Once out of the Great White North and past the Mesabi Range where even today iron ore is mined, they entered the flatter part of Minnesota's endless fields of white broken by lines of trees edging the borders of the dormant hay, corn, and soybean fields now snow-covered lakes of white. The landscape changed little as they crossed the border into northern Iowa. As they drove snow glistened in the sunlight as if the snow-covered fields had been sprinkled with diamond dust.

Annalisa looked very après ski in a red anorak over her black cashmere sweater and black ski pants that fit her form as if they had been sprayed on. The color choices accentuated her now blonde hair piled up under the Siberian hat lined with mink, a perfect match with the gloves Farley Nilsson had given her. Despite the enervating emotional turmoil of her confession to Will, her good-natured personality had restored itself. She seemed happy to the point of exuberance with the expectation of the return with Will to the duplex and her room on the first floor of the apartment.

On the trip down she said she had loved every minute but one with him at the cabin, and he knew and understood the oblique reference. He reminded her that he had sworn an oath to protect the Constitution and people of the United States against all enemies, foreign and domestic. He reminded her that it was his sworn duty as a federal officer and a special agent of the Department of Justice to report her. Anything less would have constituted dereliction of duty.

"I know what you had to do," she said, her words measured and precise. "I also know that you could've brought me in, exposed me, done your duty, and not given it so much as a second thought." She turned to him and he nodded. "Instead, you found a way to maintain your integrity, and at the same time saved me from an inglorious expulsion from the university, and in the worst-case scenario, having to suffer the embarrassment of a trial for espionage against the United States with likely incarceration for up to twenty years." She paused for a moment to consider the full import of what he had done for her. "I will never forget what you have done for me and I will love you until the day I die, whether I am sitting next to you in a

Subaru Forester driving through Minnesota back to Iowa, or languishing in a federal prison serving time for high crimes against the state. None of those circumstances matter or affect why or how I love you." She looked at him again. "I just want you to know that."

He drove nearly five miles before he spoke. When he did, he asked, "Do you want Hardees or Wendy's?"

"Hardees," she replied, defeated.

After lunch and southbound once more she said, "If you don't mind my asking, how did you know? Was there anything other than the language mistakes that gave me away?"

With the traffic lighter than usual and the Subaru Forester on cruise control, he turned to her. "A relationship is frequently established on the basis of an initial sexual attraction between two people." She nodded. "I accepted the fact that I was sexually attracted to you from the beginning. And despite the fact that I am occasionally attracted to female graduate students, I rarely ever acted on such attractions, given the inherent problems, to say nothing of the institutional rules that now try to regulate any and all romantic relationships between professor and students. Against my better judgment, with you I acted on the obvious sexual attraction between us when it appeared that you are also interested in me."

Before he could continue, she interrupted. "I am absolutely, positively, and wildly attracted to you sexually."

"Be that as it may," he said, "I permitted myself to engage with you sexually and I take full responsibility for my actions. I acknowledge and understand on the basis of some rather painful self-analysis, that I needed to find a way to survive my loss of love and former relationship with Sylvie Schumann. I thought she was the love of my life and inexplicably, I lost her, and I could not then understand why. In spite of all my training in semiotics and psychology, I did not understand why I lost that woman; whether to another man or to a career, it does not matter. I lost her and I now realize it was my fault. I did not want to lose her but

I also did not want to lose my way of life at that time. That realization frustrates me. It aggravates me, and most of all it humiliates me. And in the throes of frustration, aggravation, and humiliation I permitted myself to enter into a sexual liaison with you."

She frowned and wrinkled her nose. She wasn't sure if she liked being merely a sexual liaison, although at one time it had been good enough for her.

"It is one of the best decisions I have ever made in my life," he said to her. "Sexually, I've never been happier," he acknowledged.

"Were you happy sexually with Sylvie?" she asked in a very small voice.

He glared at her. "You do not have the right to ask me that question."

In an even smaller diminutive voice she said, "Sorry," and looked out the window, crossing her left leg over her right away from him.

"I was quite happy sexually with Sylvie, despite her lack of experience with men and an inherited streak of sexual conservatism it took me some time to overcome," he said with intensity. Then he moderated his voice before saying, "However, you are in an otherworldly dimension entirely when it comes to a woman freely and uninhibitedly expressing her sexuality. This is the very thing that attracted me to you and gave me the psychological freedom to once again take a chance with a woman, to take a chance with myself that this time I will not go stupid and lose her."

They drove five more miles before she swore to him, "You will never lose me."

He snapped back instantly. "But how can I know that, Annalisa? I don't even know your real name. The foundation of trust on which we built our relationship is destroyed. How can I be certain that you are in fact sexually attracted to me instead of you using that very pure, very basic, and very truthful biogenetic attraction between a male and a female to share your sexuality and your sense of self with me? How can I be certain now that what you claim is your sexual attraction to me was not merely a subterfuge used by a highly sophisticated female sleeper agent doing her duty for mother Russia as an agent of the SVR?"

"Alina Augustans," she whispered in a voice so small she doubted if he could hear her. "You know I passed a lie detector test."

He glared at her. "I also know that Russian spies receive in-depth training in how to defeat the polygraph."

She turned again to her window and began to cry. "You are the only man other than my father who has ever made me cry," she said, as if that bald statement alone should suffice as an explanation and atonement for her tears.

"But dammit Lisa, or Alina, or whoever the hell you are, how do I know that your tears and now your repeated profession of your love for me are nothing more than the work of a highly sophisticated and well-trained spy?" With a finality and an ineffable sadness that surprised even himself he said, "I have no reason to ever trust you again."

After another five miles, the quiet sobbing stopped, she dried her tears in the crook of her arm. With deliberate cool and studied sangfroid, she turned and reached for one of her bags on the back seat, brought it forward onto her lap, took out and opened her makeup case. Without a word and to his surprise she removed first her lipstick, then the light foundation on her face, then her eyeliner. Her lashes were long enough naturally that she did not need mascara to lengthen or thicken them. With a moist towelette she wiped the eyebrow pencil from her eyebrows and cleaned her fingers. Lastly, she flipped her nearly white blonde hair back, using only her fingers to comb it out. Only then did she turn and look at him and say, "You know now that this is my natural hair color."

He nodded, wondering what the hell she was up to. She unbuckled her seatbelt. Traffic on the interstate was still light and moving at a reasonable pace as the seasonal cold regulated the traffic, most drivers in boots, bundled in parkas, gloved mittens on the wheel, hats on head. She unzipped her black boots, taking them off socks and all.

Next, she removed her cashmere sweater. As usual, she was not wearing a bra. Then she lifted her hips off the leather car seat, hooked her thumbs into the spandex of her ski pants tight as yoga pants, hooked her thumbs into the waistband and pulled her black pants with the red stripe down over her knees and off her feet. Obviously, she was not wearing panties either. She sat next to him completely naked. "This is who I am stripped bare. No lies, no pretensions, no more prevarication. I am extremely sexually attracted to you and I have uncontrollably and forever fallen in love with you. I formally renounce all that I was. I no longer want to be a spy for Russia; a doctoral candidate at university; a double agent working in service to the United States and the CIA. I no longer want to be any of these things. But I cannot renounce what I am now."

"What is that?" he asked, his curiosity piqued by the quite beautiful and quite naked person sitting next to him.

"A woman in love."

Time enough for another five miles down the interstate elapsed. "At some point, Annalisa, you have to put your clothes back on."

She turned to him and yelled. "At some point you have to trust me again!"

He sighed and passed a very impressed trucker hauling cattle to Des Moines from Hibbing, Minnesota. In appreciation he honked his horn twice.

"Can you at least permit yourself to find me sexually attractive once again?"

"That will never be a problem for us," he said, and gently but forcefully put her hand down between his legs. She immediately unzipped him and exposed his erect penis. As she encircled his girth with the long graceful fingers of her right hand, she kissed him full on the lips and said, "At least he still loves me."

As she took him into her moist hot mouth he said, "Don't make the mistake of confusing sexual attraction with love."

After five more pleasant miles had gone by, she paused for a moment to tongue her lips clean and looked at him, smiling beatifically. "For a woman, sometimes they are one and the same."

When they arrived at the duplex in Cedar City, he helped her unload the suitcases, he his one, her three, two of which he had bought for her as a set of three including the makeup kit, turned the lights on, central heating on, a pee for them both after a long and emotionally exhausting trip. He left her upstairs to the unpacking and replacement of her clothes in closets and chest of drawers. Downstairs he unpacked quickly, stowed the suitcase in the room set aside for storage, plugged in his laptop and got to work. After he checked his emails and wrote a few letters, he closed his computer, turned off the light to his office, and went to bed hungry. He wanted nothing more to do with seductive, intelligent, Machiavellian women. He was tired to the bone from all the travel, the talk, and the emotional pandering, and could not care less if his sour mood improved after a long and necessary sleep.

Lisa floated down the carpet stairs of the basement in her bare feet light as falling leaves in autumn. She was shocked to find his door closed, no light lining the bottom of the door. She had thought everything between them was good again; that they would start anew and quickly rebuild the foundation of trust she had undermined and caused to collapse. She stood at his door, trembling in the cool of the basement, naked under a new Victoria's Secret silk teddy she had bought to wear just for him, eager to rebuild, desperate to put things between them back as they had been before, when she was happier than she had ever been, a happiness that she would have again with him or die.

In the complete darkness of the room where he slept, with no windows to admit light or sound, he awoke the next morning, earlier than usual, lots of time for sleep still on the clock. He decided to take advantage of the early hour and empty his bladder, then return to his covers and a bed the perfect temperature for sleep. As he walked through his open door into the dark of the early morning in the basement, he almost tripped and fell over the form lying outside the door. She lay on her side, knees to her breasts, wearing something light as a spider's web and silky to his touch. He reached back into his room and fumbled for the light switch, never taking his eyes off her. In the glare of the electric light he saw it was Lisa. There was no blood beneath the pillow of her gossamer blonde hair or at her wrists. He tapped her nose and her eyes opened. Drugged with too little sleep, she fought through the narcoleptic haze to recognize him. As she reached up to him, she said in Latvian, "*Es esmu tikai jums. Sūtiet mani prom, ja vēlaties.*" When she roused enough to understand what she had said, she translated the words into English for him. "I am yours alone. Send me away if you wish."

He put a finger to her lips and from one knee, gathered her into his arms and lifted her, her hands unconsciously encircling the thick muscles of his neck, and took her into the bedroom. He carefully put her head down on the pillows, straightened her nightie, and covered her to the chin with the blankets. He turned on his reading light, turned off the overhead light and left the door open just enough to make for an easy trip to the bathroom. When he returned, he found her nightgown under his pillow, she in a deep and guileless sleep, directly in the middle of the queen-size bed. Nuzzling her cheek with his lips and spooning her, she awoke just enough to say in Latvian, "*Es mīlu Tevi.*" The few words of Latvian he had learned over the years in his reading was enough for him to understand that she had said I love you. He doubted she had heard his reply, also in Latvian. And in the spirit intended he decided, for the time being, to accept her gift of love. And like the prince kissed by the water-nymph, he wondered if it would eventually kill him.

CHAPTER TWENTY-SEVEN

Blood Brotherhood

Word had reached the remaining five. The disappearance of Blood Brotherhood member Sam Salerno was cause for concern. Albert Young called them to assemble and once more swear their vows and fealty to the union of brothers. The brothers had lost one of their own and it was time to renew allegiances and test the durability of the Brotherhood by oath and by action.

Young greeted them as they arrived at the compound. Buck Miller, the sheriff, still in uniform came first; Kenneth Black, president of Black Insurance entered with the Honorable Robert Franklin, the county judge who had dismissed the DWI case against him; Lawrence Rosenstein, president of Farmer's National Bank came in a bespoke blue suit and red power tie. Already there, pig farmer and local butcher Maynard Cheska, who had arrived earlier to help with the preparations for the important ceremony.

The men mingled, shook hands as each member arrived, then relaxed in the hunting room while drinking single malt Scotch whisky half their age and smoking Cuban cigars as they discussed the politics of the day. An electric current of anxiety undercut the laughter, the racist and sexist jokes, and the bonhomie. Young called them to order and the talk ended. "Tonight is a full ceremony in full regalia."

They turned to each other and clapped shoulders and smiled in anticipation. Young waited for them to quiet down again. "As you no doubt may remember, whenever a former member—despite his signed contract and sworn oath—asks to be removed from the lists of the Blood Brotherhood, his wish is granted. Sam Salerno joined us in blood and per his contract, he was removed in blood."

"Always pays to read the fine print," quipped Judge Franklin.

"I'll second that," added Ken Black, no stranger to the importance of fine print. The rest nodded nervously, wondering or trying to remember what the fine print said in the contract they had signed in their own blood.

Young continued after the nervous laughter abated. "Where we were once seven, we are now six, leaving an opening for a new member. Very early in the new year we will meet in committee and discuss the inclusion of a new member. And now I invite you to robe up and meet me in the ceremonial hall at precisely 11:30 p.m."

At the appointed time, five men in red robes, black hoods covering their heads, filed solemnly into the ceremonial chamber lit by candles. Young, clad in an all red robe with a red hood, welcomed the Brothers to stand around the ceremonial table of polished stainless steel that glistened in the faltering candlelight.

"With our hoods up and masks on gentlemen, let us prepare to welcome our honored guest." A door at the far end of the darkened room lit by the gentle flickering light of seven candles, each a foot tall, opened to reveal Maynard Cheska clad in his ceremonial robes. He led a young woman draped in a white tunic to the table. She stumbled and Cheska caught her. Her pupils were fixed and dilated and she had been warned not to speak. Her white blonde hair had been shorn above the nape of her neck in preparation for the ceremony. Cheska positioned the young woman so that she faced the end of the table.

Young said, "Gentlemen, I present for your consideration...." He flipped a switch at the end of the table and the young woman was bathed in a soft circle of light from above. At this point Cheska, released the drawstring holding the white robe together just below clavicle of the young woman who stood in offering, dazed and confused by the Rohypnol in her system. Her robe dropped to the floor, covering her naked feet. The Brotherhood examined her. She was nearly alabaster white and thin, her thinness accentuating her small breasts sitting high on her chest, which rose and fell as she struggled to breathe, wrapped in a tunic of fear. Cheska turned her at the shoulder. They studied the delicate vulnerable neck centered between thin shoulders, spine running down into and disappearing into the sudden swell of her rounded buttocks.

Even with her legs together at the knees, the Brotherhood were able to discern the delicate outlines of her sex, couched in the natural pocket formed by the buttocks curving into the top of her thin white thighs. It was impossible to tell if she had been shaved or whether she stood before them naturally bereft of any hair on her body below her head. At his signal, two of the Brothers came forward and assisted Cheska. She was bent over the table at the waist, forced to lie on her stomach, the coldness of the steel on her breasts and stomach causing her to gasp. Her arms were extended and buckled into leather straps; her head placed on a thin red pillow. Her legs were splayed and buckled with leather against the legs supporting the end of the sacrificial table.

After each of the men standing around the table laid hands on the woman, taking the warmth and softness from her skin, Albert Young came around the end of the table. He opened his robes and approached the young woman quivering on the table. He repositioned his feet, grabbed the young woman's hard buttocks, and pulled her closer, hips flexing. She screamed, but it might have only been in her head, the pillow silencing any noises she was able to produce. After he had finished, Young withdrew and began the examination. With satisfaction, he announced as he cleaned himself with a white linen towel,

"Brothers, behold the purity of her hymenal blood. She is a virgin no longer. Please feel free to partake. May her blood bind us all in everlasting brotherhood."

Each man took his turn at the foot of the table, with Cheska going last, each man sharing in the virginal blood by rank within the organization. By the time the third brother had finished, the young woman was motionless on the table, only her shallow, unconscious breathing signaling the life still left in her. After everyone had partaken and satisfied themselves, Young spoke once more, reciting the oath of the Blood Brotherhood.

"We six brothers stand as one." He heard them echoing his pledge. "From blood and in blood we stand united. We are the Blood Brotherhood now and forever." He waited for them to finish the vows. "So it will always be."

Two of the members remained behind as the others solemnly filed out, removed their robes, and dressed. The restraints were uncoupled from the unconscious woman's meager wrists and legs, where the bruises, the shadows of her struggles, had already formed. Using one of the six towels at her feet, Cheska cleaned and wiped the fluids from her thighs. "I'll take it from here," he told the other two, who were only too glad to leave the room, which stank now of bodily fluids and guttering candle smoke.

He placed her on the table stomach up and taking one of the folded towels with both of his thick powerful hands, sealed her mouth and nose. As she struggled one last time for her life, he took his pleasure, a personal and private bonus. After cleaning up again he joined the other members for celebratory cigars and single malt Scotch. Young impressed on the Brotherhood the need to recruit another member so the ranks once again stood at the sacred number seven. They all agreed to begin a careful search for a viable and trustworthy candidate.

With work still to be done, Cheska changed and with the help of two other members, wrapped the sacrificial victim in her white robe and loaded her into the back of his panel truck, covering her with the stained towels. He locked the two back doors of the van and drove to his slaughterhouse. Once more among the long, razor-sharp carbon steel knives, electric saws and the meat grinders, he knew he had a long night of work ahead of him under the glow of the selenium moon, rendered gray by the passing clouds.

He sat at the round kitchen table, slurping a bowl of chicken noodle soup while he read the latest issue of a research journal in language philosophy. Lisa came skipping in from her bedroom, hair up and off the back of her neck. It was long enough now to put into a short ponytail. Otherwise, she was as usual gorgeously naked. "I find clothes too inhibiting," she once explained. "I am never happier than when I am naked. Except when I'm happily naked for you." Knowing her as he did, he put his spoon down. She did a half pirouette and stood on her toes, tightening the muscles of her perfectly shaped behind. What do you think of my ass?"

He shrugged; maybe this would be easy for once. "I don't think five gods working together in harmony could have given Venus or Aphrodite a more perfectly sculpted rear end, and that is my professional and aesthetical opinion. I have seen enough shapely keesters in my time to speak with authority on the matter."

"Don't brag," Lisa said and put a bottle of hydrogen peroxide on the table. "Lisa needs help bleaching her bum."

"Lisa, really. This is too much. I've never met another woman so blatantly and candidly willing to smash through all sexual and social boundaries, and at the same time be so enduringly enticing. That said, why in the hell do you want to bleach your already perfect behind?"

She stood naked in front of him hand on one hip, the other jetting to the side. "I've been doing some research. All the best porn stars are doing it. I don't want you to think, oh my God, what have I gotten myself into when I make you fuck me anally."

Will could not help himself and laughed at her creatively design pun. "All right. The things I don't do for country and queen." Bend over and let me have a look."

Lisa locked her knees as she bent at the waist. Both cheeks pulled open, she offered herself for inspection.

"Your ass is perfect, just as I said, you silly goose. Go put this bottle back in the bathroom."

She shook her head no, looking back at him, but kept herself spread open. "Tongue," she commanded.

"What?" he said, startled.

"Tongue," she repeated, so he tongued her.

CHAPTER TWENTY-EIGHT

Practicum

A patchwork of snow quilted the drab ground of plowed cornfields and filled in the dry sloughs Will and Annalisa had left behind about three weeks ago. The landlord had been kind enough to arrange for a snowplow service to clear the driveway, otherwise they would not have made it out of the garage and onto the main road. Judging by the height of the snowbanks lining the driveway, the depth of the snow would have challenged the very competent symmetrical all-wheel drive capabilities of the Subaru Forester. When they arrived at the university, they found the parking lot plowed clear of snow. Three or four vehicles with dead batteries wore snow hats fully two feet high.

The second half of Will's two semester course was designed and designated as a practicum for which returning graduate students still enrolled would receive ten credits toward their respective degrees. The students were required to meet at the beginning of the Spring semester in early January for three hours. On the first evening of class in their usual seminar room, Will welcomed back his graduate students. He greeted and personally shook hands with Mike, Karin, LB, and Lisa. Larry Davidson had dropped the class early in the Fall semester after Lisa had whipped his ass and sent him home crying to his mother. Yuriko Sumitomo, after completing the Fall semester, had been called home to Osaka where she was helping her father who had suffered a mild heart attack and needed her help with the family business, a kimono factory. Will gave the four returning students time to reacquaint themselves and all seemed in good spirits, healthy, and rested from their semester break.

"I hope you all enjoyed your time off and had a good holiday. They say the average weight gain over the holiday is about five pounds. To hell with that. My goal was ten." They laughed at the little joke. "As you know, today marks the first day of your ten-credit practicum, available to those graduate students who survived the Fall semester with me." The class grinned as one, LB slapping high-fives with the other three. LaDamian wore what could only be called a white sequined Elvis jumpsuit, a long broad white silk scarf hanging from his skinny shoulders. "Not used to the cold yet, LB?"

"Amen to that, Dr. Sheridan. It don't snow like this in Baton Rouge, where my *gran'maman* lives."

"Don't worry," Will joked. "Another six months or so and spring will be here." LB groaned, wrapped his silk scarf more tightly around his neck and palmed the sides of his hair, which he had straightened and slicked back. "I love the jumpsuit, by the way," Will said.

LB curled up the corner of his lip into a mock snarl and said, "Thank you very much," and for an instant Will thought Elvis Presley had entered the room. LB stood, legs apart and turned in first one, then the other knee, did a full pirouette, and came up on the toes of both black boots. The class applauded as he took his seat. "Y'all are very kind," he said, in an eerily perfect imitation of the King's Tupelo, Mississippi drawl.

Will waited for them to settle their attention on him again. "Okay, let's get to work," Will directed and the graduate students took out their notepads and pens "This segment of the course is designed to give you an opportunity to take what you have learned in semiotic theory and apply it to a real case in the field. In the academic world this is called a movement from *theoria* to *praxis*, in other words from theory to practice. Accordingly, we are ready to begin our investigation."

"As you have already noticed, Yuriko Sumitomo is no longer with us. Her father's unfortunate illness has forced her to withdraw from classes for the Spring semester. She has been called home to help with her family's business until her father recovers. She sends warm greetings to all and invites you to Skype whenever possible. Do keep in touch with her, but please do not discuss our cases with her or with anyone else for that matter, understood?" He looked at each student in turn, awaiting affirmation before he went on to the next. "For your protection this is what we call a black operation, as Mike well understands."

"Roger that, sir." he said, pointing a thumb up.

LaDamian raised his hand in a flurry of waving. "Yes, LB."

"Dr. Will, don't you mean an African American operation?"

Will could not help but laugh. He really liked this kid and his unbundled and unbridled runaway horse enthusiasm. "It may not be politically correct but let's keep it black ops for the time being."

Elvis said, "Thank you very much."

"Now the news you've all been waiting for. I had time over the Christmas break to give each of your cases additional in-depth consideration and analysis. I'll share with you some of the criteria I used to make the selection. And by the way, these criteria are different from the ones used to evaluate the quality of your papers and the grades you received as a result. I just wanted to let you know that the grade was not based on whether or not your case was chosen for investigation. I wanted a case where we have a good chance of achieving a positive outcome. The case had to be logistically feasible. For example, although Yuriko gave us an excellent case for consideration, given the financial limits of my grant and the possibility that some or all of you might not have passports for a trip to Japan, I had to eliminate her case for consideration. Mike, your case had great possibilities, but again the logistics of getting everyone to Afghanistan posed unsurmountable obstacles. LB, your case too had its merits, but unfortunately, all the principals in the case are now dead. Under such circumstances a case of this type usually involves the examination and interpretation of whatever evidence has survived. Although this is indeed a valuable and applicable context for semiotic analysis, I decided the two remaining cases would give you a broader playing field and a greater chance for success. After discussing her case with me, Annalisa and I decided in fairness to the rest of you that she should withdraw her case from consideration."

"Why in the world did you do that?" Karin wondered.

Will looked to Annalisa. "We want the rest of you to know that Annalisa and I are now a couple." He waited for the spontaneous applause to end.

LB quipped. "I'm very upset with you, Dr. Sheridan."

"Why is that, LB?"

"Because there's no hope for you and me now since that white hussy has stolen you away." Elvis looked sad.

"Don't worry LB, there is still hope. We're not exclusive," Lisa consoled him.

Elvis raised an eyebrow in question, but patted his hands together in glee. Will smiled and shook his head no. LB reached over and patted the top of the Ranger sniper's hand. "No hope here either, brother. But if the wife ever leaves me, you get the first call."

Karin sat up straighter in her chair, as if that were possible. Her eyes widened. "That means you picked my case."

Will nodded. "Karin presented the case of Deputy Sheriff Delbert Copeland, who was recently tried and convicted of murder in Fort Charles, Iowa, Karin's hometown and not too far from here. She believes her father was framed by at least two of the town's most notable citizens, one Albert Young, owner of the Ford dealership in Fort Charles and Deputy Sheriff Copeland's boss, Sheriff Buck Miller. After I read her proposal, I believe Karin is correct. I'll give you all more details on the case and the case folder when we meet next." Will turned to Karin. "Your case gives us the best chance of success, but I think there is something you still need to tell us."

"How did you know?"

"It's what I do," he said.

As tears streamed down both cheeks Karin Gladstone said, "Deputy Sheriff Copeland is my father. Gladstone is my mother's name." Lisa reached over and put her hand atop Karin's. LB took his scarf off and gently wrapped it around her throat. She cried a bit more, took a handkerchief from her purse, dried her tears and said, "Thanks guys, this really means a lot to me."

"The next thing we need to do is form a rapid response investigation team, an RRIT if you will. For example, I want Mike to go undercover and start working at Al Young's car dealership. Don't worry Mike, I'll teach you all there is to know about selling cars. It's a form of persuasion. I want you to infiltrate his inner circle."

"No worries, sir," Mike acknowledged. "We will adapt and overcome."

"Very well. But I'll need you to send back intel on a secure cell phone to our Director of Communications, or the DOC and that very important job falls to LB." Instead of being delighted, LB was crestfallen.

"No disrespect sir, but I want to be a field agent too. Is this because I'm gay?"

Will chuckled. "Not at all," he assured him. "Karin, how many blacks live in your hometown?"

She grinned, her upper lip curling at the edge. "Exactly zero."

"See the problem, LB?"

"Got it, sir. But for the sake of the team I'm prepared to go whiteface, à la Michael Jackson." They all laughed.

"That won't be necessary. But don't think you aren't a field agent. Even though I have established you as our DOC, that doesn't preclude you from setting up in the field when and as needed."

"Oh, goody," LB said, clapping his hands.

With LB placated, Will turned to Karin. "For obvious reasons we have to limit your presence in the field. We don't want Young getting suspicious and thinking that you are snooping around." She nodded. "That said, your presence in town during the weekends is a normal part of your routine, is it not?"

She confirmed that it was. "Especially now with dad incarcerated and me having to look after the house," she explained.

"Okay," Will allowed, "this will provide Mike a contact point with another agent in the field but any contact between you two should be 100% clandestine. None of the principals or persons of interest to this investigation should ever see the two of you together. Later on, I'll instruct you both in tradecraft, or spycraft as some call it. And one more thing, Karin. I need you to liaise between us and your father in prison, but you can't visit him when we are there. However, you might be able to glean additional information from your weekly meetings with him and this intel and anything that Mike gives you should immediately be sent across to the DOC," Will said, indicating to LB, who was taking notes.

"And dear LB," Will added, "write this down and underline it. You are to contact me night or day at any hour when you receive a field communiqué either from Mike or Karin."

"Any time night or day, boss man," LB recited.

Will nodded. "It has to be this way LB, for the protection and security of our team. I need to know immediately when you receive intel reports so I can determine if it is actionable intelligence. Lastly," and here he turned to Lisa, "Annalisa and I will begin an investigation into the disappearance of young Amish girls who do not return from *Rumspringa,* their opportunity to temporarily leave the church and experience life on the outside. Some return, some don't, and I'm interested in those who for some reason have lost contact with their families. According to Karin's paper, this is an issue Deputy Sheriff Copeland was also investigating and I have reason to believe it is somehow linked to those who conspired to frame him for murder.

"One last thing for tonight before I dismiss you. I require from each of you the utmost secrecy when you are under-cover. This protects the mission, but more importantly, it protects you. We are dealing with some very bad actors who have no qualms about killing other human beings, so be very, very careful out there. I can't stress that enough." From the serious expressions covering their faces, he saw his message had gotten through to them.

"Mike, your cover is that you are researching the routine everyday communication practices that constitute persuasion in the car buying interaction between seller and buyer. Karin, you are researching the communication structure within state and federal prisons. LB, you are looking into the most modern communication technologies currently deployed by the NSA, CIA, and FBI. Lisa and I will be doing an ethnographic study of the ritual practices in non-mainstream religious sects such as the Amish and the Mennonites, with particular interest in *Rumspringa.*"

"Everyone understand their cover and the need for secrecy?" All nodded in the affirmative. "I will also give you a code word to be used only if you believe your cover has been blown, your safety is compromised, and you require immediate extraction. Anyone remember Aristotle's term for an indisputable sign, that is, a sign whose meaning is unambiguous?"

LB immediately raised his hand and threw one end of his silk scarf over his left shoulder. He stood and shouted, "*Tekmērion!*"

"*Tekmērion* it is," Will acknowledged. "And don't be afraid to use it if you are in trouble. With that said, every two weeks we will meet together here at the university or at my duplex and we will do a full debriefing. However," Will announced, "we will convene as a class at my house next Wednesday, same time. Don't eat dinner. I will have pizza and beer for all of you. At that time, I will brief you in greater detail on the case, go over specific assignments and we'll have a strategy session. See you then," he said, formally dismissing the class into the bitter cold and crystalline dark of the Iowa night.

CHAPTER TWENTY-NINE

Assignments

On Wednesday he had everyone seated around the oval kitchen table, Lisa taking drink orders. After everyone had settled, drinks in front of them, Will called them to order. "Pizza will be here in about one hour so let's get to it. For your information I have contacted and informed my colleagues at the FBI of our case and our plans. They will assist us with technical resources and share intel. More importantly, they will provide overwatch for us."

Next to each student he distributed handouts of case folders detailing the particulars of the case. "You can read this in more detail at your leisure but here are the high points. Deputy Sheriff Delbert Copeland was arrested and charged with the crime of murder. He supposedly raped and killed a woman named Penny Prescott. He was apprehended by the sheriff as he tried to leave the scene of the crime. He was quickly tried and found guilty of second-degree murder and sentenced to a minimum of 30 years in the state prison. He maintains his innocence and swears he had nothing to do with the crime. He strongly believes he was framed because of the work he was doing on another case. That case concerned the investigation of a series of unsolved missing persons and possibly implicated some of the other more notable citizens in the town of Fort Charles, Iowa."

"And as you might remember from our last meeting, he also happens to be the father of our dear Karin who, of course, despite her familial bias is absolutely convinced her father has been caught in a cruel and vicious frame-up. After I researched the facts of the case, and did a deep semiotic analysis of the crime I concluded she is correct. Our job then, is to further investigate the charges against Deputy Sheriff Copeland and bring forth the facts that exonerate him so we can free him and bring to justice whoever actually committed the crime. You will also notice in the handout I have given you that I have not provided the details of my semiotic analysis of the case. You will receive those after we have finished our work together and absolved Karin's father of all charges in this matter. I do this because I do not want to bias your own thinking and analysis at this time."

"Your first assignment is this. After you have read all the material in the case folders I have handed you, using the semiotic theories, information, and knowledge you learned during the Fall seminar, I expect you to do a formal and written analysis of the case with your conclusions stated and supported. I also expect you to submit your written recommendations for how we can proceed on the basis of your conclusions. Notice too, I have provided you with all the references you might need, such as case law precedents and citations, the facts and evidence of the case against Copeland, and his defense. You have also received a relevant list of web addresses, URLs, and Internet postings of anything that was written at the time about the crime. I have also arranged for you to have access via the computer to the full pdf transcripts of the case for and against Deputy Sheriff Delbert Copeland. I'm also available to you to handle any questions you might have in the process of your work. To that end we will continue to meet during our regularly scheduled seminar day every other Wednesday so we can brief each other and keep each other apprised of our progress as we build our team and begin working together as a rapid response investigation team."

He looked around the table at his students diligently taking notes and asked, "Any questions for me at this time? Very well, hearing none, after you have finished with your notetaking, I want to give you your specific assignments." He waited until he saw all his graduate students looking at him. "We will start with LB."

LB raised a hand in protest. "Don't you start with me, sir!" he said facetiously, looking elegant in the tight cut of his very narrow haute couture Hugo Boss suit, the coat worn over his bare chest. Will was certain LB had borrowed the suit from Lisa. LB sucked in his cheeks and pursed his lips.

"Runway model, or runaway model?" Will asked, the rest of the students curious as well.

LB laughed and nodded and added a wrist flip for clarification. "Gay supermodel."

"LaDamian, as I explained last week, despite your theatrical talents I can't put you in the field, much as I want to."

The gay supermodel sucked in his cheeks again, giving the slim features of his face an even more gaunt appearance, his eyes gone suddenly vacuous. He waited for an explanation.

"There are simply no African-Americans in all of Fort Charles. I checked. And Karin can confirm this."

"Time to integrate these white folks," LB declared.

"I couldn't agree more," Will said, "but I need your technical skills more than I need your acting and social skills. All commo will go through you. In addition, you will be our IT guy and our systems analyst."

"You can depend on me," LB said.

"I know I can and I appreciate the offer. Karin, for obvious reasons, I can't put you in the field, at least at the start. I need you to provide for the team an enriched context and understanding of the ethnomethodological practices of the folks in Fort Charles. You know some of the people there and some of them know you. Which is not to say I can't use you later in the investigation because if anyone has a legitimate reason for being in town, it's you."

Seated next to him, as she nodded her can do agreement, he could smell the perfume of her hair. He looked at her again as she furiously scribbled her notes and out of the corner of his eye noticed Lisa smiling at him. Both women had keen observational abilities that no doubt would later come in handy.

"Mike, I need you in the field as deep cover. As stereotypical as it sounds you fit the bill for insertion into Fort Charles. You're smart, you're tough and well-trained, you can think your way through things and I need you to get as much intel from on the inside as possible." Mike Brisbane positively beamed under his military haircut. "That reminds me, Mike, no more haircuts for a while and even though the wife might not like it, grow me a mustache."

"Already on it, Dr. Sheridan," he said, fingering a two-day stubble below his nose.

Will paused and took a minute to look down at his notes. "One more thing, Karin. I forgot to add that I need you to prepare in-depth dossiers on the principal actors in your dad's case. And I need them soon as possible. I'll review them with the rest of the team. He paused and looked again at his graduate students. "The more we know about who we are dealing with, the better for us. I'll ask Lisa to assist you."

"Of course," Lisa said without looking up from her notetaking. He turned to Lisa, waiting patiently until he caught her eye. "I also need your forensic and analytical abilities in the field with me, not to mention your language skills. I will brief you on your role in just a bit."

"How did you know I had language skills?" she asked for the sake of the class and for the sake of maintaining her cover.

Before he could answer, LB said in sublime solemnity, "It's what he does, Lisa; and of all people you should know that by now." She squeezed his dark blue sharkskin cloth pant leg just above the knee with her thumb and index finger. "Give me some sugar," she said, as he jumped in his chair. He quickly kissed her cheek and she released her grip on his skinny leg.

Will ignored the horseplay and looked at his watch. "We have about another twenty minutes or so before the pizza gets here. I want you to start thinking of yourselves as an integrated team with specific roles to play as I give you an overview of the case and lay out a strategy for us to pursue. After that I want your critiques, your reviews, your questions, your comments and your strategies to proceed, written up and ready for presentation next week, please."

"Let me review the case as we now understand it. Deputy Sheriff Copeland is charged with the crime of killing one Penelope Prescott, a female in the employ of Albert Young's Ford dealership. Although convicted of second-degree murder because no evidence of intent or planning was discovered, a first-degree murder warrant was not filed. For your information, a first-degree murder conviction in Iowa carries a sentence of life without parole, with the first five years served in solitary confinement. Del Copeland has steadfastly maintained his innocence, which is not unusual in crimes such as these even when the person is guilty."

Next to him Karin said, "He didn't do it" in a whisper just loud enough for everyone to hear.

"My study of the court transcripts leads me to believe that you are correct," Sheridan agreed. "Our job as the investigative team is to discover substantial evidence that will support your claim. This is our team mission. We start with the assumption, our working hypothesis, if you will, that your father did not kill Penelope Prescott. This assumes logically that someone else killed her. Our job is to discover irrefutable evidence that supports the conclusion that someone else killed her and in our best-case scenario, discover who that person is."

"Could be more than one killer," Mike suggested.

"Exactly. This is the type of thinking and input I need from you guys. Remember, we're a team now. This is no longer about a grade. Everybody gets in A at the end of the practicum whether we solve the case or not. This is about a man's life, his family, his career, and his reputation." The team look quickly at Karin, as she held her chin up. That's what he wanted to see from her.

"The sheriff, first on the crime scene and the law enforcement officer who arrested your father, is definitely a prime suspect for our investigation," he said to Karin. "I'll need a full workup on him first. Not just the facts of his life, but everything you know about him. I need to know the routine practices of his day. Who does he talk to, where does he go, what does he do in his off time? What do others say about him? This is the ethnomethodological analysis of your investigation. I know it's a big ask, but Lisa has already offered to help and I'm certain LB is willing to assist you as time permits." Karin wrote fiercely. He waited until she finished.

"Mike, big dog, I think Albert Young is also in play. He is the central power in town and much of what goes on in Fort Charles seems to revolve around him. He's an alpha dog like you, so I need you to be a pack dog. Ever sold a car?"

"No sir, but I've stolen everything from an Army Jeep to a Soviet-era T-72 main battle tank. If I can bullshit my way into stealing a commanding officer's Jeep, I sure as hell can sell a brand spanking new Ford F-150 pickup truck. In fact, I can put you in one tomorrow morning, Dr. Sheridan," he said, grinning. "Mine's for sale."

Will nodded. This was the gung-ho attitude the team found so infectious. "Let's not get ahead of ourselves. Before you go, I've got a book for you to take home written by an industry insider in the car sales business. Read it and learn it. Once you feel comfortable with the routines and language of selling a car, I want you to get a job at the Chevy dealership across from Young's place."

"Why there?" Mike wondered. "I would have thought you would want me to work for Young."

"I do. When you start setting sales records at the Chevy dealership, he'll come calling. I want him to think it's his idea to put you in his organization. Besides, there's a very good chance he is looking for someone to hire."

"Why is that?" Lisa asked.

"Penny Prescott sold cars for Albert Young."

"Hmmm," LB said, now wearing a monocle in one eye and holding in his left hand an unlit cigarette sticking out of a six-inch-long ebony holder. "Devious," he said, "and at the same time, brilliant."

Will had to laugh at FDR's affected New York accent. "Well, I don't know about that," Will said, "but we will certainly find out if it works. There is something else that really bothers me about this case that I want to share with you guys. Call it instinct or intuition if you will—and this is something I want you guys to know—there will come a time when after all the analysis, investigation, and consideration of the facts, you might have to trust your gut feelings. Here's what I know. Over the last few years, it seems a number of young women have gone missing from the area surrounding Fort Charles. But no bodies have been found, there is no evidence of their reappearance, and also no contact whatsoever with the families who filed the missing person reports. This is an anomaly in the case and anomalies are, to quote myself, highly significant. I don't know if the missing persons are runaways from the religious sects that have settled here in Iowa or what. In terms of semiotics this is a highly significant sign. Yes, people disappear, yes people run away, but not one missing person has been found or been in contact with other family members. This significant event warrants further investigation." The team agreed with his assessment.

"This aspect of the case, if it indeed becomes pertinent to the case, will provide cover for Lisa and I. I will be a professor from the university doing research on *Rumspringa* in different religious communities like the Amish and the Mennonites. Without seeming suspicious, this will provide us cover and permit us to ask questions of culture that we can use as a bridge to learn more about the missing young women. Lisa will be my doctoral graduate student research assistant. I'll see to it that any calls concerning our research work or our bona fides are directed to Dean Carpenter. He and my contacts in the FBI are the only outsiders who have been briefed on the case. LB, that's where you come in. The contact numbers Lisa and I will give out will ring directly into a service you will set up. The gear is on its way and should be here by Friday."

The monocle dropped as he clapped his hands, the cigarette holder clenched between his teeth in the corner of his mouth once again casting him into the look of a black FDR.

"All communication from the outside will come into you first. Everyone will have a burner throwaway cell phone," he said handing them out, "and I'm waiting for a wiretap subpoena to come up out of the West Des Moines FBI office. No recordings until then," he said to LB.

"Thereafter?" FDR asked, in a passable New York accent.

"Everything goes on record," Will said, chuckling to himself. The doorbell rang and Lisa's phone buzzed, indicating a message had arrived.

"Pizza's here," said Lisa, looking at her cell phone message as she ran to the door.

"Meeting adjourned. Let's eat. Beer and sodas in the fridge," said Will. After one more meeting same time Wednesday, we go into action. Karin, how are you holding up?"

With a layer of steel showing below her resolute green eyes she said, "Ready, willing, and able."

CHAPTER THIRTY

Karin's Show

After the meeting with the graduate students officially ended and the pizzas were all wolfed down, the team sat and talked and relaxed and had a good time. LB had come with Mike since he did not have his own car in Iowa. On the way to the meeting Mike picked him up from on-campus graduate student housing in his four-wheel-drive truck. Mike needed to get back to his wife and with apologies and thanks for the food and beer, he and LB shook hands all around and took off. After they left, Karin asked if she could stay a while longer. "Of course," Will said, and invited her to stay as long as she liked. "Another beer?"

Already a bit tipsy through the eyes, she shrugged through her shoulders and said, "Why not? It's been a tough time for me and I finally feel a sense of hope now, thanks to you guys."

Will poured her another glass of beer from the bottle. She drank half of it down, licking the foam mustache from her upper lip. Seated on the couch next to Annalisa, Will moved and settled into the recliner, feet up, socks showing, and sipped a single malt Scotch whisky, his new position affording him a better view of both Karin and Lisa. They talked for another half hour after which Karin excused herself to pee before she said her goodbyes. "I've had such a good time tonight. I can't thank you two enough.

And just between the three of us," she said, a note of conspiracy in her voice, "I think you two make a great couple."

Will helped her into her blue thigh-length parka and Annalisa opened the front door. She held the storm door open to look through the porch light before quickly closing it. "Wow!" she said. Outside, a thick sheet of snow painted the glass storm door white. As Lisa opened the door again to give them both a look into the swirling maelstrom, Karin stumbled past Lisa to have a better look. "I can't see my car," she said, wonder and a little trepidation in her voice. She hiccupped once and with her hand covered her mouth and a rueful smile. Will had seen enough. He pulled her back inside.

"That settles it. You are our guest tonight. You may have the spare bedroom across from Annalisa.

"This is so very kind of you, Dr. Sheridan," she said, struggling to extricate herself from the constriction of the tight blue parka. Lisa helped her get her arm out and showed her to the bedroom, watched Karin hang her coat in the empty closet, sit and take off her boots before she came back into the living room and retook her seat on the couch next to Annalisa. She rearranged her long hair with her fingers and said, "Since I don't have to drive tonight, may I taste one of those Scotches you're drinking?"

Will got up and got a shot glass from the kitchen, then poured her finger of the amber liquid. "This is a single malt whisky called Glenmorangie." He poured one for Lisa too, who held up her glass in anticipation. They clicked glasses and toasted each other with a quick sip and Will stretched out again in the recliner.

"Oooh," Karin said, savoring the sip of the whisky. "This is so good. I can smell flowers and honey. "How do they do that?"

"All in the making of a good Scotch," Lisa explained. "Good water, good malt, good sherry oak casks, and a good distiller."

"I'll drink to that," Will said, and drank to that.

As he poured the girls another round, Lisa asked Karin, "Would you permit me a small indiscretion?"

"Sure," said Karin helpfully, wondering what it might be. Karin had the top two buttons of her pale blue Oxford button-down shirt open. On the occasions when she leaned forward the shirt fell away from her bra like a spinnaker luffing in the wind, allowing Lisa to see the full tight curve of her fellow student's breast as it disappeared into the soft padding of her bra cup. Lisa unbuttoned the third button, further exposing the white cleavage of Karin's breasts. "One more, just to be daring?" Lisa asked, daring her.

Karin covered the fourth button with the hand not holding her shot glass. "I'm not a lesbian," she said with a little giggle, and took another sip of the cold Scotch.

"Neither am I," Lisa told her.

Karin looked dumbfounded. "I thought you like to have sex with girls." She looked quickly at Will, who was enjoying the show more than he should. "No disrespect to you, Will Sheridan."

He smiled and graciously said, "None taken."

Lisa continued. "I am a sexualist. I enjoy having sex with attractive men and women, but if I had to choose..." She tipped her shot glass at Will.

"I think that is so cool and so liberating," Karin said, finishing her drink. "But I don't think a small-town girl like me is quite ready for that. But I do want to say you are the most beautiful woman I have ever seen, and I've been to Minneapolis and Chicago. You are intimidatingly attractive. Sometimes I can't take my eyes off you."

"Well, thank you for that wonderful complement. I think you're very pretty, too."

In exasperation Karin blew the chestnut bangs from her forehead. "I don't know." She looked at Annalisa. "Pretty enough to take to bed?"

"More than enough."

Will grew increasingly interested to see where the repartee between the two gorgeous women would lead.

"Okay," said Annalisa. "Here's what we will do. We both have had too much to drink, so no sex tonight but I want you to do me a favor."

Karin went from sad to alcohol happy again. "Okay. I agree. No sex tonight," she said carefully articulating each word. She flashed a mischievous grin. "But you can do whatever else you want."

Annalisa grinned. "Just a small favor. I want to see those beautiful breasts of yours, that's all."

"You really think the girls are beautiful?" she asked, looking down and sizing herself up. Lisa nodded vigorously, as did Will in support. "I don't know," Karin said, looking rather doubtful again, then suddenly brightened and laughed. "I'll show you mine if you show me yours. You go first!" The results of her liquid courage brought a flush from the top of her breasts up through her throat and into her ears.

"Very well," said Lisa. "If that's what it takes; as our guest you get to call the shots." She uncrossed her long elegant legs, the top of her thighs shining under her mini-skirt, stood and settled the hem of the short skirt just above midthigh. She removed her sweater and set it aside. She took the bottom of her silk camisole in both hands, inverted the material over her head, and dropped it on the couch so that part of the silk flowed over Karin's arm. Karin felt the warmth of Lisa's body in the silk and could smell the perfume lingering there. She sat as if transfixed, mouth slightly agape, shocked to see Lisa was not wearing a bra.

Lisa stood before her smiling, hands on her hips, like a supermodel, legs crossed. Then, like a ballerina, she raised her arms, extending them from her sides, hands bent at the wrists. The delicate movement of a swan accentuated her long graceful lines. Karin could see the pectoral muscles of Lisa's chest lengthen and lift the breasts of the dancer. Lisa turned slowly, stood partially in profile and used her fingers to lengthen her already erect nipples. She turned her back to Karin and heard the gasp of excitement behind her. Lisa's back was as beautiful as her front, exquisite in form and physique. Her trapezius, rhomboids, and erector spinae stood in natural relief, shaping the lithe muscled contours of her back.

Whether she had planned it or not, her posing had a remarkable effect on Will as he studied the living, breathing human work of art standing across from Karin. Lisa completed her dancer's turn, combing through the silk of her white blonde hair with both hands, an action that raised her breasts even higher on her chest, at the same time lengthening the rectus abdominus of her stomach muscles. Now Will understood why she had set the waist of her skirt so low on her hips. Her stomach muscles flowed into the cut of her obliques and into the wall of muscle just above her shaved mons pubis. At this point, Will was ready to rip the skirt down to her knees and take her in front of Karin, but he did not, preferring to see what might yet unfold in the dramatic dance of sexual tension developing between the two women.

Lisa smiled and sat on the couch next to Karin. "Your turn."

Karin shook her head slowly from side to side "I can't compete with that. You have the most beautiful body of any woman I've ever seen." She looked at Will for confirmation of her assessment.

"One of the best I've ever seen."

Lisa tried to assure her. "It's not a competition, dear Karin. It's a show of liberation. We are women and we have the power to do as we please. If we want to show our breasts, we have the courage and the right to do so." As they sat shoulder to shoulder, hip against hip, one of Lisa's breasts grazed the soft part of Karin's upper arm, exposed in her short-sleeved blue shirt.

"I did say I would," she said sheepishly now, as if she had no other choice. She stood and smiled her lip into its characteristic curl at the top of the corner of her mouth. "But I just want you to know I sure as hell can't top that."

"Remember, it's not a contest, Karin," Lisa assured her. "It's a show. Each body is unique and each body has a beauty to it. Show us the unique beauty of your body."

Emboldened by Lisa's words, Karin stood in front of Lisa, their knees almost touching, Will noted, and with trembling fingers unbuttoned the chambray blue shirt, and pulled the tails out of and over the tan khaki pants she was so fond of wearing. The tails of the shirt out, she undid the last two white buttons on the shirt and let it hang tantalizingly between her breasts for a moment. Then she slowly opened the unbuttoned shirt, settled it over her shoulders and pulled her arms clear. She dropped the shirt on the couch next to Annalisa.

"Beautifully done," Lisa said, clapping her elegant, long fingered hands in studied appreciation.

Karin used the encouragement to slide first one bra strap down over her muscular shoulders, then the other. She turned her back to the couch, smiling at Will, reached back and unhooked the three prongs of her bra strap, letting the two loose ends fall open against her back. Her hands held the cups of her bra to keep it from falling to the floor. Much to Sheridan's chagrin, she then turned back to face Lisa and let the lacey brassiere fall, her breasts covered only by the cup of her hands. In a final dénouement, she clasped her hands behind her back. She was slim like Lisa, but also hard-muscled, the result of many years walking the cornfields in the hot humid summers of Iowa, pulling the tassels from the plants before the seed corn matured and cross-pollinated, costing the farmer tens of thousands of dollars per field.

Her breasts were tight and high, resplendent in form and fitment. When she moved, they did not jiggle; they dropped and immediately reset themselves on her chest. She was at least a C cup and her nipples were uniformly bound in pink at the tip. Her nipples were half the length of Lisa's, but both were erect and reddening. To conclude her presentation, she did a small curtsy and nearly stumbled into the couch, the fall seating her next to Annalisa. Karin laughed at her little tumble, her bare chest rising and falling as she breathed her excitement in and out, the sleek muscles of her belly rising and falling.

"May I touch?" Annalisa asked decorously. "You have such beautiful skin."

"Oh, what the hell," Karin replied, flipping her thick long hair over her shoulder and out of the way. Lisa drew a manicured hot red fingernail under the curve of Karin's breast, tracing a rising line to the top of the crinkled aureole. She delicately squeezed the nipple with her thumb and forefinger, and then bent forward and kissed its tip. "Your turn."

Karin leaned forward and nursed Lisa's nipple into her mouth, her lips encircling the base of the nipple and like a baby suckled rhythmically at her breast. Lisa held Karin's head until it suddenly went limp and dropped into her lap, her mouth still open, her lips wet. She looked at Will as if to say what the hell and laughed. "You're not going to believe this. I think she just passed out."

Will laughed at the incongruity of the act. "These young graduate students simply have no tolerance for excellent whisky these days. Too much dope and cocaine. And it doesn't say a lot for your ability to seduce."

"Oh, don't be an idiot. I was going to stop there anyway. Get over here and help me trundle her off to bed." Will came over and despite his obvious and apparent physiological difficulties at the moment, waited as Lisa turned Karin over onto her back. He bent over, put one arm under her shoulders and the other under her knees, and lifted her up off the couch in one smooth turn. "Damn, you're strong," Lisa commented.

"I don't think she weighs a hundred and ten pounds," Will said, with expert analytical certainty. "Let's put her in the bed in the spare room and you go get her a nightgown, please." Will switched the light on with an elbow, Karin's long hair cascading in a dark blonde and chestnut waterfall over his arm. Half-naked in his arms, he could barely resist the impulse to kiss her rose red lips, partly open above her white teeth. He put her down on the bed and took her white socks off. Lisa came in with one of her sheer nighties in hand.

"It's all I've got," she said defensively. "I'm a very sexy girl."

"Yes, you are," Will agreed.

"Now let's skin these pants off her," Lisa said and undid the button holding the waist together. And as she unzipped the khakis in one smooth pull of the zipper, she said, "This girl is all about buttons. I wonder why that is?"

"You're the forensic psychologist," Will said. "You figure it out."

On the bed Lisa knelt and sat her behind on the backs of her heels. "She wants the security of the manly button but she's smart enough to know she's repressed and conservative. wants to take the chance that at some point she can unbutton herself for someone."

"Isn't that what she did tonight?" Will asked. "She undid herself for you."

"I'm not so sure of that. Don't forget she undid herself for you too, probably more so than me. She knew very well you were watching us. You lift her ass, big man, and I'll pull at the knees. This girl wears her military khakis one size too small."

"It sure does a wonderful job of accentuating the curves of her excellent behind," Will declared.

"So I've noticed. And I've noticed you noticing."

"Only in aesthetic appreciation of her comely female figure."

"Is that why you're still showing that big boner?"

He didn't respond. "Ready? Pull!" he commanded, lifting Karin's hips to clear the bed. As Lisa pulled the tight khakis over Karin's slim hips, like a baker rolling a thin strip of dough, her panties rolled down over the fine hair of her pubic bone. One more good pull and Karin's ass let go of the pants but her white panties, also edged in lace to match her bra, bunched just above her knees.

Lisa remarked as she observed the sleeping woman, "Someone needs to take this woman for a Brazilian. She's got a cute little pussy, if you can get through the jungle of her pubic hair to find it. These panties are soaked and by the looks of it she's still wet. I think she might have come sometime during the show."

"I know I almost did," Will said, and pulled the thin white cotton panties off her heels. "You're right. Definitely soaked through in the middle."

Lisa left the room for a moment and came back with a towelette which she used with the efficiency of a nurse to clean and wipe the moisture that looked like hot wet silk from Karin's vagina. "She'll be more comfortable like that," she said, observing her handiwork. Working together, Will and Lisa got Karin into the nightgown, first pooling the sheer cloth in a circle like a silk scarf around her neck, then pulling an arm through, then the other, then draping material over her breasts and her belly to reach the top of her thighs.

"Her breasts do make quite a positive impression on that nightgown," Will said, admiring the effect.

Lisa pushed him off the bed. They gathered up Karin's clothes, turned off the lights and closed the door. Lisa ran downstairs and started a short load in the washing machine as Will waited for her on the couch in the next room. When Lisa returned from the laundry room, they worked together to draw down the sexual tension that had been building in both of them during Karin's show earlier in the evening. They both came as the buzzer sounding the end of the washing machine's cycle signaled their time was up.

After a short cycle in the dryer, just long enough for a serious cuddle, Will helped Lisa fold Karin's warm clothes in a neat pile, returned upstairs, carefully opened the door to the spare bedroom and checked on her. Lisa put the clean and folded things on the night table next to the sleeping figure, who did not stir.

"Remind me to wash that pillowcase tomorrow," Will said. "That's a healthy and generous amount of drool for anybody that isn't mooing."

They switched off the light, closed the door and Lisa pulled him into her bedroom for a short but warm hug before Will kissed her good night, wished her a good sleep and found the comfort of his own bed downstairs. Outside, an unrelenting blizzard piled snow nearly two feet deep, higher in drifts that rose like frozen waves atop an ocean of white.

CHAPTER THIRTY-ONE

Breakthrough

The next day around 10:30, already at the breakfast table, Lisa sat spooning milk over her apple muesli, Will eating a piece of buttered toast with ham on it. Karin flitted into the bathroom, her hair a mess. Ten minutes later she padded into the kitchen on bare feet, her shirt fully unbuttoned down the middle, breasts flaring the fabric, her hair combed and in place and smelling of hairspray. "Well good morning to you," Lisa said, and Will mumbled a greeting through a full mouth.

"Morning guys," she said, standing there looking sheepish, young, fit, and attractive all at once. She had put her laundered panties on, Will and Lisa noticed.

Will waved her into a chair next to Lisa. "Come and sit and we'll talk while I make you breakfast. Eggs?"

"Two, please. Sunny side up. And two pieces of toast, if you don't mind."

"Not at all. I'll get right on it," he said, taking the last bite of his toast with him as he pushed away from the table.

"Orange juice?" Lisa offered from the carafe at the table.

"That would be swell. My throat is parched. I feel like I've swallowed a cat." She sat at the table and crossed her legs at the knees, pooling the tails of her shirt together to hide the white of the V of her panties. "I want to apologize to you both for my behavior last night. I got drunk and did things I probably shouldn't have done."

"Don't be silly," Lisa said. "We are all adults here. You didn't do anything you shouldn't have done," Lisa said, took her by the chin and gave her a quick comforting kiss on lips tasting of mouthwash. "You did last night what you needed to do, no more."

Karin took a deep breath, exposing the inside slope of her breasts to them both. "I had a ball last night, I really did, but I gotta ask. Did we do anything else in bed last night?"

As Will brought the shiny eggs and buttered toast next to a thick slice of ham browned in the pan and set the plate before Karin, Lisa reassured her. "You fell asleep on the couch. Will carried you to bed, we undressed you, put you in my nightgown and you were gone from the world."

Karin laughed at herself. "You mean I passed out."

"Yes, you did," they both said.

She took a bite of eggs, ham, and then chomped the toast. "I know this may sound weird but were my panties very wet when you took them off?"

"Yes," Lisa said. "As a matter of fact, your panties were truly and finely soaked. That's why we washed everything for you."

"Milk?" Will offered.

"Yes, please," Karin said and quickly drank down more than half her glass and waited patiently for Will to refill it. "Can I tell you guys a secret?"

"You can tell us anything you want. Your secrets are safe with us," Will promised.

"I think I had a wet dream last night. Can girls have wet dreams?"

"Only the lucky ones," said Lisa as if she knew something about the subject. "It's your body releasing a very great deal of tension that you have kept tightly buttoned up within you these past few months. Last night you let go a little bit. And look at you now," she said, indicating the unbuttoned nudity of Karin's breasts.

"I really don't know why I came to the table dressed like this. It seems so wanton and sinful and yet I feel so safe and comfortable with you guys."

"The sexy look suits you, I might add," Will observed. "And that makes it all the more fun. For the first time in a very long time you had fun."

"I did. I really had a lot of fun last night."

"And how do you feel now?" Lisa asked, playing the role of the forensic psychologist.

"Honestly, except for the fog of a slight headache, I feel strangely liberated, like a weight has been lifted from my chest and I can breathe again." She demonstrated for them.

Lisa opened both hands, palms up. "Well, there you are. Liberated."

Karin asked for another piece of toast with grape jelly, drank another glass of milk, stood, took off her shirt in front of them and said, "Liberated." They laughed at her boldness and after she thanked them for breakfast, she went back into her room and slept another three hours.

"She's not that liberated yet, despite what she thinks," Will said, "and no matter what the two of you may believe."

Lisa stopped a bite of toast in midair. "What could possibly make you say that?" she asked, a little hurt that he would reject her analysis.

"Oh, don't get your virtual panties in a bunch."

"You know I don't wear panties, not even to breakfast, and not even virtual ones."

Will explained. "I noticed a significant semiotic action or, in this instance, the lack of an action, I should say."

"What do you mean?"

"You saw it yourself."

"The open shirt and no bra."

"Nope. The panties."

"Oh, the panties. I see."

"Yes, the panties you saw. Had she been truly and fully liberated, as the two of you say, in fine echo I might add, she would've come to the breakfast table without any underwear on at all. And I offer yourself as a prima facie case of one who is truly and fully liberated."

"No panties," Lisa confirmed, offering herself in evidence. "Your point is taken and well-made. Thank you for the generosity of your analysis. What do you think we should do about it? You know, should we further assist her on the path to full and complete liberation? I'm certainly willing to help if you are willing to assist me."

"And that is why I love you as I do, darling Lisi," he said, kissing the taste of orange juice from her lips. "But I think not. She is still too vulnerable; the wounds are still too fresh. Granted she has come a long way down the road to liberation and dealing with the trauma of her father's false incarceration. You have given her guidance and shown her what is possible. The next step has to be hers, or there will be no growth, only dependency. Even though last night was about sex at the surface level of her psychology, it was not about sex," he said, continuing his analysis. "This was, as you so rightly put it, about psychological stress and tension symbolically manifested in Karin's actions, first by getting drunk, and then by her first playful steps with you as her guide holding her hand and leading her to having a bit of fun. She has made significant strides consciously, to a lesser degree unconsciously in dealing with her father's horribly fucked up situation, and how she has had to deal with a mess not of her own making."

Lisa kissed her index finger and put it to his lips. "And that is why I love you as I do."

The blizzard outside stormed away all the noise not natural to wind and blowing snow, steeping the house in quiet inside and Will and Lisa took advantage of the silence and resumed their work and study. Karin came to lunch fully dressed and Will made her a bowl of beef consommé with German pancakes cut into strips.

"Wow. This is good," she said between appreciative slurps.

Lisa came in for a sandwich so he left the two alone to chat. He had more work to do and calls to make.

Before he took his robust roast beef sandwich and went down to the work cave, he admonished the two. "Karin. I need a full dossier on the sheriff, on Al Young, and whatever you might know or can find out about Penny Prescott. And you Lisa, I need a full research report on the religious sects within 100 miles of Fort Charles and please include the languages and dialects they speak." He put his hand up to his ear. "Here that? That's the sound of me cracking the whip. Let's get some work out of you two today."

"Right away, boss," Lisa said, saluting.

Will pointed to Karin. "You too."

Karin executed a snappy salute. After all, her father had been in the Army. Satisfied that his message had been heard in no uncertain terms, he went downstairs, closed and locked the door to his computer room. He knew Lisa would call if anything important came up.

After he disappeared into the basement, Lisa leaned in to Karin's ear. "You want to have some fun?"

Karin nodded conspiratorially. "But what about work?"

"Screw work. We'll get it done later. He'll be down there a good four hours before he comes up and gets something to eat. We should be back by then. There's a short window opening in this storm before the next one roars in. But first there is something I want to show you." By the hand she took Karin into her bedroom and sat her on the bed. Karin looked puzzled and not a little afraid. Lisa stepped out of her warm-up pants and stood completely naked from the waist down. She opened her legs and waited while Karin observed her.

"I'm not sure what you want me to do," Karin said, a note of caution edging her voice.

Lisa shook her head. "Just look and tell me what you see."

"Oh my God. You are completely shaved. Your pussy looks like a baby's."

"It's just as smooth," she agreed, going to her dresser and pulled out a tight pair of yoga pants, "but I'm not shaved, I am waxed, which is even better. It makes it easier for us girls to keep things clean down there, it feels and looks sexy as hell, and it heightens the sexual experience for women and men both." Karin looked skeptical, thinking of her own physiognomy, natural and undisturbed from the time she was thirteen years old. "You and I are going to get you waxed, and then we will buy you some panties sexier than something with the days of the week stamped on them." She pulled on a pair of socks, put on a sweater, stepped into her snow boots, and after sneaking out the front door, off they drove down the street slick with ice and snow.

Three hours later they returned, giggling like school girls as they tried to sneak in unnoticed, hurried to their rooms, got out their laptops and got to work. About an hour later Will came up and got a candy bar and a glass of milk. Very good, he thought to himself. I'm finally getting some production out of those two. He yelled to both closed bedroom doors "Dinner at seven. I'm cooking hamburgers and baked fries."

The next morning, Karin went into Lisa's room, having spent another night quarantined by the second blizzard coming in a chained wave down out of the Canadian Arctic and forecast to last another day or so. Lisa, still in her warm bed slid over to make room for her new bestie and Karin sat on top of the covers facing her. "I had another wet dream last night. My panties, my new sexy cotton panties were soaked in the middle again. And by the way, you're right. Much easier to keep myself clean now. And I love the feel of the fabric on my clitoris," she offered as a friendly aside.

"Are you sure you didn't masturbate last night? Lisa asked.

"Oh, no," Karin assured her. "I never do that," she confessed with some embarrassment.

"No matter. Throw them in the laundry. But tonight I want you to do something for me. I want you to try and remember your dreams. And keep a notepad and a pen ready on the night table next to your bed so you can immediately write down the dream while it's still fresh in your mind."

"Okay," she agreed but was puzzled at the unusual request. "I think you should know that I can never remember my dreams. In fact, I'm pretty sure I don't dream at all."

"Karin, darling," Lisa said, taking her by both hands, "everyone dreams or we would all become psychotic raging lunatics. Tonight, when you go to bed remind yourself to remember. You will."

The following morning the storm had not broken, snow flying incongruously sideways. Karin was up early and out the bedroom door in the silk nightie borrowed from Lisa. After a quick visit to the bathroom she discovered to her horror that her panties were once again wet. After removing them and throwing them into the laundry basket, she cleaned herself and then ran downstairs to Will's open bedroom door where she found him still asleep. She woke him with a gentle press of his shoulder.

"What's the matter, Lisa? he asked, concern in his voice but not yet turning over.

"It's Karin, Will. Sorry to bother you so early, but I really, really need to talk to you."

He turned on his reading lamp, flipped the switch for the overhead light after his eyes adjusted and invited her in. She shivered as she stood at his bedside in her negligée. He could tell she had been crying. He scooted over and lifted up a corner of the featherbed. "Close the door and get in before you let all the heat out. I don't have the furnace set to come on until 9:00 a.m."

She crawled into the warm envelope of heat where his body had been. "Could we turn off the overhead light please?"

He reached across her and flipped the switch, pitching the room into the soft muted light of the reading lamp. "Tell me what's the matter."

She cried a little before she started, wetting his pillow. "Please hold me," she said and quickly turned her backside to his front. "Last night before I went to bed, Lisa told me to try and remember my dreams."

"Why did she want you to do that?"

"I don't know. I honestly don't know. I never remember my dreams but she told me everyone dreams and so do I and I could learn to remember them."

"What happened?"

"I woke up again this morning with my panties soaked. I had to put on a fresh pair before I came down to see you."

"I can tell." She had been unconsciously pushing her behind against his crotch. For warmth, he told himself. She rolled over on her back and pulled the negligée down between her legs to cover the red panties.

"I'm afraid this pair is getting wet, too."

Will decided this was a good time to try and change the subject. "Where the hell did you two go yesterday anyway?"

"Lisa took me to get my pubic area waxed after she showed me hers."

"That woman has absolutely no shame about her body. How did it go?" he asked.

"I found out it's morbidly erotic; a strange mix of pleasure and pain, but I really like the end result. I feel truly liberated now."

"So why are you here, if I may ask?"

She turned into him, her hands closed above the meridian of her breasts, crying softly again. "Because I remember my dream. I'm a horrible, horrible person. In my dream I was having sex with my father. I knew it was wrong and yet I wanted him inside me so badly. I encouraged him and told him it was all right. It was almost as if I could feel it when he entered me. I think that's when I came and I immediately woke up. Will, I'm dreaming about having incest with my dad. What the hell is wrong with me?" she asked, pleading for an answer.

He let her sob for a minute or two and held her until she stopped. He offered her Kleenex from the nightstand and waited as she dried her eyes. "Okay," she said. "I can take it."

"There is nothing wrong with you. Two things are happening with you. As a healthy and vibrant female, you have sexual needs and urges and you have been unable to find an outlet for those needs. Annalisa tapped in to your sexual tension, an uncanny skill of hers, and out of her concern for you, tried to help you in that regard. That's the physical side of what is happening to you. Your body is trying to release those built up sexual tensions nocturnally. At the psychological level, as you know, our unconscious mind creates symbols and works through symbolic actions when we dream. Our dreams thus become interpretable symbols and that's what the semiotic interpretation of dreams is all about. Remember your Freud. He showed us there are two types of meaning in our dreams. What we remember in our dreams is called the manifest content."

"You mean me seducing my father and having sex with him?"

"Yes. But the latent content is the symbolic act of you seducing your father and the meaning we can derive from an interpretation of such symbolic actions. Would you like me to analyze your dream for you?"

She took a deep breath and nodded her head on the pillow next to him, her eyes searching his. "Yes, I want to know what's going on with me."

"How have you felt during your father's difficulties?"

"Helpless and out of control, anxious and afraid, depressed and desperate. Only in these last few days with you and Lisa have those feelings lessened somewhat."

He pushed her hair from her face where it had fallen across and obscured one of her pretty green eyes. "The unconscious mind handles our anxieties and our repressed wishes and desires. All these are expressed in our dreams."

"You mean I've always wanted to have sex with my father? "

"That's a different question for a different time. In the dream you are taking action, even if it is a sexual action. You are helping your father, trying to make him feel good, trying to ease his emotional pain and give him comfort. You remember the dream because you have now come to terms with your helplessness and lack of control. You are finding a way to regain some semblance of that control. Your father is a symbol of security and of love. You have lost that very important sense of security every person needs. You want your father back and you want to console him, to heal his pain, in other words, to love him as you know he loves you. When we love another person, we want to give them pleasure. The unconscious mind, or the id as Freud calls it, seeks pleasure. In the pursuit of pleasure, it does not recognize sexual barriers or taboos. These are socially constructed limitations. Your dreams are primal and instinctual. Your sense of self, your ego, that is, your contact with the world, is trying to heal itself."

"So I don't really want to have sex with my dad?"

"Of course not. I believe these dreams were actually triggered by a deeper, more repressed traumatic event you experienced as a young girl, a time when you did not yet have the psychological tools to deal with the fear and anxiety that traumatic event caused in young Karin."

Her eyes widened as he continued the analysis of her dream.

"I believe your father's incarceration—his being suddenly taken from you—has revived deep-seated repressed anxieties experienced when your mother left you. It is possible you were unable to fully understand her actions at the time and internalized them, thinking perhaps you were somehow responsible for your mother leaving your father. Your current dreams, thanks to Lisa having you try to remember them, are most likely an unconscious attempt to relieve the guilt of what you incorrectly thought was your responsibility. In your dreams you are symbolically taking the place of your mother, trying to be a love substitute for your father. Now that you are a fully mature young woman, you have other things to offer a man in addition to emotional love. Take it for what it's worth, but this is what I think your dreams are trying to tell you. Once we peel back the onion of meaning using our semiotic analysis of dream symbols, it permits us to understand their deeper symbolic meaning and the message becomes more understandable and relevant."

She wrapped her arms and legs around him so tightly he could barely breath. "Oh my god! I think you are right. I hated my mother for the anguish and pain she caused my father. And I hated myself because I thought I was the reason she left us. I felt I was responsible for pushing her away from him. Even as a young girl I was determined to fill the void in my father's life by loving him and being the best daughter I could be for him."

"You did a wonderful job supporting and loving him and I'm certain he knows and appreciates you for that. And one more thing I might add. The id sometimes throws us symbolic curveballs. Your father in the dream might not really be your father after all."

This puzzled her. "Who could it possibly be?"

"What does a father symbolically represent according to the Jungian archetype?" he asked her, hoping she remembered that part of lecture from class.

She thought for a moment before she answered. "Strength, security, courage, and love," she suggested.

"Very good. Now do you know anyone else who might embody those qualities and to whom you might be attracted but unwilling to engage with because of social constraints? Here Freud would say your superego, that is, your inculcation of societal rules and cultural norms, is restricting your behavior. The superego, if it is highly restrictive, could very well be the cause of your more conservative behaviors."

She said, "I have another secret to confess. Sometimes it's you in my dreams instead of my father." She searched his eyes again for any sign of condemnation, her own open and wide in the shock of inspiration that is the result of a sudden and unexpected realization. Without saying a word, she removed her negligée and put it under her pillow. She pulled her panties down, bending her legs at the knees, threw them on the floor next to the bed, and rolled back over onto her side. She pushed the pliant feminine curve of her behind against him with a newfound urgency and insistence. He discovered she was wet again.

"Karin?" he said, stopping her with a hand on her naked hip.

"Don't worry, I'm on the pill."

"I want you to know that sometimes in the clinical setting between a client and a therapist, clients form an emotional bond with their therapist and believe on the basis of this bond that there is a sexual attraction between the two of them. It is a natural psychological attempt on the part of the client to incorporate into their own psychology what the therapist symbolically represents as a person who cares, comforts, and nurtures. This is called transference. Your attraction to me may be the result of this type of transference."

She rolled over to face him again and moved his hand up to cup her breasts. "I very much appreciate the insight, the analysis, and your caution, but as far as I'm concerned, this is the next step in my personal and sexual liberation, as Lisa would say. I give myself to you freely and without any strings attached. I do so because I want to share pleasure with you. This is also my way of thanking you for caring so much about me during this extremely difficult time in my life. And I don't want you to worry that handsome head of yours for a minute. I wanted to screw you from the first day you walked in to the classroom. This is my way of finally acting on those feelings, especially now that I've come to know you not just as a professor but as a man who I want very much to be with at least once in my life so I don't regret hiding behind the wall of my conservative upbringing. And I also hope there won't be any more wet dreams at night after this, will there?" she asked.

"I don't think so. At least not for the reasons we discussed. That's not to say that in the future you won't have them again if sexual tension builds without release."

She took a deep cleansing breath into her lungs. "So, on the face of it the dream wasn't really about incest at all," she said, whimpering just a little, hoping.

"It is a little bit but not in the way people think. It was about you once and finally being able to relieve your father's pain by giving him pleasure in all this misery he has suffered. Unconsciously, now as an adult, the mind knows the greatest and simplest pleasure we can give each other is sexual."

Her breathing calmed, and across the pillow she smiled into his eyes before she kissed him. Shortly thereafter, she gave him the greatest and simplest pleasure she could, and received the same in return.

At the breakfast table later that morning, Karin sat in Lisa's white bathrobe, loosely cinched at the waist. Lisa flowed in, naked as usual from her shower, hair wrapped up in her towel like a turban, not yet ready for the imposition of clothes that confined her body.

"Morning. You certainly look well-rested. What's Will up to?"

"He said he needed another hour. I guess all this semiotic and psychoanalytic analysis is wearing him out."

The two laughed at his misfortune. As she sat across from Karin, Lisa noticed the robe had fallen casually open across freshly shaved thighs and she took the liberty to run a naked hand up the length of one silky-smooth naked thigh, opening her legs, meeting no resistance. "Breakthrough?" Lisa asked.

"Breakthrough," Karin acknowledged, sliding her hips down and opening her knees to afford Lisa unfettered access.

Outside, a brilliant blue sky and a new sun reflected light off the thousands of mirrors embedded in the freshly frozen snow. All was still and calm. Later that morning, the snowplows made their breakthrough, the curved steel blades shaving the snow into great white coconut curls piled in banks along the sides of the roads, and the streets were once again clear, clean, and smooth.

CHAPTER THIRTY-TWO

Prisoner

In the visitors parking lot of the Iowa State Penitentiary in Lee County, Iowa, signs led them to visitor reception and in-processing. After they were wanded, signed in and personally met by the warden, Will and LB were ushered into a seminar-like room with a long table and three non-descript gray chairs on each side, one at the head of the white table. Ironically, Will observed how much prison architecture and design reminded him of university buildings and classrooms. At the far end of the room, in the middle of the run of the wall, a glass and metal door stood. After a five-minute wait, tumblers turned and fell, metal bars within the door retracted and a guard in highly polished black boots stepped through, followed by a prisoner, hands manacled in the front, then a second guard. Both guards were armored, wore leather work gloves, boots with black laces and carried black nightsticks. The warden indicated the prisoner should be unmanacled and seated. The guards were excused to stand behind the glass wall separating the interview room from the prison proper.

The warden asked if they needed anything. Will assured him they did not; his contacts at the Iowa Department of Corrections had come through in facilitating the arrangements to visit the maximum-security prison. The prisoner, Deputy Sheriff Delbert Copeland, a medium-size man diminished in the oversize coveralls of his prison uniform, sat across the table from Will and LB. As a reward for his excellent work in command-and-control, Will rewarded him with a field trip to the state prison. LB took the occasion to outfit himself in what could only be called high-end defense lawyer chic. He rocked his blue Armani suit with a red power tie worn over an Ermenegildo Zegna slim fit shirt perfectly draped to his skinny frame. He stood without socks in Salvatore Ferragamo calfskin leather shoes.

For obvious reasons, Will had left Lisa home despite the fact she had offered him inmate sex, whatever that was. He knew she would be more of a distraction than anything else in a visit to a prison that held just under 1000 inmates deprived of female company for long periods of time. Besides, she needed to work on her dissertation research. Karin, the daughter of the incarcerated Deputy Sheriff, was also a no go: Will could not trust her to maintain control in the presence of her father, stooped by the weight of his incarceration and seemingly without hope. Mike Brisbane, of course was busy selling cars and had infiltrated Albert Young's Ford dealership in Fort Charles.

"You must be one powerful dude," Copeland said, "to get me here in front of you without shackles." He massaged the red marks left by the manacles deeper into his wrists.

"Professor William R. Sheridan. Your daughter has told us a lot about you. This is my graduate student, LaDamian Baker, a classmate of your daughter." LB rose to shake the prisoner's hand, which he found firm and dry.

"My pleasure," Copeland said not without a touch of skepticism in his voice. He looked at Dr. Sheridan. Will waited for him to retake his seat and the two prison guards waiting behind the glass wall visibly relaxed.

"As you may know, Deputy Copeland, I've had some success solving cold cases here in the states and internationally. I have written textbooks for the FBI on the techniques I pioneered and subsequently I work as a special consultant for the Justice Department, specifically the FBI."

The deputy sheriff nodded, inwardly grateful for the respect Sheridan showed him by using his former title. "I've heard of your work and guys I know in Interpol have nothing but good things to say about you."

"I'm glad to hear that. I've enjoyed being able to work on both sides of the Atlantic. However, let's get to the business at hand. As your daughter—also my graduate student—no doubt told you, I'm currently an adjunct professor at Iowa Polytechnic State University, teaching a graduate seminar on semiotic theory and its applications to criminology. LB," he indicated, "is another of my best and brightest." LB put a hand on Will's arm. "If you don't mind, I want him to lead the questioning. But before we start, man-to-man, how are you doing?"

With his fingers, the deputy sheriff combed his thinning light brown hair, now showing flecks of gray. He grimaced. "Don't come here for the food or for the company and I never knew how noisy prisons could be at night. I'm not sleeping very well." He had bags under his eyes to support his statement, the reason Will had asked. Will looked over to LB, a signal for him to ask the next question.

"How are you being treated, sir, if I may ask?"

"Call me Del. There is a hierarchy in prison, son. At the very bottom of the barrel are the sex offenders who violate and victimize children. Then there are the other sickos who rape grandmothers and other elderly women. Then come guys like me who put a lot of those guys in jail in the first place. I've been lucky that most of my time on the job was down in Des Moines so no one here has tried to stick a shiv in me yet. The fact that I'm in for murder helps, although I haven't had time to have the teardrop tattooed under my eye."

"I'm sorry Del, I don't understand the significance of the symbol. Does it mean you are sad to be in jail?"

Del coughed into his closed fist, stifling a laugh in deference to the young man's naïveté and his need to come across as a professional.

"A perfect example of the semiotic significance of a potentially ambiguous symbol whose meaning must be deciphered in a specific context," Will said, professing a bit.

"Yeah. What he said," Copeland agreed. He explained for LB. "Around here ink is taken seriously. Tats are a public expression of your affiliation, just like a cop and a badge. The symbols you have needled into your arm have significance. You kill somebody outside and in prison culture inside you have earned the right to wear the teardrop tattoo under one of your eyes. Some guys in here have one or two at the corner of each eye. If other prisoners find out you are lying about your tats, they kill you."

"Geez," exclaimed LB, "this is some real shit." All three took a drink of water from the plastic cups sitting around a thermos of water. LB opened his briefcase and took out a tablet computer. "Dr. Sheridan and I have reviewed the transcripts of your trial and we would like to ask some questions for clarification."

"I'm impressed," Copeland said, interlacing the fingers of his hands atop the white Formica table. A white ring of skin on the third finger of his right hand had replaced the wedding ring he once wore as a token of remembrance of Karin's mother, formerly worn on the third finger of his left hand. After his trial and before his incarceration he had given the ring to Karin. "Fire away. But before we start, let me ask you a question, son." LB nodded. "Do you think I did the crime?"

LB shook his head emphatically. "No, sir. I do not." Copeland looked to Will, awaiting his answer.

"Del, I can assure you we wouldn't be here if I thought you were guilty. To explain, the final project for my graduate class last semester required each graduate student to review, analyze, and present a case to me based on a semiotic analysis of the facts of the crime, a crime they believe constitutes a miscarriage of justice. Based on its merits, and its merits alone, I then chose what I thought was the best case. Without us knowing it was about you and before we knew of her relationship to you, your daughter Karin presented your case for our consideration. My personal analysis of her work showed your case clearly constitutes a miscarriage of justice and we are here to rebalance the scales. Any information you share is likely to assist us in our attempts to have you freed and bring the true perpetrators of Penny Prescott's murder to justice."

Deputy Copeland heaved a sigh up between his shoulders, slumped into his chair, legs extended. "I can't believe somebody other than my daughter actually believes me."

"It's not that we trust or distrust your claim of innocence, sir—with no disrespect intended—Dr. Sheridan has taught us that it's the facts of the case as we have analyzed and interpreted them that permit us to arrive at an objective conclusion of your innocence," LB said.

Sheridan smiled. LB sounded like a professor.

Copeland sat up again and put his hands on the table, fingers splayed in front of him. "Son, however you arrived at your conclusions is irrelevant to me."

LB grinned. "Given our understanding of the case, why do you think you were framed? If we can establish a motive for the act, and use that to develop a context in which we can center our analysis, we might be able to establish a deeper understanding of the events that led to your incarceration."

Will said, "LB, if you would be so good, please enumerate for the deputy sheriff what we have established so far."

"My pleasure, Dr. Sheridan," LB said and formally took a quick look at the open screen of the tablet. "We have a body identified as Ms. Penelope Prescott. We have a crime scene. You were at the crime scene. You were discovered by the sheriff himself to be in possession of the weapon that forensics show was used to commit the murder. Your fingerprints were found on the weapon, to be expected, as the gun was found in your possession. There was gunpowder residue on the hand that held the weapon, your throw down. At the autopsy semen was discovered in the vagina of the murder victim. Subsequent DNA analysis of that seminal fluid matched your genetic profile." LB closed the lid of the computer.

Copeland scratched and shook his head. "This is essentially the same case the prosecuting attorney presented. But I didn't do it. Penny's body was there and I arrived on the scene but only after she called me there to help her with a car problem. Phone records prove she made the call to me but the judge, for reasons my defense attorney still can't understand, did not allow the records into evidence."

Copeland rubbed his wrists and took a drink of water from his Styrofoam cup. "I know I made a critical mistake. I found the weapon before I found the body. At the time I picked it up, I did not know it had been fired or used to commit a crime. I found what I thought was a lost or stolen weapon. I was astonished when I looked at the serial number and found it was my gun, which I reported stolen out of my locker sometime before. When I cleared the gun, the fresh gunpowder residue got on my fingers, not unusual when handling a recently discharged weapon. I had no knowledge that the gun had been fired until after I examined the weapon, cleared it, and dropped the magazine into my hand. I walked down the dirt road another ten yards or so where the fishermen back in their trailers and launch their boats. It was then and only then I discovered the body and to my everlasting shock and horror I saw that it was Penny Prescott, with whom I had been intimate earlier that evening after our dinner date together. I knelt down next to her, checked her carotid artery for a pulse and found none. I also ascertained she was not breathing and only after that and as I was returning to my car to call it in, Sheriff Miller arrived on the scene and the rest, as they say, is history. And here we sit."

LB said, "We find it curious and significant that your version of the facts as you just presented them to us here today is not recorded in the official court transcripts." At this point, Will wanted to reach over and kiss the cheek of the very good smelling young black man wearing a Lagerfeld Kalona aftershave.

"Yeah, ain't that a bitch. The shyster who represented me said he would not put me on the stand to testify. He said the research on juries showed that when cops are on trial for murder, even if they are innocent, they don't come across well to the jury. Nobody likes cop killers, but they hate killer cops. So much for presumed innocent until proven guilty."

"A psychological flaw in the belief system of human beings, one of a thousand fallacies of belief I could describe for you," Will admitted.

"So, no one got to hear my side in court and that's why it's not in the court transcripts. What did show up is my lawyer's flimsy and incompetent attempt to discount the DNA evidence, which failed miserably. I never denied the semen was mine. I admitted we had been intimate earlier in the evening. What I denied was that I had raped her and then killed her.

"I also found that to be highly significant," Will said and LB tried to hide a grin. Deputy Copeland new it had to be an inside joke but he really liked the kid and so he smiled at his two questioners.

"Sorry about that," Will explained. "Graduate student having one over on the old professor."

LB interjected. "Whom we all love and respect." Deputy Sheriff Copeland was a good enough cop to know the kid wasn't kidding.

Will continued. "There was something else that troubled me during the course of my analysis of your case. Though you were tested for and the tests confirmed gunshot residue, that is, gunpowder residue on both your hands, there was no blowback. Forensics showed the bullet entered Miss Prescott at close range. Your clothes were tested but no blood was found on you, no spatter, no biological material on your hands or your shirt and pants. Only gunpowder residue. That is highly significant. Says you held the gun all right, but you did not pull the trigger."

Delbert Copeland, a good guy and a tough cop, slowly shook his head. "I swear I did not pull the trigger and kill Penny Prescott. I had absolutely no motivation to do so."

"And that is exactly why the prosecution had to fabricate a false case of rape as the source of motivation for the murder," Will said. "This is another highly significant action. And if we can establish why someone wanted you framed for this killing and draped it in the sham curtain of sexual assault, it will go a long way to help us determine who the actual killer or killers were. Delbert, I want you to think back one or two weeks before the murder. What were you working on? No matter how large or how small, I want to hear it and I will judge its potential significance."

"Wow. This has all happened so fast. My life has been trapped in a blur of events I can't seem to control. I can't seem to get my head fully wrapped around what has happened to me yet. It's like I'm a character in a bad movie and I'm trapped as the bad guy when I know I should be playing the role of the good guy."

Will reiterated. "What I am asking you to do is potentially very important and could become highly relevant in establishing your innocence. I want you to take a deep breath or two, close your eyes and think back one week before the crime. See yourself at your desk. What do you have to do?"

Copeland took a deep breath and settled himself more comfortably in his chair. He had used the same techniques when questioning witnesses or interrogating suspects of crimes. In his wildest dreams he never thought that one day he would have to use the same relaxation techniques to help himself discover the truth of what happened. "There was some run-of-the-mill stuff. Rattling chains and shaking locks, and driving by the bank. Arrested a farmer who got drunk and shot one of his pigs for fun. A high school kid stole a tractor and took it for a joyride, plowing up the principal's front yard. That's it."

"Well done," Sheridan told him. "Okay. Now clear your mind again and this time go back two weeks."

Eyes still closed, Copeland squirmed in his chair. "Sorry. Again, a lot of routine daily policing in town and around the county." The deputy sheriff stopped his recitation of the daily grind, suddenly went rigid and sat up. "A missing person report on the computer caught my eye. A Pennsylvania Dutch girl from down in the Amana Colonies. No big deal. Sometimes they run away from the church and the family to escape the restrictions. Many of them come running back after trying the lifestyle outside. The freedom is too much and the lack of discipline causes too much anxiety. Then I caught another report not too far out of my district. And then another report just two weeks before my fan clogged with my shit. I printed out all the reports and I told the sheriff I thought I had found a pattern in the missing person reports. He said it was a waste of time for all the reasons I just mentioned and I should get my ass back to doing real police work. So I said I would investigate it on my own time. And I did. I went around asking some questions, which did not seem to make me any more popular around town, at least not in Fort Charles."

"Outstanding," Will said. "You can open your eyes now." Deputy Sheriff Copeland rubbed both his eyes with the knuckles of his index fingers. "Is there anything else you can tell us that you think might be of importance to the case?"

Copeland slowly shook his head no. He furrowed the space between his eyebrows and tapped the surface of the table with his index finger. "I don't know if this is relevant but I'll throw it out to you guys. We had a guy around town by the name of Sam Salerno. He owned a gas station or two in Fort Charles and in the neighboring towns. I think he was a pal of Al Young, and maybe even supplied the gas and diesel for the dealership. I know the Sheriff's department had a contract with him to fuel our vehicles. Not too long ago he up and disappeared. Vanished into thin air. And nobody has heard from the guy since. Rumor had it that he got in a fight with Young and lost that contract so he picked up and went to Canada. I didn't believe that for a minute. I asked a few questions around town but ran into nothing but dead ends and stonewalls. The sheriff didn't seem too interested and I put the case aside until I had more time to come back to it. My instincts told me there was something not right with the whole damn situation. It just didn't make sense to me but the other missing person cases pulled me in another direction. That's all I've got," he said with a shrug under his prison coveralls.

Will said, "You've given us plenty and I think your instincts about Mr. Salerno are dead on. The circumstances of his disappearance are highly significant and the signs point to Al Young. Please make a note, LB. Now one more question for today Del, as I see our time is just about up and the guards are getting nervous. Who would you say are Sheriff Miller's two closest friends in town?"

"Hell, that's easy. The guy who owns the Ford dealership in Fort Charles, Albert Young, and the judge who sat on my case, Judge Franklin."

LB had already written the names into his tablet computer but looked up at his professor and asked, "Highly significant?"

Will grinned. "Highly significant, indeed." Will signaled to the guards that they were finished with the interview. LB and he watched with some dismay as Copeland offered his hands to the manacles. Before he turned to be led away and shuffled back into the prison, Will told him to hang on and assured him things would be breaking his way very soon. Copeland thanked Will and asked him to tell his daughter Karin that he loved her. Will promised to do so. As they walked back to the car in the parking lot, Will told LB he had done a fine job and asked the name of his tailor.

CHAPTER THIRTY-THREE

Rumspringa

Upstairs in the room she shared with her younger sister Kristal, Adelgunda Berghammer pushed the troublesome tendrils of blonde hair up under the lace edges that fringed her white bonnet and looked in the small mirror atop the desk where she dressed. In the soft wavering light thrown by the candles lighting her room, she applied lipstick to her naturally red lips, eyeliner under her naturally blue eyes, and mascara on her naturally long lashes. She took the makeup tools from a leather pouch her brother had made her as a Christmas present. She put a touch of rouge on the apples of naturally red cheeks and studied the effect. Her red lips were now darker and glistened. Her skin, the color of fresh cream, glowed in the natural golden light thrown by the candles burning on her chest of drawers. Her bed frame, her night table, her chest of drawers, and her dressing table had all been hand-built by her father and his brother, her uncle, both master carpenters who made money selling their wares to the *Englisch* in the shops in the Colonies not far from where they lived, bringing in money for the church and the family.

After one more look into the mirror, she corrected the rouge. Now looking five years older, she was satisfied with her corrective work. She doubted that she was beautiful, but she was pretty enough for the Amish and Mennonite boys. Her blocky black shoes made her seem taller, accentuating her slim figure, narrow hips below breasts that were taking forever to emerge. Her mother, much better endowed than she after two daughters and three sons, gave her hope. She stuffed the makeup pouch into a backpack ready beneath the bed, filled with the clothes she would change into at the party.

She hugged her little sister goodbye and with Kristal's wishes for "*Viel Spass*," Adelgunda snuck down the stairs, avoiding the wooden risers that creaked, into the darkened living room and past the bedroom where her parents slept, her father snoring his way into a deep and profound sleep, his just reward from his day's labor on the farm and later in the outbuildings where he had his woodworking shop. His shop contained the materials and tools for crafting the rocking chairs, bed stands, chest of drawers, tables, and other furniture the *Englisch* fawned over and paid exorbitant prices to carry home.

Once out the front door and down the stairs fronting the porch, she shouldered into the backpack and ran down the dirt road that connected the farms with the main road. Where the road intersected with the black top, an old Ford Fiesta rolled up and flashed its lights. On the passenger side the rear seat door swung open and she climbed in, holding the stuffed backpack on her lap. The young boy driving, and not much older than sixteen, said hello and she greeted him and the other two young males crammed into the front seat, shoulder to shoulder, already dressed in their *Englisch* clothes: Nike sneakers, the latest expensive denims, T-shirts stenciled with Midwestern professional sports teams or long-sleeved Western shirts with snap closures down the front and at the cuffs. They wore no hats.

She held hands with her best girlfriend, Simone, and greeted another girl about her own age, a friend of Simone's. The other two young women were dressed in their normal habits and as the old Ford did its best to roar down the road, as if on a timed signal, all three girls removed their bonnets and combed out their hair, good-naturedly banging elbows in the narrow confines of the backseat.

Five minutes later they pulled off the blacktop and drove a mile or so over the dirt track toward the distant sound of bass thumping deep into the night. As they parked among five or six other cars, their excitement grew. The girls immediately ran from the back seat to the barn door that had been pushed open a crack for them upon their arrival. The boys checked their wallets for condoms and the girls found a side room where they quickly changed into thong string bikinis, short tube skirts, low-slung crop tops, Victoria's Secret push-up bras; slid bangles over hands and onto forearms, clipped earrings into place, perfumed their exposed bellies taut from farm work and labor in the kitchens, and they were ready to start their *Rumspringa*. If and when they came back from their excursion, and not all did, they would be formally baptized into the church and would then be required forever after to follow the church's rules and regulations, the *Ordnung*.

Shortly after their arrival, a white Ford Econoline van pulled into the field where the cars were parked toward the front of the barn, headlights facing the barn doors and the hay loft above. The driver, a short, powerful man, hair cut en brosse, put on a leather jacket and took a large black briefcase from the seat next to him. Briefcase in hand, he was waved in by the two young men in straw hats working the sliding barndoor. They clapped him on the back in welcome and showed him to a folding table set up against a wall from which working halters depended, the black leather buckles polished and shining under decorative lights lining either side of the barn's walls. Other red, white, yellow, and blue lights hanging from the rafters had been turned off except for those spotlighting the massive stack speakers, turntables, CD players and stereo amplifiers perched atop a series of hay bales. The young sons of the barn's owners DJ'ed the music. Already five or six couples were writhing ecstatically to the steady beat of the thumping bass overpowering the rest of the music. A group of four young men, shirts unbuttoned to the sternum, pulled shots through the neck of a shared bottle of Jäger-meister.

Three girls standing together watched the couples writhe and grind, boys behind the girls simulating copulation in time to the music, the girls grinding their asses back against the boys or twerking as the beat changed. Adel's group of three young women watched fascinated, all three wanting desperately to dance, hoping the young men would soon drink down enough herb flavored courage to come over and ask them to dance. Adelgunda recognized an older boy, perhaps already out of his teens, who worked part-time with the *Englisch* as a mechanic in the gas station in town. He waded across the music, the siren smiles of all three girls pulling him toward them, rewarding his courage. He reached into the left top pocket of his Western shirt, unsnapped it and took out a pre-rolled joint. Behind cupped hands, he sucked in the flame of a long stick match. The end of the joint crisped and he drew a hit deep into his lungs, held it, and let it slowly steam out both nostrils.

It was an impressive show and when he passed the joint to Adel's best friend Simone, she eagerly accepted, took a hit and passed it on to Adel. She breathed in the silky sweet smoke curling off the lit end of the joint as she had seen others do, and sucked more smoke into her lungs. She coughed most of it out and the other three laughed at her distress. The young man clapped her on the back as two other young men emboldened by the success of the first, came over and offered shots of Jägermeister to the ladies. After drinking down the liquid courage, all six moved to dance in front of the throbbing speakers' exposed cones, pushing the music high up into the barn's rafters, the reverberating noise shaking dust from them.

The stocky man with the briefcase sat uncomfortably on a metal folding chair next to a Formica-topped table that stood on thin green metal legs, opened the briefcase and began a brisk business selling rolled joints, drops of LSD on sugar cubes, and his bestsellers, tabs of Ecstasy. As the night wore on and sales slowed, his customers sated or out of money, he watched the dancers with growing interest. One young blonde, a head taller than her partner, sported a tattoo of chains hanging from an empty cross inked into her naked back, swayed in rapture to the music. The two tabs of Molly she had dropped heightened the pleasure of movement and the sonic impact of the music on her senses. As she let the music overwhelm her, she felt two probing and sluicing fingers seek and then enter her vagina through her denim cutoffs. She was wet with excitement as she held her partner closer and ground her shaved pubis into his palm during the slow dance.

Won't be too much longer now, the dealer thought to himself, as he watched Adel, unsteady in her new heels, supported by the muscular arm of the young man who had given her a first experience with marijuana and was now seeking to give her a second. He steered her out the oversized sliding door of the barn and into the welcome cold of the fresh night air. He maneuvered her past a young woman, her miniskirt pulled up to her hips. She squatted, feet apart, stretching her thong panties below her knees like a slingshot pulled back to fire, as urine gushed into the packed dirt below her naked bottom. They passed two cars rocking and swaying, old springs creaking, young boys grunting between the legs of the young girls willing and eager to give up their virginity in the back seats of the old vehicles.

He took her to his car, an older model four-door Chevy Impala, and handed her into the back seat. From the cooler he kept in the trunk he handed her a cold Budweiser, which she guzzled after snapping the top, only too happy to wash the dryness she had smoked into her throat, parched from too much weed, cheap whiskey, and dancing. His needy mint-laced kisses thrilled her and she opened her mouth for the first time under a kiss, letting a boy touch her tongue with his. Before she could stop him, he lifted her spandex top over her breasts and began caressing them. She gasped when he kissed first the nipple of her right breast, then the nipple of the left. She arched her back trying to make her breasts look bigger. How could anything feel so good, she wondered as she ran her fingers through his black hair, longer on top, cut short and high on the sides.

He slid his hand atop one satin-sleek thigh, pushing her skirt up to her exposed belly. She laughed a short high nervous laugh, grabbed his hand and pulled him off her breast and up to her mouth for another kiss. As she pushed her tongue against his, he unbelted his blue jeans and took out his penis, already hard and hot. He took the hand holding his, wrapped her fingers around the shaft and said, "Suck it for me baby. I promise I won't come in your mouth."

Panic flashed through her like a lightning bolt striking the black metal rooster above her father's woodworking shop. As she tried to control her breathing, she let him move her hand up and down the length of his penis. She covered the swollen head of his penis with the palm of her hand and felt the moisture of his pre-cum. She knew she had to get out of there, but she also knew he was too strong for her to resist physically. Unlike the other girls who left their hymenal blood on the back seats of the cars where they fucked with dazed, bewildered exuberance, their drug-induced ardor swimming in the haze of the ecstasy enveloping them, Adel was not yet ready to give in.

She whispered breathlessly into his ear as she squeezed. "I really have to pee, but when I get back, I'll let you fuck me."

"Okay," he agreed, still hard and high and impatient to take her. "But don't take too long. I don't want to lose my boner. "

"You can put a condom on it while I'm gone," she said with a bit of sexy encouragement in her voice.

"*Nein*," he said, "*Nicht für mich*. Not for me. "I want to feel your wet heat on my cock. Don't worry. I'll pull out and come on your tits."

"I can't wait," she said as she rearranged her short skirt, found the handle to the door and was out of the car in a flash, stumbling on her high heels, breaking one off the right shoe. Jumping and balancing on one leg, she removed both shoes and ran and did not stop until the smoke of panic surrounding her dropped away and dissipated under a night scarred with stars and her head finally cleared. Her bare feet felt the rough skin of the tarmac covering the blacktop. Sweating now, she slowed to a walk, unsure how far she would have to go in the dark. She heard the engine of the van prowling behind her, and stepped to the graveled shoulder of the roadside, trying to escape the blinding beams of the headlights. The van stopped across from her, the passenger door swung open and she took the callused hand that lifted her up and into the passenger seat as if she were made of starlight. She looked over at the smiling face of the dealer from whom she had bought the joints. "Bad boys a bit too much for you to handle tonight?"

"You can say that again," she admitted as he drove her into the tunnel of the night.

"Where to?" he asked, and she directed him. She knew her girlfriend would bring her backpack to her at the cafeteria where they waited tables in town.

"I've got a terrible headache all of a sudden," she said, putting one hand to her forehead, unconsciously trying to put a tendril of hair back under her bonnet, forgetting her head was bare.

He turned on the cabin light and pointed to the glove box. "I've got a bottle of aspirin in there and a can of warm Coke, if you want it."

"Thank you for your kindness, sir" she said and pulled out the plastic bottle, opened the top and shook out two tablets. She popped them into her throat, and swallowed both with a long draft from the soda can. Inadvertently she burped before she could cover her mouth. She said excuse me and he laughed at her indiscretion. Shortly thereafter the Rohypnol put her to sleep and he grinned as he drove north to Fort Charles where he would prepare her for the ritual ceremony in the coming days.

It had been a surprisingly successful trip for Maynard Cheska. He had a shitload of cash stuffed in his briefcase and sleeping next to him in the passenger seat, a young woman perfect for the needs of the Blood Brotherhood. Albert Young would be pleased. He drove for a while into the night, waiting for the drug to fully take effect. When he was certain she could no longer resist, he pulled off the macadam and down onto a dirt road edging a plowed forty-acre field of corn. He went around to the back of the van and opened both doors before returning to the passenger side of the vehicle. He undid her seatbelt and let her fall toward his powerful shoulders. Lifting her dead weight like a slaughtered hog across one shoulder, he wrapped one arm across the back of her bare legs to steady his load. The movement hiked her short skirt up across the meridian of her buttocks. She gurgled a little as his massive deltoid pushed the carbonation from her stomach.

With less than five quick steps to the back of the van, he gently lowered her and laid her flat so that her head did not bounce as he put her down onto the vinyl tarp covering the floor. He took a good long and hard look between her thighs. His military grade flashlight illuminated the cotton V of her thong, which had slipped between the two outer lips of her vagina. He was barely able to resist the impulse to touch and caress her there, to slip the sliver of moist red cloth aside and explore her with his fingers, just like the young bucks back at the rave, trying to take full advantage of the young revelers all too eager to give up their virginity during their *Rumspringa*.

Why shouldn't he help this one on her adventure outside the protective boundaries of the church? He would give her an experience she would never forget. Instead, he pulled her skirt up to her belly, the seductive rise of her pubic mound very much in evidence. He pulled the moist cloth of her panties from the junction between her lips and shined the flashlight there as he moved in for a closer look.

Luck was with him. His preliminary inspection showed she was still a virgin. With both hands under her heels, he placed her legs together at the knee, pulled the short skirt back down and checked the rise of her small breasts to see if she was still breathing. Satisfied, he closed and locked the doors to the van, got into the front seat and the butcher from Fort Charles drove another fifty miles to his slaughterhouse.

Off the highway and on the road leading to his outbuildings, the gravel crunched under his wide tires. He backed into the ramp used for deliveries. He punched in the code for the building's alarm and unlocked the door to the vinyl-sided structure with rotating scoop fans on the roof. Once inside he turned on the powerful mercury vapor lamps hanging high above the polished stainless steel of the slaughter tables, made by the same company that supplied autopsy tables to morgues and medical examiners. He went out and opened the doors to the back of the van, pulled the vinyl tarpaulin forward until her legs dangled over the bumper, and carried her like a lover in his arms into the slaughter room where he carefully laid her atop a clean table. He hurried back to the van, closed and locked both doors and put the tarp into the dumpster for collection. He parked the van on the other side of the building, big as a barn, where it could not be seen from the road.

Once again inside he changed his clothes in his office and put on overalls and a disposable white butcher smock. He decided not to glove up. He wanted the pleasure of feeling her under his fingers as he worked. He opened a green plastic disposal sack and put in her stiletto heels, which she had put on the seat between them in the van. Only then did he notice one was broken. That could be a problem, he thought, but there was nothing to be done about it now. He pulled down the zipper of her miniskirt, then grabbed the skirt at her hips and tugged it out from under and off her butt. The red thong string bikini worn under her white skirt, he would save for last. He removed the three cheap gold-plated bands from the wrists of her arms where they had coupled and overlapped and threw them into the bags with regret. Like grapes, he plucked her earrings from unpierced ears next, and threw them into the bag.

He placed both arms above her head as if she were preparing to dive into the pond back behind her farm house at the edge of the forest. He lifted the sparkling spandex top just over her breasts, rolled it toward her throat, and lifted it over her chin and out from under the back of her head, moving her thin blonde hair out of the way. He finished the removal by pulling the shirt down the length of her extended arms. Into the sack it went after he smelled her perfume and her naturally sweet body. He posed both her hands under her head and admired her breasts. They were small but perfectly formed across the pectoralis muscle of her chest. Like her thwarted lover in the old Chevy Impala back at the barn, he took the liberty of kissing first her left breast, then the right, sucking both raspberries that tipped her nipples up off the breast tissue before allowing them to snap back into the reddening pool of pink flesh.

He sweated now from the labor of undressing her, from the labor of trying to resist her, and took a minute to towel his forehead dry with the blue shop towel pulled from the case he kept on the brushed stainless-steel counter near the slaughter table. Now for the prize. Now for the reward. He grabbed the strings of her thong at both hips, pulled them under her buttocks, which splayed slightly on the cold steel table, and then with exquisite slowness lifted up the soft cloth of the triangle that had rolled together and lodged between the lips of her naked flesh. As he pulled the filament of cloth down over her knees and off the tops of her feet, he was disappointed to see she would not require shaving. He put the gossamer cloth, less than a handful within the maul of his enormous hand, up across his nose and breathed in the heady fruity scent of her perfume and the natural smells of a healthy young woman. Then he threw the string bikini into the disposal sack.

He pulled back the light pink skin that hooded and protected her clitoris and examined the peanut-sized organ, glistening under the sodium vapor lamps above the tables. With two fingers he carefully opened the lips of her vagina and stared. To all appearances she was still a virgin. Unlike some of the others, this one hadn't ruined everything by sticking homemade candles or the carved wooden handles of a hairbrush into her cunt, confirming his earlier inspection. He knew there would be hell to pay if he brought Al Young and his fellow brothers damaged goods.

The young buck at the barn had just missed his prize. He let the delicate skin of her lips fall closed and put his fingers in his mouth as he savored the delicate flavors. By this time, he could barely control himself; he wanted to take her so bad, but he knew better. Instead, he dropped his pants and masturbated his erect penis with his right hand, using his left hand to stroke and caress her breasts. In less than two minutes he came across the well of her belly, squirting semen from the rise of one hip across to the rise of the other. The force of the ejaculation surprised him. The little bitch was that pretty. A shame he couldn't come on her face and into the white shock of her hair.

He cleaned himself up at the deep sink, then pulled down the portable spray nozzle above the table and rinsed her from throat to toe. He rolled her over and rinsed her back, pried apart the slippery muscles of her buttocks and held them open with one hand while he directed the geyser of warm water into the cleft of her buttocks and across the ring of her anus. He grinned to himself. Just like the table shower in the Korean massage parlors in Des Moines. He released the showerhead and grabbed the soap, sudsed her shoulders, under her arms, the well of her small buttocks, down into the valley below, and down her hamstrings all the way to her feet. Then he rinsed her clean of all the soap and turned her once more over onto her back. He lathered her breasts, her arms, the defined muscles of her stomach now relaxed, the tops of her thighs and down to her toes. Then with deliberate and particular pleasure he soaked her vagina outside and between her lips. He rinsed her free of all the soap and opened the lips of her vagina once more. Satisfied she was perfectly clean, he narrowed the aperture of the spray and directed the warm water toward her clitoris. He watched her eyes move beneath closed lids, her eyelashes quivering. Just a little treat for you, the thought. He knew she had felt every single sensation and could do nothing about it. After he thoroughly dried her using two large blue bath towels, he put her into a new fresh white smock and laid her atop the bed kept in the room adjoining his office. He closed and locked the door behind him, and finished his cleanup of the work area. The garbage bag and its contents would be burned tomorrow.

It had been a good night's work and Maynard Cheska was pleased with himself. His boss would be proud, happy with the money he had earned for himself and the cabal. He switched off the lights, watched the mercury vapor lamps above him fade away, locked the door behind him and reset the alarm. He went to the main house, took a shower and went to bed. As he recalled with pride the force of his ejaculation, he fell instantly asleep.

CHAPTER THIRTY-FOUR

Interviews

The investigative team comprised of Will's graduate students was producing results and working well together. LB, with Dr. Sheridan's help, put together a communication center in Sheridan's office at the duplex where LB was coordinating interaction between team members. With Karin's help, two weeks earlier Mike had found an apartment in Fort Charles and had been successfully placed in the Chevy dealership. Less than a week later, based on his sterling sales figures, he got a call from Albert Young at the Ford dealership, inviting him in for a meet and greet and a formal interview. Immediately thereafter he was offered a sales position, which he accepted. That evening Mike called LB on a secure line and had him relay the information to his professor. LaDamian promised to call Mike's wife Regina and let her know everything was going well and that Mike sent along his love. The wife of a former Army Green Beret, she fully understood the necessity for secrecy and the limited amount of information she could receive while Mike was away on a mission. As a former Army wife, she was used to Mike's secretive deployments, and therefore ready, willing, and able to sacrifice her personal needs in service to the requirements of his duty. This was her contribution to service and to her man.

After assisting Mike with the search for accommodations, Karin briefed him on the routine practices of everyday life in Fort Charles, such as where the bank is located, how long the gas station stayed open at night, where the town regulars ate breakfast and at what café, in other words, the comings and goings in a small town in rural Iowa. Karin had also given Dr. Sheridan her dossiers on the shakers and movers in Fort Charles.

Lisa had provided him with a series of reports on the locations of the various religious sects that had settled in Iowa seeking to avoid religious persecution elsewhere. Having found inexpensive and fertile land, the congregations migrated west, crossed the Mississippi, put down religious roots and raised red barns in their new sequestered communities. As he had thought, most of the sects spoke a recognizable dialectical version of German, as most of the religious immigrants historically originated in Germany or Switzerland. In fact, the residents of the Amana Colonies spoke English, German, and a mixture of both called Amana German.

Having digested the intelligence provided by his team, it was time for Will to accelerate the investigation into Deputy Sheriff Del Copeland's false incarceration and the roles played by Sheriff Buckminster "Buck" Miller and Albert Young—evidently the town's mayor, number one businessman, and de facto center of political power—in fostering and perpetuating the brazen injustice against Copeland. This was the case Will and his team of graduate students made their mission to solve, bringing to bear their enthusiasm, their training, their learning, their willingness to translate theory into practice, and most importantly, their resolute motivation to see justice done.

Will and Annalisa prepared for their trip to the Iowa Amish and Mennonite communities under the auspices of doing research on *Rumspringa,* the opportunity for younger church members to experience life outside the community of the church. If and when they returned from their run around, they would be baptized into the church and forever after be beholden to its regulations, practices, and beliefs. It was Will's working hypothesis that some of the younger members of families who were church adherents and who did not return might very well have been kidnapped or abducted. Will also knew that many law enforcement agencies in communities surrounding the placements of the religious orders often did not treat missing person reports with highest priority, given the cultural practices of the Amish and Mennonites, among others.

Before they left for Hazleton, an Amish settlement closest to Fort Charles, Will took the time to brief Annalisa. The two had decided for security purposes not to use her real name, Alina Augustans, until she was free from her duty to the CIA as a double agent and no longer afraid of reprisal by her masters in the Russian FSB and SVR.

"I want you along because in the culture of these types of religious sects, a man often will open up and be more forthcoming to questions when a woman is present. The interviewee forgets the man is there and focuses on the woman. I've seen it a thousand times, and not just in religious contexts. I want that focus on you. There is also a very good chance we will have to interview a female or two if they are permitted to interact with us. When that happens, I want you to take the lead."

She nodded her understanding. "How do you want me to dress?"

"An important question, semiotically. How you present yourself makes an immediate impression symbolically on those with whom we interact. How we dress is semiotically significant at both the conscious and subconscious level to those who perceive us," he explained. "Number one, you are a woman, a young woman at that and you are exquisitely beautiful. In many cultures this will make you immediately suspect, and an object of envy. Never underestimate the power of envy as a human motivation. Wars have been won and lost on the basis of wanting what others have. Therefore, I want you to dress down. Please wear dark nondescript clothing, black if at all possible." He saw her shudder. "Wear a skirt that falls at least to the knee, but no pantyhose or nylons, and do not shave or wax your legs." She looked at him as if he were crazed. "For shoes buy a black pair without heels, no fancy buckles or straps," he continued, ignoring her growing distress.

"Do you want me to wear a veil?" she asked sarcastically.

He chuckled. "Let's leave that for your Muslim sisters, but I see what you're getting at. But let's keep the mission in mind. This is not about liberating the sisters of the holy cross." She wrinkled her nose but nodded her agreement.

"Number two. Your interactions with me will be carefully observed and are thus highly significant to the observer. You must show obedience and deference. That means I go first through the doors. I take the best seat and sit first, and you speak very little if at all, and respond only to direct questions. You must be controlled at all times in the presence of men. However, the fact that I allow you to be present during the questioning will at first cause some confusion, but ultimately will confer on you higher status than an ordinary woman in their society. I will explain your presence as my graduate student and my assistant and they will accept it as part of English culture."

"Number three. Semiotically we will be perceived and understood as foreigners who are temporarily and by their invitation visiting their culture. We are the others, *les autres*, as Simóne de Beauvoir pointed out. We will be objectified and seen as unequal in their eyes. Our English culture is perceived as a very real threat to theirs, and as a result, out of politeness they will agree to interact with us but most likely will be less than forthcoming. Anything less is a violation of their cultural code. They won't want us there and will be relieved once we are gone. Expect them to be somewhat nervous and arrogant at the same time. Remember also that women are not equal to men in their culture. According to the Bible, women were put on Earth for the sole purpose of serving men. As a female, your role," he said looking at her, "is to serve men. You keep the house, you cook, you have sex to reproduce, you bear children and raise them to work the farm and to serve the church. This is your life."

She slowly shook her head. "The parallels with the Taliban are frightening."

He nodded. "Treasure and respect the freedoms you have to express yourself in this country, despite the daily erosion and the continued attacks on those freedoms by the ultraconservatives who would welcome a government of religious theocracy with open arms," he gently reminded her. "And the ultimate irony is that they have the freedom to repress women as they do, all in the name of religious belief and democratic freedoms." He paused for a moment. "These are sociological and anthropological concerns that I point out to you because they serve to enrich our semiotic basis for understanding how I expect the true believers will interact with and react to us. On that basis, you must now play your new role. This is not the time for liberating oppressed women or inviting others to join you in your quest for universal girl power. Our job is to solve this case and to free a man unjustly convicted of a capital crime. We will settle for nothing less. Agreed?"

"Agreed," she assured him.

"The Amish settled in Iowa mostly in the towns of Kalona, Hazelton, and Bloomfield," she told him in the car on the drive up to Hazelton in Buchanan county. "There we will find the most conservative of the Amish communities. Hazelton only has a population of about 850 persons. The town was founded in 1873 amongst a grove of hazelnut trees. Here's an interesting tidbit for your trivia notebook. When the railroad first came to town, they missed it by about a mile. The enterprising townspeople picked up the town and moved it lock, stock, and barrel, literally, next to the railroad."

"Very industrious of them," Will commented.

By prior arrangement through the university, in Hazelton they located and spoke with an elder of the church, black boots dusty, black pants worn above white sox. His white shirt, taken off the line that morning, seemed new, starched, and freshly ironed. He shouldered into a coat to meet them and pulled a hand through his beard as they greeted each other. They sat at an oak table in the community hall where the townspeople congregated and ate their communal dinners. Already in full preparation for the noon meal, good smells and the bustling sounds of many persons cooking came from the kitchen. The older women moved and directed their younger helpers among the stoves, pots, wooden tables and cabinets.

Will's research indicated that in the last two years seven males and three females chose to take part in the *Rumspringa.* According to church records all but two males and one female had returned to the church and all the others had dutifully accepted baptism and were now following the rules and dictates of the *Ordnung*, required by the church of all its members to live an orderly and godly life. Upon further questioning, the church father said records indicated the two boys had left the church to work in the nearby recreation vehicle factory where they installed doors, couches, beds, and bunks into the shells of large RVs. At least one of them was sending money home to help support his parents, who had lost three cows from the herd due to the severity of last year's winter when the heavy snow falls made it nearly impossible to get hay to the animals. The other young man had gotten married to an English girl and the two shared an apartment in a town nearby. The girl, age 15, had disappeared. After finishing her schooling at 14 she went on a *Rumspringa* and her family never heard from her again. Not a letter, not a postcard, not a single call to the community phone shared by all.

"The fact that there has been no contact whatsoever with her family is highly significant," Will told the older man.

"If you say so," he allowed, stroking his beard again. "We would be very glad to have her back," he said after a shared moment of silence, as if Will somehow had a vested power to bring her back. The elder kindly invited them to stay for lunch, but Will politely declined, saying that they had two more appointments yet today. The church elder thanked the professor doctor and nodded to Annalisa, showing them to the door. They had lunch in a café in Marshalltown where Will used to pheasant hunt, then headed south toward Iowa City. Their next destination, Kalona, was in Washington County, one of 99 in the state. An hour and a half later, they took a short break in Iowa City, home of the University of Iowa, reprogrammed the sat nav and topped off the gas tank.

Will had Lisa continue her briefing to help pass the time as the freeway took them through the rolling hills of plowed corn and soybean fields resting under a meager blanket of snow, corn stocks in regularly spaced clumps of two and three pushing up through the snow and into a heavy layer of cold.

"As you know from your language studies, the Amish in this area speak a linguistic dialect called Pennsylvania German, which is derived from the German spoken by the original immigrants who left Germany in the early 1800s. Presently in Iowa there are communities of old order Amish and old order Mennonites as well as less conservative offshoots of these two religious sects.

"As you might expect, their migrations to the United States were the result of ideological squabbles and divisions within the churches of their homelands. For example, the Amish, led by Jacob Amman separated from the Mennonites as far back as 1693. The Mennonites take their name from Menno Simons, leader of an Anabaptist group called the Swiss Brethren, and follow the teachings of the Jesus of the New Testament. Kalona is a town of about 1200 among the rolling hills of Johnson and Washington County and the Amish settlement here in Washington County is the oldest and best-known in Iowa, with no less than ten church districts. The town was founded in 1846 and also has a new order church, which explains the modern tractors seen working the area in the fields and on the farms."

Lisa looked up from her notebook. "I was wondering about that. It seems a contradiction to their extremely conservative religious beliefs."

Will explained. "Some technology is permitted among the less conservative and less strict of the sects, but anything new requires a meeting of the church elders and a vote."

They slowed as they approached a black buggy, pulled by a single brown horse, a triangular shield of caution hanging on the back-left side of the cab, a young bearded farmer in the front, no mustache, and no gray in his beard. His single horse smoked white mist from his nostrils and his ears perked up at the sound of the approaching car. In German, Will wished the farmer a good day and asked him for directions to the community hall in Kalona. There they learned that in the last two years fifteen young adults had chosen to experience a *Rumspringa,* eleven boys and four girls. An old churchman read from records that showed that seven boys had returned and all but one of the girls. The four boys had left the church, to the chagrin and shame of their families and had moved to Iowa City, where they lived together in a shared apartment. One was in county jail for possession of marijuana with intent to sell; the other three worked as carpenters for a building contractor in Iowa City. Three girls had accepted the *Ordnung.* The missing girl had disappeared and had made no contact with her grieving family. There was a rumor that she had run away with a boy to live in Missouri. Lisa took her name, but it seemed unlikely they could track her down, and Will told the churchman as much. With the forbearance that comes with age and the resolute faith already lined deeply into his face, he thanked them for their interest and Will promised to be in touch if their research investigation turned up any leads.

CHAPTER THIRTY-FIVE

Little Sister

Will made Lisa a promise. "One more stop on the outskirts of Kalona to interview a family of a recently reported missing girl, and we're done for the day. Afterwards, we'll stop at the Amana Colonies, and have dinner there in a restaurant I know."

Lisa nodded. "Lisa is interested and still curious to learn whatever we can, but is getting hornier by the taciturn minute, because men in beards and straw hats turn her on. As a warning to you, not too much further down the road she intends to impose herself on the driver of this vehicle with a religious fervor that will force you to take the name of God in vain."

"Good to know," Will said, and for the safety of the all the occupants in the SUV, took a side road and then a two wheeled gravel track down to an iced over river where he parked among the trees. Five minutes later, Lisa's energetic and religious ardor had steamed the windows closed and rocked the SUV on its chassis.

Earlier Will had made the necessary arrangements under the auspices of the university to visit the town of Kalona about thirty miles south and west of the Amana Colonies. This gained him access to the Amish, a Pennsylvania Dutch religious community, and the Amana Society, whose adherents had settled in and around Amana, Iowa, after leaving Germany and the restrictions of the Lutheran church. The congregation settled first in New York state and moved on to Iowa in 1856. The so-called Amana Colonies, actually a collection of seven villages in east-central Iowa, was located about one hundred miles from Des Moines, south via Grinnell, the location of Grinnell College, a small private liberal arts college of about 1700 students. He reminded Lisa that the residents of the Amana Society were not Amish, had different cultural traditions, and spoke a different dialect despite their proximity to the old order Amish in Kalona

Will and Lisa drove to the small town of Kalona, about an hour's roundabout drive from the Colonies, then out to the house of Rudolph Berghammer. Will parked the Forester in a pullout on the shoulder of the blacktop that led to an unpaved road that ran past the farm house a short distance away and then on to the buildings of the next closest neighbor. During their five-minute walk they were passed once by a black cart, open to the front, pulled by a shining black horse in black halter, reins in the hand of a man dressed all in black, including his wide brimmed felt hat. He did not wave or stop to offer them a ride.

Three well-worn wooden steps raised them to a screen door that opened upon a broad porch that faced the house. A two-person swing depended from the roof shadowing the porch. At the oak door, Will knocked the iron door clapper against its metal seat and stepped back. Lisa stood three paces behind him and to the right. She wore a long-sleeved black shirt covered by a delicate white laced shawl worn over the shoulders and a black cotton skirt, thick enough to be uncomfortable on even a slightly warm and humid day. Her shoes, unpolished black brogues, had been bought at the local Goodwill store along with the rest of her outfit. Will told her it would be best not to wash her ensemble, but on this point she refused to budge. Instead, she had promised not to wash her hair, which she wore pulled back and gathered into a soft honeybun. She wore no perfume, no makeup, and no deodorant. She did sneak on a quick swipe or two of clear anti-perspirant. He too was dressed all in black, foregoing his omnipresent polos for a black collared long-sleeved shirt that buttoned at the wrists. He wore black pants and a pair of black work boots bought at the local Walmart. He had taken the time to re-condition the boots to make them appear they had been worked in. He carried nothing with him. Lisa carried a black leather attaché case in which she had placed her notebook and pencils.

In response to a second forceful knock with the metal clapper, the door opened in. A man finished shouldering into a plain black coat shiny from washing and wear, worn over a much-laundered white shirt, the white going to gray, and stood before them, watching. He did not speak. Will wished him a good day in German. "*Guten Tag.* I am Professor Doctor William R. Sheridan from Iowa Polytechnic State University, and this is my graduate student Annalisa Allen. I wrote you a letter requesting an interview with you regarding the disappearance of your daughter Adelgunda. My secretary called you earlier today informing you of our arrival." Will did not extend his hand, but the door opened wider to admit them.

Will entered first and said, "*Vielen Dank, Herr Berghammer. Sehr angenehm von Ihnen.* Many thanks, Mr. Berghammer. Very nice of you.

Rudolph Berghammer stared at Will. "*Wie ist es daß Sie Deutsch so gut sprechen können?*" Berghammer wanted to know why Will could speak such good German.

Will smiled inwardly. His use of German had produced the desired effect. He explained why he was able to speak German and informed the *Hausherr* that both he and Lisa had been born in Bavaria, Germany. Satisfied with the explanation, *Herr* Berghammer led them into the kitchen and offered Will an oak chair at a hand-polished oaken table that nearly filled the room. He stood uncomfortably by, not knowing what to do with Lisa. He asked if she preferred to sit with the women in the living room, offering to show her the way with the sweep of his arm. Lisa bowed her head in thanks. Good girl, Will thought, but it was time to exert some interpersonal dominance.

"If it is not too much trouble, Berghammer, please permit Lisa to sit with us. I need her to take notes of our conversation so I do not forget essential details that might help us solve the case of your daughter's disappearance. As I wrote you in my letter, I am an anthropologist studying the return rates of Amish and Mennonites who have left on a *Rumspringa*. In the course of my research, and in the missing person reports law enforcement has been kind enough to share with me, I noticed a small percentage of girls have literally disappeared without a trace. Is it possible your daughter is one? This is the reason we are here today."

Berghammer seemed doubtful, but indicated a chair for Lisa next to Will, and only then sat at the head of the table he had crafted with his own two hands, using the tools he had made for woodworking.

"Beautiful craftsmanship," Will said appreciatively, rubbing his hand over the highly polished and hand-rubbed oak table.

"Ask your questions, *Englisch,* I have work to do," he said rather brusquely.

"Where is your daughter, Adel?" Will asked without a pause, giving as good as he got.

The question caught Berghammer by surprise, and he blushed from his black beard up into the lobes of his substantial ears. "Only God knows," he said obliquely, as if that were the end of the matter. "No one in this household has reported her missing."

"Since I'm not an elder of the church, I cannot purport to know the mind of God," Will said and smiled disarmingly. "I can only hope to ask you." He did not disclose who had reported Adelgunda missing.

"I do not know where she is," Berghammer said, placing both his broad suntanned hands on the table. "For all I know, she is dead. I can tell you this. If she does not return from her *Rumspringa,* and accept her baptism into the *Ordnung,* she is dead to me." He watched Lisa closely, trying to gauge the effect his words were having on her. She wrote dutifully on the yellow pad taken from her attaché, her expression neutral. "As a professor, I have no doubt you know what *Rumspringa* is."

Will nodded. "I know from previous research that nearly eighty percent of the young persons who do decide to take advantage of the church's permission to go and freely experience the life of the *Englisch,*" Will said, giving the word a German inflection, "very happily return home to the *Kirche* and take the initiation into the orders. But twenty percent do not."

Berghammer showed them his open hands, raised calluses the color of butter evident on the palms. "God has other plans for them."

Will nodded. "I'm not concerned with their choices. I'm concerned with the fact that your daughter, for all intents and purposes, seems to have disappeared off the face of the earth. No one reports having seen her after she left the house. I have also run across other examples of young women who left and were never heard from again. It is highly likely that some of them were abducted."

"In that event," allowed church elder Berghammer, "it can only be the work of the Devil."

"Of that I am absolutely convinced," Will said. "My job as a scholar, sir, is to discover and try to understand the nature of that work."

Elder Berghammer looked at him for very long time. "Then I wish you every success with your investigation." He paused for a time as if struggling with what he wanted to say next. "If it is God's will, her mother would like to see her daughter again sometime."

Despite his training, Will was unnerved by the man's iron control. He took a minute to regain his composure before he asked his next question, knowing full well that he was bouncing the handball off an intractable prison wall. He decided to take another tack. "With your permission I would like to speak with Adel's mother, preferably alone, but with my assistant present."

Berghammer pushed his wooden chair away from the table, rose, opened the door to the living room and nodded at his wife. Fully dressed in the mufti of the old order Amish, she came in, hands clasped nervously in front of her, uncertain, unsure what was required of her. Berghammer introduced her with the sweep of an arm. "*Mein Frau.*" She bent her head in supplication.

Will rose and Lisa quickly followed. "*Frau Berghammer. Sehr angenehm Ihnen kennen zu lernen.*" She blushed and smiled as Will said it was very nice to meet her.

Defying Will's request to speak with his wife alone, Berghammer retook his seat at the head of the table. She offered the two visitors each a glass of fresh buttermilk, Berghammer declining. Both accepted with pleasure. Will drank his down to half the glass, Lisa took a restrained feminine sip from hers, and Mrs. Berghammer sat patiently if not nervously, waiting for the first question, a tic in the hollow of her cheek betraying her.

"I apologize for the inconvenience as I know we're getting close to dinner time but I need to ask just a question or two and we will be on our way and not trouble you further." Will took the cold milk down to the bottom of the thick glass. "Best milk I have tasted since I left Bavaria."

"*Ach, Sie stammen aus Bayern?*" With happy surprise on her face Frau Berghammer asked if he came from Bavaria. "My grandmother came from the Allgäu region in Bavaria," she elaborated, and replaced the tendril of hair that had escaped the confines of her lace cap.

Will doubted if she was much older than Lisa. "My birthplace," Will informed her. Berghammer seemed none too pleased with the direction the conversation was taking and glowered at his wife. "There is still work to be done before our evening meal," he informed the table.

Before he could rise, Will asked his first question of *Frau* Berghammer. "Did Adelgunda show any signs of depression before leaving on her *Rumspringa?*"

"*Ach, nein,*" *Frau* Berghammer answered immediately. "She was always a very happy girl, always did her chores without question or complaint, and never spoke back to me or her father, unlike so many of our youngsters today." She lowered her head after the admission, accepting the responsibility for the bad actions of other young church members.

Will waited for Lisa to finish her notes. "Do you know if she had a boyfriend she might have run off to see and stay with?"

"*Nein, nein,*" *Frau* Berghammer adamantly stated. "She was much too young to see a young man unaccompanied. It would never have been allowed, unlike some of the *Englisch* girls she works with in High Amana." Elder Berghammer nodded.

At this point Will thanked her for her answers to his questions and the excellent buttermilk. As Rudolf Berghammer showed them to the door, Will looked directly into his brown eyes below bushy eyebrows and asked, "If I do learn what happened to her, whether it is God's will or the work of the Devil, do you want me to inform you?"

For a brief instant, elder of the church Berghammer abandoned his piety and permitted one red drop of love for his daughter to escape his pious heart. As he looked away from Will and at his wife, without further pause he said one word only, "*Ja.*"

As they walked back to the car, Will congratulated Lisa on a job well done. "I wanted to sock that guy in the face," she said, letting her anger out. "What a bastard."

"What did his body language tell you? Based on a semiotic analysis of his unconscious nonverbal behaviors, do you think he was telling the truth?"

"Absolutely not," Lisa said with conviction.

"Okay, said Will. "What about *Frau* Berghammer?"

"She was lying, too, but not as much."

"I agree, Lisa. She was not lying to protect herself, but to protect her husband. Both those two are grieving the loss of their daughter, and cannot bring themselves to admit it, to share with each other, to say nothing of sharing it with two strangers in their house. My semiotic analysis tells me they are both desperate to learn more about their daughter but are afraid to ask. I think we're not done yet with the family Berghammer, not by a longshot."

As they walked the mile or so back to the Forester, they heard the commotion of someone calling and running. A young girl, her blonde hair covered by her bonnet, tie strings and white apron bouncing as she ran in long strides on impossible shoes, waved and shouted, "*Hallo!*"

Will and Lisa stopped and turned and waited for the young girl who ran up to them with all the energy of a twelve-year-old and waited for her to catch up with them.

"*Hallo, Junge. Macht's du jetzt dei' Rumspringa?*" Will asked her in Bavarian dialect, wondering if she was now going on her *Rumspringa*.

"*Noch nicht,*" she laughed and waited for her breathing to catch up with her after the long run through the mowed barley field. Not yet, she had said. "I'm Adel's sister, Kristal."

Will introduced himself and Lisa. "Are you looking for my sister?" she asked, her breathing not yet under control after her nearly one-mile run to catch them.

"Yes." Will told her.

"Do you want to help?" Lisa asked.

"*Doch.*" Of course, Kristal said.

Will took Lisa's notebook out of her attaché case, clicked a pen and leaned back against the Forester, letting Kristal, now beaming white irregularly shaped teeth at them, catch her breath. Her cheeks glowed red atop the buttermilk white of her skin.

"When did you see your sister last?" Lisa asked.

"On the evening of her *Rumspringa,* about a week ago."

"Was she very excited?"

She nodded vehemently. "She couldn't wait to go to the party." In all cuteness she tapped her finger to her chin and said, "I think you *Englisch* call it a rave. She couldn't wait to meet boys and dance. She had been preparing for two weeks."

"What do you mean?"

"You know, putting together her modern clothes, her makeup, and planning with her girlfriend Simone."

Will asked, "Was she going to meet Simone at the party?"

Kristal nodded and adjusted the ties of her bonnet. Lisa asked, "Do you know Simone's last name?"

"Eberhardt. She works with Adel at the café in High Amana. She should be there now."

Will wrote down the name Simone Eberhardt. Lisa wanted to reach down and pinch her cheek back into ruddiness like a troublesome auntie. "You have been a great help," she assured Kristal, who was now looking back over her shoulder toward the farm from which she had run.

"I have to go," she said suddenly. "I'm worried that I will be missed and get my mother in trouble."

"She sent you," Will said.

Kristal nodded.

"One last quick question," Lisa promised, "and we will send you back. "Was Adelgunda happy at home?"

Kristal pursed her red lips as if she were about to whistle. "She loves us, but not the life. She did very well in school and wanted more learning, but Father forbade her."

"You think she ran away?" Will asked her gently. This time she shook her head no.

"Why not?"

"She promised to stay until she could take me with her. We are going to run away together when I am old enough for my *Rumspringa*."

Will thanked Kristal in German. She asked him, "Do you think my sister is coming back home? I miss her very much. If you do find her please tell her that I love her and want her to come back. Please find her and bring her home."

"*Versprochen*," Will said, promising her.

On impulse Lisa hugged her. "We will do everything we can. Now back home with you," she said as she tied the laces of Kristal's bonnet under her chin. She turned and skipped away, the movement of her knees flouncing her dark blue calico skirt until she broke into an easy lope that would take her back toward the farmhouse and its neighboring barn.

They watched her for a minute or two and then got in the car. "That certainly puts the matter entirely in a different perspective," said Lisa and put on her seatbelt. She pulled her hair free of the stricture of the twisty she had used to tie her hair back and shook it out. She kicked off her shoes and wiggled her toes as Will started the car and pulled onto the tarmac. "Would love to hear your thinking," she said, flapping and fanning the heat from her thighs with her heavy cloth skirt.

There was almost no traffic on the blacktop so Will engaged the onboard navigation and said, "Kristal was telling the truth. I am convinced now Adel intended to return, if only to keep her promise to her sister. Tomorrow, we find her girlfriend Simone Eberhardt in town. Next, we find a quaint room at a little inn nearby and get a bite to eat. I'm tired from dealing with people all day and I'm starved, as I'm sure you must be. You might have noticed we were not invited to stay for dinner at the Berghammer's."

CHAPTER THIRTY-SIX

High Heels

After an early breakfast of blueberry pancakes for him, strawberry waffles with whipped cream topping for her, sausages, and eggs over easy for both in a nearby waffle shop, they took a little break from interviewing and went shopping. Adel had never seen this part of east-central Iowa before, despite a trip or two down to the University of Iowa in Iowa City to use their larger and better-equipped research libraries. Will remembered having to do the same during his tenure at IPSU. Besides, the day had brightened and was warming and for once in a very long time, the sky was blue and uncluttered with clouds.

The Amana Colonies, a regional tourist destination, sprawled out over nearly thirty thousand acres of towns and surrounding farmlands. Will reminded her that the early settlers were German Pietists escaping from Germany and the Lutheran Church. The village of Amana, also known as Main Amana, where they stopped, one of the six among the settlement, had also given its name to a famous producer of washers, dryers, and refrigerators, many still fabricated by workers from the church communities.

Will and Lisa decided to forego the formal tours, opting instead to visit the furniture shops, clothing stores, souvenir shops, and took the time to taste the local fruit wines, raspberry, plum, cherry, blackberry, or peach. Other than their distinctive fruit signatures, the wines tasted all the same, too sweet and too flabby from a lack of acid to balance the cloying sweetness. "Good for a reduction to syrup and then drizzled over ice cream, but certainly not noble wines," Will whispered to Lisa, so as not to offend the pregnant pourer, looking helpful and expectant, in face and in her belly that pushed her apron out at her patrons. Lisa agreed, her tongue insulted by all the overpowering sugary sweetness in the wines.

"Give me a big cab or a merlot any day," she declared.

Will raised an eyebrow. "Just one more reason for me to love you."

"I'm keeping count," she assured him and he laughed.

Then he said something in a throw-away remark intended as humor, which stole the core out of her happy-go-lucky good nature. "Now if I can only find a similar number of reasons to trust you." His thoughtless and unfeeling statement sent her into the dark brew of a bad mood; one, however, she was determined not to let him see in an effort to hide its effect on her.

In one of the textile shops in the neighboring village of High Amana she fondled a beautifully woven wool blanket, yellows and blues interspersed among the whites. She casually examined the price tag before she sighed and replaced the blanket on the shelf with others of the same size and design, but not before giving its near Kashmir softness one more longing caress. She moved on to handle and examine other goods and determined to buy something for herself in an effort to lessen the doldrums of her mood, she bought herself a finely woven red and black wool scarf to throw around her neck and over her shoulders. It came with a pair of matching five finger mittens. They met at the door, their shopping done and walked to the Forester. "I bought myself a scarf and some wool mittens," she said with pride. "What did you buy?" she asked, indicating the bag he carried.

"Oh, nothing much. Just an old blanket to throw over my toes on these cold spring nights. I think it will look good on my bed, don't you?"

Curious, she reached over and opened the bag and saw the blanket she had wanted so much but could not afford on the stipend salary paid to a doctoral student. She looked up into his smiling eyes and when she got it figured out, squealed in surprise and kissed him unabashedly on the mouth to the embarrassment of the women and girls walking by, white bonnets under black outdoor caps. "You knew it would look even better with Lisa cuddled under it."

It was his gift to her for saying something stupid and he was pleased his present had restored and brightened her mood to the effervescent glow he preferred. "We will have to see," he suggested. "Let's eat and get back to work. If we have a little luck on this fine fresh day, we might be able to accomplish both at the same time.

"I love my blankie," she said, using the soft nap to caress her cheek.

The Subaru's onboard navigation led them to a small restaurant in Amana. They parked in front, walked in past the Please Seat Yourself sign posted by the cashier station, past the stack of revolving pies, apple, cherry, banana floating in white meringue, and one glazed donut sitting by itself on the bottom of the carrel. They took a booth about halfway back, across from the counter where two men sat, reading the local paper. The tables were clean, Formica topped, the glass salt and pepper shakers full, catsup in a red squeeze bottle, mustard in yellow. A sheaf of napkins in a polished stainless-steel dispenser awaited dirty hands and lips.

The young waitress arrived promptly with the Pyrex coffeepot, waiting for them to turn up the two heavy porcelain coffee mugs sitting next to the condiments and packets of sugar, natural and artificial. Lisa presented hers for a fill. The young woman, with little enthusiasm and practiced routine said, "Hi guys. My name is Simone and I'll be your waitress today." She finished filling Lisa's mug with the steaming black liquid from the clear pot and turned to Will. "Anything for you to drink, sir?"

"A large glass of iced tea, please, with a slice of lemon, Simone. Is Adel not working today?"

The question from an obvious stranger caught her by surprise. She stammered and after a false start said, "I don't know if she's on the schedule or not today." She put the hot pot down on the table. "Do you know her?"

Without answering, Annalisa looked to Will who said, "When do you go on break, Simone?"

With two fingers from the back pocket of her tight jeans she fished out a small smartphone. "I have a break in ten minutes." She got that question all the time from men trying to hit on her in the cafeteria and rarely answered truthfully, but there was something about this couple that caused her to change her mind for once. She could hardly keep from staring at the blonde. She had never seen a woman, English or Pennsylvania Dutch, so beautiful.

"Have you had your lunch yet?" Will asked.

"No," she said.

"Why don't you bring us three cheeseburgers with fries and a drink of your choice, then come and sit with us, our treat."

"Is this about Adelgunda?" she asked, her natural suspicion of strangers still evident. Will nodded. "Okay, I'll be back with the food and tell the boss I'm going to take my lunch break." She brought the cheeseburgers and fries atop butcher paper in three red plastic baskets. She returned with Will's iced tea and a straw and a long thin spoon for stirring and a Coke for herself. After she served Will and Lisa and placed a hand written bill on the table, she slid in the booth next to Annalisa. Will reached for the square-shouldered mustard bottle, Lisa for the catsup. After he had painted the bottom of his bun, he rearranged the lettuce and tomatoes and took a giant bite, mustard edging both corners of his mouth. Lisa took a paper napkin and gently dabbed him back into social respectability.

"I can't take him anywhere," she said with resignation. Simone laughed and Will shrugged his shoulders.

One third of her hamburger gone, she asked across a bite, "Are you guys cops?"

Will said, "No, we are researchers from the university investigating the disappearance of young girls from religious communities, particularly those who don't come back from *Rumspringa*."

Simone blinked once or twice through her naturally long eyelashes. "I didn't come back from my *Rumspringa*."

Will crunched a French fry, a dollop of catsup waiting to fall off the end just as he caught it with his tongue. "But you didn't disappear." He let her chew on that for a minute.

"How well did you know Adel?" Lisa asked.

"I was two grades ahead of her in school. We've known each other all our lives."

"Besties?" Will asked.

"Besties," Simone said, smiling again.

"Kristal told us her sister met you and some boys who drove you to the rave about a week ago."

"*Ja*," she acknowledged. "I knew some boys who had a car and were willing to take us to the dance. The driver is a friend who for a few bucks picks up Adel and I and drives us here to work. Adel wanted to see what it was like on the outside and experience music and dancing with boys for the first time. The two of us plan to run away from the Colonies, get an apartment with another girl and live in the *Englisch* community when Adel's sister is old enough to come with us. Adel wanted very much to go back to school and maybe someday go to college."

"What about you?" Lisa asked.

"Oh, I'm too dumb for more school. The eighth grade was more than enough for me. I'm a good waitress, I work hard, and in six months the boss promised me I'll be the next shift manager."

"You will make a good one," Will said with certainty. Simone was genuinely flattered. "I'd like to know a little bit more about what happened at the party," Will said, "if you don't mind."

"Not at all. Once we got there, we changed into our rave clothes so the boys would find us attractive like the *Englisch* girls and want to be with us. Then we waited for the boys to ask us to dance." She paused.

Will took the opportunity to jump into the conversation. "Usually there's booze, dope and drugs at a rave... at least at the good ones."

She laughed and flipped her reddish blonde hair over her shoulder. "This was a great one. Everything you wanted was available."

"Did Adel partake?"

Simone hesitated and dropped her eyes. Lisa gave her a sisterly pat on the back of her hand. "Don't worry. She's not in trouble. We're only interested in finding her for the sake of her little sister and her parents."

Simone decided Lisa was telling the truth. "She smoked a joint or two with Martin, one of the best-looking guys there. He's a couple of years older and left the Amish after his *Rumspringa*. I warned her about him. He only wants to do it with virgins and he won't use a condom." As an afterthought born of a bad remembrance, she added, "He forces girls even if they don't want it bare."

"Like he forced you?" Will asked.

Surprised that he somehow knew the truth, she looked up at the cafeteria menu above the counter. "Yes. But I was lucky."

"How were you lucky? Lisa asked gently, wondering to herself how a young woman could be lucky having been raped, and possibly losing her virginity to a male screwing her without a condom.

"I had just finished my period. And I immediately went home and drank a Mountain Dew."

"How did that help?" Lisa wondered, puzzled.

Now Simone patted the back of Lisa's hand and explained. "You know, if you drink MD soon enough after sex, you won't get pregnant." All three at the table together nodded at her good luck.

"Where did the drugs and pot come from?" Will asked.

"Oh," she said matter-of-factly, "there's a guy who shows up at the barn parties every month or so. He drives a white service van, sits at a table in the back and sells to us."

"Interesting," Will said. "Does he ever dance or talk to the girls."

"Not that I know of. Once things start to die down, he closes his big attaché case full of drugs and leaves."

"By any chance did he talk to Adel that night?"

Simone shook her head no. "He just asked her what she wanted. I warned her to stick with smoking joints for the first time, but she might have taken some Ecstasy. You never know what some guys will put in a girl's drink or get her to try."

"And you don't recall seeing her leave with the dealer?" Will asked.

"No. In fact she left with Martin. He told me he was going to fuck her. That's what he said."

"Did she know this when she left with him?"

"Yes. I told her when we went outside to take a pee together. That's what besties are for. She told me she wanted to try fucking for the first time so she could fit in better with the *Englisch* girls in town."

Will asked, "So she went willingly with him, but she was high?"

Simone nodded and nervously looked at her watch. Will knew she was exceeding her lunch break time. "But she didn't come back after she went outside with Martin?"

"That's right," said Simone, "but Martin did and he was pissed as a raccoon who just got his tail stepped on."

"Why was that?" Lisa asked.

He said that bitch Adel, his words, left him in the back seat with a high hard-on and never came back. The bitch bounced on me, he said, and said because she was my best friend, I had to fuck him instead."

"And did you?" Lisa asked. "Just between us girls."

"No. Not this time. I may be dumb but I ain't stupid. I don't want a kid at sixteen or seventeen like my mother and my sister. To get rid of him I gave him a blow job behind the barn, got Adel's backpack from the barn where we had the rave, and he drove me home. When Adel didn't show up at my apartment that evening and missed her morning shift the next day, I called the cops. I know she might have hooked up with some boy for the evening but it was not like Adel to ever miss work."

"They told me they would take the report but there was really nothing they could do since I was not a family member. They told me not to worry and that she would come back when she was ready. I know Adelgunda. She would not miss a morning shift for anything. That's when she made her best tips. She was saving money for herself and her little sister Kristal. After Kristal's *Rumspringa*, they were planning to leave the farm and move in with me. After we saved enough money, we were going to leave the Colonies."

"Would you like dessert?" Will asked her. "Remember, I'm buying. She thanked him but declined. She had to get back behind the counter and finish her shift.

"Before you go, one last thing if you don't mind. It's crucial to our investigation. Can you give us a description of the drug dealer?"

She hesitated before she said, "He doesn't look like a drug dealer at all. He wears clothes that you would expect of a farmer who just changed after his workday on the farm running the tractor. He has red hair balding on top and a very short haircut, but there's one thing I'll never forget about him."

"What's that?" Will and Lisa inadvertently said together, making Simone laugh. They were such a cute couple.

"He has hands like a butcher."

Will reached for his wallet and read the check Simone had written in a beautiful cursive hand, substituting small hearts for periods where she had written it was my pleasure to serve you, please come again. "You have greatly helped us in our investigation and I want to thank you. He opened his wallet and in addition to the charge, gave her two twenty-dollar bills.

Her eyes widened at the size of the tip. "You don't have to do that," she said, eyes never leaving the money. "I told you guys what I know because I love Adel."

"The tip is yours," he assured her. "And soon as we learn anything more about Adel, we will let you know."

They drove northbound out of the Amana Colonies. Will looked over at Lisa, her skirt folded up above her sleek and well-muscled thighs, her shirt now unbuttoned to her belly, the long sleeves pushed up above her elbows. She had managed to remove her black bra without taking off her shirt, a magical move of female prestidigitation that never ceased to amaze Will. She looked religiously ravishing. "You approve?" she asked.

"You have my approval no matter what you wear. But to finish the look, I would have you pull your hair back and add tortoise shell bifocals."

"Ah, I understand," said Lisa. "Librarian rather than sectarian."

Will laughed. In all seriousness he then asked her, "Based on Simone's description of the drug dealer, who would you pick out of the dossiers Karin provided for us, photos and all?"

Without missing a beat, Lisa the librarian said, "Maynard Cheska."

Will nodded. "The butcher of Fort Charles. We gotta go back." He pulled to the side of the road and executed a rolling U-turn. About five minutes later, they were back at the Amana Café. Will went in. Lisa stayed with the car, wanting to stay with her look a while longer.

Simone smiled when she saw him approach the cash register. "Forget something?" she asked helpfully and in mind of the biggest tip she had ever received.

Forgoing the need for pleasantries Will immediately asked, "How much longer do you work today and how much money will you make in that time?"

Despite being surprised by the question she used the calculator at the cash register. "With tips about $50."

He said, "We need you for about an hour. I'll pay you $100 for your time."

With unerring accuracy, she reached behind her back and pulled loose the knot of her apron strings, took the name badge off her uniform blouse, yelled back to the fry cook she was sick and needed to go home for two hours, but promised to return when she got her medicine. There were two diners sitting at the lunch counter. Only one looked up from his paper.

"By the way, I'm Will," he said and handed her into the back seat, "and this is my partner, Lisa. We need you to take us to the barn where the rave was held."

She directed them and under thirty minutes they arrived. Will asked her where the boys who drove her that night had parked. They got out and she put them as close as possible to the same spot in the sections of grass where the partiers had parked. From there she led them two spots over to where she thought Martin had parked his car. "What are you looking for?" Simone asked.

"Anything you can find," Will said. "I want to see it."

Minutes later, their search circle expanding away from where the car had been parked, Lisa bent over and picked up a shiny, thin black object about four inches in length. She called Will and Simone over. "I think it's the heel off a pair of high heels," Lisa said and handed it to Simone, who turned it over from front to back.

"OMG," Simone gasped. "Adel was wearing a black pair of high heels at the rave."

Will told her, "Think carefully. Was she wearing them when she went outside with Martin to his car?"

"Absolutely," she said, no uncertainty in her voice. "I know they're hers because we were shopping together when she tried them on and bought them specifically to wear after we got to the dance that night."

Will kissed her on the cheek. They took another half an hour to canvass the area of the makeshift parking lot and then took Simone back to the café $100 richer for her experience.

Once again traveling north on the darkening road home Will asked Lisa, "What does the found broken heel indicate to you semiotically?"

Lisa mulled the question over before answering. "Based on where it was broken, and the force required to do something like that, I would say she was running away, possibly from Martin."

"I agree. What else is significant about the find?"

"I'm not certain," Lisa admitted.

Will helped her. "Except for a surprising number of discarded condoms and wads of toilet paper used by the young ladies going outside to have a pee, we didn't find anything else of significance. Not even one of her shoes. This indicates to me Adel must have stopped in midflight and removed her shoes, as it was becoming nearly impossible to walk or run any farther with one broken heel. Since we did not find her shoes, I deduce she continued on in her bare feet. This also suggests Martin was not chasing her or she would've thrown the shoes off in a panic and left them. I think she walked to the blacktop, hoping for a ride to come by and unfortunately, I think one did. Much as I hate to say it, I conclude that Maynard Cheska picked her up off the side of the road and gave her a ride in his service van. Otherwise, it seems certain to me, based on our interview with Simone and Adelgunda's family members, most likely she would have returned home, at least in time to make it to her morning shift at the cafeteria. No. I don't think she's simply a missing young woman who has taken off with some young boy to experience the life and culture of freedom outside the constraints of her family and the strictures of her church."

"What do you think it is, then?" Annalisa asked, curious to see where his line of reasoning was taking him.

He looked over at her, his lips compressed, serious and grim. "She is a victim of kidnapping and, much as I hate to say it, a possible murder."

Lisa nodded in silence. The way he laid it out, the conclusion was inescapable

They continued on in silence as they pondered the potentially devastating consequences of Will's reasoning and Cheska's actions, their mood flat and dull as the surrounding the Iowa landscape, the day gone cloudy and windy. Inevitably, they arrived at the same conclusion: they were too late.

CHAPTER THIRTY-SEVEN

Grandmother

The word came from the dean's office. Dean Carpenter walked down to tell Will personally during his office hours. Will thanked him for the information and after a chat and informal progress report, made a quick call to LB, who said he would be there in about half an hour. When the young man arrived, there was no artificial color in his hair, the earrings were gone, he wore no makeup and he was dressed all in black. He looked thinner than usual, if that were possible. For an instant Will thought the theme of the day might be Johnny Cash, but when he saw the grief in the young man's face, Will knew. After LB seated himself Will said, "I was going to inform you of your grandmother's passing, but I see the bad news has already reached you."

"Thirty minutes before you called. I'm devastated, Dr. Sheridan."

Will pushed forward a box of tissues. Will was certain LaDamian had loved his *grand-maman* more than anyone on earth. His tears confirmed Will's supposition. "Tell me about your grandmother, LB."

"That woman meant everything to me, Dr. Sheridan," he said between uncontrollable sobs. He took a deep breath, looked at Sheridan with shame and desperation in his reddened eyes, and dabbed at the tears. "She raised me from the time my papa left my mama for a white woman when I was two years old. After he left her my mom didn't have much need for me or for herself anymore and got hooked on crack." He took a drink from his water bottle, which almost all students carried in their ubiquitous backpacks. "Not too soon afterwards she got hooked up with a dude at the local crack house where she got her dope and he turned her out. He forced her to do a minimum of ten tricks a day and if she ever missed her number, he beat the shit out of her. But he never hit her in the face so the cops wouldn't stop her on the stroll and start asking questions," he said, anticipating the question.

"Three years later the drugs and the whoring dried up that poor woman from the inside out and one day the cops got a call and found her lying dead atop an old bare urine stained mattress there on the floor where they did their drugging and fucking. They said the needle was still in her arm. Of course, I didn't learn about any of that shit until much later."

He paused for a minute to blow his nose, took a deep breath, and another long pull from the ceramic water bottle. "So *grand-mère* took me in. She made sure I had enough to eat, had clean clothes, and went to school every day. She read to me every night before I went to sleep."

Will smiled when he saw the love and affection that temporarily replaced the grief in LB's face.

"She was there for me at my high school graduation, when I graduated from LSU, and when I finally had enough courage and self-confidence built up to come out, she hugged me and loved me all the more."

"She was an exceptional woman and I can see you loved her very much."

LB looked him directly in the eye and nodded. "That's why I have to go home and take care of her. But I can't stand the thought of leaving the team, or you." The anguish in his face was real. "I'll do everything I can to get back soon as I can," he promised.

Will took a minute and looked the young man over, his café au lait cheeks shiny from his tears. "Are you taking any other classes this semester?"

"No sir, just yours."

"Okay, here's what we do. I will contact Dean Carpenter and see that you are placed on temporary bereavement status. This will guarantee your position in your master's program. With this semester nearly at an end, I don't see the need for you to formally withdraw. Let's not complicate things too much for the administrators."

LB almost managed a smile. He knew Will's opinion of upper administration.

"Since you are doing a practicum with me this semester, we will do it this way. I'll submit your final grade so you receive all ten credits even if you don't get back in time. At the end of the summer, when things have settled down for you and before you return to write your master's thesis, send me a copy of your proposal and anything you might have written and I'll send you some feedback. How does that sound?"

LB beamed. "I couldn't ask for anything more."

"One last thing. When do you leave?"

"There's a bus leaving early tomorrow morning for Baton Rouge."

"Tell you what, if you can meet with Karin and square her away this afternoon, I'll put you on the evening flight to Baton Rouge via Chicago. Ticket is on me."

LB stood, eyes brimming again, cheeks glistening. "Bring it in close, Doc," he said.

Inside the thin young man's heavy hug, Will realized just how much he would miss LB. "Promise me you will stay in touch. We'll put Karin in charge of the command center and you can reach me through her at any time."

"No worries, Dr. Sheridan. You and semiotic theory are now a very important part of my life. And thanks for everything. I'll never forget what you've done for me and I promise to pay you back every dime."

"LB, the best way you can pay me back is to stay in touch and make certain you finish your master's degree. Do that and we are even."

Soon as LB left, Will called the executive administrative assistant in the dean's office and had her book a flight for LB. He made certain she billed him personally. He next called Karin and brought her up to date. She said she was sad for LB and offered to drive him to the airport in Cedar Rapids. Will told her to expect a call or an email from LB and once squared away, he invited her to dinner with Lisa at his place so he could answer any questions she might have directly. She accepted an invitation to dinner for the next evening, thrilled to be considered, and eager to get started with her new duties.

When Karin arrived, Will took her downstairs to the room next to his bedroom where he had installed the computer and communications equipment for the team. He gave her the passwords, all the secret login names for each of the team members and showed her how to use TOR to set up untraceable and secure Internet connections to make certain their interactions over the computer could not be traced. She took to it eagerly and with enthusiasm. He was glad to see the spark of life, the *élan vital* that usually made her so vivacious and attractive reappear. When they finished, she asked if she could have a private word with him before they went back upstairs to help Lisa, preparing a Chicken Kiev in the kitchen. He sat her on the couch next to him.

She kicked off her tennis shoes and pulled a leg up onto the couch, bent at the knee, hand on the ankle. "You know I think the world of you and Lisa and I'm so glad you found each other. I really love you guys. And you are the best professor I have ever had." He smiled at the compliment but knew there was more to come. "What you and I did the night of the blizzard is a night I will never forget and I do not regret one moment of our time spent together." She paused, searching for the right words.

"Tell me what is troubling you, Karin," Will prompted.

"It's really about what I did with Lisa the next day. I've just decided for my own very personal reasons I don't want to do it again. I'm glad I got to experience being with a woman and I'm very glad it was with Lisa, but for me, once is enough. I just like boys too much." She giggled at the admission of her realization, then turned serious again. "My problem, dear Will, is I don't know how to tell her. I would be crushed if I hurt her feelings or even worse, lose her as a friend." She turned up both palms, hands open and shrugged. "I don't know what to do."

Will nodded. "You are right to trust me. Let's go up and clear the air. Then we three will have a nice dinner and drink a toast to LB and his grandmother."

Karin seemed relieved a thousand different ways. Impulsively, she hugged him and gave him a kiss on the cheek. "You know, Will, if you ever want me again, just say so."

"What a wonderful offer, dear Karin. I just might take you up on that when the time is right." He followed her up the stairs and remembering her figure beneath her khaki slacks and blue long-sleeved shirt stretched across the rounded contours of her bra, the top three buttons open, he wished for once that he could bend time to his personal needs.

In the kitchen, Lisa had on an apron that read "Kiss the Chef," and turned from her knife work to greet them.

"Put the knife down, Lisa, and walk away," Will commanded in fun. She did so immediately and without question. Will waited as Karin used a thumb to clear kiss of greeting from Lisa's cheek. "No more sex with Karin."

Lisa looked at Karin, who blushed. Lisa pouted, kissed her on the cheek and said, "Okay. Come help me set the table."

"That's all it takes?" Karin asked, incredulous, and then laughed at the simplicity of it all.

"Of course. We're all adults here. In this house, as I have been informed by the good Professor Doctor, no one does anything one does not want to do. House rules. And no one is jealous of anyone else."

"Then kiss me on the lips one last time, you sexy beast," Karin said, and Lisa gladly obliged after pushing Karin's hair out of her face with the back of her fingers.

"Now let's get this food on the table while the good doctor opens an outstanding chardonnay from California's Central Coast, wherever the hell that is." They drank a toast to new understandings and a new wine region that seemed to be producing world-class wines at a fraction of the cost, Sheridan informed them.

After dinner the two walked Karin out to her car, a late model Chevy Caprice. She turned and said to Lisa. "I had Will tell you because I couldn't bear the thought of losing you as my friend."

"Not going to happen," Lisa said and assured her with a hug that cemented the new foundation of their redefined friendship. Karin gave Will another quick cool kiss, this time on the lips in the European fashion. "See you both soon."

They waited arm in arm until she backed down the driveway and found the road past the berm left by the snowplow and waved their goodbyes. Once inside and out of their coats and boots, she jumped into his lap, forcing her hands under his arms. "Lisi was begging me for another night with that wildcat."

"You'll just have to settle for me later tonight."

She shoved a hand still gloved in cold from outside into his pants. "Lisi says now!"

At the prearranged time, exactly three o'clock in the afternoon, Karin sat in the Fort Charles Public Library in a carrel placed against the far wall of painted cement block where it offered readers a quiet and unobtrusive place to sit and read. There were no other patrons nearby, no one in the other two carrels next to hers. One person slow-walked the aisles set aside for recently published mysteries and two patrons using the public computers sat up front by the reception and checkout desk. Otherwise the library was under a siege of heavy silence. At 3:15 p.m. Karin looked up from her notetaking, picked up the book she was writing from, pushed back her chair and strolled the aisles looking to replace the reference book. Two additional books remained at her desk next to her open notebook and her backpack. When she returned, a third book had been placed atop the two on the desk. She sat, took up her pen, took the top book from the stack of three and opened it. From within its pages she found and took out a blank piece of paper that had been carefully folded in half and slid it into her notebook with a few other loose-leaf pieces of paper. Mike had made the drop.

Karin wrote another five minutes or so, replaced the three books, gathered her backpack and drove to her father's house. Once there, she removed the folded blank piece of paper and slowly passed it over the flame of a large candle. As if by magic, writing filled the once blank page. She quickly transcribed the message written there before it faded into illegibility. She touched one end of the page into a pearl of flame, watched the tip of the paper blacken and curl into a yellow flame tipped with black and dropped it into the kitchen sink. She quickly read the transcribed notes she had made and immediately called Will.

Mike had been invited into the Blood Brotherhood that morning, with a full initiation ceremony to take place one week hence on Friday night at midnight. Al Young would drive him to the compound Wednesday after work, show him around the clubhouse, and introduce him to the other five members. Will told her job well done and she beamed into the burner cell phone. The call completed, she took the page on which she had transcribed Mike's message and fed it into the shredding flame. Before the heat scorched her fingers, she dropped the burning page into the sink and washed the ashes down the drain.

The news could not have been more timely. The semester was in its last two weeks with an additional week reserved for finals. Will had hoped to bring the case to a close before the Spring semester officially ended and students went home for the summer. His funding covered the summer term but he did not feel good about holding his graduate students over. Another call to FBI headquarters was also in order. Will needed to brief his contact once he had formulated his action plan. He sat at the kitchen table and thought.

Through the kitchen window that looked out into the large unfenced backyard, a doe meandered by, stopping for a minute to take advantage of the cover under the spread of whip thin branches hanging from a massive willow that shaded a large portion of the yard, the branches just coming into greenleaf. He wondered if the appearance of the doe was a significant sign. Probably not, he concluded. Annalisa was at the university research library and would not be back until six or so. He watched the deer for another moment or two, her head up and alert, ears pitched forward. Across the way a neighbor's dog barked in the distance. The whitetail doe, unperturbed by the noise, walked out of his view. At that moment he took out another brick from the wall of distrust he had erected between himself and Lisa. From that moment on he decided to think of her only as Alina, reserving the name Annalisa for their public interactions only. Satisfied with his decision, he got his workout bag, gym shoes, and left to play handball at the YMCA in Waterloo. He did not think to leave Alina a note.

When he returned, he told Alina they needed to drive to Fort Charles and do overwatch for Mike that Wednesday. She seemed genuinely excited. Here was a chance to put her nascent espionage training back into action, this time for the good of the team and her friend Karin. Another message had come in from Mike via Karin informing the team that Mike and Young would leave for the clubhouse Wednesday at an undetermined time before it got dark so Mike could have a look around the facilities, shoot a few rounds at the range on the property, meet the other members, and enjoy a barbeque dinner and beers in the evening. He did not have an address for the meeting place but from speaking with Young, gleaned that it was south of town...and that there was a gated fence surrounding the compound...and security cameras around the perimeter. This was enough information for Will to find a compound on Google Earth. Wednesday morning, a cold front dropped in out of Canada and sucked another week of spring back into winter.

Will Sheridan knew there was little time to waste. He also knew the importance of human intelligence, the HUMINT derived from surveillance, personal and electronic. After he received Mike's message that Young was setting up a meeting for him to introduce the other members of what Young was now calling the Blood Brotherhood, Will immediately called his contacts at the NSA and FBI and secured FISA wire taps for Al Young's home, business and cell phones. Mike's description of the property had been good enough for Will to locate it south of Fort Charles and after he found the satellite photos for it, he keyed the GPS coordinates into the onboard navigation system of the Subaru and into his smartphone. Alina—and he was not yet used to thinking of her in terms of her given Latvian name—was uncharacteristically quiet and he did not disturb her as he drove. He liked the fact she was working things through in her mind. She had been well-trained by the FSB. His seminar work with her convinced him he was merely putting the polish on the diamond.

He parked the rented truck on a side road leading to a copse of woods that had not been cut, stumped, and farmed about a half mile from the compound. He shook his head as Alina, clad in camo from hat to boots exited the white rental truck. How in the world she could manage to make camo sexy was beyond him, but she rocked it. He made certain she kept her white blonde hair tucked up under her watch cap, which she wore over a full facemask. He pulled his down over his sunglasses and pulled on his gloves. He shouldered a pack onto his back. She carried

Will's camoed 30.06 Savage rifle with scope, loaded but with safety on.

They moved silently as possible through the woods until they reached the perimeter of the two-meter-high fence that surrounded the compound and its two buildings, one a log cabin and next to it a metal structure large enough to hold a Boeing 777 for full teardown and maintenance. A covered walkway connected the two buildings. A twenty-meter kill zone had been cut from the outside edge of the fence to the edge of the forest and surveillance cameras monitored the open space. Will pointed them out to Alina, just to be safe. She nodded in affirmation. In the woods and out of sight of the cameras Will unshouldered his backpack and took out a high-powered pair of Vortex binos. As he adjusted the fog-proofed lenses, he checked for tire tracks in the thin skim of snow covering the road into and through the gate. The snow blanket lay undisturbed. Good. He read the numbers on the buttons of the touch pad that controlled the opening and closing of the gate. "Get comfortable," he said to Alina, sitting next to him, shoulder to shoulder, backs against an ancient oak, the rifle laid across her lap. The elephantine bark of the massive tree trunk bit into the muscles of their backs, keeping them awake.

After one hour of waiting in the cold, he checked his watch. Alina shivered next to him in the 28-degree cold. For once there was little or no wind pushing them back into the trees. He whispered into where he thought an ear should be. "Go back to the truck and warm up. Relieve me in one hour." She grabbed his gloved hand and gave it a squeeze, her eyes watering, her breath fogging his cheek. He watched her merge into the oaks, ash, black walnut, and pines.

Shortly before the hour and minutes before he was about to get up and relieve his bladder, he heard a branch snap behind him. He carefully looked back over his shoulder in the direction of the sound. It might be nothing more than a whitetail buck moving through the forest. After inadvertently stepping on the downed branch, she had frozen in place behind an elm. He saw her only as she started to move toward him again. Once she had settled next to him as comfortably as possible, he told her, "I'll be back to get you in one hour." He left her the binoculars. When he returned, she reported no vehicles. "Okay," he said. "Time to change up our tactics. We have to get smarter than the average bear in the woods." She did not understand the reference. No Yogi Bear in the pine forests surrounding Livani, Latvia.

He established a line of sight from their position to the code pad by the gate. On a pinnate oak he strapped a high-power, high definition miniature camera that also contained a ranging laser that could also serve as a motion detector. Any sensed movement automatically triggered the camera to record. He programmed the camera and watched the image being sent back. It was crystal clear and he centered the focus on the alphanumeric keypad by the gate. "I love my friends at the CIA," he whispered to her and set the camera on automatic.

In silence they walked back through the woods to the white Ford pickup truck. Will turned the engine on and set the powerful heater to high. As they warmed up, he opened his laptop and checked the reception of the telemetry coming from their spy camera. The image was sharp as a manufactured diamond. "Time to warm up and let the electronics do the work," he told her, her eyes wide in agreement, as yet unable to control her chattering teeth. She leaned in, grabbed his arm, and held on.

About thirty minutes later a ping from the computer awakened them both. He swung the laptop screen around so both could see it. A white Lincoln Continental had triggered the camera's motion sensor. It stopped at the gate, steam curling from the tailpipe and they watched a gloved hand press four numbers on the keypad. Seconds later the wrought iron gate slowly swung open, admitting the sedan, and then closed behind it. Will paused the camera's recording function, digitally rewound it to the time stamp when the motion sensor had been triggered by the movement of the vehicle, and set the playback speed to slow motion and enhanced the resolution. He read out the numbers as Alina wrote them down. "7777. Now that is highly significant. Mike said there were seven members in their so-called club."

"I can't believe we got the numbers."

"Sometimes a little luck goes a long way." She kissed him to sanctify their luck.

He fiddled with the camera settings on the laptop. Two minutes later five more vehicles spaced a minute or two apart drove up to the gate.

"Are you confirming the code they enter?" Alina asked.

"No," Will said. "I'm recording the license plate for each vehicle that enters."

"Oh, what a smart man I love," she said. "Are we going to stay here on overwatch for Mike until all the cars and trucks leave?"

It was a good question and he thought about it as she copied down all the plate numbers. "Mike can handle himself and my semiotic analysis of the situation leads me to conclude he will be safe given the number of persons who have showed up. If Al Young has anything bad planned today, I don't think he wants five witnesses milling around."

She concurred with his reasoning.

"But I do have bad news for you," he said, remorse in his voice.

She leaned away. "What is it?"

"Someone has to go back and get the camera."

She nodded in acquiescence, but sighed with resignation. "If I have any strength at all left in my body after my trek through the cold, bright woods and back, tonight I want to try with you a marvelous new tantric position from the Kama Sutra...if I have the strength, that is."

He retrieved the camera in record time as she rested and regained her strength.

CHAPTER THIRTY-EIGHT

Decisions

As usual, when things break, they break quickly, Will thought, and usually in unexpected directions. Mike's latest signal to Karin confirmed his initiation into the Blood Brotherhood was scheduled for Friday at midnight. Upon receiving the news, Will immediately called Mike and Karin home and briefed them on the team's new action plan. He thanked them for a job well done, cautioned them to keep their guard up, and sent them back to Fort Charles. He noticed the excitement and nervous intensity in their faces as they left in separate vehicles.

"How far do you want me to go with this guy?" Alina asked, preparing herself emotionally for a potential interaction with Al Young.

Will said, "I leave that up to you. Fall back on you FSB training and do only as much as you are comfortable with. You don't have to marry the guy, if that's what you mean."

She laughed. "You know exactly what I mean. You won't care if I have to lay him in the line of duty?"

"Of course, I'll care. But you are a professionally trained spy and I have my own training to fall back on. However, my semiotic analysis of this man's psychological profile suggests that however much he might be attracted to you Friday night, I have no doubt in my highly trained academic mind that he will want to save himself for a sexual performance at the ritual. Because that is what I think is going to happen with some poor kidnapped young woman they intend to offer up in sacrifice as part of their perverted initiation ritual. And we are going to stop it at all costs, no matter what it takes. I promise you this."

She hugged him, absolutely certain that he meant every word.

"If anything, seduce him to the point that his blood boils in his ears, his brain coagulates like a fried egg, and his eyes cross. I want all the blood drained from his brain and forced down into his pecker. Throw him off his game and break his concentration; you know, just how you do with me. I want him thinking about doing you so obsessively he starts to make mistakes and fucks up. Any advantage you can give Mike is a positive."

She understood what would be required of her. She went to pack an overnight bag. Will made one more call to the director of the FBI office in West Des Moines and brought him up to date. Satisfied with the support he could expect from them, he packed two black nylon tactical bags with an assortment of weapons and ammunition and loaded them both into the rear of the Forester. Despite Alina's best efforts to relax him, he slept fitfully through the night, troubled by dreams of a young blonde girl in a bonnet and apron running barefoot through the emergent green grasses of a hayfield.

Albert Young had a decision or two to make before he left for the compound. He examined the written copy for the TV ad produced by his sales staff. It read like boilerplate for a bad car commercial run late at night on the higher cable channels. He grimaced at the hyperbole, but that's what the rubes who bought his overpriced vehicles wanted. They loved the show and dance and if that's what they expected, then that's what they would get. To sell rusting metal sometimes you have to put on clown shoes and a red nose. Once he determined the entertainment value was in the script, he looked for the more important and subtle cues that really sold the cars and trucks.

He read carefully and underlined the themes he demanded appear in each and every ad he ever ran: patriotism, family, and most importantly, community and trust. The first three values were designed to engender the last two. After he had established a trust between his potential customers and himself, his sales group, and his organization, the deal was good as done. Selling cars and trucks was all about building an essential bridge of trust over the river of distrust. Once his customers crossed that Rubicon the only remaining challenge was to see how much profit he could squeeze out of the good folks who came from miles around to get the best deal possible from the number one Ford dealership in the tri-county area. Satisfied with his annotations, he signed off on the go ahead to run the ad. The film crew would be in tomorrow. He made a mental note to return from the compound a bit earlier than usual after a full blooding ceremony so he could get up the next day early enough to have his hair cut and his makeup done for the TV spot.

That decision made, he pushed back and put his booted feet atop the lacquered oak desk, crossed them at the ankles, the polished silvered points of his cowboy boots pointing to the ceiling. Nothing symbolized the middle-class values of trust and solidarity better than a strong, shiny oak table and the suspended rocker he had strategically placed in the corner of his office. He interlaced his fingers behind his head, careful not to disturb the lay of his hair. There was the matter of the initiation to consider next.

In the short time he had known the new shaker and mover, Young came away impressed with his work ethic. In his private conversations with the former Army Green Beret, he heard him say all the right things, leading him to believe they shared the same ideas and philosophies. He decided the young man was trustworthy and had earned Al Young's respect and consideration for inclusion into the ranks of the Blood Brotherhood. Of one thing he was damn well certain: if the young stud was smart enough to accept and enjoy the full benefits accorded to the membership, his financial and social status was assured. In fact, he made a note to promote the young hard-charger to lead salesman on the floor the day following his initiation. The war fighter's inclusion would bring the club's numbers back up to seven, for him a number of near magical significance. He came from a family of seven brothers. The number six did not sit right with him and made him nervous. Sam Salerno's removal from the lists of the Blood Brotherhood had brought the number of members to six and that was intolerable. It had to be seven or he could not rest.

Young mulled over the offer he had made to Mike to get him to join and take part in the social and economic brotherhood of the top men in Fort Charles. He had accepted the offer with genuine enthusiasm but Young wanted to be certain in his own head that the decision to include the former Green Beret sergeant first class was not only correct but in the best interests of the club. Al Young hoped the young man was smart enough to go through the ceremony and drop his pants when it came time for him to step up and take part in the initiation ritual. Even more important, he hoped that afterwards the new initiate was smart enough to keep his mouth shut. Young hated the messy work of killing a man but not enough to let a common murder destroy everything he had accomplished over the years. He reflected on what he had achieved and built for himself and the membership and at what cost to himself personally. The thought troubled the mayor of Fort Charles.

Maybe it was time to close the membership once and for all. He was enough of a gambler to know at some point his good luck could turn bad faster than an Iowa fall turns into winter. Perhaps the incident with Sam Salerno was a harbinger of things to come. The butcher Cheska was having to range farther and farther afield to find and bring back the young girls who served as the sacrificial offerings during the bloodletting ceremonies. One trip not too long ago took him south into lower Missouri. Young seriously considered the idea that it was time to shut down that aspect of the ceremonies. He would come up with something else for the boys to do. Maybe have them all fuck a goat and then kill it there on the table. They could roast it for dinner afterwards. He laughed out loud. His crew were all a bunch of dumb goat fuckers anyway. Then the vision of white thighs splayed open and him moving forward toward their center intruded and got him hard again in his chair. He decided one more time only, this one last time for the benefit of the young Green Beret sniper, and that would be the last time. It was getting too damn dangerous.

He recalled the situation with Penny Prescott and that dick of a deputy sheriff. That incident convinced him he was making the right decision. As he dropped his booted feet to the floor and reached for the intercom, he wondered if he should have his secretary, fuck it, his executive administrative assistant, as the bitch wanted to be called now, come in and blow him before she collected the text for the TV spot. Just to take the edge off, he thought. It had already been a very stressful day in Fort Charles' number one top-ranked Ford dealership in the tri-county area. As she came through the door he decided to pass. An edge for tonight's activity is exactly what he needed.

Albert Young was sweating into his down overcoat when he climbed up into the leather seat of the black Lincoln Navigator. He was running late. His wife was on the rag and in high bitch mode when he told her he would be working late on the TV promo. She was certain that he was going to fuck his secretary, excuse me, executive administrative assistant, behind her back. Even the truth of his denials did not seem to placate her. The bitch was already halfway through a bottle of chardonnay. He no doubt would return later in the night after the ritual ceremony at the compound was over to find her passed out on the massive leather sectional that filled one third of the living room, the large screen smart TV having shut itself off automatically. At least he had been spared the trauma of having to deal with his two tweener brats, spending the night with their mother, his first wife, across town in the house they had grown up in. His house goddammit, given to his ex in the divorce settlement only because of the brats, but he had paid for every square foot of that house, goddammit. As he started the mammoth vehicle, he took a red bandanna from his pants pocket and wiped the sweat intermingled with the first snowflakes of the late spring evening from his face and forehead. Great. Now winter was trying to make a comeback, delaying the much-anticipated Iowa spring once again. He shouldered out of the coat, not wanting to steam the windows and set his Stetson next to him on the passenger seat.

He drove to the east side of Fort Charles, to the new apartment complex he owned and where he had ensconced Mike Brisbane at a very favorable rent. He parked next to Mike's loaner work truck, another employee perk and good advertising around town, the snow nearly obliterating the dealer plates on the rear of the Ford F-150 truck. He parked next to the vehicle, the big tires of his Navigator carving black canals into the light snow, the snowflakes swarming like bees through the white beams of his head-lights. He decided against the coat for the short run to the apartment door illuminated under the yellow light above the apartment number, but put on his white Stetson hat so he could take it off again in a show of gentlemanly cour-tesy. He pressed the button for the doorbell once, then once again, and was just about to get pissed off enough to hammer his fist through the goddamn door. What he saw when the door opened changed his mood in two tenths of one second. In bare feet and bare legs below a short white bath robe held closed about halfway above her white breasts, a stunning young woman greeted him. She was exactly as tall as he was in his cowboy hat, which he re-moved as she invited him out of the weather, and greeted him by name.

"Please come in, Mr. Young, and make yourself at home," she said, and indicated to the cheap tan couch with a sweep of her bare arm. The motion inadvertently opened the cleft of the towel at midthigh and offered him a brief glimpse of the top of her sleek, well-muscled legs. She sat at one end of a new couch still smelling of a commercial stain guard used to protect the upholstery, he at the other end. She casually closed the gap of the towel that fell open as she sat and crossed her legs. He noticed her hair was still wet from her shower but she had taken the time to comb it straight back off her forehead. It made her look like a supermodel posing in a glossy and expensive print advertisement for French perfume or handbags.

"Where's Mike been hiding you?" She grinned demurely, which seemed to enhance her beauty, and she crossed her long legs, which forced the hem of the bath towel to settle even higher up on her sleek legs, the well-defined muscles drawing his attention from her breasts. "You're about the prettiest thing I've seen in the tri-county area. What's your name, beautiful?"

"Candy." She batted the long lashes above her eyes at him and leaned forward to pat the tight gabardine of his pant leg as she said, "Mike warned me that you were a charmer." Young grinned. "Mike is finishing up in the bathroom and shouldn't be more than a minute or two. I'm a senior majoring in business at the U of I and I thought I would drive up and surprise Mike with a short visit before I have to go back for classes on Monday. He's been working so hard I haven't seen very much of him lately.

"You sure as hell surprised me. I was expecting to see Mike's ugly mug at the door." He stole a quick glance at his watch before he locked back onto her startlingly blue eyes. "We're running a bit late, Candy. Tell him to hurry the hell up."

She scooted a bit closer to Young, an action that opened the top of her robe above her left breast. She reached forward and placed her hand higher up on his thigh and said, "It's all my fault, Mr. Young. Please don't blame Mike. He didn't know I was coming to see him on such short notice. He'll be out in five minutes, he told me to tell you." She looked down at her exposed breast. "Oh dear, excuse me," she said and casually folded the terrycloth robe closed again. "I really should go and put on something more decent, but Mike told me to keep you entertained while he was getting dressed."

What a lucky bastard, Al Young thought. He made a vow to himself. If it was the last thing he did on this planet Earth, he decided he must and would most certainly fuck this gorgeous U of I coed. He was ready to strip the robe off her naked body, shove her down on to her hands and knees, spank her ass and give her what she needed and wanted. He reached over and brazenly stroked her exposed leg, moving his hand up just below the hem of the bathrobe.

"You know, and don't you dare tell him this, but I'm strongly considering Mike for promotion to lead salesman, excuse me, salesperson," he said to show her how politically correct he could be in front of such an enlightened and liberated young lady. He winked. "He will get a nice raise and a bonus to boot. Maybe he can buy you a nice diamond ring as a present. Her eyes widened and she took a deep breath that lifted her breasts toward him.

"I promise. Not a word from me," she said. "I can be trusted." Then she looked him directly in the eye. "You know I would do anything to help that man." She dropped her eyes demurely and looked toward the bedroom. He wondered if he should just say screw it and grab her pussy right then and there on the couch, but before he could act on the impulse, he heard Mike yell, "Be right out Al, just need to find my keys and grab a coat."

Young made a snap decision. He leaned in to her and said, "Before you return to Iowa City Sunday, why don't you come by the dealership. I know Mike has the day off. Maybe we can do something before you leave."

She smiled conspiratorially. "I think I would like that. She patted him once more on the thigh, her fingers lightly grazing his penis as she settled back to her side of the couch. It might have been inadvertent.

"You are a real firecracker, aren't you?"

She smiled at the corners of her mouth. "When I can find the right guy to light the fuse."

Mike came out of the bedroom, shouldering into his leather coat. "I see you met Candy. Sorry to keep you waiting, boss."

"No worries, buddy."

As Candy stood to receive her goodbye kiss from Mike, she bounced her breasts into his hug goodbye, and Young saw her grab his cock through his pants. "Sorry you have this meeting to go to. I wanted to show you how much I missed you."

Mike kissed her quickly on the cheek. "Plenty of time for that tomorrow after I get off work."

"Promise?" she asked, begging a little.

Young waited just inside the door and shook his head under his hat as Mike walked by. "What a lucky bastard you are," he said, grinning.

Candy stood next to Young as Mike walked out onto the porch. She pressed the side of her breasts against the length of Young's arm. "It was a pleasure to meet you, Al. I hope we can see each other again sometime very soon."

"Sure," Young said, feigning cool politeness. "Just let me know when you're in town next. We'll do something. The three of us," he added.

She winked and waved him out the door. "Should I wait up?" she asked Mike. For an answer he looked to Al.

"Shouldn't be later than one or two," he lied.

She nodded. "I'll still be up then."

They shouldered into their seatbelts, Mike in the passenger seat, and Young took one more look back at the closed apartment door, a grim look on his face. As he keyed the ignition and waited for the wipers to clear an arc of snow, he turned to Mike, shook his head in disbelief and said, "How in the hell does an average looking joe like you get so lucky with a bombshell like that? If there was ever the perfect picture of a suicide blonde, she's it. I hope you're hitting that ass on a regular basis."

Mike laughed. "Every chance I get and twice on Sunday, if you don't have me scheduled to work."

Young grunted. He might have to redo the walk-up schedule after all. At least on the weekends when he knew Mike's girlfriend would be in town for a visit. Besides, working Sundays would help the kid fill his pockets with cash. He would need it to keep the suicide blonde happy.

CHAPTER THIRTY-NINE

Hostage Rescue

The Driver's Privacy and Protection Act restricts the search of license plate numbers for the purpose of obtaining private and personal information to law enforcement and members of the Department of Motor Vehicles. The general public are permitted to learn a vehicle's accident history, registration, and VIN for purposes of buying and selling a vehicle. On the authority of his FBI credentials, what Will discovered surprised him into unexpected shock and dismay. Every single name the database search returned came back to a highly respected individual living and working in or around Fort Charles, Iowa. A judge, the Honorable Robert Franklin; a county sheriff, Buckminster (Buck) Miller; a bank president, Lawrence (Larry) Rosenstein; a butcher and delicatessen owner, Maynard Cheska; Kenneth Black, the president of an insurance company; and the mayor of Fort Charles and owner of a car dealership, Albert Young, were on the list.

Mike Brisbane did not seem to fit the profile of the other Blood Brotherhood members; he was too young, not successful enough, and a recent arrival in town. Based on the information developed from the case so far, Will's semiotic analysis predicted there had been a seventh member in the cult and Mike, a young up and comer, was being groomed as his replacement. It was also significant that he was being sponsored by his mentor at the dealership, mayor and owner Albert Young.

Like a physicist using all available scientific data to predict the existence of a black hole in the space/time continuum in advance of its eventual discovery by astronomers, Will's hypothetical reasoning that there was or had been a missing member of the cult opened up a new avenue of investigation for the team, and as Karin and Mike had their investigative plates full in Fort Charles, he served Alina with the opportunity. Given her exemplary research skills, she gave him an answer to the mystery of the missing person Thursday night before the scheduled initiation.

She found the name Sam Salerno, owner of Salerno's Gas Station and Oil Company. What she did not find was Sam Salerno. She reported to Will that Salerno was a missing person out of Fort Charles. The local newspaper reported that he had suddenly disappeared as if an alien spaceship had come down out of space and snatched him away from Earth using a tractor beam, which some of the locals interviewed by the media considered not at all as far-fetched as it sounded. After all, were there not still plenty of unexplained cow deaths on many of the farms in the area, to say nothing of the mysterious crop circles that only alien technology was capable of carving into the cornfields?

It was reported that Salerno's business ventures were being continued by his ex-wife and his oldest son. The ex-wife, according to reports from the sheriff's office, had taken a lie-detector test and passed. She was unaware of any enemies Salerno might have made, with the exception of herself. But she had very good reasons for throwing the cheating philandering bum out, in addition to an airtight alibi. Credit card receipts verified she was at the Mall of America in Bloomington, Minnesota with her girlfriends on the day Salerno was reported missing. She had no idea where Sam Salerno was, and did not care where he was. For all she knew he had a mistress in Canada. She was glad to be rid of him and those creeps he hung around with, the self-styled big swinging dicks of Fort Charles. Two letters were carefully elided from the word dicks so as not to offend the sensibilities of the paper's readers. No BSDs were named in the article. The interview and column ended with the statement that the disappearance of such a valuable community stalwart as Sam Salerno was being treated as an open investigation, one the sheriff promised to keep alive as long as it took, given that Salerno was a personal friend and an important businessman in town. The information Alina turned up gave Will an additional argument to swear before the federal judge on stand-by for an emergency warrant out of Des Moines. Will took possession of the warrant, thanked the woman, and graciously accepted her best wishes for success.

Two hours before midnight, in full camo and tactical gear, using a top-secret electronic jammer, Will Sheridan temporarily defeated the closed-circuit cameras sweeping the compound and entered the main facility using the stolen codes for the keypad. He disabled the alarm system, entered, and reset the alarm. He picked the lock to the inner door, closed and relocked it behind him. Using his tactical flashlight, he quickly went from room to room and decided he would be safest waiting in a back bedroom that looked unused, given the amount of dust on the dressing table mirror. He sat on the bed and waited, his eyes adjusting to the dark. The closed vinyl shades muted the light of the full moon.

With one hour to go, he heard his radio click. Joe Rodriguez, commander of the FBI Hostage Rescue Team signaled his team's readiness. They were dispersed and out of sight in the woods surrounding the compound.

"I assume you have the warrants and are already in place." It was just like his old friend to double-check. Will confirmed both. "We'll hang back until you signal us. FYI, we have the first vehicle approaching and in sight. Looks to be a white van. Good luck and good shooting," he whispered into his mike.

Will clicked twice in acknowledgement and went to radio silence as agreed.

He had known Joe for years, meeting him for the first time at the West Des Moines FBI Office shortly after Will had published his first book on the use of semiotics for crime investigation and detection. Rodriguez occasionally came north for a fishing vacation with Will after he left IPSU and moved to the cabin on Lake Kabetogama. Will knew him to be an operator of the highest competency and professionalism. He could not think of a better man to be lurking in the woods under the crystalline night light of a full moon. Having Joe's crack squad in reserve was a tactical godsend. The HRT was part of the Tactical Support Branch of the Critical Incident Response Group. Its members are often former Special Weapons and Tactics officers who made the jump from local or state law enforcement to federal. An elite tactical unit, they receive training as good as any Navy SEAL team or Army Green Beret unit, often trained by and with special forces operators. Primarily used as an anti-terrorist force, they are also tasked to assist local law enforcement as needed and help coordinate manhunts and rural operations. Will could not ask for a tougher and harder group of men and women to cover his back.

Will heard the diesel engine of the van approaching and took his position behind the chest of drawers in case someone opened the door for a quick look in. The vehicle must have driven around to the back of the building he was hiding in and he heard nothing further until lights came on inside and he heard movement. Will assumed it was a group member responsible for setting up. He heard other vehicles approaching, one after the other, then the sound of voices, laughing and hollering greetings as they donned their ceremonial robes and waited for their leader, excited by the anticipation of what was to come.

Young was duly pissed with himself. He had against his better judgment allowed Mike's dazzling young girlfriend to bore into his brain like a seductive sound worm. Running late, he gunned the big Navigator at speeds that nearly defeated its traction control system but managed to arrive just in time to help Mike robe up before he donned his own robe. He was sweating and needed a handkerchief to mop the moisture from his brow. He decided to overlook his usual safety precautions and protocols for a new member awaiting initiation and forgo the usual frisking and checking for weapons or contraband. He permitted only booze and dope at the meetings. Besides, if he couldn't trust a Green Beret special forces operator, then who the hell could you trust? He decided he was going to fuck his girlfriend anyway. He heard the first strike of the gong signaling midnight and the beginning of the initiation proceedings. He had briefed Mike on the way in and told him to follow his lead. The rest was self-explanatory.

At precisely seven minutes and seven seconds after midnight, the gong sounded seven times, calling the seven members of the Blood Brotherhood to assemble in the room set aside for bloodletting. Atop seven-foot-high wrought iron holders, seven candles illuminated the ritual table, draped in white linen. Four masked men in red robes, heads covered by their cowls, waited. Young walked Mike into the ceremonial chamber as the gong struck for the seventh and last time. Mike stood to Young's left, who was facing the end of the table, two men at the head, two at the sides, hands clasped above their bellies. A door at the far end of the ceremonial room opened and Maynard Cheska, the seventh member appropriately robed, entered the ceremonial chamber leading a young blonde woman by a red velvet rope that encircled her neck. Her eyes seemed glazed and lifeless as she shuffled forward in response to Cheska's tugs on the rope. Dressed in a white tunic that fell to midthigh, she shuffled forward barefooted.

Cheska, assuming his duties, addressed the congregated members. "I present to you and for your pleasure this virginal beauty standing before us as we welcome a new member to our ranks."

The others clapped their hands together seven times. Mike was uncertain if it was for him or for the victim. After Cheska loosened the rope around her delicate neck, whiter than a swan swimming through a pool of candlelight, he pulled the knot that held closed the thin white cotton linen above her breasts and allowed the tunic to slide off her narrow shoulders and pool above her feet. As Mike beheld the trembling figure standing not seven feet from him, he nearly let panic force him into grabbing for the throwdown pistol strapped to his left leg in the hollow above his ankle at the Achilles tendon. He was stunned into place by the young woman's unmarked and pristine beauty, the red velvet rope still wrapped around her neck as the members gently laid her atop the table, one holding her head, one on each arm and legs, now splayed apart.

If it was the last thing he did on planet Earth, he vowed to himself, he would see that no harm came to the young woman now restrained by the other members of the Blood Brotherhood.

"Gentlemen," Cheska intoned, "it is time for our exalted leader to show our new initiate the way to the blooding as he seeks acceptance into the Brotherhood."

"Thank you, Brother Cheska. You have once again presented us with an extraordinary beauty for this very important ceremony, the initiation of a new member into our lifelong brotherhood. Let us all be joined in blood." As he moved forward to draw the hymenal blood from the unresponsive girl on the table, her eyes dulled and glazed, unable to move, unable to make anyone hear the screams in her head, Mike noticed the entrance door to the ceremonial room open and Professor Will Sheridan entered silently, weapon at the ready, the attention of the other members still riveted on the victim atop the sacrificial table.

In his best command voice, Will ordered them to raise their hands but not move from the table and informed them they were under arrest by warrant and by the authority of the Federal Bureau of Investigation. "The first man who disobeys my commands, I shoot to kill," Will said and moved to the end of the table so the others could see he was armed. He moved like a wraith through the shimmering, butter colored candlelight, his father's .45 service weapon held in both hands, the forward bead centered on Al Young's forehead. With the gun he motioned Cheska over to stand with the others. As the butcher of Fort Charles moved forward, he pushed one of the candle stands illuminating the end of the table with such force that the liquid wax that had pooled in the hollow cupola of the candle surrounding the wick splashed onto Will's cheek and gun hand. His lightning reflexes saved his eyes as he turned his head just in time to avoid the majority of the hot wax that struck and splattered his hand and cheek. That second of inattention permitted Cheska to take him down with a bone crunching tackle that knocked the wind out of Sheridan, the full weight of the 300-pound man's shoulder driving into his stomach. As Cheska fought to reach for Will's dropped semi-automatic, Mike had the presence of mind to kick it out of reach. A second kick rolled Cheska on his side.

All the other members of the group except one stood frozen at the table, held transfixed by the sudden chaos in the room. Young used the fight between Sheridan, Cheska, and Mike as cover to move toward the opened door Will had come through. Just before he made his escape, he heard the word freeze shouted at him by what could only be a female voice. For an instant he thought it might have come from the throat of the young victim on the table. As he quickly turned to verify the truth of his incongruous thought, he looked over his shoulder into the intense blue eyes of the starkly gorgeous woman he knew to be Mike's girlfriend. She held a Glock 22 Gen4 semi-automatic pistol pointed at his chest. He threw back his hood and grinned at her. "You couldn't resist me so you followed me here. So, let me ask. Are you here to fuck me or fight me? Either way you get fucked," he said.

In a voice so cold that it sent chills up his spine she said, "I'm here to kill you for raping and murdering these young women."

He ran for the door. This bitch wasn't fucking around. A round fired from her pistol caught him in the back of his shoulder and spun him in a circle. He dropped to his belly and low-crawled through the open door. He heard a second round blister the wood paneling of the antechamber and pushed the door shut with his booted foot, got to his knees, and locked it. He recovered enough to make it to the gun safe in the adjoining room. He could hear Alina trying to open the locked door. He knew she would be unable to get through in time as he grabbed an assault rifle and a .44 Magnum Ruger Blackhawk revolver, boxes of ammunition for both, and ran for the Navigator.

Once more in control of his breathing, Will got to his feet, pulled out a handkerchief and removed the cooling wax from his cheek and hands, the damage already done. Will had Mike keep his .22 trained on the others, their hands still up, not knowing what to do in the midst of the chaos surrounding them. Alina ran back to the middle of the room to check on Will and Mike when Cheska tripped her with a vicious leg sweep from his prone position on the floor. The leg whip brought her down but she was up in an instant to face the stocky brutal man. His massive hands wrapped around her throat, choking the life from her. She kneed him in the groin to no effect other than to produce a surprised grunt and just as she felt her neck about to snap, she pushed both her thumbs into the bulging eyes of the butcher's reddening face. She felt his grip around her throat loosen slightly as he stepped back, trying to rid himself of the bitch's thumbs gouging deeper into his eyes, blinding him with pain and blood. At that instant, Alina dropped to one knee while simultaneously driving both her forearms up and into the underside of Cheska's heavily muscled forearms, effectively breaking his grip on her neck before he snapped her vertebrae.

She heard the shot that tore Cheska's knee off his leg and dropped him to the ground for good. Will had found and recovered his .45. Despite the hot pain radiating down the left side of his face, his aim was still good. Maynard Cheska writhed in a bloody pool of his own pain, gripping the hole where his knee had been and passed out. Alina went over and gave Will a hand up from his kneeling position.

"I thought I told you to wait with Karin and coordinate with Joe's FBI team."

She looked away. "I had a bad feeling and you told us to trust our instincts when it came down to that. Karin said she would wait and handle the communications."

Will looked over to Mike who had the other members under his gun. He signaled a thumbs up for an okay. Will keyed his hand-held radio. "Alpha team to Omega. Alpha calling Omega." He heard a click in response.

"Omega. Wait one, please. We have our hands full out here."

"Roger that," Will answered, hearing shots fired from an automatic rifle in the background. A minute later, Omega team leader Joe Rodriguez called.

Will told him," We could use a little help in here on our end when you get things under control out there."

"Roger that. I'll have a unit there in two. Out." True to his word, Special Agent Joe Rodriguez led in a team of HRT FBI agents, all dressed in full tactical gear from black boots to bulletproof vests, gloves, shielded helmets, Heckler and Koch automatic weapons at the ready.

"Good. We're sure glad to see you guys," said Will in greeting to an old colleague. "The cavalry has arrived."

Commander Rodriguez stood next to Will and indicated to his men who searched, cuffed, and took the four standing members of the Blood Brotherhood to a waiting van for transport.

"Keep a close eye on that one, Joe. He's the sheriff of the county and a prime suspect in the murder of Penny Prescott. What happened out there?"

"As per your request, I had the tactical assault team stationed and deployed just beyond the compound's main gate. We saw a vehicle, a large black SUV, no lights on, crash through and I directed my men to stop it. They took out three tires and the windshield before the vehicle stopped. Young shot and wounded two of my agents and escaped into the trees. We were preparing to pursue when you called. I had heard the shooting in the log cabin and decided we could go track Young after we helped you."

Sheridan clapped Rodriguez on the shoulder strap of his black Kevlar vest. "You made the right call, Joe. We had our hands full in here but I've got one hell of a team with me too, if I could only get them to follow orders," he said, looking over at Alina, who shrugged.

"I like a good fight," she said in her defense.

"Well, you and Mike saved my ass this time," Will acknowledged. "But there's still some work to be done. I want that bastard Young apprehended and in custody so he has to answer for his crimes."

"I second that," Mike said. "And I want to get out of this goddammed robe."

Will agreed. "You want to track this guy with me?"

"Hell yeah, I do."

"Okay. Here's what we do. Since Lisa already popped a cap in Young's shoulder, she'll stay here, secure the scene with Joe and do an evidence sweep. She knows what we're looking for."

She nodded.

"And Joe, put in a call for your best forensic criminalists. I want nothing in these facilities overlooked. And send them to Cheska's butcher shop after they are done here. I want an airtight case against all these assholes. And I have no doubt Sheriff Miller will only be too willing to cop a plea and turn state's evidence to save his sorry ass. He knows he will be killed in the federal penitentiary for what he's done to these girls."

CHAPTER FORTY

Longshot

Will walked over to the young woman sitting on the edge of the white table, now draped in a blanket and being comforted by a female FBI operative.

As she rubbed the blood back into her wrists, Will asked her name. "*Wie heisst du?*"

Able to cry now she looked at him through tear-swollen eyes. "Adelgunda," was all she said.

"*Grüsse von deine Schwester und deine Freundin.*" He conveyed greetings from Adelgunda's sister Kristal and her girlfriend Simone.

He watched a spark of life light in her face as the adrenaline in her system burned through the last of the Rohypnol. Under the care and comfort of Commander Rodriguez, she was led to an ambulance on its way into the compound. Will directed another young agent to stand guard over Cheska, still unconscious, until the paramedics arrived to stabilize and transport him. "He is not to ride in the same vehicle as our victim. In fact, I want you to stay with him until you arrive at the hospital. He is extremely dangerous, a flight risk, and strong as a steer. He is wanted for numerous kidnappings, rapes, and murders."

"We will double cuff him, sir," the young agent promised. "And I'll sit on his chest if I have to."

"Very good. Let's go gear up," he said to Mike. "The Subaru is parked back behind the utility building." Once there, from the back of the vehicle he pulled out two sets of AN/PVS 31A BNVD night vision goggles with improved white phosphor tube technology, the Savage 30.06 rifle loaded with Federal 168 grain Sierra Match BTHP high velocity rounds, scoped with a combination thermal and infrared imaging sight attached to the rifle. Coats and night vision goggles at the ready, Will drove them to where Young had crashed his SUV and fled into the forest. From his tactical bug-out bag Will removed a special monocular scope that illuminated blood in the dark and not seven yards beyond the vehicle they picked up a blood spatter atop the light coat of snow.

"Looks like Lisa hit him pretty good," Mike commented.

"I'll say," Will agreed. "He's still bleeding like a stuck pig. Got a good moon rising, a clear starlit sky above that and a running man bleeding his strength out into the evening's snowfall. This shouldn't take very long."

Forty-five minutes later they came to the end of the woods just as the blood trail diminished to intermittent and increasingly infrequent blood spatters. Young had somehow managed to control the bleeding from the exit and entrance wounds in the shoulder where Alina had shot him through. Using their combination thermal and infrared night vision goggles, about 400 yards ahead of them they spotted a figure standing in and among the short-cropped stocks of a cornfield, not yet plowed under for spring planting to soybeans.

Although Young turned and looked around him, despite the noise of their arrival, he was unable to see Will and Mike standing in the tree line at the edge of the field. Nevertheless, from the AR-15 automatic rifle still in his possession, he fired a spray of bullets into the trees that dropped snow and branches over their heads. At the sound of the gunfire, Will flinched involuntarily and dropped to one knee. He had been shot at before.

Mike was already on the ground in a prone firing position watching the target as Will low-crawled over and handed Mike his backpack, which the former Green Beret sniper used to support for his weapon. "Can you take him?" Will asked.

Mike sighted through the starlight scope, the scope's reticle trained on the figure in the darkness ahead of them, now bent over at the waist. "I think he's stopping to puke," Mike said to Will. "Light him up, sir, if you please." Will painted Albert Young's back with a high-powered infrared laser.

"Do you want a kill shot or do you want me to just drop this bastard in the snow?" Mike asked with venom in his voice, his personal choice unambiguously clear.

"I can't let you take the onus of killing him on your shoulders. Stopping him will be sufficient."

Mike looked up from the rifle. "One more dead man to my credit isn't going to cause me any lost sleep. I have a firing solution if you will help me call the shots, Professor Sheridan."

"Let's make him pay for his crimes in a court of law," Will said, not wanting the young Green Beret to shoulder the responsibility for killing a man, no matter how vile or evil that man might be.

"I'm ready if you are, sir," Mike informed his professor, eye back on the scope and the padded butt of the rifle securely placed against the muscles of his deltoid.

"Call the shot, soldier," Will said.

"Shooter on target. Distance 403 yards," Mike reported, reading the telemetry from the inside of his rifle scope.

"Confirmed," Will said, checking the laser rangefinder. Spotter on 403 yards. My best guess is we have 10 mph full value wind blowing from the left."

"I concur. 10 mph left wind.

"By my calculation using Marine Windage Formula, push it 3.5 MOA left at 403."

"I agree. Pushing 3.5 left at 403. Target steady. Shooter on. Shooter ready."

"Shooter ready," Will confirmed. "Send it."

The rifle bucked into Mike's shoulder. The noise of the explosion ricocheted through the trees, disguising its origin. Mike cycled the bolt, ejecting the spent shell and brought up the next round. He pushed the bolt forward, chambering the round, and slapped the bolt down. Inexplicably, he pushed the safety on. Will watched the shot through his night vision goggles. Downrange, under his Stetson hat, Al Young's head exploded like a watermelon. Through the scope Mike had been watching the ballistic trajectory of the bullet's flight and impact. As Young's headless torso pitched forward into the snow now the color of a red Blood Brotherhood robe, Mike imagined, he got to his knees and looked at Dr. Sheridan.

"Sorry the shot went a little high. Must have been a slight drop in elevation we couldn't see in the dark at that distance."

Will checked the figure on the ground 403 yards ahead of them. There was no discernible movement. "Put your weapon on full safe, son. That was a hell of a shot, even if you did hold a tad bit high," he said, joining Mike in the deception. "If you would like, I'll take full responsibility for the shot and the kill. Mike, this doesn't have to be on you."

"Not on your life, sir. My shot, my kill. This one goes into my logbook and no man's daughter will have to worry about that bastard ever again."

The two men stood and shook gloved hands. Will keyed his radio and reported that the suspect had been killed in an exchange of gunfire. He sent the GPS coordinates so the body could be recovered by the FBI. He was suddenly very tired and wanted nothing more than to have Alina within the safe press and security of his arms, the natural perfume of her body in his nose, the sweet and urgent taste of her on his lips, and the essential sense of her centered deep within himself.

Author's Note

I want to take a minute of your time and share with you the conclusion of the events I described in this book. I owe that much to the graduate students who played such a crucial role in resolving the case I presented. Their hard work and able assistance were instrumental in bringing the perpetrators of those horrible crimes to justice and bring closure to the grieving families and friends of the victims.

Sheriff Buck Miller did in fact cop a plea and detailed the roles of Al Young and Maynard Cheska, the principals in the kidnapping, rapes, and murders of the young women abducted during the course of their *Rumspringa*. Miller was tried and found guilty as an accessory to the murder of Penny Prescott and Sam Salerno. He received two life sentences for his crimes, but given his cooperation with the state's prosecuting attorney, was made eligible for parole after serving forty years. During his second year of incarceration in the federal penitentiary he was stabbed more than forty times and killed by members of the Aryan Brotherhood, which I find a rather delicious irony.

The other members of Young's cabal, as accessories after the fact and not having taken part in the kidnappings and killings per se, were tried on seven counts of rape and were found guilty on all counts. All four men were registered as sex offenders. Judge Robert Franklin, shortly after his incarceration, committed suicide by hanging. Neither the banker Lawrence Rosenstein nor the insurance salesman Kenneth Black will be eligible for parole during their lifetime, as their sentences are to run concurrently.

Maynard Cheska, the butcher of Fort Charles, is awaiting execution by lethal injection in Missouri, where he made the fatal mistake of kidnapping two of the Blood Brotherhood's victims from the Amish community near the town of Seymour. Iowa does not have the death penalty and so by arrangement with Missouri officials he was extradited and sentenced to death for his crimes. His Blood

Brothers testified against him and with credit card receipts from gas and food purchases, and forensic evidence taken from his butcher shop, he was convicted on all counts. Like many serial killers he made the mistake of taking souvenirs from his victims, which tied him to their kidnappings, transport across interstate lines, and ultimately, murder. Good riddance. We will all be better off the instant after he draws his last breath.

Deputy Sheriff Delbert Copeland, Karin's father, was released from prison, all charges against him were dropped, and the case against him was dismissed by a judge with extreme prejudice. This is a legal designation which means Copeland can never again be charged with the crime for which he was falsely imprisoned. He never received so much as an apology from the county or the state. He sued both and was awarded damages for false arrest and imprisonment, including an additional award from the jury for emotional pain and suffering. He was forced to sign a nondisclosure agreement as to the sum total of the settlement, but whispers in my ear from trusted sources put the total in the range of two to three million dollars. Delbert Copeland is now retired and lives in upstate Michigan.

My four graduate students in the Spring practicum received As after submitting their final paper detailing their experiences on the case and the application of semiotic theory to the resolution of the crimes we discovered and solved. Karin, Copeland's daughter, graduated with her master's degree, and despite my urging to go on for her doctorate, accepted a teaching position at a small liberal arts college in southern Iowa. She is happily married and she and her husband are expecting a son.

As promised, after taking care of his grandmother's affairs, LB returned to IPSU and finished the courses for which he had taken incompletes. I helped him finish his master's thesis and upon graduation, he applied for a position with the FBI. Unfortunately, a background check revealed two misdemeanor citations for the possession of marijuana, and his application, despite my strong letter of recommendation, was rejected. This will be the Bureau's loss. After graduation LB moved to California where he is now a forensic electronics specialist for the Bureau of Forensic Services, the scientific arm of the Attorney General's Office. I am happy to say he fell in love with and married a handsome young man he met dancing at a rave in Los Angeles.

Mike Brisbane finished his Master of Science degree, applied for and was accepted into service with the Iowa State Patrol. Adelgunda Berghammer, after a full recovery from her ordeal, went home and a year later took her younger sister Kristal and left her family and church. With the permission of the Berghammers, they became wards of Mike Brisbane and his wife, Regina. Adelgunda dotes on her younger sister, loves animals and hopes one day to become a veterinarian.

Alina Augustans, also known as Annalisa Allen, finished her doctorate at IPSU and was awarded the Ph.D. At my invitation, she moved in with me at my cabin on Lake Kabetogama in northern Minnesota. She is a tenure-track professor at the University of Minnesota-Duluth. She enjoys teaching and research but the drive from our cabin to Duluth is tiring. The head of her department was kind enough to arrange a Tuesday through Thursday teaching schedule with Wednesdays also reserved for office hours. She works from home via the internet on Monday and Friday. Next year she will look into getting a position at Rainy River Community College in International Falls, a much closer commute. I am not permitted to disclose her current status with the CIA or the Russian FSB-SVR. So far, my trust in her has been well-founded and richly rewarded. But I remain vigilant.

Two months after I submitted my final report to Dean Harry Carpenter and successfully completed in full the requirements of my one-year grant, I received a letter from the Office of the President at IPSU. Over the adamant objections of Dean Carpenter, a committee charged with investigating the matter determined that I had inappropriately placed my graduate students in positions of unacceptable risk during the events that took place at the compound of the Blood Brotherhood. Despite each of my students writing unsolicited letters of support on my behalf, the committee wrote a formal reprimand of my conduct to be placed in my permanent personnel file with the admonition that I should never again be hired or work for the university as a professor. I wrote each committee member a short letter thanking them for their wise decision.

In closing, you may expect the publication of my next and fifth novel sometime shortly after Lake Kabetogama ices over.

ABOUT THE AUTHOR

William Russell Sheridan, trained as a research scholar, earned an interdisciplinary doctorate in semiotic theory from a Research I university in the Pacific Northwest. After developing and publishing his new method for solving crimes using semiotic analysis, he served as special consultant to the Bavarian State Police, Interpol, and the FBI. He is a retired professor and lives in California.

www.ingramcontent.com/pod-product-compliance
Lightning Source LLC
Chambersburg PA
CBHW051455030726

47592CB00006B/1937